WELCOME TO THE
LEGEND OF THE FIVE RINGS!

You are about to enter Rokugan, a land of honorable samurai, mighty dragons, powerful magics, arcane monks, cunning ninja, and twisted demons from the Shadowlands. Based on the mythic tales of Japan, China, and Korea, Rokugan is a vast empire, a unique world of fantastic adventure.

Enjoy your stay in Rokugan, a place where heroes walk with gods, where a daimyo's mighty army can be thwarted by a simple word whispered into the right ear, and where honor truly is more powerful than steel.

Legend of the Five Rings™

BOOKS

THE SCORPION
Stephen D. Sullivan

THE UNICORN
A. L. Lassieur
Available September 2000

THE CRANE
Ree Soesbee
Available November 2000

Legend of the Five Rings™

THE SCORPION

STEPHEN D.
SULLIVAN

CLAN WAR
First Scroll

Cover art by Brom
First Printing: July 2000
Library of Congress Catalog Card Number: 00-101662

9 8 7 6 5 4 3 2

ISBN: 0-7869-1684-2
620-T21684

U.S., CANADA, ASIA,   EUROPEAN HEADQUARTERS
PACIFIC, & LATIN AMERICA   Wizards of the Coast, Belgium
Wizards of the Coast, Inc   P.B. 2031
P.O. Box 707   2600 Berchem
Renton, WA 98057-0707   Belgium
+1-800-324-6496   +32-70-23-32-77

Visit our web site at **www.wizards.com**

This book is dedicated to my father,
David A. Sullivan, who first introduced me
to samurai films and haiku poetry.
Thanks, Dad.

ACKNOWLEDGMENTS

Special thanks to my friend Ed Henderson: Asian language authority, oriental history advisor, and travel writer extraordinaire. Any of the cultural details in this book that I've gotten right can be credited largely to his patience and expertise. Any stuff I've gotten wrong is entirely my own fault.

Thanks go to Brian Thomas as well, for helping me track down the samurai films that inspired me while I wrote.

Thanks also to the late Akira Kurosawa for making many of those films and the late Toshiro Mifune for starring in nearly all of them.

All of history is a lie. The truth depends on who does the telling—and who does the listening."
—Bayushi Shoju

PROLOGUE:
THE GATES OF HELL

Bayushi Shoju strode through the blood-clotted battlefield, looking for someone to kill. The land around him had been lain waste by war. Bare trees stretched bony fingers to a sky painted orange with fire and black with smoke. The blood of his enemies stained the land dark and made the small stream in Shoju's path run crimson.

In the distance, the Scorpion daimyo heard the cries of the dying echo among blasted hills. Nearby, only the stream's weeping voice disturbed the silence. Shoju's eyes found no foes remaining to be slain.

The veil of bloodlust lifted, and Shoju saw that many of *his* people lay dead on the battlefield as well. Eiji had long been a retainer for the daimyo's family. Now his eyes lay open to the sky and his mouth brimmed with his own blood. The retainer was not the last Scorpion casualty, not nearly.

As he crossed the stream, Shoju noticed Rumiko lying in the water. Her helmet had fallen off, revealing a gaping hole in the back of her skull, a wound not even her long black hair could conceal. A twinge shot through his heart for the loss of the rare and brave samurai.

Further heartbreak awaited Shoju as he topped the next rise. Before him lay another hill, covered with the bodies of Scorpion retainers. At the crest, propped against a pole supporting the clan's standard, stood Bayushi Tetsuo, Shoju's cousin's son.

A black crow perched on the young lieutenant's helmet and pecked at his eyes, first one and then the other. Tetsuo's open mouth made no protest to the bird's molestation, nor did he wave his one remaining hand to shoo the crow away. Instead, he held his fist clutched tight to the pole, which supported the tattered battle flag of the Scorpion Clan. Tetsuo's other fist lay at his feet. His right arm had been severed at the shoulder.

Shoju advanced quickly up the hill. Hot wind swept yellow dust from the battlefield and stung his eyes, making them tear. He reached the top of the hill, drew his sword, and swiftly killed the bird tormenting his lieutenant's corpse. The daimyo sheathed his katana. He slid the standard pole free of Tetsuo's dead fingers, and the young man's body eased gently to the ground.

Tetsuo's mouth seemed to form an unspoken question: "Why?"

Shoju had no answer. He stared down at Tetsuo's bird-damaged eyes. A reflection in the dead orbs saved the Scorpion daimyo's life.

Instinctively, Shoju jumped back—just in time. A huge jade samurai rose up before him from the pile of bodies. The warrior appeared untouched by the battle; whether he had lain in wait for the daimyo or had arrived as Shoju attended to Tetsuo, the Scorpion leader could not say.

The jade warrior raised his long sword high. The late

afternoon sun reflected off it, splashing crimson into Shoju's eyes. The daimyo squinted against the glare and drew the sword of his Bayushi ancestors, bracing for the attack.

The samurai came at him swiftly, silently, his huge sword poised over his head. Shoju stepped aside. Their blades met. The sound of steel on steel echoed across the fields of the dead. As their swords parted, the Scorpion daimyo aimed a quick cut at the samurai's neck. The giant parried effortlessly and returned the attack in kind. Shoju caught the slice with his katana. His enemy's blade slid off, barely missing Shoju's shoulder.

The Scorpion circled left to gain the uphill advantage.

The jade warrior pressed the attack. Kicking bodies aside as he came, he forced Shoju back down the hill.

As he retreated, Shoju stepped on the helmet of a dead enemy. The lacquered bamboo gave way. There was no longer a skull underneath to support it. Cursing, Shoju toppled backward.

The samurai bore in, sword raised for the kill.

Years of practice took hold. Shoju lashed out with his right foot as he fell. His metal-shod toe connected with the samurai's left ankle—a vulnerable spot in the jade armor. The samurai lurched forward. Shoju rolled away from the intended blow.

The jade warrior caught himself before he fell and almost recovered. The Scorpion didn't give him a chance.

Lightning-swift, Shoju rolled to his knees and swung his katana in a wide arc. The sword sliced into the back of the samurai's knees, in a spot without armor. Shoju felt the satisfying bite as steel cut through tendons and muscles.

To his credit, the giant didn't cry out as he fell. Instead, he tried to turn toward the daimyo, but his legs no longer obeyed him.

The Scorpion thrust the Bayushi sword between the breastplate and the helmet of his foe. It emerged from the back of the jade samurai's neck. The giant crashed to the ground and moved no more.

Shoju pulled the sword of his ancestors from the samurai. Curiosity overwhelmed him. Who was this man who fought so fiercely? Shoju reached toward the demon-masked helmet and opened it.

A cold chill seized the daimyo's stomach as he gazed at the face of his foe. There was no one there—no body—nothing in the helmet. Only a mirror.

Shoju cursed and rose. He'd seen evil magic before— though never any quite like this. He crested the hill once more and stood beside the body of his dead cousin, Tetsuo.

A vast sea of corpses rolled down from the hill, blackening the plain below. Here great armies had met and fought until not one man remained standing. Nothing moved. No sound disturbed the gruesome tableau save the plaintive whispering of the wind. Even the birds remained silent.

Before him, at the edge of the plain, Shoju saw the Forbidden City, sacred precinct of the emperor, rising like a monumental tomb in the land of the dead. Cautiously, with his sword still drawn, the daimyo walked down the hill toward the city.

He passed more of his people on the way, their faces drawn gaunt with pain and death. At some he paused a moment in contemplation, always cautious not to be surprised again by hidden foes. No more samurai appeared to bar his path.

At last the iron gates of the palace stood before him— silent, monolithic, impassable. Shoju wondered how he would surmount them, and what he would find within the sacred precincts.

As he stood thinking, a sound came from inside the city. Slowly, almost silently, the great gates swung open to welcome the Scorpion daimyo. A droning melody washed over him as the gates parted—a song of blood and death and victory. Shoju had heard the song all his life, but he could not remember its name. The tune stirred the fires in his soul.

Someone waited for him on the other side of the gate.

Beyond the portal, Shoju saw his lovely young wife, Bayushi Kachiko. She smiled, stretched out her pale arms, and said, "Greetings, Husband. The day is ours."

1 DREAMS

The Scorpion daimyo woke from his nightmare, choking down the urge to scream. He sat bolt upright in his bed, sweat pouring from his body, his right arm aching. He clenched his teeth and rubbed the arm vigorously.

The tattoo on his right shoulder burned under Shoju's touch, just as it had the day his father's shugenja scribed it upon his flesh. Gradually, the burning spread down the rest of the withered limb and restored it to life. The arm tingled, as if ants crawled over the daimyo's skin. Through the years, Shoju had grown used to the sensation. In fact, he almost enjoyed it.

The tingling pain was far better than the alternative: an arm twisted from birth, almost useless. With spells, herbs, exercise, and the dark tattoo, Bayushi Shoju was the equal of any man in Rokugan—better than most. Far better.

As the pain subsided, the Scorpion daimyo relaxed his jaw muscles and let out a soft breath. The sweat began to cool on his skin, and he shivered slightly in the cold darkness of his bedroom. Beside him, his wife stirred and sat up.

Shoju could see her pale form in the moonlight leaking through the room's sole, high window. Even after sixteen years of marriage, Bayushi Kachiko was still the most exquisite creature in all of the Scorpion's holdings. No—in all of the Emerald Empire itself.

Her form was as shapely as a young willow; her skin pale and smooth like porcelain. Her black hair cascaded like a raven waterfall over her naked shoulders. Her eyes were as black as ocean depths and shone softly in the moonlight. Sea-green flecks danced within them. Her voice held honey and the mist of Rokugan's forested valleys.

"What's wrong, Husband?" Kachiko asked softly, her voice barely causing a ripple in the darkness. She placed a pale hand on Shoju's damp body and stroked his back. The Scorpion could feel his tension ebbing at her touch.

"I had a dream," he said, his voice deep and mellifluous. The Scorpion daimyo had spent years training his voice and even now, in the privacy of his own bedchamber, kept his tones under tight rein. "A dream of fire and death." He reached up and brushed a damp lock of black hair from his face.

She leaned forward, kissed him, and then lay back, sprawling like a contented cat, inviting him to join her. The white expanse of her body was a seductive ghost in the moonlight. "Tell me about your dream," she said, gazing into his eyes.

Despite himself, Shoju felt a smile creep over his hard face. It tugged at the corner of his lips—lips made crooked by the same accident of birth that had twisted his arm. Shoju knew he was ugly, even in the moonlight. His eyes were too large, his nose was long and hawklike, his lips thin, his chin sharp. But when he was with Kachiko, he seldom remembered this.

She smiled at him and spoke with an affectionate tone reserved for him alone. "Come," she said, stretching out her arms.

The Scorpion daimyo reclined beside his wife, leaning on his good arm and gazing into her deep eyes. He kissed her once, upon the lips. When he spoke, his voice was barely a whisper.

"I dreamed of a final battle on the plain of Heigen no Utaku," he began. "Bodies lay everywhere, and fire burned across all the land. I killed many men: daimyo and commoner, samurai and ronin alike. So many that I no longer remember their faces. I waded through rivers of blood and, when the slaughter was finished, looked for more foes to slay.

"Only then did I realize that the battle was over, and I was the last man standing. I saw the Imperial Palace in the distance and made my way there.

"The Emerald Champion rose to bar my way, but he was nothing, just a hollow shell. I slew him as I had slain the others. Soon I stood before the gates of the Forbidden City, triumphant but alone."

"Was I not with you?" Kachiko asked, her voice a distant memory of a song.

"Always," he said. "You opened the gates of the city as I reached them and beckoned me inside. You told me we had won the war. Together we walked to the throne room. The throne sat vacant, and so I took it.

"But, as I sat, a black fire coursed through my body. The arms of the throne grasped my arms, pinning me to it. It turned into a throne of skulls—laughing skulls.

"Then I was in the fires of Jigoku. Demons sprang up around me, jeering obscenely and joining in the laughter of the skulls. The walls of the palace fell away, and I could see all the land that I ruled over.

"But Rokugan was desolate, barren, destroyed—a kingdom of ash. My heart, like the kingdom, lay barren."

Kachiko reached up and stroked his long, black mane. "Was I not with you then?" she asked.

"Yes," said Shoju. "Even to the last you were at my side."

"Then you need not fear," she said. "So long as we are together, your heart will never be lonely."

He embraced her, and they kissed long and deeply. After a time they separated.

"Those you killed, did you know them?" Kachiko asked quietly.

Shoju nodded and laid his head beside hers. "Many of them. Yes."

"Tell me."

"Kisada of the Crab. Hoturi of the Crane, as well as their Emerald Champion. Ujimitsu of the Phoenix and Yokatsu of the barbarian tainted Unicorn. All of them fell before me like rice before a sickle. Even Yokuni—the Great Dragon himself."

"Not the Lion, then," she asked, her voice drifting off into dreams.

"Tsuko of the Lion, yes, but not Toturi." As he said it, Shoju felt a tightness at the base of his skull, like a snake twining around his spine.

Kachiko stroked his chest. "Have no fear. If it becomes necessary, you will slay Akodo Toturi as surely as all the others. None may stand before my great Scorpion master."

She embraced him once more, and the two of them melded into the darkness together.

⩓ ⩓ ⩓ ⩓ ⩓ ⩓ ⩓ ⩓

By the time Shoju woke early the next morning, his wife had already departed their bedchamber. Her perfume lingered, mingling with the scent of flowers. The carefully arranged blossoms sat on a low table in one corner of the room.

The room was small, square, and sparsely furnished. Its walls were *fusuma* and *shoji*, many-paned rice paper screens. Bright morning light filtered into the room through the east wall. Atop smooth, dark floorboards lay a thick *tatami* mat that held the daimyo's futon. Embroidered scorpions and mythical animals danced across the quilt.

The Scorpion daimyo rose, bathed in an adjoining room, and then dressed. His mood was still grim, so he chose a black and maroon kimono. He cinched it at the waist with a wide, midnight blue *obi*, and fastened the belt with a pin in the shape of a golden scorpion.

For his mask he chose a simple one, painted pale with impassive features. For Shoju the mask served a dual purpose. It not only denoted his membership in the Scorpion Clan, but it also hid his true face from the world. Only three living people had ever seen the Scorpion without his mask: his wife Kachiko, Kiko—the old woman who had attended him as a child—and his half-brother Bayushi Aramoro. Not even his son, Dairu, had seen the face behind the mask.

It amused Shoju that most of Rokugan assumed the mask hid a face as attractive as Shoju's words. Aramoro's mask, which barely hid his handsome countenance, reinforced this idea—as did the mask of Kachiko. In fact, the mask of the Scorpion daimyo's wife could hardly be called a mask at all. It wasn't even a veil, just silk fabric and paint applied to her face.

Kachiko's mask enhanced her beauty; Shoju's mask hid his ugliness. It was the essence of the Scorpion Clan that no one suspected the truth. Who would ever believe the most beautiful woman in the world had married a man whose face could make an ox weep?

Behind his bland mask, Shoju smiled. The art of the Scorpion was to lie by telling the truth and tell the truth by lying.

To finish his wardrobe, Shoju placed the emblem of his house, the *mon*, on his left shoulder, the shoulder closer to his heart. He had to use his right arm to do so; the arm twinged.

Shoju lifted a small blue bottle from a low table near his futon. He removed the stopper and drank. He held the warm liquid in his mouth, counted to five, and let the potion slide slowly down his throat. The tattoo tingled, and the pain in his arm slipped away—if only for a while.

Every day of his life the Scorpion had performed some combination of rituals to give his right arm strength. Now he moved slowly around the smooth wooden floor of his bedchamber, executing intricate *kata* to exercise not only his withered limb but the rest of his body as well. Soon energy flowed through his supple frame, and he felt ready to face the day.

He took the sword of his ancestors, *Itsuwari*, from its mulberry stand near his bed and tucked it into his belt. As he touched the hilt, the power of the katana hummed in his mind. In the distance, as always, came another song, soft but persistent—the song of a magical sword hidden deep within the bowels of the castle.

Shoju pushed the song from his mind, picked up a *wakizashi* he had forged himself, and tucked the smaller sword into his belt as well. A final glance in his looking glass assured the daimyo that the cut of his clothing hid his deformity. Not even his eyes could be discerned behind his mask.

He left the bedchamber and walked through the cool hallways of the Scorpion palace, Kyuden Bayushi. His wife would be breakfasting in the gardens; she always did when the weather permitted. Even at the height of summer, her beauty outshone the best of the castle's rare blossoms.

Usually Shoju joined her, but today his mood was too dark. Instead, he set course for an audience chamber off one of the fortress's eastern balconies. The balconies were a ruse, of course, to make the castle seem more vulnerable than it was. In keeping with Scorpion tradition, they created both that impression and its opposite. Could this castle be so impregnable, the thinking went, that balconies didn't hinder its defense? Not only did the balconies raise such questions, they also made Kyuden Bayushi one of the most ornate fortresses in Rokugan. People who beheld the castle's gracefully curved walls and high, balconied towers could not help being impressed. Bayushi Shoju smiled at the dual nature of the Scorpion.

He passed a servant in the outer halls near the balcony room and ordered breakfast. He also requested that his cousin, Bayushi Tetsuo, be sent to him. Most daimyos had servants follow them around, tending to every whim—but that was not the way of the Scorpion. Shoju valued his privacy too much to have toadies fawning over his every movement. He preferred to roam his castle free from such interference. When he actually needed something, like breakfast, there was always someone close at hand to fulfill the request.

He drew back the paper fusuma wall that separated the room from the hall, entered the chamber, and then slid the screen shut behind him.

Walking to the far wall he threw open the shoji and gazed out into the sunrise. The sun loomed large and golden over the mountains to the east of the castle. Seikitsu san Yama no Oi, they were called—"The Spine of the World." Even now, in spring, their topmost peaks glittered white with snow.

A wide road snaked away from the castle's eastern gate toward Roka Beiden. Behind his mask the Scorpion smiled. Many battles had been fought to control Beiden Pass, the only avenue large enough to move an army through the mountains. Though technically the emperor controlled the pass, in fact, the western end lay in Scorpion lands. Shoju's coffers had been bolstered mightily by the tolls his people collected from travelers.

On the eastern end of the pass sat the Lion, ever vigilant, ever wary of both the Scorpion to the west and the Crane to the south and east. In the last two hundred years the Lion and Crane had largely restricted their quarrels to each other—a practice the Scorpion subtly encouraged.

Recently, the daimyo of the Lion and Crane came to an "understanding," and their petty wars diminished almost to nothing. Shoju didn't like that. A distracted enemy was easier to deceive or persuade. The Scorpion Clan had many enemies.

That, of course, was the clan's job. Long ago the first Bayushi had been charged by the first emperor to become Rokugan's master of espionage. Since that time, the clan of the Scorpion had been distrusted by all the other clans of the Emerald Empire, and not without reason.

People said the Scorpion heard all whispers and knew all secrets. Largely, this was true, but only Scorpions knew how hard they worked to get those secrets. Shoju and Kachiko knew best of all. Masters of spy-craft, they were privileged to serve the emperor against all his enemies, within the empire and without. Kachiko even held a formal position at the Imperial Court, as the emperor's personal aide.

The Scorpion smiled again. He and his wife did their jobs well—too well to care that the Scorpions were despised.

Shoju's thoughts turned once again to the Lion beyond the mountains. Akodo Toturi, born to rule the Lion Clan, schooled by monks—a master strategist and fighter. Not brash and impulsive like the other Lion leader, Matsu Tsuko, but cool and level-headed, at least on the battlefield. Though they had never met, Toturi was the one man Shoju feared in battle, the one man he could never defeat in his dreams. The Scorpion daimyo wished he knew more about the man. He made a mental note to have Kachiko's spies look into it. He would tell her after breakfast.

Just then, the fusuma entrance to the room slid open. Instinctively, Shoju's hand went to the hilt of his katana. He relaxed as his cousin, Bayushi Tetsuo, entered the room. Two servants trailed behind the young lieutenant, carrying trays of food: fruit, bean paste, rice, nuts, and green tea. The servants set the food down, bowed, and left the two men alone, sliding the screen closed as they went.

Tetsuo stood a few inches shorter than the Scorpion daimyo. He had a pleasant face and a square jaw. His body was strong and supple, a fact clear even under his carefully cut kimono. Tetsuo shaved his head in the traditional samurai style and tied what was left in a topknot. He seldom wore a mask while in the Bayushi stronghold, and this morning was no exception. Tetsuo liked to show off his good looks to the ladies of the castle.

The young lieutenant bowed low to his master and laid aside his *dai-sho* swords as he sat on the floor beside the food. He kept the swords near his right hand, making them difficult to draw, as a sign of respect and trust.

Shoju nodded and took a seat beside his cousin, laying aside his swords as well. Because he was left-handed, he put his swords on the left. This was not a courtesy Shoju extended to everyone. Often, when eating in public, Shoju placed his swords on the right. He did so both out of expedience and to maintain the dual nature of the Scorpion. Only those who knew Shoju intimately realized how dangerous he was with his swords in that position. Bayushi Tetsuo knew him well. Out of respect, Shoju put his swords on the left.

"I'm honored to eat with you this morning, Lord," Tetsuo said.

The Scorpion daimyo almost laughed. "You're not speaking to a Crane, you know," he said to the younger man. "You're among Scorpions. No need to put on such a pretty mask."

Tetsuo's face reddened slightly. "Nevertheless. I *am* honored." He bowed his head a bit.

Shoju waved his hand at Tetsuo, picked up a persimmon, and began to peel it. He carefully manipulated the food up under his mask and into his mouth.

Tetsuo took a small bowl of bean paste in one hand and a pair of chopsticks with the other. He brought the bowl to his lips and shoveled in some of the paste. "You know, Cousin," he said around a mouthful of food, "your kitchens make the best *natto* in all of Rokugan. When I'm away from home, I always miss it."

Behind his mask, Shoju smiled, though Tetsuo couldn't see it. "I despise the stuff," he said. "Though the staff knows you're fond of natto, which is why they continue to make it."

"You won't mind if I have yours, then?" said Tetsuo. He'd finished his own bowl and now picked up the second. "Glorious morning, isn't it?" he said. "I saw Kachiko in the gardens. I'm surprised you didn't join her. You usually do, don't you?"

Shoju nodded. "Usually, yes," he said. "But this morning I didn't want to intrude. I did not sleep well last night. I had . . . a dream."

Tetsuo stopped eating for a moment and looked at his cousin, forgetting that all he would see was the Scorpion daimyo's mask. The pale face looked back at him, neither happy nor sad, neither smiling nor frowning. "Only a dream?" Tetsuo asked.

"A nightmare, really," Shoju said flatly. In brief, unemotional terms, he told Tetsuo of his experiences last night. Halfway through, the young lieutenant stopped eating. By the time his lord had reached the end of the tale, all Tetsuo could do was nod grimly.

"A terrible dream. Surely you were in the grip of the oni ringetsu." Tetsuo nodded his head in a slight bow and said, "*Baku kurae!*" a traditional blessing against nightmares. "But you need not worry yourself. What Kachiko said is true: so long as you and she are together, there is nothing you can't accomplish."

Shoju nodded again. Behind his mask he frowned. "Usually, I would agree with you. But this time . . ." The Scorpion daimyo rose and went out onto the balcony. He leaned his hands on the railing and looked at the courtyard below. "This time," he said, "I fear the dream may hold my future—and the future of all Rokugan."

Tetsuo rose and joined his master on the balcony. "I'm no shugenja, no expert in dreams. Perhaps you should consult one. Yogo Junzo, perhaps?"

"Junzo thinks me a fool. He believes Kachiko leads me around by my obi, as if I were a doddering old man."

The younger man's jaw dropped open in shock. "Junzo would never . . ."

Shoju turned on him suddenly, and Tetsuo felt glad he could not see the daimyo's face behind the bland mask. "Junzo would never say so, of course," Shoju said, almost spitting the words. "But I am *the* Scorpion. Little escapes my perceptions. No, Junzo may have his uses, but reading my dreams is not one of them. Not today."

Tetsuo nodded politely. "I understand that you fear the portents of this dream," he said. "But no man may know his future—save perhaps for Uikku, the Serene Prophet."

Shoju put his hand on the young man's shoulder. They walked back into the room together and sat down once more.

The daimyo said, "What a Scorpion would give to know the things the Serene Prophet saw . . . What *I* would give. . . . What Bayushi Daijin *did* give. . . ."

"They say Daijin still haunts the catacombs beneath our deepest dungeons," Tetsuo said.

The Scorpion daimyo looked at the younger man's face, holding Tetsuo's dark eyes with his own. "You believe this ghost story?" Shoju asked.

Tetsuo shifted uncomfortably where he sat. "In my youth," he said slowly, "I often ventured into the catacombs. I saw many strange things there—frightening things. Whether I saw the ghost of this retainer, I cannot say for certain. But I do believe that such a ghost *could* exist."

Shoju nodded slowly. "I believe it too," he said. "There is a tradition that the ghosts of our ancestors haunt the catacombs beneath the palace. In times of trial, Scorpion daimyos have sought answers from these spirits. My grandfather did so."

"And . . . ?" Tetsuo asked.

"He never spoke of it afterward," Shoju said grimly. "And he died horribly."

"I see," said the younger man.

Behind his mask, Shoju's mouth drew thin and tight; his brow furrowed with determination. He stood and gazed out into the lands beyond the windows. In his mind, he saw the corpse-littered plain from his dream.

"If such shades exist," the Scorpion daimyo said, "you and I shall find them and ask our questions. Together we will hunt the ghost of Daijin and wrest from it the secrets I need—the meaning of my dreams and the final prophecies of Uikku."

2 THE DREAMER

The hunter stalked through the ancient forest, looking for his prey. His every sense was alive with the fire of the hunt. His eyes darted, lighting briefly on a bent twig, a trampled bush. His ears listened for rustling underbrush. The aroma of the pine forest filled his nose; his mind set aside the evergreen smell and searched for his quarry's scent.

He'd been on the hunt since the stars hung pale in the sky, just before the light of dawn painted the Spine of the World Mountains in gold. Now, morning cast long shadows, dappling the forest with splotches of green and yellow.

A wide, clear stream cut across his path, and the hunter stopped at it. He dipped his hand in the cold water and brought it to his lips. He smiled at the sweet, pure taste. The serene isolation of the forest reminded him of his days in the Asoko Monastery.

He shook his head and sighed. Those were simpler days, and sometimes the hunter missed them. His duties had called him away from his isolation, away from his studies. For whatever reason, the Fortunes had granted him great power in Rokugan. Such a fate could not be disregarded.

A sound caught the hunter's ear: downstream, an animal drinking, shaking off the remnants of sleep, foraging for breakfast and a sip of cool water. His quarry.

The hunter quietly rose from where he squatted. His sandalled feet deftly navigated a course of stepping stones across the stream. Quietly, he parted the ferns on the other side and vanished into the brush. He slipped with stealth through the undergrowth, walking mindfully as the old monks had taught him. Not a twig snapped under his feet.

In a few moments he had ranged down the stream and had the boar in sight. The animal was foraging in the undergrowth, not fifty yards upwind. A satisfied smile came to the hunter's lips. He unslung the *yumi* bow from his back and nocked an arrow to it.

The hunter aimed at the wild boar and pulled the string of the bow to his ear. He calmed his mind and listened until he could hear his own heartbeat.

In the moment of perfect stillness, he opened his fingers. The bowstring snapped tight. The arrow flew straight and true toward its target.

At the last moment, something—perhaps a succulent bit of root—made the boar turn its head. The animal squealed in pain as the hunter's arrow lodged in its shoulder. It turned, seeking the source of its torment, and quickly spotted the hunter.

With a deep bellow, the boar charged through the undergrowth at the hunter. The marksman cursed his luck and dropped the bow to the ground. He didn't have time for another shot. Instead, he put his hand on the hilt of his katana and drew the sword in an on-guard posture.

He could see the animal better now. It was large, at least

four hundred pounds, with tusks that curved back nearly to its upper lip. Its eyes were red with fury, and its breath came in great puffs. Steam blew from its nostrils. The scent of the animal almost overwhelmed the hunter; it reeked of decay and anger and brute power. The boar smelled like death.

The huntsman cleared his mind and stood ready.

As he felt the animal's hot breath, the man jumped to one side. The boar tried to react, but it was too late. In one swift move, the hunter's sword flashed across the neck of the beast, opening a gaping wound. The boar grunted and fell to the ground, its life blood splashing on the dark earth.

The hunter stepped forward and finished the kill.

In less than an hour he had the beast dressed out and ready to carry. The hunter slung the boar's carcass across his shoulders and hiked back through the woods the way he'd come. Though it had taken him all morning to track and find the animal, it took him barely twenty minutes to return to his destination.

He stepped out of the woods and into a tiny clearing. Just ahead of him stood a cabin, small, but exquisitely built. The posts and lintels of the building had been painted a cheerful red, and its paper shoji walls shone white in the morning sun. It looked like a small piece of heaven.

The cabin stood on the side of a hill, overlooking the Kawa Mitsu Kishi, the so-called Three-Sided River, which divided the lands of the Lion from those of the Scorpion and Crane.

The hunter frowned. He didn't like thoughts of politics to intrude on this perfect world. It didn't seem fair that so beautiful a river should be at the center of years of bloodshed. No, the hunter thought, people should appreciate the river for its beauty, rather than its strategic importance.

The shoji screen of the cabin slid open, and out stepped an angelic figure, a bright *kami*—his lover, Hatsuko. Akodo Toturi adjusted the boar he carried on his shoulders and sprinted the last few yards across the clearing into the arms of the woman he loved.

▲▲▲▲▲▲▲▲

The Lion daimyo woke smiling. The late afternoon sun shone through the paper walls of the room, painting the tatami-covered floor with pale golden warmth. The perfume of love filled the small chamber, and Toturi drank it in like wine. He took a deep breath and exhaled it slowly.

On the bedroll beside him, Hatsuko lay dreaming. Toturi gazed at her slender body and sighed. So beautiful. He stroked her black, silken hair, his fingers lingering over the strands. Gently, he kissed her forehead, but he did not wake her.

This place, this time was so much like his dream. Lying here beside his love, he could almost believe the dream had been real. He could nearly imagine that the two of them were inside the mountain cabin, a fragile fortress built with his own hands.

In reality, they lay together in a small room in a large house on the outskirts of Mura Kita Chusen, one of the towns surrounding the great city of Otosan Uchi. It was a geisha house, not a cabin—a house where Hatsuko worked entertaining samurai. This special form of entertainment she reserved for Toturi alone. He stroked her hair again.

How much his dreams seemed like reality, and how much reality seemed a dream. Didn't Shinsei teach something about that? With his mind beclouded by sleep and love, Akodo Toturi couldn't quite remember.

Indeed, this morning he had forsaken the town for the solitude of the hunt. As general to the emperor, Toturi had leave to hunt in the Imperial Forest, Fudaraku no Mori. He had seen great trees and a rushing stream similar to those of his dream.

But his quarry today had been a doe, not a boar. The boar had been another day, another forest, the sprawling woods of his homeland, near the Scorpion border. No, this day he had not faced death, merely a challenge to his skills as a hunter. Of course he had triumphed. Toturi almost laughed to think how even so small a victory filled him with pleasure, but he remembered Hatsuko sleeping beside him and stifled the noise.

So sweet, she was. In his dream she had met him at the cabin step. In reality, he and his doe "offering" had been met at the gate to the geisha house by Kitsune Junko, mistress of the house. Though the Lion general had come in disguise, as he always did, Junko fussed over him nonetheless. Toturi could never quite make up his mind whether to be flattered or annoyed by all the attention.

In the end, Junko allowed him to bring his present through the inner sanctums of the house to the cooking pit out back. Hatsuko greeted him politely, as she always did. Later, the passion between them flared—as it always did.

Toturi slipped out from under the bed's soft quilt, making sure the blanket covered Hatsuko before he left. Stretching, he crossed the small room and fetched his short kimono from where it lay. The Lion daimyo put the robe on and smiled again. He and Hatsuko had slept through most of the day, but Toturi didn't care.

Here, in the Willow World of the geisha house, his responsibilities as head of his clan seemed a world away. Perhaps that was why he liked this place so much. He scratched himself and slipped his sandals onto his bare feet.

Quietly sliding open the room's shoji screen, Toturi crossed the small porch beyond and went outside. Near the house, the doe still roasted on a spit over a fire pit. The fire had grown low. Toturi fetched a few logs and threw them onto the smoldering pyre. This diminished the log pile to a point that made Toturi frown. He walked behind the house to where the unchopped wood lay.

The geisha mistress Junko would never have allowed him to stoop to so menial a task. The thought made him smile. Monks—even former monks—did many things in pursuit of a self-sufficient life, things no other samurai would consider. He selected an armful of stout logs, took them to a nearby stump, picked up an ax, and began to split them. When they were done, he got another armful to work on.

Soon a soft sheen of sweat began to bead on his forehead. This, too, brought a smile to the Lion daimyo's face. Chop wood, carry water, he thought. How simple, how *clear* life seemed here beside Hatsuko. How like his life at the Asoko Monastery.

But Hatsuko wasn't like life in the monastery. Not in the least. She was everything good that the world had to offer. Soft-spoken, kind, warm to the touch, and sweet to kiss. Lips like nectar. Toturi licked his own lips at the thought—and split another log.

He remembered the first time they'd met, at this very geisha house. His general, Ikoma Bentai, had brought Toturi here along with a number of other officers after a successful strike against a cadre of bandits.

It wasn't a large victory by Lion standards, but in the peace that Toturi and his friend, Crane Daimyo Doji Hoturi, had imposed between their two houses, any battle was cause for celebration. The bandits had not been the pushovers they'd expected, either. They'd even had a rogue shugenja working with them. Toturi lost two samurai to the magician's flame tongues before he put his sword through the man.

The bandit chief proved easier to kill. Bentai had piked his head even before the shugenja fell. Normally, the Lion daimyo wouldn't have ridden out on such a trivial matter, but the peace had made his men edgy. They needed to see him.

Toturi's monastic background made him suspect to many in his clan. His brother, Arasou, had been expected to succeed to the clan's leadership, but Arasou had been killed in the battle to take the Crane city of Toshi Ranbo wo Shien Shite Reigisaho. The city of Violence Behind Courtliness had lived up to its name. Leadership of the Lions suddenly fell to the quiet, contemplative Toturi—who was summoned home from the monastery to fulfill his family's obligation.

At first, the burden of leadership sat heavily on the young

man. Soon, he discovered that his flair for strategy served his people well. Now, there was little the Lion armies could not accomplish militarily under his command.

Had his lifelong friendship with Doji Hoturi, the Crane daimyo, not forced a truce between their clans, Toturi felt sure the Lions could have regained all the lands they had lost to the Crane previously—even Toshi Ranbo wo Shien Shite Reigisaho.

Despite his aptitude as a commanding general, Toturi was not a warlike man. In fact, he had not even been much of a *worldly* man—not until that night with Bentai.

General Ikoma Bentai was a self-made samurai. Born to a farming family, he'd joined the Lion army and—through dint of his heroism—earned the dai-sho and samurai ranks. He'd even acquitted himself nobly in the battle where Toturi's brother and their uncle, who had been Lion Champion at that time, fell.

Bentai possessed and lusted for all of the earthly experiences that Toturi lacked. After routing the bandits, Bentai had insisted with all due politeness that his daimyo join him and his men on their celebratory trip to the local geisha house.

"How can you lead men when you have no knowledge of what it is like to truly *be* a man?" Bentai had said to Toturi. "Samurai are not all high thoughts and battles. A man must learn to *enjoy* life. Why, I doubt if you've even seen a geisha perform. A man hasn't lived until a woman from the Willow World sings to him. Come!"

At first Toturi had demurred, but the general's good-natured prodding finally convinced him. Toturi remained profoundly glad he had listened to his general.

Toturi had seen immediately that Hatsuko was not like other geisha. Yes, she had the ways of the Willow World, the softness of voice and form, the skill with music and conversation, the shaved eyebrows and white-painted skin. But she also had another quality, something Toturi found hard to define. He found himself returning to that geisha house again and again.

After a time, he knew he loved her. He could not let her stay where she was. The life of a geisha was no life for the lady of the Lion Champion. He should buy her contract, sweep her away from the geisha house, build her that mountain cabin he dreamed of. There, nestled in the Spine of the World, the two of them would find the solitude that their love needed to grow and flourish. He knew this, but his plan remained only a dream.

His duties in the Imperial Court interfered with his dreams. Even in times of relative peace, there were battles to be fought, enemies to be deposed, endless processions of pomp and pageantry, and the incessant intrigues of the court. It seemed peace only increased the plotting and back-stabbing. Scorpion and Crane and Phoenix insisted on making everyday life more complex than it needed to be.

Why couldn't a man be allowed to enjoy what he'd won? Why couldn't Toturi simply ask the emperor for release from his unwanted engagement to that Phoenix woman? Why did the courage to do this one, simple thing escape him?

Yet escape him it did.

When he came to the geisha house now, the Lion arrived in disguise. He wore simple clothes, a broad-brimmed straw hat, and peasants' *zori* sandals. The disguise agreed with his monastic upbringing. In fact, Toturi felt more at home in it than he did in the elaborate kimonos he was often forced to wear at court.

Though obligated to lead his clan, this life—the simple life—truly agreed with him. Fresh air, clean water, beautiful landscapes, and of course, the woman he loved. This was all Toturi needed to be truly happy. This place was so close to his dream—so close. The Lion daimyo wiped the sweat from his forehead and split another log.

A soft sound, like the voice of a nightingale, disturbed his reverie.

"Toturi-sama," the nightingale said, "I have made dinner for us."

Toturi split a last log and embedded his axe in the stump. He turned and saw a sight that made warm fire run through him.

Hatsuko bowed. The late-afternoon sun flashed off her black hair. She had dressed in a flowered kimono, cut modestly, and plain sandals. Her face was lovely, even though she kept it painted in geisha fashion: white, with arching eyebrows and red lips. Toturi longed to see the true face behind the mask, but he never had. He knew he never would until he bought her contract.

In his mind he imagined how it might be—how it had been in his dream that morning. Her face would hold a hint of the sun from living outside. He would make her stop painting her face and shaving her eyebrows. "You are no longer a geisha," he would tell her. "You are my love. I will look upon your true face."

That was the future. In the present, still painted as an entertainer, she was nevertheless lovely.

As her bow ended, Hatsuko met Toturi's eyes. She smiled at him. The Lion's heart melted all over again. "Your meal awaits, Toturi-sama," she said.

"Not so formal, Hatsuko-chan," he said, his voice warm with love. "Never so formal with me."

"You are my love," she replied, "but you are also my lord."

"As you are the ruler of my heart," he said. He closed the distance between them and embraced her. They kissed, long and passionately.

When they parted, she said, "After dinner, we will have tea."

Toturi smiled. Hatsuko performed the tea ceremony better than anyone he'd ever known—even those experts he'd seen at court. The ceremony affirmed and renewed their love.

No wonder I smile so much, he thought.

Holding hands, they went inside.

⋏⋏⋏⋏⋏⋏⋏⋏

After the glow of the tea ceremony had died away, the couple left the cabin for a walk in the woods. Hatsuko is lucky, Toturi thought, to live this close to nature.

The trees in this part of the Imperial Forest were old. The preserve's larger stands had never been cut for timber. Tall pines predominated the landscape, some so wide that Toturi would have needed two other men to encircle the trunks with their arms. In the tallest part of the forest, the underbrush thinned; wide branches overhead blocked the light smaller plants needed to grow.

Here the lovers could walk on a blanket of pine needles and listen to the wind whispering through the boughs. Hatsuko had resisted leaving the geisha house at first, but Toturi convinced her. He wanted to show her the natural world as she had shown him the Willow World. Though she held his hand as they walked, her steps were cautious, tentative.

The pungent aroma of the big trees filled the air. Toturi thought of the morning's deer hunt and suddenly realized he'd left his bow and dai-sho behind. He didn't care. Wrapped in love, he feared nothing in the broad forest. Surely no real threats could lurk so near the Imperial City.

All that mattered was *here*, beneath the wide boughs. He was here. His lover was here. The sun, the sky, the trees, all lived in a perfect world with him and Hatsuko. Nearby, he could hear the friendly babbling of the stream as it coursed down the hillside.

Hatsuko found a flower growing at the base of a tree, a pale lily. She picked the blossom and pleated it into Toturi's long hair behind his left ear, just above his heart. The daimyo dyed his mane yellow like most Lions, and Hatsuko appreciated it. She ran her fingers through the silky black strands as she wove the flower in. Her work completed, she kissed him.

He seized her shoulders and kissed her back. When they parted, he saw sadness in her eyes.

"What is it, my love?" he asked softly.

"I cannot believe . . ." she began, and then faltered.

"Cannot believe what?" Toturi asked.

She spread her delicate hands and indicated the world around them. "All of this," she said. "This world we live in. I love it, as I love you, but I know it cannot last."

The Lion daimyo almost laughed, but didn't when he realized how gravely serious she was. Instead, he took her round chin in his large hands.

"Some things," he said, "will never pass away. This hillside, these trees, the sky above, the water flowing in the stream nearby. Our love is like these things: eternal."

She closed her round, dark eyes and looked away from him. "Eternal, perhaps, but not unchanging. Even the tallest trees may be felled by men or insects; water may be caught and trapped in still pools; the sky darkens with clouds and weeps with rain. In time a mountain may become no more than a small hillock."

Toturi took her in his arms once again. "But that would take an age, and in that age, I will love you as no man has ever loved a woman."

"I fear that it will not always be so."

"So long as you are in my arms," he said, "you need never fear."

"But your position, responsibilities at court, my . . ." she hesitated, ". . . my *situation* . . ." She trailed off.

"You are my love," he said softly. "You rule my heart; even the emperor cannot change that."

"And your fiancée . . . ?"

"I will beg the emperor to dissolve our engagement. I will buy your contract. You will become my lady in name as well as in my heart. I will pledge my allegiance only to you. You will be free."

"Free," she whispered softly, as if loosing a delicate bird from its cage.

She put her head against his strong, broad chest, but her apprehensions did not vanish. Instead, they grew greater, as the shadows of the trees filled the forest in the lengthening afternoon.

Toturi took her hand, and the two of them continued their walk.

Soon they came to the wide stream that Toturi had encountered both in his dream and in his hunt that morning. They paused and drank, and sat on large, flat rocks they found by the waterside. Toturi told her of battles he had fought since becoming daimyo, and things he had learned while a pupil in the Asoko Monastery. He even sang songs to her.

Occasionally, she joined her voice to his, and their music drifted up into the leafy canopy like sweet smoke in the afternoon air. Hatsuko had the voice of a songbird, and Toturi marveled every time he heard it. He wondered whether it was her voice that he'd first fallen in love with, or the gentle soul behind the white paint of the geisha.

Long minutes they spent rapt in nature and music and the wonders of love. Then Toturi asked, "What lies in that direction?" With one long-fingered hand he pointed upstream.

"I do not know," she said. "I never venture far from the house. I would not be here now except that you are beside me."

Toturi stood. "Let's find out."

He took her hand and helped her up. Together they hiked upstream. Soon the stream opened into a broad, clear pool. Fern fronds and smooth rocks lined the pool's banks. At the far end, a waterfall tumbled down the face of the hill, leapt over a tall precipice, and cascaded into the pool, causing soft music as it landed. The setting sun played off the falls, sending shimmering rainbows of light dancing around the forest.

Toturi and Hatsuko, stunned by the beauty of the scene, caught their breath.

"This place," he asked, "does it have a name?"

"I do not know, my lord. No one has ever spoken to me of it."

He looked at her, and love filled his eyes. "Then I will name it Hatsuko Falls," he said. "The sunlight glinting on the water reminds me of the shine of your hair, and the sound it makes suggests the music of your gentle voice."

Hatsuko blushed and turned away. "My lord," she said. "You cannot."

He smiled broadly. "I am the daimyo of the Lion," he said. "I am the general of the emperor's army. He who owns all this land listens to my counsel. Who is to say that, with the emperor's permission, I cannot name things as I like?"

"Not I, my lord," she said, still avoiding his gaze.

"Come then," he said, taking her by the shoulders and giving her a hug. "Gaze at the beauty that I behold in you." She turned and did as he bade. Together, they stood there, in that perfect place, in silence for a while.

Then he stepped away from her. "Can you swim?" he asked, beginning to strip off the top of his robe.

"No," she answered shyly.

"Then I shall teach you." He let the robe fall to the forest floor and took her hand. "Come," he said. "Let us see if the purity of these falls can wash away the paint of a geisha."

But as he turned back to the waterfall, Toturi saw the immense, serpentine form of the dragon.

3 THE SCROLL

Bayushi Tetsuo jumped. He swung his sword in the direction of the menace. It was only his own shadow, cast from the torch held in the right hand of his daimyo.

Bayushi Shoju chuckled. "Nervous?" he asked.

"I would be lying if I said no, my lord," the young lieutenant answered. "I have not been in these catacombs since I was a youth."

"Were you braver then, or more foolish?" the Scorpion daimyo asked.

"Both, I think. Less wise, certainly," replied Tetsuo. "I wonder if we should have the audacity to try to commune with the dead."

"Audacity is a Scorpion trait," said Shoju. "As is loyalty. I would dare anything for the empire. Anything."

Tetsuo nodded. "As would I. Still, I think I'd rather face an army of Crab soldiers than these catacombs."

"Brace up, Tetsuo. Only your fear can harm you."

Tetsuo looked at his daimyo and forced a smile. The Scorpion's face remained hidden and unknowable, though the mask he'd chosen for this task was far more fearsome than the one he'd worn at breakfast. Tetsuo wished they'd worn their armor instead of simple robes.

Shoju had insisted that to wear armor in their own fortress would be an insult to their Bayushi ancestors. "I am master of this place," he had said. "Let the specters fear *me*; I shall not fear them."

Tetsuo had reluctantly agreed, but now, so very near the entrance to the sprawling underground, he wished he hadn't. His thumb fingered the hilt of his katana. He edged the sword up from its scabbard just a crack, firmed his resolve, and pushed the sword back down.

"This way," Shoju said. "I had Soshi Bantaro fetch the best map of the catacombs. Bantaro's not as good a shugenja as Junzo, but he is easier to manage."

"Naturally, he wanted to come along," said Tetsuo.

"Naturally, but I forbade it. He may be a Scorpion, but he is not Bayushi. This test—this challenge—is for those of our blood."

Tetsuo nodded, wishing secretly the sorcerer had come with them. Bantaro was a toady, yes, but he was also powerful. Tetsuo hoped they would not need the magician's skills before the night was through. He brushed aside a thick mass of cobwebs, and the two of them continued deeper into the bowels of the castle.

Ahead, their torch light gleamed off damp paving stones on the floor of the corridor. Occasionally they passed niches in the wall. Most lay empty, but a few were filled with the bones of forgotten ancestors. Always the samurai took care to avoid touching these unclean things.

Deeper they went. The floor of the catacombs changed from flagstone to native rock. They had come below the depths of the castle's many cisterns. In the distance they could hear the trickle of water. A foul smell permeated the underground; Tetsuo wondered if the stench would ever wash out of his clothes.

Soon the map Bantaro had given them grew fragmented and inadequate. Shoju consulted it less and less. Three times they came to places where the passage branched off. Each time Shoju chose the leftmost passage—a course that took them ever farther below.

They were now deeper than Tetsuo had ever been in his youthful explorations—far deeper. The young Bayushi felt uncertain if he could remember his way back to the surface; he hoped his master could.

No, he *knew* his master could. Bayushi Shoju never undertook a task he could not complete. As far as Tetsuo knew, there was no task beyond the daimyo's undertaking. Even now, so deep within the ground, the Scorpion daimyo exuded confidence and control. He never paused in his journey, but pushed ever onward.

Eventually, the passage debouched into a large, cobweb-filled cavern, a place so enormous that the dim torch light did not reach the other side. The sound of water echoed from somewhere in front of them.

The Scorpion daimyo rolled up his map and put it away. "From this point on," he said, "the map is useless."

Tetsuo nodded. "Where are we, Master?" he asked.

"In Kokorono Sukima, the 'Cavern of the Mind,' as our ancestors called it."

"I like to think that my mind is considerably more open and airy," Tetsuo said.

The Scorpion chuckled again, a deep sound like thunder on distant mountains. "You're young yet," he said, stepping into the great open space.

"Where do we go from here?"

"From here, our ancestors will guide our way. We will be given a sign."

"I hope we won't have to wait long."

As if in answer to Tetsuo's thought, a strange noise echoed in the cavern. Not the babbling of water, but a kind of skittering noise. Tetsuo looked around to find that the Scorpion daimyo had set down the torch and drawn his sword. The ancient weapon gleamed yellow like a tiger's eyes in the torch light.

"Not our ancestors?" the youngster asked.

"No," Shoju said. "Look!"

Above them and to the right, shadows moved among the cobwebs.

"And there!" said Shoju, pointing now to their left.

Tetsuo swung in that direction and drew his katana. The spiders descended toward them on long strands of silk and skittered across the floor.

They were horrible, hairy things the size of small dogs. Red eyes glowed. Green venom dripped from curved fangs. Pale, skull-shaped marks adorned their backs.

Shoju attacked. His sword whisked through the air, cutting several descending spiders in two. A spider landed near the daimyo's foot and reared back. Shoju kicked it. The black, crusty body sailed into the darkness.

"I wish we'd brought more torches!" said Tetsuo. He'd seized the torch Shoju had dropped and was using it as a second sword. Fire seemed to repel the spiders better than steel.

Shoju whirled in a wide arc. He danced among the spiders and cut down several more. "I'll remember that the next time we come here," he said grimly.

Tetsuo smiled and set one of the spiders alight with his torch. He spitted another on the point of his sword and side-stepped a third. With a quick motion, like the *shiburi* used to clean a sword of blood, he flicked the punctured body from his katana. Still writhing, the creature sailed across the cavern and smashed into the bodies of two others.

"Our ancestors need better servants to clean their house," Tetsuo said.

"We shall have to tell them when we see them." The Scorpion daimyo continued his dance of death. The bodies of the spiders now lay heaped around him, though the tide of hideous arachnids showed no sign of ebbing.

A thought occurred to Tetsuo as he kicked aside a spider. He reached up with the torch and set the nearest cobweb ablaze. One web set off the next, like a series of fuses. In an instant, the room filled with blazing light.

A river ran through the middle of the cavern. It was about six feet wide and filled with bubbling, black water. Neither man could see any spiders on the other side.

"Make for the river," Shoju ordered. He slew a few more spiders and then ran.

Clutching the torch in one hand and his katana in the other, Tetsuo followed.

Spiders rained down on them. The samurai batted the creatures aside with their swords or kicked them with their feet. When one arachnid landed on Tetsuo's back, the Scorpion daimyo killed it without even breaking stride. Soon, they reached the bank of the black river.

"I hope it's not deep," Tetsuo said as they charged in. It wasn't. Even in the middle, it reached only halfway up the samurai's calves. The water was cold, bone-chillingly so, and black as charcoal. They couldn't see their feet on the bottom.

On the far bank, they whirled and stood at guard. Flames burned everywhere in the great webs. Spiders danced in pain and fury by the firelight. Several of the hideous creatures approached the river, but the Bayushi cousins charged in and killed them easily enough. Soon the fires died down, and no more spiders came. Gradually, even the hideous chittering grew still. The only sound in the cavern was that of the river and the labored breathing of the samurai.

"I see why no one comes down here," said Tetsuo.

Shoju nodded. "Not a trip to take lightly."

Tetsuo looked around, peering into the babbling ebony waters. "What is this?" he asked.

"Omidowe no Kawa, The River of Memory," Shoju said. "Drink from it, and you'll forget everything you ever knew."

"I'd like to forget those spiders."

Behind his mask, Shoju smiled. "Unfortunately, the river is not so selective. We had better move on."

Before them, several passageways beckoned. All were natural hallways formed out of living rock and worn smooth by running water. All led deeper into the ground. No footprints disturbed the dust at their entrances. No signs, man-made or otherwise, distinguished one passage from another.

A shiver ran down Tetsuo's spine. "Which way?"

"Hold a moment," Shoju replied. "Listen."

The samurai stopped and held their breath. A long minute passed, and then another. Tetsuo began to wonder what they were listening for. He exhaled and quietly drew another lungful of air—after the manner of his Scorpion stealth training.

Whether the daimyo breathed or not, Tetsuo could not tell. So complete was Shoju's mastery of his clan's art that, had Tetsuo not known better, he would have thought the older man a statue. His cousin's grim mask only enhanced the effect.

"Do you hear it?" Shoju whispered.

Tetsuo quieted his thoughts and concentrated. After a minute he whispered back, "Yes. Yes I do."

Faintly, in the distance, Tetsuo's ears could make out a strange moaning—as of a dying man on a battlefield. "The shade!" he said.

"Perhaps," agreed Shoju. "There," he said, indicating one of the tunnels with the point of his sword. He flicked the spider ichor from the blade and resheathed the weapon. "Come," he said.

Tetsuo cleaned and sheathed his blade as well. He followed his cousin into the dark passage beyond.

They passed more wall niches but saw no bones in them. The nooks grew more frequent, and the walls of the tunnel more rough.

"Could we have enough ancestors to fill all these?" Tetsuo asked.

Shoju shook his head. "Who can say? The line of the Scorpion is long. Perhaps these niches are so deep within the catacombs that they have never been used."

"Otherwise, what has happened to the bones that once rested here?" Tetsuo said.

"*Hai*," Shoju said, nodding.

Tetsuo wished, not for the last time, that he could see his daimyo's face behind the mask. It would have comforted the young samurai to know that his lord felt the same apprehension he did. The mask gave no clue, and Tetsuo knew that his cousin preferred it that way. In all the years of his life, Tetsuo had never caught more than a glimpse of Bayushi Shoju's face. He had no idea what his cousin really looked like.

Shoju paused and listened again. The moaning had grown louder, closer. A shiver ran down Tetsuo's spine.

"Not far now," Shoju said somberly.

Tetsuo nodded and unconsciously pushed the *tsuba* of his sword up with his thumb. This time, he did not push the hand guard back down again. His sword remained ready for an attack.

Up from the passage came a rustling noise, like wind blowing across twigs and dry leaves. Shoju and Tetsuo looked around warily, but could not find the source of the sounds.

Once again, the passageway opened up before them into a large cavern. This time, they saw no spider webs. Instead, the walls of the room were lined with niches. The light from the samurai's torch could not illuminate what, if anything, lay inside.

"Look!" Shoju said, pointing.

On the far side of the room was a raised dais, and on the dais sat a stone altar, and above the altar floated a scroll. Dim green foxfire bathed the scroll in eerie luminescence.

Before the cousins could enter the vault, two samurai stepped forward to bar their way. The men were dressed in black and red, traditional Scorpion colors, but the armor was tarnished and in poor repair. The samurai in the armor had been dead a very long time. The creatures made a noise like rustling leaves as they walked.

"Bayushi's spirit!" said Tetsuo, drawing his katana.

The Scorpion daimyo drew his sword as well, but he uttered no oaths.

The dead samurai attacked.

Tetsuo blocked the first cut with his katana. Green sparks flew from where his blade met that of the dead creature. Though the samurai's blade looked rusty, it didn't break as Tetsuo countered the blow.

"What are these things?" Tetsuo shouted.

Shoju, fighting for his life, answered, "The Lost—*Jigokuni Ochimuratachi*. The remains of Scorpions who wandered into these catacombs, never to return."

With a deft move, Shoju cut through the sword arm of his foe, just below the wrist. The hand and sword fell to the earth.

The creature didn't notice. It bore forward, clawing at Shoju with its remaining hand and trying to bite him with its teeth. The teeth made a sound like breaking twigs as they gnashed together.

"I should have thought our ancestors would treat us better," said Tetsuo, masking fear with bravado.

"These are not our ancestors," Shoju replied. "They are but husks reanimated by the dark magic of this place." His blade whirled around his opponent and separated its head from its shoulders.

Headless, the monster lashed out with its one bony hand.

"Then let's return their bodies to eternal rest." With swift strokes, Tetsuo severed the middle of the creature facing him.

It fell in two parts, but each piece kept trying to fight. Paper-skinned arms dragged the torso across the floor toward Tetsuo. The creature's legs wobbled after the young Scorpion as well, as though it might butt him to death with its bony hips.

Quickly, the cousins severed limbs from undead bodies. The disparate parts continued to quiver and shake, though they could no longer fight.

Tetsuo suppressed a shudder. He had hoped destroying the creatures would quiet the clamor in the chamber. Instead, the clacking sound grew louder, and the moaning increased. A baleful howl emanated from the altar on the far side of the room.

"*Yosh*," said Shoju, unconcerned about the noise. He kicked a bone away. "Now to have a look at that scroll."

"Master . . . !" Tetsuo pointed his blade toward the wall niches. Suddenly, they came alive with movement. The bodies of the Lost crept out of their niches and shambled toward the crypt's invaders.

"It seems the scroll won't be easy to obtain," Shoju said. "But the altar is where our answer lies. Run toward it . . . now!"

The Scorpion daimyo sprinted into the vault and toward the altar. Tetsuo followed.

The Lost swarmed out of their niches and met the samurai in the middle of the room. Many were mere annoyances: crawling headless torsos, hopping bodiless legs, rotting skulls that pushed themselves across the floor with bloated tongues. These posed little threat to the cousins. Shoju and Tetsuo avoided some and stepped on others, shattering long-dead bones.

Some of the dead, however, still retained the weapons and skill of the samurai they had been in life. They shambled forward, bones creaking, dry skin cracking. Some held katanas, others spears. These monstrosities coordinated their attacks. They scuffled past decrepit brethren and cut the living samurai off from the dais.

"Be like grass before the typhoon," Shoju said. He whirled and danced among the dead, his blade flashing. Where the Scorpion met the creatures, the Lost fell. His sword disconnected heads from bodies, torsos from hips, arms from shoulders. He left a pile of quivering parts in his wake.

Tetsuo marveled at the skill and grace of his master, but he didn't have time to reply. The corpses crowded in on him. His breath was drawn away in fear. The touch of the living was uncomfortable to most Rokugani, but touching the dead . . . The Lost clattered and clutched. Their dead mouths soundlessly gaped. They smelled of rot and mold and decay. This was what it was like to be in Jigoku.

Tetsuo fought back with all his might, parrying swords, hacking arms and necks. Many fell before Tetsuo's blade.

A corpse seized Tetsuo's sword arm, another his leg. The bony arm of a third wrapped around his waist.

Tetsuo started to scream.

The sound never left his mouth. In a flash, his lord stood beside him. The daimyo's sword moved like wind through the trees. Shoju clove the monster clutching his cousin's waist. Those holding Tetsuo's limbs lost their arms. Shoju kicked the remaining pieces away from the young Scorpion.

Tetsuo turned and swung his blade in wide circles, as he had seen his daimyo do. His katana found the most vital spots on the corpses: their necks, their waists, their joints. Body parts flew across the chamber. In a moment Tetsuo fought free of his oppressors.

The cousins once again ran toward the altar.

"Thank you, Shoju-sama," Tetsuo gasped.

The older man merely nodded in reply.

Behind them, the dead, damned things regrouped and shambled forward. Ahead, the path of the samurai was not yet clear. A last phalanx of undead barred their way.

"Be like the wind among the reeds," said Shoju, darting into the midst of their enemies.

Tetsuo tried to follow, but his courage faltered. Though he and his cousin had butchered many, the remains still attacked. Bodiless arms crept across the floor, skulls hopped about by opening and closing their jaws, legs pushed and twisted like crippled serpents.

The cavern reeked of death. The rustle of desiccated

corpses sounded like an army of crabs marching over a dry beach. Pieces of parchmentlike skin swirled in the air. The Lost would never stop. They would fight until Tetsuo and Shoju had joined their army of undead.

"Calm yourself, Tetsuo!"

"I shall try, Master," Tetsuo said. "I . . . Aaa!"

"Tetsuo!"

The young lieutenant had momentarily dropped his guard, and the sword of a dead samurai found its mark. The sword cut Tetsuo's kimono and traced a long gash on his left shoulder. Tetsuo staggered back.

Undead advanced, weapons raised.

Shoju reached the altar dais. His foot touched the bottom step. The moan in the vault turned into a fierce howl. Winds gushed from behind the floating scroll.

A shape formed in front of the altar. It resolved into the figure of a Bayushi retainer, the design of his armor and clothes many hundreds of years old.

The specter screamed. Hot, fetid winds blasted from its mouth. The bodies of the dead fell before the wind like twigs in a typhoon. The Lost moved no more. Tetsuo scrambled to his feet, clutching his wound with one hand.

"Shoju!" he cried, fearing for his daimyo's life.

The Scorpion raised his katana over his head. "I am Bayushi Shoju," he said, "daimyo of all the Scorpions. I have come seeking the shade of Bayushi Daijin. I crave answers."

The ghost undulated through the air, waving its arms. It was far larger than a mortal man. Shoju looked like a doll before it. Its eyes blazed in the darkness. Its tongue lolled like that of a drunkard. Its fingers were long talons. Its legs ended in torn and bloody stumps.

Tetsuo could hardly bear to look at it. His feet would not move, no matter how he tried to press them forward.

"Then you crave your death," the specter bellowed. "For I am Daijin. Whoever finds me finds his doom."

"The scroll you guard, what is it?" Shoju demanded.

"The future," said the ghost. "Nightmares no living man should know. Secrets I gave my life to defend. Secrets I am bound to protect even now."

"The dreams of Uikku, the Serene Prophet?"

The specter merely dipped and bowed.

"Then I will have them," Shoju said, taking another step forward. "Come, Tetsuo. Fear not this bag of wind."

Tetsuo tried to will his feet forward. "Master!" he cried. "I cannot!"

Shoju glanced back at his lieutenant, but kept walking. He stepped into the ethereal body of the spirit.

It howled, "To touch that scroll is to bring your own doom, Bayushi Shoju!"

Tetsuo wanted to cover his eyes. The Scorpion daimyo stood amid the body of the specter. Its insubstantial limbs flailed around him. Its ghostly eyes glowered.

"For the empire," Shoju said, "I will dare anything."

He stepped through the ghost and seized the scroll. As Shoju's hand touched the parchment, the specter vanished like mist melting before the day.

The light around the scroll dimmed. Shoju opened it.

The scroll resisted him, trying to keep itself rolled tight. Green sparks flew from its parchment, nearly blinding the daimyo. The runes that he saw in the moment before the scroll snapped shut burned themselves into Shoju's mind:

"Know that these are the words of Uikku, the Serene Prophet, as told to Bayushi Daijin. Though long hidden, they will be revealed again when the end of the world is nigh."

4 THE DRAGON

Time stood still as the dragon walked Rokugan.

Toturi saw its scales shimmering in the cascading water, its great back heaving in the rushing stream, its mane tossing at the waterfall's head. The creature shook itself into wakefulness. A fine mist flew from its body, making rainbows in the afternoon sun. It yawned and fixed its awesome gaze on Toturi.

The Lion daimyo stood naked before the fabulous creature, amazed but not afraid. He'd seen dragons before. They'd appeared to him a number of times, in moments of great importance.

Before being called home from the Asoko Monastery, he'd seen one. Another had danced high in the clouds on the battlefield at Shiro no Yojin. A third had appeared in his dreams before he made peace with Doji Hoturi and the Crane clan. And when Toturi lay wounded by barbarians before the mountains of Kyodai na Kabe sano Kita, a dragon had told him how to turn the day and win the field for Emperor Hantei the 38th. Dragons also appeared as portents in his dreams. In dream, dragons conformed to their mythical appearance—scales, manes, horns, claws, serpentine bodies. In reality, they were nearly beyond description.

This one was as translucent as running water. Its long body snaked in and out of the stream like waves heaving on the ocean. Scaly ripples ran along its back in ever-changing armor. Sunlight danced along the dragon's body, splashing light around the small clearing. Where the dragon touched the banks, droplets sprayed in the afternoon air. They spun and danced like tiny perfect worlds, never quite returning to the stream. Soon the air was saturated with the liquid jewels of the dragon's aura.

The dragon yawned. Fog billowed from its huge mouth. The mist circled its head like a wreath and drifted up into the sky. The creature kept its gaze leveled at Toturi.

The Lion steeled himself and waited for the dragon to speak.

Hatsuko stood beside him, her mouth frozen in mid-word, the top of her kimono just beginning to slip from her shoulders. She looked like a lush, beautifully-fashioned statue—the perfect image of a perfect woman.

The words of the dragon were for Toturi alone.

The dragon rumbled. Its voice sounded like waves crashing on a distant shore. "Akodo Toturi, your fortunes have been great."

Toturi bowed and smiled. "Thank you, great master."

The dragon shook its head. A halo of rainbows surrounded it.

"Your fortunes have been great," it repeated. "And your climb to fame spectacular. But your fall will be even greater—if you do not obey the ways of honor."

Toturi almost laughed. The Lion daimyo had contemplated honor for many years, even back to his days at the Asoko Monastery. "I serve the ways of honor in all things," he said.

"Not in all things," the dragon replied, its coils dancing in the stream.

"Was it not for honor that I left the monastery and returned to the lands of my father?" Toturi asked.

The dragon nodded. "Yes, it was," the creature said.

"Was it not for honor that I took up the mantle of my father and led the Lion?"

Again, the creature agreed, its voice soft like the waterfall itself. "Yes."

"Was it not for honor that I fought against the barbarians during the battle of Kyodai na Kabe sano Kita and nearly died for the emperor's cause?"

Once more the dragon nodded.

"And did I not, for the honor of my family, accept the position of general to Emperor Hantei the 38th?"

"In all these things," said the dragon, "you have been above reproach."

"How then, have I been remiss?"

The dragon turned its head and looked at Hatsuko. "This, then, is your fiancée?" the creature asked, its voice reverberating.

Toturi felt burning anger rise within him. Balling his sword hand into a fist, he said in measured tones, "She is not my betrothed."

"If not the woman chosen for you by the emperor . . . if not Isawa Kaede of the Phoenix . . ." asked the dragon, the waterfall of its voice building to thunderous proportions, "who is she, then?"

The Lion daimyo clenched his fist tighter. "Not my betrothed," he said, "but rather the woman I love. Her name is Hatsuko."

"She is geisha," said the dragon.

"Not in my eyes," said Toturi.

"Always," the dragon rumbled.

"No," Toturi said firmly. "I will make her my courtesan. I love her."

"In love's name men do things they would never consider doing for honor," the dragon said.

"I will marry her," Toturi said, feeling as though the dragon's gaze would burn his bare skin.

The dragon reared its watery head. "You have spoken of this to your emperor—and your fiancée—then," it said.

The Lion daimyo turned his face away, no longer able to meet the dragon's eyes. "No," he said.

The dragon laughed, and the forest shook.

Toturi fell to his knees beside the dragon's pool.

"Beware, Akodo Toturi," the dragon said. The power of its voice forced Toturi to look at it once more. "Love for the emperor is the highest love of all. No other can compare." It paused and then said, "Not all threats to the empire come in the form of Crane or Scorpion."

Toturi nodded, unsure what the creature meant.

The dragon peered directly into his eyes, as though it were looking through his soul. "A lion's heart, once divided, will not sustain him."

The dragon lost substance. It returned to the waters whence it came.

Toturi drew a deep breath and stood once more.

"My lord?" said Hatsuko, her lovely voice tinged with fear.

He turned and saw apprehension in her eyes. She clutched her kimono tightly to her chest, though it had slipped down to reveal white shoulders.

"You saw it, then," he said.

Her eyes filled with confusion. "Saw *what*, my lord?"

"The dragon," he said impatiently.

She gasped and stepped back, drawing up her kimono. "I . . . I saw no dragon, my lord. One moment you were talking to me, and the next . . ."

"The next?" he asked.

"The next you merely stood, staring at the waterfall. You stood so for a long time."

Toturi nodded grimly.

"Did you really see a dragon, my lord?"

"Yes," he said, "but you needn't worry about it. I should have known it wouldn't appear to you. Come here."

Cautiously, almost fearfully, she stepped forward. He reached out his arms and embraced her.

"So long as you are in my arms," he said again, "there is nothing you need fear."

She put her head on his naked chest and whispered, "Yes, my lord."

In her heart, though, her fear of losing him deepened.

5

THE SECRETS
OF FU LENG

The Scroll of Bayushi Daijin lay on a long, low, black-lacquer table in a high room at the Scorpion fortress, Kyuden Bayushi. The room was dark, lit by a single lantern set on the table next to the scroll. Shadows danced across the fusuma walls.

Shoju, Kachiko, Tetsuo, and Soshi Bantaro sat on the floor. Side by side but not touching, they peered at the artifact. No one had opened the scroll since Shoju gazed at it briefly in the catacombs.

"This is a thing of wonder, my lord," said Bantaro, his eyes darting over the rolled parchment. "A pity we cannot share it with the world, and thereby spread your fame."

Shoju looked through his mask at the old man. Bantaro had aged prematurely due to his magics—or perhaps to the vices he secretly indulged. The shugenja's mouth twitched nervously as he spoke. He rubbed his bald head with one long-fingered hand.

"We are not the Lion, Bantaro," Shoju said. "We do not seek fame and glory. We merely serve the emperor—and we do it in secret, as is the Scorpion way."

"Of course, lord," Bantaro said, bowing. "I only meant that it is a pity the world will never know how well you serve Rokugan and the emperor."

"The emperor knows, and that is enough," said Kachiko. Her eyes caught those of the old man, and the shugenja felt his bones turn to jelly. Bantaro loved her or feared her or both. Seeing his subtle confusion, Kachiko smiled slightly.

"Master, this scroll is an evil thing," said Tetsuo. "No good can come of it. I feel it in my bones. Better we had never found it in that forgotten vault."

"Knowledge is neither good nor evil," Kachiko said. "It is merely a tool in the hands of one who knows how to use it."

Shoju nodded. "We will know better what Daijin's words hold once we have read them." He looked at Bantaro. "When I open it, you know what to do."

Bantaro nodded as well. Fear glinted in the shugenja's eyes. "My life, my power, my service are yours, my lord."

Shoju reached for the scroll. The room seemed to darken.

Tetsuo swallowed hard, his hand straying to his obi, where his swords usually hung. His fingers found only his belt. His swords lay on the floor to his right. Tetsuo resisted the urge to take them up. He swallowed again.

The Scorpion lord's hands hovered over the parchment. The power of the artifact made his palms tingle. Shoju fancied he could see a dim green glow around the scroll. Slowly, he lowered his hands.

When his fingers touched the artifact, cold spikes rushed through them. His bones ached, and the tattoo on his shoulder burned. As though it were a living thing, the scroll fought his attempt to open it. He concentrated, gritting his teeth behind his grim mask.

Kachiko drew a sharp breath as he forced the scroll open

just a bit. Green sparks jumped up from the parchment. Bantaro's eyes grew wide. The shugenja began to chant in the ancient language of magic.

Beads of sweat ran down Shoju's forehead. He forced the scroll to open wider. The sparks grew taller, dancing like tiny demons across the artifact. One leapt from the page, arcing toward Tetsuo.

The young lieutenant gasped and threw himself away from the table. The others took no notice.

Inch by precious inch, Shoju opened the scroll. Bantaro droned his chant. Kachiko looked from her husband to the sorcerer. The green light from the scroll played on the masks of both men, making them look strange and evil.

A form took shape in the green sparks—hands, clawed hands. They reached toward Shoju. The daimyo saw them, but no fear shone in his eyes. The hands lunged for Shoju's throat.

Bantaro's voice rose, adding new syllables to his chant. He waved long fingers over the scroll. The green hands dissipated before they reached the Scorpion lord.

The green sparks died down until they burned only on the runic characters covering the page.

Bantaro chanted more softly. When Shoju had unrolled the scroll fully, the shugenja stopped his drone and let out a long sigh of relief.

Shoju peered at the burning words. Kachiko and Bantaro leaned closer for a better look. Recovered from his fright, Tetsuo joined them.

"I . . . I cannot read the words," he said, wiping sweat from his brow.

"The language is archaic, difficult," Kachiko said.

Shoju nodded.

"I can translate it easily enough," Bantaro said. " '*Long is the grasp of thrice-damned Fu Leng. His fingers reach into the souls of the unwary, the dishonored, the unclean. . . .*' Hmm . . . the commentary rambles quite a bit."

"So I see," Shoju said. His eyes hurt from gazing at the burning green letters. Behind his mask, he blinked.

" '*Lightning and fire presage the final days of the empire,*' " Kachiko said, reading from another portion of the scroll. " '*Men shall be as beasts and beasts as men. The heavens shall be torn asunder and the son of heaven shall give up his throne to the dark one. Born not of mother, but of spite, he leads them.*' "

Shoju traced his fingers down a line of enchanted characters and read. " '*The last days of Hantei herald the last days of Rokugan. Who shall be called to join the righteous? Only those with honor unimpeachable. Who fights for the dark one? All others, even unto him who sits on the throne.*

" '*Though the throne be destroyed, three emperors will give obeisance—the last a beast in the form of man. Fu Leng is his name. The first will have noble intentions, but his heart is led astray. The second will hold the throne in good hands, but his reign will not last beyond his name. The third will be called the last of the Hantei and Fu Leng also.*

" '*His power will shake the pillars of heaven, and the world shall be rent asunder. The sky shall fall to the soil and the soil be assumed to the sky. Fu Leng's demons will overrun the land, and the sky, and the oceans, and . . .*' " Shoju trailed off, reading silently to himself. Finally, he looked up.

"Tetsuo is right," he said, taking a deep breath. "The knowledge here is a terrible thing. The scroll speaks in riddles, but even these fragments make the message plain to me."

"And to me also, my lord," added Bantaro.

"The return of the Demon Lord Fu Leng is imminent," Shoju said, continuing as if the shugenja hadn't interrupted. "And with his rebirth comes the death of the empire . . . the death of all Rokugan. This is what my dreams foretold."

"I do not believe in prophecy," Kachiko said calmly. "I believe in the will of men to shape the world as they see fit. I know that you believe this too, Husband."

"How could I not believe it?" he said. "For hundreds of years the Scorpions have secretly worked their will on the world, serving the emperor and ensuring that none of the clans grew strong enough to challenge him."

"None but our own," Kachiko added.

"But it is not our place to challenge," said Tetsuo. He looked pale in the lantern's dim light. "It is our place to serve. How could we serve if others surpassed our might?"

"We could not," Bantaro put in.

"Just so," Shoju said. "The other clans do not know the devotion with which we serve. They think we are like them, involved in petty squabbling. The Crab may be stronger, the Lion bolder, the Dragon wiser, the Crane smarter, the Phoenix better at magic, the Unicorn more versed in the ways of the *gaijin*, the outside world—but all their great powers they use only to further their own ends. No one serves the emperor as the Scorpion does."

All at the table nodded their agreement, and the room sat silent for a moment.

The fusuma door to the chamber slid suddenly open.

The four Scorpions spun at the sound. Tetsuo reached for the hilt of his sword, where it lay by his right hand.

Through the entrance came a youth of about fourteen. He wore an ornate red and black kimono, decorated with gold filigree. His mask was plain and youthful, and it revealed a great deal of his handsome face. He wore no swords, but his dress indicated his rank as a samurai in training.

Kachiko gasped. Shoju scowled behind his mask. Bantaro glanced from the scroll to the boy and back again. Tetsuo stood and moved quickly toward the youngster.

Breathless, the boy knelt.

"Dairu," Kachiko said, worry tingeing her voice. Quieting her heart, she added more affectionately, "My son."

"Why have you come?" Shoju asked coldly. His palms remained flat upon the parchment, lest it roll up again.

"Forgive me, my father," said Bayushi Dairu, heir to the Scorpion dynasty. "I beg to be included in your plans." He bowed low to his father, touching his head to the tatami mat covering the floor.

"The boy has not yet reached his majority, has not endured his *gempuku*," Bantaro said, frowning at the heir's display. He twined thin fingers around themselves and glanced at the scroll again. "His presence at this council would be a bad omen."

From the boy's side, Tetsuo said, "He's in peril here. This scroll is dangerous."

Dairu looked up from where he knelt, "I do not fear danger," he said. "Though my gempuku is two years away, I have the heart of a warrior now. Our secrets hold no dread for me. I need to learn the workings of our clan. Great lord, if you will not have me now, move up the date of my majority. I am ready to pass the tests; Swordmaster Masayuki says so."

The Scorpion daimyo looked at the boy. Behind his mask, his thin lips drew into a slight smile.

"He is *your* son," Kachiko whispered proudly to her lord.

"So you remind me," Shoju shot back, so quietly that only she could hear. Kachiko turned away from him, and the Scorpion lord straightened. "My son," he said, "though you are wise beyond your years, the time is not yet right for you to join my council. What we do is dangerous, as your cousin Tetsuo has said. Too dangerous for you to help."

The boy hung his head in disappointment.

"But your time may soon come," Shoju continued. "I will consider moving up the date of your gempuku."

Dairu bowed low again. "*Domo arigato gosaimasu*, father. Thank you."

The Scorpion daimyo nodded at his son who was not his son. Kachiko was right. Despite the boy's bloodline, he was Shoju's son. As the Scorpion smiled, another figure shambled through the open fusuma door to the sanctuary.

It was an old woman. Though she entered the room as quickly as she was able, by no means could she be called fast. Her manner was extremely deferential; she bowed repeatedly and looked around nervously as she came. "Lord Bayushi," she said, her voice quavering. "Forgive me. I was drawing the young lord's bath. . . . I turned my back but a moment. . . ."

The boy interrupted, "It is I who should be forgiven, Father. I tricked Kiko-san. She did not know I planned to come here."

The daimyo nodded. "You should have expected this from the son of the Scorpion, Kiko," he said to the old woman.

The old woman bowed low and touched her head to the tatami. "I know, great lord. I have no excuse."

Shoju laughed loud and long. "Are you sure your mother did not find you in a Crane's nest, Kiko?"

Kachiko reached out her hand, stopping just short of Shoju's arm. "My lord . . ." she said.

"Very well," Shoju said, still laughing. "Kiko, I forgive you for being deceived by the Scorpion's son. In future, you should remember who it is you are preparing the bath for."

"I will, great lord," Kiko said from her prostrate position.

Shoju motioned to her with his left hand. "Now get up. Tell the kitchen to send up some food. We're likely to be here most of the night. No one is to enter the chamber, though, under penalty of death."

The scroll burned under his right hand.

Kiko stood and bowed. Dairu did the same. "Yes, great lord," the old woman said.

"And see that my son takes his bath," Shoju added.

Dairu bowed and turned red. The old woman just bowed. "Yes, Lord Bayushi," she said.

The mismatched pair exited the room and slid the fusuma door shut behind them.

"Your boy has fire," said Bantaro.

"Like his father," Tetsuo added.

Kachiko looked at her husband, but could not read the face behind the mask.

Shoju merely brought his left hand to the chin of his mask and said, "Yes."

Soon the food arrived: pickled vegetables, rice, natto, dried seaweed, and sake. Retainers placed the meal outside the entrance. Tetsuo brought it within the chamber. The food sat, largely uneaten, for most of the night as the four Scorpions reread the scroll a second and third time.

Tetsuo had serious trouble translating.

Kachiko was more than happy to help the young samurai.

Shoju could only admire his wife's skill. He understood why she had nearly every man in the empire eating out of her hand. The subtlety and grace of her ways soon put even the most suspicious off their guard. Only Bayushi Shoju was her equal in guile. Only he was worthy to be her husband.

Finally, all of them stopped reading and leaned back.

"The end of the world," Tetsuo said quietly. He looked pale.

"Not necessarily," Shoju said calmly.

"I don't see how to escape it," Bantaro said. "The scroll's meaning on this is plain. The last emperor of the Hantei will bring the darkness of Fu Leng back into the world. Rokugan will burn. Its seas will boil. Demons will overrun the land, and people shall be their fodder. Not even the righteous shall escape."

"I agree with Bantaro's translation," said Kachiko, "but not with his conclusion. Prophecies are fulfilled by men who use them to explain their own weakness. Fortune favors the strong. Strong men and women make their own fates. Under the guidance of the Scorpion, this terrible prophecy need never come to pass.

"I will whisper in the emperor's ear," she continued. "Encourage him to build up forces on Kaiu Kabe, the Carpenter's Wall. Make sure that the Crab are watched as they guard the wall, to see that Fu Leng doesn't influence them. We can use our guile to protect the empire, as we have for millennia. The wall that keeps Fu Leng and his minions in the underworld will grow stronger, not weaker. It will never crumble."

"No wall can withstand the will of fate," said Shoju. "And it is fate's will that speaks to me now." He stood and paced the room. "The dreams I've had lately were sent to me for a reason—as a warning of things to come. I believe that. How could I not?"

Tetsuo and Bantaro nodded; Kachiko stayed silent.

"The dreams led me to the catacombs, and my fate led me to this scroll. The prophecy of Uikku says that the last Hantei emperor will bring the ruin of Rokugan," Shoju continued. "None of you can dispute that."

Again, Tetsuo and Bantaro nodded. Kachiko pulled her kimono tighter around her, as if to ward off the cold of night.

"But Kachiko is right as well; there is a way to avert this danger—a swift and certain way."

Shoju paused and turned away, looking out of the room's sole window. Outside, darkness enshrouded the Scorpion lands. The night was black. No moon hung in the sky.

Tetsuo swallowed and said, "How, my lord?"

Shoju turned back to them. All three fancied that they could see the Scorpion daimyo's eyes blaze red behind his mask.

"If the imperial line is ended," Shoju said softly, "the doom will not come."

Silence, as thick as the darkness outside, hung in the room.

"Kill the emperor," Bantaro finally murmured.

"And his heir," added Shoju.

Tetsuo got to his feet. "But this is . . ."

"Treason?" Shoju asked, looking at his young cousin. "Is it treason to save all of Rokugan? Is it treason to sacrifice two people for the sake of the empire?"

"But the emperor and his son . . . ." said Tetsuo. "Who will we serve if they are gone?"

Kachiko rose and stood next to her husband. "We will serve the empire, as we always have."

Bantaro stood as well. "And the new emperor, whomever he may be. The Hantei line may die, but the Emerald Empire will continue." He looked from the scroll to the Scorpion lord. His face drew into a thin smile.

"For the good of the emperor, a man may give up his honor," Shoju said. "For the good of the empire, should a man do anything less? I devote my life and honor to averting this terrible fate."

Tetsuo rose and joined the others. His stomach felt as if it had clenched into a fist. He looked at his lord's mask and saw the iron will of the Scorpion behind it. He swallowed his fear.

"You are right," Tetsuo said quietly. "If it must be done, it must be done." He took a deep breath and drew himself fully erect. "I will follow you wherever you may lead, my cousin, even into the gates of Jigoku."

"As will I, my lord," Bantaro added quickly.

"Where you go, my lord and husband, I go as well," Kachiko said. "Thus it will always be, even past the end of the world. Perhaps, though, there is still another way."

Shoju shook his head. "If there is," he said. "I cannot see it."

Kachiko nodded. "But, my lord, there are others who could," she said. "I am reminded of the Dragon daimyo, Togashi Yokuni. Our spies tell us that he has the wisdom of the ages at his disposal."

The tone of her voice conveyed her meaning to Shoju easily enough, and reminded him of something he'd almost forgotten: a secret learned by a clever Scorpion long ago.

"He may be able to see what we cannot," she continued. "Surely we should seek his council before setting our feet on this path of destruction."

For long moments, silence reigned in the chamber. Bayushi Shoju thought.

"Yes," he said finally. "Though it is my belief that the Hantei line must be destroyed to prevent the return of the Demon Lord, before I set this doom upon our clan, I will seek the wisdom of the Dragon."

6   THE COURT OF HANTEI

Spring brought great beauty to the court of Hantei the 38th. The lotus blossoms were in bloom, and outside the graceful walls of the Forbidden City, the Lotus Festival had already begun. Visitors from all over Rokugan crowded the city, vying for space at the festival and hoping beyond hope for a glimpse of the emperor.

Those who were not lucky enough to see His Imperial Majesty consoled themselves with Otosan Uchi's other magnificent sights: the towering cliffs, the swift, clear River of the Sun, the great waterfall, Fudotaki, and the Imperial Palace and gardens. Flowers filled the sprawling miles of the emperor's gardens to overflowing. Even the most jaded visitor to the city could not help noticing their sweet fragrance. "The scent of heaven," was a phrase often used by guests.

Indeed, in the blossom of spring, there

was no place on Rokugan closer to heaven than the "City of the Shining Prince." The great city was clean and well ordered. Even its back streets and alleys were spotless. The towers of the Imperial Palace shone white as sunlight within the Forbidden City. When the scent of flowers did not dominate the atmosphere, the clean sea breeze did. Even the sky seemed bluer within Otosan Uchi. The song of the great river and the roar of the waterfall mingled with the music of birds in the emperor's gardens.

The weather was unfailingly perfect. Warm cloudless days followed cool moonlit nights in an endless procession across the sky. In such a place people found it easy to see that their emperor was descended from the Sun Goddess, Amaterasu.

On perfect spring days like this, the Hantei emperor often forsook the high towers of his palace and held court in his gardens. The magnificent plantings sprawled for miles beyond the walls of the Imperial Precinct, but the emperor seldom conducted his business outside the secure courtyards immediately adjacent to the palace. Sometimes, though, he and his retainers ventured beyond the walls to see the wonders in the rest of his city.

This morning, the Sun Goddess found her heir visiting his gardens in one of the outermost baileys of the Forbidden City. The view from this cliff-top vantage was spectacular, affording a panorama of the vast curvature of the sea beyond Otosan Uchi. White sails dotted the water, darting back and forth like kites in the sky.

Hantei took a deep breath of the clean salt air and let it out slowly. A garden stream flowed quietly here, rejoining the river nearby. The emperor watched serenely as a lotus blossom floated past. He knew he was supposed to be attending to court matters, but at the moment, he couldn't keep his mind on them.

Kakita Yoshi of the Crane sat at the emperor's left hand. His position as personal advisor and aide to Hantei gave him the favored spot.

Also to the left, and slightly behind the emperor, sat Shosuro Taberu of the Scorpion, a dark balance to the light of the Crane. Usually Bayushi Kachiko would have been in his place, but she had recently returned to her homeland to consult with her daimyo husband. Though Taberu wasn't as sinister as most Scorpions, the emperor secretly missed the Scorpion mistress.

The seat reserved for the Lion, at the right hand of the emperor, remained conspicuously vacant.

Members of the imperial house hovered nearby as well: Miya Yoto, the emperor's herald; Seppun Bake, Hantei's religious advisor and yes-man; Seppun Daiori, military advisor to the Emerald Throne. Descended from offshoots of the Hantei line, they stood outside the other clans. Their only purpose was to serve the emperor himself. They had no clan agenda— which made them unique within the power structure of the empire.

Others graced the gardens of the emperor as well, chief among them Isawa Kaede of the Phoenix. She sat beneath a cherry tree under the watchful eye of the emperor's captain of the guard. Nearby, the Moshi twins played music on flute and *Shamisen*, charming a gaggle of teenage girls sitting by the river's edge.

Doji Hoturi, daimyo of the Crane, had come to call on the court today. Doji Ameiko—formerly of the Kitsune, the Fox Clan—came with him. Hantei thought the handsome man and beautiful young woman a fitting couple. He nodded with approval as they politely approached him and made all the usual obeisances and spoke the traditional honorifics.

They had brought with them Doji Shizue, a promising young courtier left lame by an accident of birth. The girl had spent time in Hantei's court before, and the emperor was always glad to see her. "You are another ray of light from our heavenly mother," he told her as she bowed low before him.

Shizue smiled and blushed at the praise. She carefully stepped back into the shadows of her more illustrious relatives.

"How goes your war with the Lion?" the emperor asked Hoturi.

Hoturi smiled and bowed. "The fighting has all but ceased," he said. "As per your order, Majesty. Only a few rogue elements remain, but Toturi and I shall soon quell them."

"Good. Good. And where is your partner in this new peace?" the emperor asked, looking at the Lion's vacant seat.

"I do not know, *Otennoo-sama*."

Hantei frowned. "Well, when next you see him, tell him we hope he will visit us in court soon. His absence has been noticed."

The ancient herald, Miya Yoto, leaned close to the emperor's ear. "I believe such a visit is already scheduled to take place in the near future, Majesty," he said with a voice made of gravel. He fumbled with a scroll, looking for a reference. "Within the month, I think, though I could check my records. . . ."

"I am sure that, by then, Toturi will have returned from his tryst—whatever it may be," added Shosuro Taberu of the Scorpion.

"We sometimes suspect," the emperor mused aloud, "that the Lion does not care for our court."

Isawa Kaede, seated beneath a nearby cherry tree, spoke up. "Hantei-sama," she said, "my fiancé was raised in a monastery and is, perhaps, still unaccustomed to the splendor of the Imperial Court. I myself had difficulty making the transition, Your Majesty, and I was raised in considerable comfort."

The emperor nodded at her words, he noticed uncertainty on her face.

The Scorpion said, "It is true the Lion prefers simple things. I would take that as no slight to Your Majesty, however." His eyes smiled, though his clan mask hid the rest of his face. "Some men are born to the palace, while others find more comfort in the lush hills and forests."

Kaede, the Mistress of the Void, looked at the Scorpion,

trying to read the intent of his words. For all her magical training and enhanced perception, she might as well have been looking at a wall. Standing nearby, Seppun Ishikawa, the captain of the emperor's guard, gave Kaede an encouraging glance. She turned her eyes back to the emperor.

Hantei addressed the Crane delegation once more. "Spring," he said, "is a time for love, even here. I hope you and your bride will avail yourselves of all the pleasures our court has to offer. May your union be fruitful."

Hoturi bowed his head; Ameiko did so too, but blushed as well. "By your grace, Majesty," said Hoturi.

With a wave of his hand, the emperor indicated they were free to go. The couple bowed low before him and then left. Shizue did the same.

As the Crane left, a courtier arrived and bowed.

"What is it, Matsuo?" the emperor asked.

"The royal heir begs a few moments of your time, Most Esteemed Majesty."

The emperor nodded his graying head, and a smile cracked his thin, weathered lips.

Miya Matsuo bowed again and backed away, allowing the royal heir, Hantei Sotorii, to approach.

The adolescent who was next in line for the Emerald Throne bowed and spoke. He was a strapping youth, good looking and full of vigor. "Greetings, Celestial Father," he said. "I am pleased to find you looking so well on such a fine morning. Your radiance truly lights the world."

"Have you come to bask in our reflected glory then, Hantei-chan?" the older man asked.

"No, Father," the younger Hantei said. "I merely came to request permission to visit the festival tonight."

"Would this, perhaps, have anything to do with the troupe of traveling Kabuki players we have had word of?"

The heir turned bright red and bowed slightly. "Nothing escapes your eyes, Father. Have I your permission?"

"Kabuki is a base form of theater, unworthy of the

Hantei," Seppun Bake said from behind the emperor's right shoulder.

The emperor nodded and said, "Our advisor Bake is correct. We shall order a Noh performance instead, to be held in our imperial theater."

"But these players have traversed the breadth of Rokugan," Sotorii said impetuously. "I have heard that there are no finer anywhere."

The emperor looked as though he might have a fit of temper, but the Scorpion advisor leaned close to his left ear. "Great One," Taberu began, "it is said a man may not rule the people without truly knowing them. Perhaps going to this . . . performance . . . could be part of your son's education." He added in a lower voice, "Once the heir has seen the Kabuki, it will no longer hold fascination for him."

Hantei the 38th leaned back on his platform. "The Scorpion speaks with the wisdom of his house's mistress."

Taberu bowed, taking the compliment.

"A fine idea," said the Crane, Kakita Yoshi, from his place in front of the Scorpion. "Though perhaps if a suitable teacher were to accompany him, the education of the heir would be enhanced even further."

"An excellent idea as well, Yoshi-san," the emperor said.

"If I might suggest . . . ." said Bake, trying to break in.

Hantei fixed the aging Seppun courtier with a cold stare. "We will decide whom to ask for advice, Bake-san."

Bake bowed and backed away, taking the cloying scent of his perfume with him. "Of course, Your Majesty," he said.

The emperor looked about, taking inventory of those present. "We have not heard from your kinsman recently, Bake," Hantei said, turning toward Seppun Daiori.

Daiori was leaning against the trunk of a nearby tree. He was a tall man with a stern face and hawklike features. A long, black braid of hair fell down his back. He had a faraway look in his eyes, as if he were not paying complete attention.

"Whom would you suggest?" the emperor asked Daiori.

"Majesty, of military matters I know much, but of theater . . ." He let his voice trail off, causing some laughter among the other courtiers.

"And though a fine military advisor, lately you've been a bit of a bore," Hantei said, smiling to show that it was a joke.

Daiori bowed. "The truth may be seen in the emperor's light," he said self-effacingly.

The emperor laughed. "A remark worthy of Bake, if we are not mistaken." This induced laughter from the rest of those present. The emperor turned back to the man on his left. "Well, we know that the Crane never lack for anything to say. What is your advice, Yoshi-san?"

"There can be no better teacher to separate the mind's wheat from its chaff than Isawa Kaede," said Yoshi.

This startled Kaede, who had started to drift away under her cherry tree. "Yes, of course, Majesty," she said. "It would be my honor."

"Perhaps young Doji Shizue would benefit from the experience as well," Yoshi added.

"And make a fine companion for the heir," Taberu put in.

Yoshi looked at the Scorpion but couldn't tell if the man was being serious, or subtly pointing out that the Crane sought to advance the lame girl's standing with the future emperor. The Crane cursed the Scorpion's practiced nuances.

Young Hantei Sotorii watched this political volley with bewilderment. He hadn't expected to be given permission to go, but Taberu—whom he did not consider his friend—had stuck up for him. Then Yoshi mucked things up by suggesting an escort. The young man wasn't sure whether to be happy to be going to the theater, or disappointed to have so many people tagging along.

"Well," said his father, "since your mother died, we never could refuse you anything. You have our leave to go. What do you say to that, Hantei-chan?"

The heir bowed. "Thank you, Majesty," was all he could manage.

The emperor turned to Ishikawa. "See to a suitable escort," he told the captain of the guard.

Seppun Ishikawa bowed, turned, and left to arrange it.

The emperor turned back to the others. "Now begone, all of you," he said, waving his hands as if flinging water from his fingertips. "We would like to enjoy the rest of our morning in peace."

The members of the court bowed, gathered themselves, stood, and did as the emperor bade. Soon Hantei the 38th sat alone in his garden, contemplating the clouds.

▲▲▲▲▲▲▲▲

Isawa Kaede caught up to Ishikawa before he reached the inner wall of the palace grounds. He slackened his pace slightly so that the diminutive Mistress of the Void could keep up with him.

"We've been dismissed," Kaede said, "so I thought I should help you arrange this sojourn to the festival."

Ishikawa grunted his assent. Kaede laughed.

"You're even less pleased about this than I," she said. Then, in a moment of insight, she asked, "Or is it the heir you disapprove of?"

"It's not my place to say," Ishikawa said.

"I give you leave," she said. "And, upon my honor, I won't repeat it. To tell you the truth, I sometimes worry about the young Hantei myself."

"He is undisciplined and lacks manners," said the captain of the guard.

"He misses his mother," Kaede said.

Ishikawa huffed. "She's been dead for years," he said. "And the emperor indulges the boy. That's bad enough in itself, but when he drags the rest of us into his pampering . . . well, let's just say I have no stomach for it."

"Sometimes a kind hand can accomplish what a harsh word cannot."

He turned and looked at her. Kaede was short, but she was as beautiful as a newly-fledged dove. She had deep black eyes and hair, dark skin, and a pleasing figure. She dressed impeccably, though not as well as Kachiko of the Scorpion—but who on Rokugan did? Ishikawa admired her greatly and was proud to be her friend. There was no one else in the Imperial Court with whom he could talk so freely.

"I just don't think," he said, "that you can turn a cub into a lion by feeding it goat's milk."

Kaede nodded thoughtfully. "Possibly you are right. But maybe this trip will give the heir a whole new perspective. Perhaps it will show him his true place in life."

"Only if his place in life is to be a bad actor," said Ishikawa. "This expedition is beyond all sense. I wonder who puts ideas like this in the emperor's head?"

Kaede pondered a bit. "The Scorpion, I think."

"What?" Ishikawa asked, stopping in his tracks so quickly she almost tripped over his sword.

"I said I think it's the Scorpion. I've watched their people carefully at the court, but I still can't figure them out. They say one thing, mean another, and seem to get their way no matter what happens. Even when I think they've lost, I sense that they feel triumph."

Ishikawa spat. "Sometimes I think they have more than one face behind those masks—or maybe no face at all. The emperor should have them all killed. I don't know why he doesn't."

"I suspect that would prove harder than you might think," Kaede said.

"Why should it? The Lion and Crab are mightier, the Dragon and Phoenix more skilled with magic, the Unicorn and Crane better equipped."

"But I've noticed," said Kaede, "that those who step on the Scorpion are most often stung and die themselves."

Ishikawa scowled and began walking again. Kaede followed. They passed through the inner wall of the Forbidden City and into the courtyard of the palace.

After a few minutes of silence, she asked, "What do you think the Scorpion meant? About my fiancé, I mean?"

"I'm not sure I understand you," Ishikawa said.

"When he said that Toturi preferred plain things, what do you think that meant?"

"Am I to know the mind of a Scorpion, then?" Ishikawa asked. "You know your fiancé. What do *you* think Taberu meant?"

"I don't know," she said, turning her eyes down. "No more than I know Akodo Toturi. We've seldom met. Our parents arranged our marriage when we were but children."

"Hai," Ishikawa said thoughtfully. "Such things can be difficult at first. But you have to trust that your families and the emperor knew what would be best."

"I do trust . . . but I've also *heard* . . ."

He turned to her. "What have you heard?"

"That Toturi loves another."

"He's a fool if he does. Who's been telling you such things? The Scorpion, I suppose."

Kaede shook her head. "Never the Scorpion. Others."

"Isn't that their way," Ishikawa said, snorting. "Look for the Scorpion, and he's never there."

"I just wish I knew the truth," she said.

Ishikawa grew pensive. "Truth," he finally said, "is a scarce commodity at court."

Kaede sighed and nodded. They'd reached the walls of the great keep itself now. The huge castle towered over them like an ivory mountain.

"I'll go round up my guards," he said to her. "See what you can do with the young Hantei's party."

She nodded, but her mind still seemed far away.

"Perhaps you can change the heir's mind about this."

Kaede smiled and chuckled slightly. "Perhaps I could, if I were Bayushi Kachiko," she said.

"But then," Ishikawa said smiling, "you'd have to sleep with a Scorpion."

"I'd sooner sleep with the worms," Kaede said.

7   PERILOUS JOURNEY

Just before dawn, a great host assembled behind the gates of Kyuden Bayushi. Shoju rode in front of the party astride his great gelded war-horse, a gift from the Unicorn clan. At his side, Tetsuo and Bantaro rode on horses of good but lesser quality. In all of Rokugan, the horses of the Unicorn were the best—but the strange clan, sometimes referred to as "barbarian influenced" by the Scorpion, seldom bestowed their animals on others. The daimyo of each clan had one, but rarely more than one.

Next in the host came the ladies, hidden behind the screens of their palanquins. Noble ladies never walked long distances in Rokugan. They were always carried by bearers. The small, ornate boxes hid the ladies from the elements and the prying eyes of peasants.

Foot soldiers, archers, samurai, and priests filled out the company. All were dressed in their finest clothes. Visiting the daimyo of another house required the utmost in courtesy and deference.

Shoju had sent Bayushi Yojiro ahead to announce their visit to the court of the Dragon. Of all the Scorpion retainers and diplomats, Yojiro was the one best liked by the other houses. In fact, many people called him "The Only Honest Scorpion." Shoju had to smile at that. Sometimes honesty was the best lie.

In the predawn light, the great host looked like an army ready to ride to battle. Every man stood at attention. Every horse held its place in line. The banners of the company flapped in the wind.

As the sun peeked through the mountains, the Scorpion daimyo raised his hand and commanded that the great gates be opened. Silently, the gates rolled back, revealing the mist-shrouded countryside. Kyuden Bayushi faced west, toward the River of Gold. To attack the gates, an enemy would leave his back to the water, limiting the route of his escape. Many times in the past, the Scorpion Clan had used the river to trap an enemy army and crush it. Those who did not die by the sword drowned or were killed by Scorpion assassins patrolling the banks.

This morning Bayushi Shoju saw only a misty, uncertain future before him.

The trek ahead would be long—twenty-five days at least, thirty more likely. The Scorpion did not like being out in the open for so long, but to visit the house of the Dragon, he knew he could do nothing else.

"It is not wise to sneak up on a sleeping dragon," Shoju had told Tetsuo. "Far better to announce yourself and walk into his lair boldly. The dragon still may eat you, but at least you will see his eyes before you die."

Tetsuo had mumbled his agreement. The Scorpion daimyo could sense his young cousin's nervousness. Even before they set out, he saw trepidation on the young man's face—on the parts not hidden by Tetsuo's Scorpion mask.

For himself, Shoju had chosen a proud, dignified mask. It

told of the daimyo's power without being ostentatious: his best face.

The rest of the company wore their best masks as well, even the foot soldiers and priests. They would wear everyday masks during most of the journey, and even at the Scorpion strongholds between here and their final destination, but for leaving home and for arriving in the Dragon lands, nothing less than the best would be acceptable. Every man and woman in the company had seen impudent Scorpions lose their heads for choosing the wrong face.

The Scorpion daimyo lowered his hand and gave the order to march. Slowly, deliberately, the great column moved through the gates of Kyuden Bayushi.

From inside her palanquin, Bayushi Kachiko watched the walls of the castle glide past. Her sea-black eyes observed every detail, from the plastered walls to the graceful arc of the roofs. She often journeyed into the far reaches of Rokugan but always held this image—the strong, well-ordered, honorable castle of her people—within her heart. It gave her courage in times of doubt and confidence that she would one day return.

As they moved away from the fortress and into the samurai village beyond, she caught a glimpse of something moving in the topmost tower: a person. Her son.

Bayushi Dairu stood in the high window, watching the procession leave the city. He had begged his parents to let him go along on this mission. Both Shoju and Kachiko had refused. It was best that he not come. Dairu was still young and impulsive. Despite his training, he was not used to the ways of the world, and this mission would require a delicacy the young Scorpion lacked. Notwithstanding the might of their host, this journey still held great danger.

The lands of the Dragon were perilous. No one knew much about the Dragon, not even the Scorpion. They were elusive at best, preferring to stay hidden in their high mountain keeps. Those who did show themselves were powerful in the arts of war and magic. Only their self-imposed exile kept them from dominating the clans of Rokugan. And Togashi Yokuni, the leader of the clan . . . he held a secret strength that only the Scorpion daimyo and his lady knew. Even Shoju could not stand before the Dragon's power, and Shoju was the equal of any man in the world. Any meeting with Yokuni could have unpredictable and disastrous results. For this reason Kachiko insisted that her son stay home, despite the boy's resentment.

Yes, Kachiko knew her motives for not wanting Dairu along. Her husband's motives were less clear.

Shoju knew, of course, that the boy was not his own. He'd known it since the first moment Kachiko told him that she was with child. Had other people been allowed to look upon the face of the Scorpion daimyo, they would have known it too. Shoju's countenance had been a curse upon him since his birth; Dairu, on the other hand, had the face of an angel. "Handsome as a Crane," was a comment often heard about him in the courts.

Kachiko prayed that her husband did not hear those words too often. For all her perceptive wiles, the Mother of Scorpions could only guess her husband's true thoughts about the boy he had raised as his own. Yes, her dalliance with the boy's father had ended long ago, two years after her marriage to Shoju, but the Scorpion's memory was long indeed. That was part of his power. Shoju's other great power was to hide his mind from others—even, at times, from her.

Kachiko could only guess whether her husband had left "their" son behind because he feared for the boy's safety, or because Dairu was not truly one of them. It was something the Scorpion lady and her husband had not discussed. They never would. Some secrets the Scorpion daimyo held tight, even from her.

Kachiko's heart hid secrets as well.

As she watched the white tower disappear into the blowing mist of the morning, Kachiko wondered—as she often did when she left—whether she would ever see her son or her homeland again. A single tear ran from her eye and dampened the soft silk of her mask. She turned from the castle and faced the palanquin's forward viewing slit. She felt her will returning to iron. Beyond her ornate box, no one could have seen that her resolve had ever slipped.

While these thoughts about home and fate plagued Kachiko, similar worries crossed the mind of Bayushi Tetsuo. The young lieutenant rode at his master's side, trying to discern the future, but seeing only blowing mist. The footfalls of horses and men were muffled in the fog, and Tetsuo felt as though the world itself might end just beyond the range of their sight.

He gazed at his cousin. Shoju's mask showed only what he wanted it to show: power and resolve. Tetsuo wondered for a moment if the daimyo felt the same confidence he displayed to the world.

Of course he did. Tetsuo had never seen his cousin lacking in courage. Never. Even when they had been outnumbered ten to one in the catacombs, the Scorpion had never shown fear. Perhaps that was what troubled Tetsuo. In the vaults below the Scorpion fortress, Tetsuo had felt his blood turn to ice water. He had known fear, a fear so deep that, even now, days later, he could not shake the feeling. Fear that he could not live up to the tasks set for him, fear that he would fail his daimyo, fear that he would fail Rokugan itself.

As if sensing the doubt in his cousin's mind, the Scorpion daimyo suddenly turned to Tetsuo and said, "Let's ride ahead of the column for a while."

Tetsuo nodded. The two of them spurred their horses and separated from the mass of the company. Soon their retinue had vanished into the blowing mists behind them, and the Bayushi cousins rode through the hills alone.

"Should we get so far ahead?" Tetsuo asked.

Shoju turned to him and said, "There are only two things to fear in life, Tetsuo: death and dishonor. Which is it that troubles you? Death?"

Tetsuo shook his head. "No, my lord. I've faced death many times at your side and will gladly do so again."

"Is it my death you fear, then?"

"I do not think so, my lord. Your son is strong and your wife wise. Together they could lead the Scorpion until your son is of age to do so."

Shoju nodded. "And they would lead our clan well. So, it must be dishonor that you fear."

Tetsuo took a deep breath. "No, my lord. Not exactly."

"What exactly is it, then?"

Tetsuo glanced at the fog-shrouded countryside. The mists had closed in around them. Hills loomed in the milky white haze like lurking giants. He took another deep breath.

"I fear, my lord, that I will betray you."

Shoju seemed surprised. "Betray me?" he said.

"Not by action," Tetsuo quickly added, "but by my own inadequacy. I fear I will not be up to the job when you need me."

"Do you think that if I feared this, I would keep you at my side?" Shoju asked. "Tetsuo, are you the best fighter in my lands?"

"No, lord."

"Correct. You are good with a sword, and getting better all the time. But my half-brother Aramoro would slay you in an instant. There are others as well. So, with all the warriors in all my lands, why do I choose to have *you* ride at my side?"

"That is what I do not understand, my lord."

Shoju looked at his young cousin, and Tetsuo fancied that he could see the daimyo's eyes gleaming behind his mask.

"I choose you," he said, "because I trust you implicitly. You would never put your own interests before mine, or those of our clan."

"But there are others who—"

"Are dedicated to the Scorpion, yes, but they have other concerns as well. My wife has her . . . *our* son; my brother is devoted to his sword; Yogo Junzo loves only his black arts."

"Soshi Bantaro?" Tetsuo asked, glancing back to where he thought the old shugenja might ride.

Shoju smiled behind his mask. "Despite what he may think, Bantaro is devoted mostly to himself."

"But he loves you, my lord."

"Only in relationship to himself. He loves being close to the head of the Scorpion."

Tetsuo nodded, and a feeling of pride welled up in his heart. He could feel his fears and doubts slipping away. "I will never fail you, my lord," he said.

"I know you won't," Shoju said.

Tetsuo could almost see the smile behind his lord's mask.

Suddenly, the thunder of hoofbeats broke the silence of the morning mist. A horse charged out of the fog ahead and reined up before them.

"My lord," said the woman on horseback—Rumiko, one of their warriors who had drawn outrider duty that morning. "It's terrible! You should return to the column at once!"

"What's terrible?" Shoju asked, his voice like steel.

"A creature, like nothing I've ever seen before," Rumiko said. "It came out of the mist and attacked our scouts. I was the only one to escape."

Shoju nodded. "Ride back and alert the others. Then bring Bantaro and my guard. Tetsuo and I will ride ahead."

"But, my lord . . ." Rumiko said.

Shoju turned his eyes on her and said, "Now!"

"Hai!" Rumiko wheeled and rode into the mist in the direction of the column. Shoju and Tetsuo spurred their horses and galloped in the opposite direction.

It didn't take long for the daimyo and his cousin to find the monster. It sat in the road amid the bodies of two Scorpion scouts and their steeds, stuffing its horrible face with horse-flesh. It looked up at the sound of the cousins' approach.

The creature was manlike, though much larger than an ordinary man. Great tusks and horns sprouted from its hideous face. Gore dripped from its wide mouth. The monster rose, brandishing a broken tree clublike in its huge hand. The beast was dressed in animal skins and had a necklace of finger bones around its throat. It roared as it saw the samurai.

"Ogre," Shoju said flatly.

Tetsuo nodded.

Simultaneously, they drew their katana and charged.

The ogre kicked aside the body of a fallen scout and stood ready to meet them. It raised the broken tree, as thick as a man's leg and about twelve feet long. The creature itself was nearly eight feet tall and massively muscled. It swung the tree trunk effortlessly as the cousins bore in on it.

The samurai split formation, one attacking either side of the monster. Shoju ducked beneath the monster's blow and aimed a cut at the ogre's underarm.

The beast proved faster than it looked. The ogre dodged the daimyo's blow but received a long slash on its right side from Tetsuo. The monster bellowed its rage.

The samurai rode off. A short distance away, they wheeled their horses around.

"Again," said Shoju.

Tetsuo nodded. They charged, splitting to either side.

This time the monster was ready. It swung its tree-club to one side and lashed out to the other side with its huge foot.

Tetsuo deflected the club with his sword. The tree whizzed over his head. The monster's foot caught Shoju's horse full in its side. The Unicorn-bred beast lurched, shuddered, and went down, taking the Scorpion daimyo with it.

Shoju tried to jump free, but his withered hand didn't release the reins fast enough. The horse pinned the daimyo's right leg under it as it fell. Shoju grunted in pain.

The ogre closed in for the kill.

Shoju's right hand found some loose stones and sand on the road. He seized them and flung the dust into the monster's eyes.

Momentarily blinded, the ogre staggered back. The daimyo's horse scrambled to its hooves and limped off. Like a rampaging bull, the ogre roared out of the mist.

Shoju had lost his katana in the fall. He couldn't reach it before the monster would be on him. His wakizashi seemed poor defense against so huge a brute. He drew it anyway and tried to rise. His right leg protested. Rather than standing, the Scorpion daimyo merely staggered.

The ogre raised its club for the kill.

The creature stopped. It glared down at a length of polished steel protruding from its massive chest. The blade withdrew, and the monster spun drunkenly to face its attacker.

Tetsuo's sword separated the ogre's head from its shoulders. The massive body crashed to the ground. The head landed in a mulberry bush some distance away.

Shoju got up, rubbing his injured leg. He nodded at his cousin. Tetsuo leapt from the back of his horse and ran to the daimyo's side.

"Are you all right, my lord?" he asked.

"Just bruised, I think," Shoju replied. "I'm more worried about my horse. Find it for me, will you?"

Tetsuo nodded, marveling at his master's bravery and resilience. He remounted his horse and rode into the mists to seek the daimyo's steed.

When the young Scorpion had ridden out of sight, Shoju turned his attention from his leg to his withered arm. He hadn't noticed how stiff the limb had become. It nearly cost him his life. His fingers traced the design of the tattoo under his kimono, and the familiar fire returned to the arm.

Even in my own lands, I must ever be on guard, he reminded himself. I must never allow myself such moments of weakness. He sat down on a large rock until the tingling went away.

A few minutes later, Tetsuo rode out of the mist, leading the daimyo's horse by its reins.

"Badly bruised, I think," the young samurai said, "but not broken."

"Like myself," Shoju grunted. "Yosh!" He stood and took the horse's reins. "No more riding for you today, eh, boy?" he said to the animal. The horse snorted in agreement.

Tetsuo laughed.

His laughter was interrupted by the thunderous arrival of Rumiko and Shoju's guard.

Bantaro rode with them. Sweat dripped off his bald pate, and fear for his lord shone in his eyes. The shugenja looked much relieved to find the Scorpion lord standing.

"Master, are you hurt?" Bantaro asked.

"My horse took most of it," Shoju said.

"What happened, great lord?" asked Rumiko.

Tetsuo replied for his master. "Found an ogre," he said, indicating the body. "We killed it."

The samurai of Shoju's guard rumbled their approval and nodded.

"Actually, Tetsuo killed it," Shoju said. "After my horse had been knocked from under me."

Rumiko and the guard nodded. New respect for Tetsuo glinted behind their Scorpion masks.

"A pyre for the dead," Shoju ordered. "Then we ride on. Tetsuo, Bantaro, and I will rejoin the column."

Rumiko dismounted and offered the lord her horse, which he accepted. "Let my steed stay here and recover its breath with you," he said to her. He turned to the others. "And see that my orders are carried out."

The guards bowed in their saddles. "Yes, my lord," they said in unison.

Shoju and the others rode back into the mist, toward the main part of the Scorpion retinue.

They were greeted with concern when they arrived at the column. "An ogre killed some of our scouts," Tetsuo explained. This raised a worried murmur among the retainers, warriors, and priests until he added, "But the lord and I slew it readily enough."

The murmurs turned to grunts of approval and sighs of relief.

Kachiko ordered her palanquin brought forward, next to Shoju. "Were you wounded, Husband?" she asked, detecting in his carriage something no one else might notice.

"Not to concern yourself with," he said, looking down at her carved box. He wished he could wrap her in his arms, but the situation would not permit it. His right arm twinged at the thought, and he resisted the urge to rub it.

"Shall we move on, then?" she asked.

Shoju nodded. "Yes." He waved for the retinue to continue their march.

As the column fell into step, Bantaro rode up beside the daimyo.

"This ogre is a bad omen, I think," he said. Fear lurked behind the shugenja's elaborate mask.

"Nonsense," said the Scorpion daimyo. "If anything, it proves the rightness of our cause. The beast was sent to show us that the Demon Lord, Fu Leng, is very near."

"That could be one interpretation," Bantaro conceded.

Shoju snorted a laugh and rode ahead. Tetsuo joined him.

Before lunch they linked up with Rumiko and the Scorpion's guard. The pyres of the dead scouts burned brightly, but did not abate the mist that still clung to the landscape.

Shoju chose to continue riding the samurai-ko's horse so that his would have more time to recover from its bruises. Rumiko made no objection to walking, and even seemed honored by it.

This, Shoju thought, is as it should be.

▲▲▲▲▲▲▲▲

After the battle with the ogre, the Scorpion retinue pressed on toward the Spine of the World Mountains.

Along the way, they passed through Shiro no Shosuro and the jade walled city of Ryoko Owari Toshi. They paused at these places only long enough to replenish their supplies and replace their lost guardsmen.

The passage through the Seikitsu san Yama no Oi Mountains went smoothly. The retinue followed the course of the River of Gold through the peaks, crossing over to the western bank near the castle of Shiro no Soshi.

Soshi Bantaro had sent some of his people ahead, and the Scorpion daimyo and his retinue were greeted with full regalia by the people of the shugenja's land. Though Bantaro tried not to let it show, Shoju could tell that the old magician felt glad to return to his home.

Bantaro was not so pleased to find Yogo Junzo—Shoju's master shugenja—waiting at the castle. "I thought," Junzo said to Bantaro and his lord, "you might need my services. The most perilous part of this journey lies ahead."

Shoju accepted Junzo's offer, despite grumbling from Bantaro.

On the next day, they left the Soshi castle and struck out through the mountains. Good weather made the passage less treacherous. The company soon emerged on the far side of the Spine of the World. The pass debouched across the river from Yama sano Kaminari, the Mountain of Thunders.

This sacred mountain lay in Lion territory. Shoju's party had no desire to provoke a confrontation. Scorpion spies reported that the lord's retinue was being carefully watched by Lion scouts, and there had been considerable movement in the town at the base of the Lion castle, Kyuden Ikoma.

The Scorpion carefully kept his retinue west of the river, unclaimed land between the holdings of the Lion and those of the Unicorn. The Lion forces seemed content to watch the wily Scorpion and avoid a showdown.

Ahead lay the lands of the Dragonfly—who challenged all those who sought the Dragon. "The Dragonfly guards the Dragon's path," as the saying went. Shoju knew they would let him pass. His mission was just.

On the second day after they left the mountains, the Scorpion retinue woke to an amazing sight. Fog had descended on the foothills during the night, painting the landscape in gray and white. The mist hung heaviest over the river and danced like ghosts atop the water. As the sun rose, the fog turned a brilliant white, like smoke. A strange sound came from the river. It was a soft regular sound, like waves lapping on a beach. The noise came closer. Soon it sounded like fish jumping out of the river at regular intervals.

Many in the camp made their way to the water's edge and peered into the mist. What they saw sent them scurrying back. Some even screamed.

The screams brought Shoju and Kachiko out of the daimyo's pavilion. The lord, a mask already on his face, wrapped his kimono about his waist and stuck swords in his obi. Kachiko pulled her robe tight against the chill of the morning.

As a cry went up from the guard, Shoju raced to the river. Out of the fog, Tetsuo and Rumiko appeared at his side, both ready with their weapons.

"Call out," Shoju bellowed to the guards on the perimeter, "what is it you see?"

"A great beast, my lord," a sentry called back from the fog-shrouded distance. "Swimming upon the river." After a pause he cried, "I think it is a dragon!"

8 THE WAY OF THE DRAGON

The samurai beside Shoju gasped, but their drawn swords did not waver.

Yogo Junzo dashed up, followed by Soshi Bantaro. The older of the two men fumbled with a scroll as he came. He seemed to be having difficulty putting on his clothes.

"Could the guard be right?" asked Junzo.

"We'll know in a moment," Shoju said.

The samurai strained their eyes to see into the mist. Gradually a huge shape took form. Its face was blood-red, and as green as the deep sea, and gold. It had frightful fangs and horns. Its broad breast pushed the river apart as it came. Tongues of flame flicked across its back. It made hardly any sound as it moved through the water, only a soft, regular splashing.

"A dragon!" Rumiko gasped.

Bantaro dropped his scroll.

The Lord of the Scorpions laughed out loud. "A dragon boat," he said. "It's a boat!"

"I am glad to hear you have not lost your sense of humor, great lord," said a voice from the dragon's back. The form of the dragon ship resolved itself out of the mist. Shoju's diplomat, Bayushi Yojiro, stood at the prow.

"How came you to ride such a beast?" Shoju called out.

The dragon boat shipped its oars and glided gently to shore. Its bow had been cleverly carved to resemble the face of a real dragon; the flames along its spine were burning torches.

As the dragon touched land, Bayushi Yojiro hopped ashore. He was a young man, spry, and fair of face. His kimono had been expertly tailored and impeccably trimmed. He bowed low before the Scorpion daimyo.

"I sought the Dragon, as you bade, Shoju-sama," Yojiro said. "But they found me first. It seems the Great Dragon knew of your plans to visit almost before you did. He has sent this ship to meet you and bear you the rest of the way to his hidden palace in the mountains."

Yojiro looked back along the gunwale, where a figure appeared. She wore the swords of a samurai but no armor. The tattoo of a dragon wound up her neck and curled over her left eye. Her kimono was white with gold filigree which flickered like fish scales, even in the dim light of the fog-bound morning. A wry smile played across her pretty face.

"This is Reiko, captain of the dragon boat," Yojiro said, indicating the samurai-ko.

Shoju nodded in her direction, and the woman bowed.

"I will see you safely on your journey," Reiko said.

"Forgive my impudence, great lord," Bantaro said, "but the boat hardly seems big enough for all of us."

Overhearing him, Reiko said, "Your guards will not be necessary. My lord Togashi Yokuni guarantees your safety. Your retinue may return to the base of the mountains and wait for you there."

Yogo Junzo edged close to his daimyo and whispered, "If this were a trap, my lord . . ."

Shoju shook his head. "I have come to seek the advice of

the Dragon. I will not insult him by refusing or doubting his hospitality."

Junzo bowed. "As you wish, my lord."

As the shugenja withdrew, Shoju turned back to the boat's captain. "My household and I will come aboard," he said, "along with those of our party who are necessary for our comfort."

Reiko nodded. "At your leisure, my lord," she said, bowing low.

By late morning, the Scorpion had loaded all his necessary people and equipment onto the dragon boat. Tetsuo went with him, as did Kachiko and a number of their servants. Yojiro accompanied the Scorpion daimyo as well.

Bantaro complained bitterly about being left behind, or as bitterly as he dared in the presence of his lord. Shoju quelled his complaints by arranging with Reiko that, when he and the others returned, the dragon boat would take them as far as the Soshi castle. That way, the Scorpion retinue could wait in the comfort and security of Bantaro's home rather than camping under the watchful eye of the Lion.

"I will return to my studies and excavations, great lord," Yogo Junzo said, "and I will rest easier knowing you are so well guarded now." He glanced at the older shugenja as he said it.

Bantaro merely folded his arms over his chest and snorted at the suggestion.

Shoju nodded. "I hope your studies prove enlightening."

Junzo bowed. "They already have, my lord."

When all the preparations had been made, the dragon ship cast off. It made a leisurely turn in the river and headed upstream toward the lands of the Dragon.

The boat moved swiftly up the River of Gold. Tattooed samurai pulled on her oars with patient regularity, never complaining. Standing on the deck, the Scorpion daimyo's company watched the rest of their party quickly recede into the fog.

"This boat almost seems to be flying," said Tetsuo, leaning on the gunwale and peering over the side.

The comment brought a smile to the captain's lips. "How do you know that we are not, young samurai?" Reiko said.

The Scorpion daimyo watched as the water swirled around the bow of the ship. He thought of the tides and eddies in his own life. The battle to save Rokugan would be like piloting this boat upriver—difficult, but it could be accomplished with willpower and enough strong men.

Kachiko stood beside him, but they did not touch, nor did they look at each other. Finally she broke the silence. "What we do is right."

He nodded. "We shall see," he said.

The journey from the base of the mountains to the Castle of the Dragon would take the better part of five days. On the second day, they left the placid River of Gold and rowed into Oboreshinu Boekisho Kawa, the Drowned Merchant River. Despite the legend that gave the river its name, none in the Scorpion company saw any ghosts in the river's slow waters.

Not long after they entered the Drowned Merchant River, though, the ship turned north onto a rapidly running side water. Tattooed Dragon warriors from the Mirumoto family stood guard at the river's head. Shoju consulted his traveling papers but could find no sign of the river on his maps.

Behind his mask, the brow of the Scorpion lord furrowed. "This is odd," he said quietly.

Yojiro stepped forward. "I found no trace of it either," he said, seeing his lord's confusion. "Yet, when I rode my steed to this point, there it was—with guards indicating the way to the hidden palace. The ship met me part way. I never got to the castle itself. I've heard, though, that all roads lead to Kyuden Togashi."

Shoju nodded. "The power of the Dragon is great indeed."

The Scorpions saw many wondrous sites after entering the lands of the Dragon. Strange rock formations sprouted up out of the river, looking like the heads of giants or the backs of sea monsters. Some resembled the tops of sunken palaces or the castles of an unknown race of rock-men. The trees that topped these stone outcroppings were dwarfed and twisted into intriguing shapes.

Shoju didn't like them; they reminded him of his own deformity. He found himself unconsciously rubbing his right arm whenever the ship passed one. Kachiko noticed it too.

At night the retinue slept under a pavilion erected on the deck of the ship. In the morning the silk walls of the pavilion were rolled up so the visitors could see the countryside.

Tetsuo struck up a friendship with Captain Reiko, despite a slight difference in their ages. Yojiro seemed to know the ship's mistress well already. The three of them often stood conversing together on the afterdeck.

Behind his mask, the Scorpion smiled. Friends were good. Friends told you secrets. Secrets were the Scorpions' stock in trade. What one Scorpion knew, Bayushi Shoju knew.

Next morning, the character of the hidden river changed. The ship followed a wilder, more rugged course as the waterway led deep into the mountains. The tattooed samurai at the oars had to work harder to make the same progress, but still they never complained. Reiko gave them no words of encouragement or condemnation; she merely expected them to do their best—which was only right.

As the samurai pulled, the lady captain steered her ship around rocky shoals and dangerous eddies. The dragon boat handled lightly on the water and traversed the most difficult rapids with ease.

"Even were this river not hidden," Kachiko said, "an enemy would have trouble navigating it."

Shoju merely nodded.

In the middle of the fifth day, the great ship rounded a bend and came within sight of the Dragon palace. The castle rose out of the mountain mists like a mirage, shining gold and white, as if a piece of the sun had come down to the ground. Its walls sprang up from the living rocks and seemed almost a part of them. The Dragon castle looked grown rather than built. The swift-flowing river ran from a huge carved gate in the cliff side. Reiko steered directly toward the gate.

Few people were permitted to glimpse the heart of Dragon country. In his heart of hearts, Shoju felt honored to see it. This particular mission, though, afforded little time for such enjoyment.

As the boat drew up to the great gates, Kachiko stole to his side. She surreptitiously squeezed his left hand in a rare public display of affection. "This is only fitting to be *his* home, this pillar in the clouds," she said.

Shoju nodded his agreement. "A suitable home for a Dragon."

The great outer gates of the castle rolled back on their massive hinges. The dragon boat surged forward as if eager to be home. It sailed into a small lagoon within the walls of the fortress. A dock of ivory and gold awaited them, and Reiko expertly steered to it.

Thus, Bayushi Shoju and his people entered Kyuden Togashi, the palace of the Dragon, only twenty days after they had left Kyuden Bayushi.

▲▲▲▲▲▲▲▲

Great pomp and ceremony accompanied the Scorpion's visit. Shoju and his retinue were greeted at the dock by Togashi Hoshi, son of the Dragon daimyo. Hoshi did not come undisguised, of course, but appeared as a well-dressed advisor to the Dragon lord. Shoju and Kachijo recognized him nonetheless, and realized the honor that was being done them. The blood of the Scorpion ran through Hoshi's veins as well as the blood of his Dragon father. His mother had been a Scorpion—and though Hoshi never paid call on the clan of his long-dead mother, it still pleased the Scorpion lord and lady to see him.

If the Dragon's son felt any of this fellow feeling, he gave no sign. Instead, the greetings between the "lost child" and his mother's clan were very formal. Long ceremonies followed.

The afternoon drifted into evening. Dusk set the skies around the Dragon castle afire, turning the clouds to gold and silver.

Bayushi Shoju admired the sights and elaborate ceremonies used to greet him. Even so, his Scorpion senses told him the Dragons were not comfortable with Scorpions in their midst. Even Hoshi showed it, though he hid it well. Behind his bright, formal greeting mask, the Scorpion smiled. If even the Dragons feared the secrets of the Scorpion, his people had done their jobs well.

The ceremonies lasted past dusk and threatened to stretch well into the night. The attention of Tetsuo and some of the young retainers flagged. Finally, near midnight, Hoshi rose from his seat.

"The Great Lord Togashi Yokuni will see you now," he said.

Shoju and Kachiko rose from their honored spots on the great hall's tatami.

Hoshi stepped forward and said, "My lord will see his brother, the lord of the Scorpion . . . and no one else."

Though the fire of resentment burned in her belly, Kachiko bowed. When Hoshi bowed in return, she smiled her most winning smile at the Dragon heir. Hoshi looked away from her, and Kachiko felt the fire die down.

Hoshi motioned for Shoju to follow him. They walked to the back of the assembly room. A great wooden door stood there, sealed with a huge bar of sinuously carved gold and silver. The door was easily thirty feet tall and, like its bolt, had been carved with mystic symbols and draconian shapes.

As the Scorpion and the son of the Dragon approached, the bar slid back and the massive door opened of its own accord. Beyond the portal a huge stone staircase stretched up into the darkness.

Hoshi stopped at the threshold, bowed, and motioned for Shoju to enter. "My master awaits," the Dragon's son said.

Shoju nodded and set his foot on the step that led to the

inner sanctum of the Dragon. As he entered, the great door swung shut behind him.

Shoju's withered arm twinged slightly as he heard the bolt slide into place. He traced the design of the tattoo with his left fingers, and the pain subsided. Custom had forced him to leave his swords in the reception chamber, and only his status as daimyo had allowed him to carry them that far. All other swords had been left at the first door of the castle.

Still, Shoju wished he had them now. The katana and wakizashi would do him no good, but he longed for them nonetheless. For all his power, the Scorpion felt naked within this place.

Slowly he climbed the huge steps. They seemed to have been built more for the stature of a god than that of a man. As Shoju went, his eyes adjusted to the darkness. The walls and stairs were formed out of the living rock itself. No carvings or decorations adorned this passageway to the inner chamber. None were needed. The scale of the place alone was enough to inspire respect. The ceiling was lost in darkness above.

Eventually the long staircase ended, and Shoju found himself standing on a broad, flat platform. Bright stars spread overhead. He wondered when he had come outside—if, indeed, he was outside. The stars moved, slowly, but far more perceptibly than they did in the night sky of Rokugan.

As he watched the stars turn, Shoju suddenly realized he was not alone.

"Welcome to our home, Bayushi Shoju, lord of the Scorpion," said a deep voice from Shoju's left.

Looking in that direction, Shoju saw a man sitting on a low platform made of ivory. He wore a fabulous kimono that seemed to reflect the stars themselves. Shoju tried in vain to see the man's face. His countenance was wrapped in shadow, though the glow from his golden eyes did pierce the darkness.

"I am honored, Togashi-sama," Shoju said, bowing formally to the Dragon lord. "I have come because I need the guidance of your wisdom."

"We see your true face, Scorpion lord," the Dragon said, "and we know what is in your mind."

"Tell me then," said Shoju, "do I read the signs and omens correctly?"

The Dragon nodded. "You do."

"Then the last of the Hantei will bring disaster to all of Rokugan and release Fu Leng into the world once more."

"The final Hantei emperor will do this, though those who hold the throne before him will hasten the day."

"And that day is soon?" Shoju asked.

"Very soon indeed," replied the Dragon.

"Then we must act to stop him."

"There is no 'we,' Bayushi Shoju. You know my nature just as I know yours. You know that I will not meddle in the empire's affairs."

"Great Lord, you must. The people need your strength and wisdom. Together we could—"

"Together we would destroy the world just as surely as Fu Leng—just as the Hantei will do, if left unhindered. None may see his own future, Bayushi Shoju, not even I."

Shoju thought for a while, and then finally said, "The stone thrown into the pond never sees the ripples it creates."

"Just so," agreed the Dragon Lord.

"Then tell me," Shoju said. "Can I prevent this catastrophe without your aid? Can one clan alone be enough? Will my plan work? Do I have the power?"

The Dragon nodded. "If your plan succeeds, the empire will be saved."

Behind his mask, Shoju smiled. He took a breath of the sweet, cold mountain air and let it out slowly. "But the cost will be terrible," he said somberly.

The Dragon's golden eyes gleamed in the darkness. "Some futures are plain to all of us," Togashi said.

"Again, I beg you, help me in this endeavor."

"I cannot," said the Dragon. "This path you must walk alone. Now go."

Shoju bowed low. "Thank you, Mighty One." When he looked up, the Dragon was gone.

The Scorpion daimyo turned and walked back down the long stone stairway. His withered arm ached fiercely, and he rubbed it as he went.

A future of fire and blood plagued his mind, but he realized no one else could help him. The Dragon had declared his neutrality; the Scorpion would stand alone. His retinue had come a long way for so simple an answer.

With this meeting, Bayushi Shoju knew his course had been set. From now on, he would have to keep his own counsel, even if it meant his doom.

9   DUELS

Akodo Toturi rode to the entrance of the Imperial Palace in Otosan Uchi and reined in his Unicorn-bred steed before the gates. The guardsmen recognized the Lion daimyo; the gates opened, and they waved him through.

Toturi looked at the palace with mixed emotions. The beauty of the grounds, the gardens, the castle itself, nearly overwhelmed his senses. The flowers, the waterfalls, the exquisite carvings and sculpture, and the high towers overlooking fabulous vistas enticed him with their magnificence. What man in all of Rokugan would not want to live in such a place?

Toturi also knew that the castle was a cage, a coldly beautiful cage from which he could never escape. As daimyo of the Lion Clan, Toturi was chained within the Imperial household forever.

His every instinct rebelled against such imprisonment, but his sense of honor and duty made him do what he had to.

For nearly a month Toturi had put off his visit to court, always finding some excuse—a border skirmish, a supernatural incursion—to delay his trip. He could put it off no longer. His courtiers said the emperor grew impatient to see him. It was wrong to keep the emperor waiting.

It was not the emperor that the Lion Champion feared to see.

He had tried to talk Ikoma Bentai into making the trip with him, but the wily Lion general had refused.

"This is something you have to brace yourself for," Bentai had said. "All your legions can't do it, nor can all the sake in the world. I cannot do it either. A cub once burned is twice shy, but sooner or later, a lion must face the wildfire."

Bentai's double meanings had not been lost on Toturi. The general did not refer to the fire of the Celestial Son, but to the eternally renewing flame of the Phoenix.

The Phoenix, his fiancée, Isawa Kaede—the woman he did not love. He thought of her and could not recall what she looked like; instead, Hatsuko's painted face danced before his mind.

Despite his brave words to Hatsuko in the woods, Toturi found his courage waning within the walls of the Imperial Precinct. He reined in before the stables, and a groom came to take his horse.

As he dismounted, the doors to the great hall opened. A small committee came out to greet him. At their head stood Hantei Sotorii, the heir to the throne. He was dressed in a ceremonial kimono and looked rather uncomfortable. The rest of the party ignored the boy as he scratched himself and shifted from one foot to the other.

Behind the heir stood Shosuro Taberu, the emperor's Scorpion advisor when Bayushi Kachiko wasn't at court. Doji Shizue, the young Crane courtesan, and Seppun Ishikawa, the captain of the guard, also accompanied the young Hantei, as did several other people whom Toturi did not know.

The Lion fought hard not to frown. The emperor knew Toturi was coming and yet he had sent the heir and some second-rank dignitaries to meet him.

Usually, a clan daimyo would be greeted by the emperor himself or, if the Celestial One was unable to attend, a large body of his courtiers. The size and composition of this retinue clearly indicated Hantei's displeasure with his general. Doubtless the boy heir was honored by this duty; Toturi was not.

Akodo Toturi walked toward the committee, forcing his budding frown into a pleasant smile. At least, he thought, Isawa Kaede is not with them. The Lion didn't feel ready to confront his fiancée just yet.

The heir cleared his throat and stepped forward to greet Toturi. "Akodo Toturi-san," the boy said, trying hard not to appear nervous. "My Celestial Father sends his greetings and welcomes you to the Emerald Court. We are pleased you have honored us with your presence."

Toturi bowed at this, though he wondered if the Scorpion diplomat had helped the young Hantei with his speech.

"The Most High Emperor regrets he could not greet you himself, but he has other pressing matters at present. In his stead and at his behest, we have planned a feast this evening to celebrate your return to court. We pray you will honor us with your attendance."

Again, Toturi bowed. Again, he suspected the hand of the Scorpion in the message. Of course he would attend the feast; it would insult the imperial household to do otherwise. The emperor would know that very well, as would all senior members of his court. To imply otherwise was almost an insult. No, it *was* an insult. Still nervous, the young Hantei seemed oblivious to the double meanings in his words.

Hantei Sotorii looked to Taberu the Scorpion on his left, and then to Shizue the Crane on his right. The heir seemed lost. Seeing his confusion, Shizue stepped forward and produced a small scroll from her robes. The boy fumbled with the ribbon that sealed it, unrolled the parchment, and read.

"We pray you will honor with your attendance," he repeated.

Toturi and the rest of the retinue pretended not to notice the lapse.

The heir continued. "We also hope that you will entertain our court with tales of your recent endeavors, both on the field of battle and off."

Toturi fought hard not to let his face redden. He bowed low to let the momentary flush past. Could the emperor, or someone else, suspect the reason he'd been away so long? Could they know about his dalliances with Hatsuko?

"We are sure," Sotorii continued, "that your stories will thrill us, as they have in the past." Here the heir put the parchment roughly aside and spoke from his heart. "I want to hear of your boar hunt in the mountains. Is it true you slew one of the creatures on your own?"

Toturi might have laughed, but both decorum and a remembrance of his dream with Hatsuko made him bow instead. "It is true, young Highness. I shall be happy to tell you the tale whenever you like."

For a moment, enthusiasm filled Sotorii's eyes. Then he seemed to remember his place. He became cold and regal. "Now," he said, assuming a tone of command. "You will tell us now. By the lotus . . . By *my father's* lotus pond."

Shizue stepped forward. She limped slightly, her right leg somewhat lame. "Young master," she said quietly, "what about the ceremonial tea?"

"Let the tea come to us," Hantei Sotorii said. "We shall await it by the pond."

The rest of the retinue bowed. Taberu, the Scorpion, said, "As you wish, Shining Prince."

Toturi detected a look of concern on Doji Shizue's face, and a slight scowl of disapproval from Ishikawa, the captain of the guard. Though the Scorpion's mask hid little of his face, Toturi could not see past Taberu's smile.

▲▲▲▲▲▲▲▲

The Lotus Pond at the palace was a place of tranquillity and delight. Surrounded by cherry trees, the still waters of the pond were disturbed only by occasional ripples as the pond's huge goldfish came to the surface. Toturi wondered if the fish were merely inspecting the grove's visitors, or if they had some other purpose in mind. Perhaps they expected to be fed; perhaps they expected to be fed *upon*.

Eating the fabulous fish was forbidden under penalty of death, but occasionally one went missing. Idle courtiers speculated that the fish ate each other if their daily rations proved inadequate. Superstitious kitchen hands whispered of ninja and black rites requiring golden scales. Toturi suspected large birds.

The cold-blooded creatures refused to give up their secrets. Perhaps that was why they came to the surface, to see if their kidnapper had returned.

Toturi smiled. Such fancies nearly took him away from the white towers of the castle. At such times he almost felt at home here. Almost. The heir to the Hantei throne dropped a crumb into the water. The splash of feeding fish brought Toturi out of his reverie. He became the bird in the ivory cage once more.

Around the pond with him sat the young Hantei and the retinue that had greeted Toturi. As news of the Lion's visit drifted through the castle, others had arrived as well. Toturi recognized the Moshi twins and the three daughters of Miya Matsuo among them. The middle girl, Yumika, kept a careful watch on the heir to the throne. The other two seemed far more interested in the Lion general.

Toturi felt glad his reputation still meant something in the castle. Soon a small crowd had gathered to hear his tales of battle and honor.

The Lion daimyo kept them amused, mixing war stories with proverbs and myths he'd learned at the monastery. He included a few colorful tales told to him by Ikoma Bentai.

These last he edited judiciously for the ears of the heir and the more genteel members of his audience.

Soon the garden of the lotus pond buzzed with activity, more activity than its scaly denizens had ever known. Toturi was in the middle of the tale of the monkey and the tiger princess when the murmur around him suddenly died away.

Emperor Hantei the 38th walked into the garden. Behind him came Toturi's fiancée, Isawa Kaede, and other members of his retinue, including Seppun Daiori, Kakita Yoshi, and Seppun Bake. Toturi bowed low, touching his head to the ground. All the others with him, except the royal heir, did the same. Hantei Sotorii merely bowed politely.

"Celestial Father," the boy said, "you honor us with your presence."

The emperor nodded, and several of his retainers brought forth a short lacquered chair for him to sit on. The emperor took his seat; Kaede and his retinue sat on the ground beside him.

"We are pleased to see you, Lion," Hantei said, addressing Toturi.

"Your light shines upon us all," Toturi replied, rising and bowing once again, though not as low this time.

The emperor smiled, his mouth drawn and pale. "Then why do you not visit us more often?" he asked.

Toturi felt embarrassment burn his flesh, but he fought it down. "The moth—though he wears the face of a lion—does not dare fly too close to the flame," Toturi answered.

The emperor smiled, and then laughed; his son laughed with him.

"Your words please us, Toturi," Hantei said. "Our friend Shosuro Taberu could not have said better himself."

At this the Scorpion envoy bowed; Toturi bowed as well, but he felt a slight anger well up at being compared to a Scorpion. He hid the feeling and bowed again.

"If I speak well," Toturi said, "it is because I am inspired by your Celestial Presence."

Hantei produced a colorful fan from the sleeve of his kimono and waved it open. "Enough flattery," he said. "We have heard that the Lion is in good form today, and has greatly entertained our people with his stories." He looked directly at Toturi and smiled warmly. "We hope you will not exhaust your tales before the greeting feast."

"If I run out of stories, I will invent new ones just for you, Majesty."

"I could not have said it better myself," Taberu whispered to the young heir, loud enough that everyone could hear.

The emperor, the heir, and all those present laughed, even Kaede. It took a moment for Toturi to warm up, but soon he joined the rest. Better to laugh with your friends than to be laughed at by them, he thought. He reminded himself to watch the Scorpion carefully.

When the laughter died down, Toturi returned to the tale of the monkey and the tiger princess, making sure to recap it so that the emperor and his retinue would not feel they came into the story late.

Navigating the court is like conducting a war, Toturi thought, though no one gets killed—at least not right away. He avoided Kaede's gaze and noticed she did the same. He tried not to think of Hatsuko, which, of course, made him think of her all the more.

As the day drew on, the emperor's attention seemed to flag. Soon, it looked as though he might doze off. Toturi wasn't sure what to do. The rest of his audience seemed in rapt attention. Was the emperor's demeanor an indication that he found Toturi boring, or that he trusted the Lion enough to fall asleep in his presence?

Fortunately, the Scorpion stepped in. Before Toturi had to decide whether or not to begin a new story, he said, "Your prowess in storytelling is indeed great, as is your prowess in war, Toturi-san. Though it is late in the day, the sun is hot. Perhaps we could adjourn inside and you could demonstrate for us your martial skill."

"Hai, Taberu-san," Toturi said. "If it is the emperor's wish."

The emperor roused himself enough to say, "If you so please, Lion. Ourselves, we shall stay here and enjoy the late afternoon sun. We shall rejoin you for the feast." He waved his fan. "Begone with you all."

The others gathered themselves and left the garden.

"You shall need someone to spar with, Toturi-san," Taberu said as they left. A small contingent, including the heir, continued to follow Toturi as he strode toward the great keep of the castle. Much to Toturi's discomfort, Kaede came with them. So did Yoshi, the emperor's Crane advisor—who had lately arrived at the lotus pond—and his young apprentice Shizue.

"Do you offer yourself, Taberu-san?" Toturi asked.

The Scorpion shook his head. "Only if this is to be a battle of words," he said good-naturedly.

"You then, Yoshi-san?" Toturi offered.

"I'm a poet," Yoshi said, "not a fighter."

Toturi could see from their faces that Daiori and Bake were likely to decline, too—which was just as well. Daiori had never recovered from an old war wound and Bake was permanently hunched over from his long hours of study. Testing his mettle against such opponents could only bring the Lion shame.

"I'll spar with you, Toturi-sama," said Ishikawa, stepping from the crowd.

Sotorii, the royal heir, stood nearby, and he seemed to want to say something. Perhaps he meant to answer the challenge himself. When Ishikawa stepped forward, Sotorii clamped his mouth shut.

Toturi looked at the captain of the guard and nodded. A girl in the back of the crowd clapped. A look of disapproval flashed in Kaede's eyes.

"The dojo of the swordmaster has wooden practice swords," Ishikawa suggested. "It is empty at this time of the day."

Toturi nodded again. "A fine setting," he said. "Let's adjourn there." They changed direction and walked toward the dojo; the crowd followed along.

10 WORDS BETWEEN MAN AND WOMAN

As they walked, Ishikawa sized up his opponent. Toturi was a master strategist. Unparalleled in the art of war, he had devised schemes that allowed his forces—and those of the empire—to achieve victory when otherwise they would have suffered bitter defeat. Whispers around court said the Lion general's prowess as a swordsman wasn't great. Looking at Toturi, Ishikawa couldn't tell.

The Lion was tall and lean, almost ascetic in his frame, despite his years away from the Asoko monastery. He wore loose-fitting brown robes spangled with ochre Lion crests and decorated with golden trim. Toturi's hair was golden, and he wore it tied back in the traditional style. Like all samurai, he carried the dai-sho swords, and since he was a daimyo, his weapons appeared to be of exceptional quality. On his feet he wore simple sandals.

Ishikawa wondered whether the simplicity of his attire was an affectation or a reflection of the inner man. Many a warrior had downplayed his skills through the manner of his dress. Though the captain of the guard had seen the Lion at court numerous times, he could never remember seeing Toturi fight. The Lion's garb could mean either thing.

Ishikawa upbraided himself for thinking like a Scorpion. Not all things in life had meaning. Some things just were.

As the captain of the guard studied his opponent, Toturi concentrated on the match ahead. He knew Ishikawa only by reputation, but one didn't rise to a captaincy without proficiency at arms. He recalled tales of the battles in which Ishikawa had fought and the Lion's keen mind analyzed the stories, looking for some weakness.

Iajutsu, the fast-draw sword technique, would not enter into the contest. This was just as well. It was one of Toturi's weak spots and, according to reports, something Ishikawa was good at. Beyond the draw, Ishikawa was a straightforward fighter. He came in boldly and tried to overwhelm an opponent with his strength. Toturi was the man's equal on this account; his strength would not fail him. The captain's boldness could be a weakness as well. A clever feint might trap him into committing a stroke too soon.

Pleased with his analysis, Toturi smiled. His hand unconsciously stole to the hilt of his katana. Isawa Kaede noticed the move.

The Phoenix Mistress of the Void was worried. What had possessed Ishikawa to challenge her fiancé? She could see no good outcome of the contest. Either the captain would win and Toturi would be disgraced, or Toturi would win and Ishikawa would gain nothing. Of course, there was always the slim chance someone could get hurt. Sometimes a samurai's emotions could get the better of him during combat, even in a friendly contest such as this.

Kaede could not stand the thought of either man being

hurt. She said a quick prayer to Amaterasu, the Sun Goddess, and continued to follow the two men.

They soon arrived at the castle's training dojo. As Ishikawa had said, the chamber was deserted. The small retinue seated themselves around the room on tatami mats. Toturi and Ishikawa removed their dai-sho, carefully setting the swords aside in a manner that would neither impugn the honor of their clans nor the honor of their opponents. Then they stripped off any of their ceremonial outer garments that they deemed might hinder their movements during a fight.

Each man selected a wooden *bokken*, a practice sword, from one of the many stands resting along the dojo's walls. Toturi and Ishikawa made some practice moves and cuts, testing the weight and balance of their weapons. Presently, the two men bowed and faced each other across the large tatami mat in the center of the dojo's broad, wooden floor.

Toturi held his sword high, in a defensive posture, the wooden blade close to his ear. Ishikawa kept his sword low, angled behind him, the tip of the blade nearly touching the floor.

He hopes to use his iajutsu skill for the first blow, thought Toturi. I must be ready for it.

"Ready?" the captain of the guard asked.

Toturi nodded grimly, his mind playing over a thousand outcomes. Most battles were won before the first blow was struck.

Silence fell over the dojo. The audience hardly dared breathe.

Toturi watched his opponent, careful not to be misled by the man's eyes; Ishikawa did the same. Each man waited for the other to make a mistake or, alternately, for the perfect moment to strike. Toturi listened to the sound of his own heart.

The moment came.

With a wild war cry, Ishikawa charged. He swung his wooden sword in a wide arc from his hip, aiming for Toturi's chest.

The Lion was ready for him. He whipped his sword around, blocking the blow.

The two spun on each other, their swords meeting a second time. After the third clash, they stepped back to assess the situation.

Ishikawa charged again.

Toturi met his opponent's bokken with his own and stepped deftly aside. Ishikawa staggered forward, but Toturi didn't take advantage of it. Instead, he resumed his defensive posture.

Ishikawa turned, embarrassed by his mistake, and faced his opponent once more. He cursed himself for being a fool and felt glad Toturi hadn't taken advantage of his lapse. He brought his sword up into a defensive posture similar to the Lion's.

The men stared at each other, sweat trickling down their brows. Ishikawa's eyes showed grim determination; Toturi's eyes seemed detached, distant.

The Lion's coolness made a fire spring up in the belly of the captain. How can a man with blood so thin lay claim to Kaede? Ishikawa thought. He charged again.

Toturi parried and stepped aside once more. This time Ishikawa was ready for it. As the Lion stepped, Ishikawa thrust at him with the point of his sword.

Toturi's reflexes saved him. He hopped back at the last instant, and the point never found his gut. He batted at the sword with a sweeping motion.

Ishikawa pressed forward, sensing the Lion was off-balance.

That was what Toturi wanted him to think. Ishikawa bore in, making himself off-balance. Toturi spun quickly away from the point of the captain's sword. For a brief moment, the Lion looked like a dancer doing a pirouette. His bokken described a short arc through the air and landed solidly across his opponent's shoulders.

Ishikawa fell to the mat, landing hard on his chest. His breath rushed out in a great huff.

The small crowd gasped and applauded. Toturi bowed and

offered his hand to his opponent. "A worthy match," he said.

Ishikawa looked at the hand for a moment and then took it. As he did, he felt his anger subside. Toturi had beaten him fairly; the Lion proved himself the better man on this day.

With Toturi's help, Ishikawa rose. He bowed to the victor of the match. Toturi bowed back to his opponent. In his heart, Ishikawa vowed not to underestimate the Lion daimyo again.

Toturi rose from his bow and scanned the assembled crowd.

Hantei Sotorii, the royal heir, applauded wildly, thrilled by the outcome. Kakita Yoshi and Seppun Daiori nodded appreciatively. Their faces conveyed their respect. Yoshi's Crane ally, Doji Shizue, clapped politely. Her intelligent eyes took in every detail of the scene. Shosuro Taberu smiled and applauded— but who could know what a Scorpion *really* thought? The Moshi twins, the men-at-arms, and the retainers who had accompanied the contestants cheered, nodding to one another. Toturi had impressed them. Toward the back of the group, the Miya sisters and several of their girlfriends clapped enthusiastically and chattered to each other like birds.

Only Isawa Kaede didn't seem to appreciate the match. True, she applauded politely, and her face showed no displeasure, but she was no Scorpion. The Lion could tell she either didn't like the fight, or—at least—didn't like its outcome.

Words from Ishikawa brought Toturi back to reality. "Well struck, Toturi-sama," the captain said. "I thank you for doing me this honor." He bowed to Toturi again.

"As you have honored me," Toturi answered back. He bowed again as well, but not as low as Ishikawa had. The Lion brought one long-fingered hand to his face and wiped the sweat from his brow back into his long, golden hair. "I pray that we both have time for a bath before the feast."

This brought laughter from the crowd.

"I doubt you need one," Ishikawa said. "I fear I hardly made you work up a sweat."

Toturi smiled at him. "Then the roof of this dojo needs fixing, for I believe I am covered in rain."

Again, they all laughed.

"Well done, Toturi-san," said the heir.

Toturi thought he could see a new respect in the boy's eyes. "Thank you, O Child of the Light," he said, bowing. After he stood up, Toturi said, "With your permission, Highness, I go to bathe."

Sotorii held his nose in mock disgust, "By all means," he said, the fingers on his nose pinching his words as they came out.

Toturi and the retinue laughed politely.

Toturi headed toward the bath house, and Ishikawa watched him go. "After you, my lord," the captain said.

The rest of the crowd stood to leave. They filed out of the dojo and returned to their courtly business. Only Isawa Kaede lingered behind. Ishikawa stood at the door of the dojo, staring toward the main keep of the castle.

"Why did you do it, Ishikawa?" she asked him.

The soft sound of her voice startled the captain; he'd almost forgotten she was there. "Do what?" he asked.

"Why did you challenge Toturi?"

Ishikawa shrugged, but he didn't look at her. "I wanted to see what he was made of."

"And that is all?" she asked demurely, her breath so close that he could smell its perfume.

He looked at her and realized she stood closer than he had thought—almost intimately close. "And I wanted to see if he was worthy to be your husband," he said gruffly.

"And . . .?"

Ishikawa reached under his kimono and rubbed his left shoulder. "His sword arm seems strong enough," he said. "And no one can doubt his prowess on the field." He smiled a crooked smile at her. "You could do worse."

Kaede turned her eyes toward the floor and blushed.

▲▲▲▲▲▲▲▲

The feast to welcome the Lion daimyo was held in one of the palace's huge feasting halls. Tall, dark timbers supported the chamber's high ceiling. Fusuma, painted with trees, mountains, and waterfalls, made up the walls. Thick tatami covered the floor.

The emperor's low dais occupied one end of the room, and Hantei the 38th sat cross-legged atop it. A place of honor next to the platform had been reserved for Toturi. The other guests seated themselves on the tatami in carefully ordered rows, their food and drink placed on the floor in front of them. The center of the room remained bare, for the entertainment to follow.

The celebration began with a tea ceremony for three hundred, expertly performed. A dance presentation came second, followed by a poetry reading by Yoshi. Toturi had to admit that the man had talent. Then the food—many courses, all meticulously prepared, each presented precisely far enough apart for the guests to consider the tastes and textures they'd just experienced.

Toturi enjoyed the food, though it did make part of him long for the simple meals of the monastery. A blind flutist played during the dinner, enchanting all those who heard her, but never distracting from the meal itself.

After the meal, Doji Shizue dazzled the court with a story of men and gods and monsters. Toturi had to admit that her storytelling was superior to his own. The story segued seamlessly into quiet conversation. Several courtiers played shamisen softly in the background.

Seated on the floor near the Imperial tatami, Toturi wondered if he had imagined the slights of earlier in the day. The emperor smiled and nodded when he saw the Lion. Hantei Sotorii took delight in telling of Toturi's duel with Ishikawa. By the end of the evening he'd retold the story dozens of times.

As conversation died away, courtiers drifted out of the dining room and into the many gardens surrounding the palace. Most bade good-bye to Toturi, the emperor, and the heir as they wandered out.

"I hope we shall see you at court more often," Shosuro Taberu said to Toturi. Taberu stopped to whisper something in the emperor's ear as he went, leaving Toturi to wonder what the Scorpion envoy had meant. The emperor nodded and Taberu flashed Toturi a final smile before exiting the room.

Suddenly uncomfortable, Toturi got up and stretched. He was trying to decide which garden to visit when he suddenly realized that the emperor had appeared at his elbow. Toturi bowed low, "Otennoo-sama," he said.

"Walk with us in the garden," the emperor said, indicating an exit with his fan. Toturi swallowed hard, but did as he was told. The emperor led him through several winding passage-ways until finally they debouched into a splendid garden behind the palace. The moon overhead painted the elegant castle in a pale blue radiance.

"We are pleased with how you and Doji Hoturi have quieted the feud between your two clans," the emperor said, leading Toturi along a path beneath the cherry trees.

Toturi nodded. "We but live to serve," he said. "I only wish I could report that all the quarrels had ended."

The older man chuckled. "We fear that will not happen until all of us are in the grave," said Hantei. He continued walking as he spoke, leading Toturi deeper within the garden. The emperor set a brisk pace, despite his advancing age. Toturi lost track of exactly where they were. The grounds of the palace were immense, and few people knew the whole expanse of them. Hantei the 38th was certainly one of those people.

"As we grow older," the emperor continued, "we come to see that such bickering is of little importance. Cranes will be Cranes, and Lions will be Lions. Each acts according to his nature. We wonder . . . what is your nature, Akodo Toturi?"

The question caught him by surprise. All Toturi could think to say was, "I live to serve you, Majesty."

Hantei waved his fan at the younger man. "So you've said. So you've said. Yet, we seldom see you around the palace."

"I am your general, Celestial One," Toturi said, beads of

sweat forming on his brow. "There are conflicts I must attend to, affairs I must set right . . . ."

"Hmm. Affairs. Yes. So we gather."

This made Toturi flush, and he turned away momentarily.

The emperor didn't seem to notice. "There are affairs you must attend to at court, too," Hantei continued. "One such affair you have neglected far too long." With this the emperor smiled and stepped into a small clearing.

Toturi followed him and was shocked to find Isawa Kaede waiting for them inside. She bowed her head as the emperor and the Lion arrived.

"G-Great Lord . . ." Toturi stammered.

"No need to thank us, my boy," the emperor said. He took Toturi's hand and Kaede's and placed them together.

Toturi and Kaede looked at each other, both shy and nervous.

The emperor turned and left the couple together. "We're sure the two of you have much to discuss," he said as he exited the clearing. The Lion and his fiancée held their breaths until the emperor was gone.

Then, as if by silent agreement, they let their hands slip apart.

Finally, Kaede spoke, "It has been a long time, Toturi-san."

Toturi swallowed and took a deep breath. The fear he'd felt upon entering the castle earlier in the day bubbled up inside him once more.

"Yes, it has," he said. "Are you well?"

"As always," she replied. "And you?"

He nodded. "I too am well."

"Would you like to walk?" she asked. "The moonlight is very beautiful."

"Perhaps a walk would be good."

She extended her hand to him, but then drew it back when she perceived that he would not take it. They walked in the garden together, but not truly together at all. Toturi sensed that she knew the paths well; personally, he felt lost.

How can a man face death without fear and yet feel terrified by such a maiden? he asked himself.

"Was your trip to the palace difficult?" she asked.

"No more than usual."

"I had hoped," she said, "that you would visit more often."

"A common refrain this visit," he said, more brusquely than he had intended.

She turned her eyes away from him. "It is good for people to get to know each other before they are wed."

This sent a cold spike through Toturi's heart. For a moment, his brain fumbled for an answer that would not insult her. Finally he said, "I gather the emperor feels so too."

She nodded. "Hai," she said quietly.

Toturi looked around, but saw no easy avenue of escape. "The gardens are beautiful in the moonlight," he said.

"The palace is lovely throughout the year," she said.

Her voice sounded wounded. Toturi knew he had inflicted pain on her. Moisture clung to the corners of her eyes. Kaede's long lashes batted the tears away. Proud and fair of face and form, she looked beautiful beneath the summer moon.

"Not half as lovely as you," he said, and wished immediately that he hadn't said it.

A burning contradiction welled up inside the breast of the Lion. He did not want to hurt this fair creature, he knew that. He couldn't bear the thought of the pain he was causing her even now. Yet, he loved Hatsuko with all his heart. Even in Kaede's dark, sumptuous orbs he saw the eyes of his geisha lover. The modest cut of the Phoenix lady's kimono reminded him of the soft pleasures that awaited him beneath Hatsuko's robes. Even her smell and the scent of the gardens reminded Toturi of the woman he truly loved.

Hatsuko.

He could almost hear her voice on the wind.

Kaede looked at the Lion daimyo as if she wanted to read his mind. Toturi felt glad that she could not.

"Tell me what you're feeling," she finally said.

"I must leave," he said stiffly. "My couriers are bringing news of skirmishes. I have dallied too long here."

"Is that all I am, then, a dalliance?" she asked.

Toturi could feel his Lion's heart breaking, but he remained firm. He forced distance into his voice, though part of him wanted to crush her to his bosom and comfort her. "Of course not," he said. "You are my fiancée. But I am general to the empire. Duty must come first. I need to check the reports."

"I understand," she said quietly.

Part of Toturi thought that she did. He stepped away from her. "Thank you for the walk, Kaede-sama," he said, bowing formally.

"You're welcome," she said, not looking up.

Toturi looked around, sighted the main tower of the palace, and strode off through the garden in that direction. Hatsuko's fire danced in his brain, but it still took all his resolve not to look back.

From a hidden spot in the flowers nearby, Ishikawa watched Toturi go. Kaede sank to her knees and wept. A fist clenched inside the captain of the guard. His regard for her honor prevented him from going to her, though all his heart cried out that he should.

So Isawa Kaede knelt alone in the royal gardens, crying in the moonlight.

11   AMBITION

The return to Kyuden Bayushi took the Scorpions less time than had their journey to the Palace of the Dragon. The dragon ship of Reiko ferried them all the way back to Shiro no Soshi, cutting two days off their journey.

Bantaro hoped the Scorpion lord would linger in the shugenja's keep for a while, but Shoju insisted they press on quickly. The Scorpion never spoke of his meeting with the Dragon to anyone save Kachiko, and she kept her own counsel on the matter.

The morning after their lord's arrival, the Scorpion host left the Soshi castle and marched back through the mountains toward the castle of the Bayushi. The trip took the better part of two weeks, and the Scorpion lord kept to himself for most of that time.

Occasionally, he could be seen in the company of Tetsuo or checking the ranks of his soldiers. Even as he rode at the head of the company, he seemed distant—as if he were in another world.

Hidden in her palanquin, Kachiko wondered what thoughts coursed through her husband's mind. Aside from a brief confidence about his meeting with the Dragon, Shoju had kept himself distant from her too—which was unusual. The Scorpion lord and lady were partners in all things; they had no secrets from each other. No secrets, save their own inner thoughts, and even these they usually shared with one another.

Whatever thoughts Bayushi Shoju had, he kept to himself. Kachiko had never seen her husband like this before, and it disturbed her. There were momentous decisions to be made, decisions that would affect the entire empire. Surely they should face the trials ahead together—just as they had in the past, just as they had when they pored over the scroll in Kyuden Bayushi.

Separately, she or Shoju might falter, but together . . . together they were invincible—he the hidden face and well-·tempered sword, she the soft, outstretched hand that held either the lotus blossom or sweet poison. The Scorpion lord and lady perfectly represented the dual nature of their clan. No one in all of Rokugan could stand against them.

Now, the mask of the Scorpion lord hid his face from her just as it did from the rest of the world. What lay behind the mask? When their journey was over, would she even recognize Shoju's face?

This was nonsense. He removed his mask every night before they went to bed—even while in their pavilion on the road. It was a sign of their trust. Kachiko sometimes wondered if, despite all his power, Shoju feared he would lose control of the clan if his true face were revealed.

She liked to think that it would make no difference, that Scorpions were trained to see the worth of a man behind his face. An ugly leader—for there was no other word to describe Shoju's countenance—was no less worthy than a beautiful one. This was a basic difference between Scorpion and Crane. For the Crane, truth and beauty went hand in hand.

One good thing had come from a beautiful Crane: Dairu, her son—no, *Shoju's* son. Kachiko wondered again if the Scorpion lord had left his heir at Kyuden Bayushi for reasons of security, or if somewhere deep inside, he still harbored resentment over the boy's lineage.

Kachiko's gilded palanquin box felt suddenly hot. A tense pain filled her head. She rubbed her temples and calmed her breathing. Such thoughts were useless.

Shoju had never treated her boy ... *their* boy with anything but respect. Nor had he treated her badly. In fact, he was the only man in her life who had not. The Scorpion lord had earned his wife's respect by giving her his own.

She had earned his trust by not shying away when he revealed his true face to her on their wedding night. Growing up with her brother had shown her that the way things looked mattered little. Shosuro Hametsu was fair of face and form, but his soul was empty. He was hardly worthy to be a Scorpion. He would have made a better Crane.

Of course, their father could not see that. He judged Hametsu worthy to be his heir, though Kachiko was firstborn. Her father thought her beauty and sex ill fitted her to lead their clan. He considered her a trifle, a poisonous butterfly. He and her brother had judged Kachiko by her appearance. How wrong they had been.

How many times did the Scorpion masters teach that a man or woman's value should be determined by actions? Kachiko's actions, her intellect, had proved her worthy to be advisor to the emperor and the Mother of Scorpions.

It was no wonder Shoju kept his countenance hidden. Though time and again he had proved his worthiness to lead the Scorpions, still some part of him must have feared to show his face to those unworthy to judge him.

Kachiko felt unworthy as well. A mother's fears pulled at her heartstrings. The Master of Secrets betrayed his own

deepest thoughts to no one. Thus, she wondered about her
son—and Dairu's future.

▲ ▲ ▲ ▲ ▲ ▲ ▲ ▲

As they neared the castle, the Scorpion host was surprised
to see decorative banners unfurled from the keep's high tower.

Tetsuo leaned close to Shoju, who rode beside him. "Is
there a festival I've forgotten about?"

The Scorpion lord shook his head. Behind his mask, his
face grew grim.

Golden banners, decorated with the Bayushi Scorpion
mon, hung from the castle's balconies. The sight surprised
Shoju. The Master of Secrets didn't like surprises.

"What does it mean, do you think?" Tetsuo asked.

"We'll find out soon enough," Shoju replied. The fact that
he had no better answer disturbed him. His thoughts on the
return journey had been dark, terribly dark. He had shut himself off from others, even from Tetsuo and Kachiko. The business of the Scorpion was often bleak, but what waited before
them . . . . Shoju saw no reason to burden others with it until
he had sorted out his own thoughts.

The banners disturbed him. They flapped like the wings of
birds circling their prey; the rustling of the fabric grated on his
ears, like standards on a battlefield. In his mind's eye he saw
the battles before him clearly, just as he had in his dreams. The
dead would form mountains higher than Kyuden Bayushi's
tallest tower.

This banner-shrouded keep was not his home—not the
home he expected to return to. Who could have done such a
thing? His mouth grew tight and, absent-mindedly, he rubbed
his lame shoulder.

As they rode toward the castle, the gates of Kyuden Bayushi
opened. A great company of men rode out. All were samurai,
dressed in their finest kimonos. At their head rode a man on a

half-Unicorn steed, wearing a fine mask and a brilliantly decorated robe. He carried the mon of the Scorpion.

Though all the samurai wore Scorpion colors, Tetsuo's hand stole to the hilt of his katana. Had some other lord usurped the castle in their absence?

Tetsuo fought down a shiver. He joined his daimyo as Shoju rode to meet the column. If the Scorpion felt any fear, he did not betray it. Other samurai, including Rumiko, quickly fell in behind their master.

As they rode closer, Tetsuo recognized many of the men in the column. They were retainers from the castle, some he had known all his life. This fact did not make him feel any more at ease.

Shoju reined up in front of the leader of the column. Before the Scorpion lord could speak, the man dismounted. In his hand, the man held the banner of the Scorpion. All the other samurai climbed down from their horses as well. The leader of the group bowed low, but made sure not to touch the banner on the ground.

"Father," he said from behind his ornate mask, "we welcome you home. The sun and the moon have returned to Kyuden Bayushi this day."

Tetsuo breathed a sigh of relief. Amid all the finery, he had failed to recognize Dairu, the young Scorpion prince. The boy they had left behind now carried himself like a man. Could he have grown up so much in the month and a half that they had been gone?

Bayushi Shoju wondered the same thing but, behind his mask, his face betrayed nothing. The tattoo on his shoulder tingled; he ignored it.

"Dairu," he said sternly, "what is the meaning of all this?"

The boy looked up at the Scorpion lord, and Shoju could see the youth and worry in his eyes.

"I thought to welcome you home, Bayushi-sama," he said. "You, and mother. We are glad at your return. We are proud to be your people." He tried to make the words brave, but

Shoju—and even Tetsuo—could hear a slight tremble in the voice.

Behind his mask, the Scorpion's mouth drew into a broad smile. His thoughts had been so lost in conspiracies that the simplest explanation for the banners had completely escaped him.

"Did I do wrong, Father?" Dairu asked.

Shoju dismounted and stood beside the youth.

"No," he said. "You have done well, my son." He gestured to the gates of the castle and walked toward them with the boy. The host and the greeting column fell in behind them.

Within her ornate palanquin, Kachiko sighed. The fist within her breast uncurled its fingers.

As Shoju walked, he heard a song emanating from somewhere deep within the palace. The melody spoke of battle, and death, and victory. Shoju had heard it many times before, though it seemed closer now.

He ignored the siren call and concentrated on enjoying the moment with his son.

▲▲▲▲▲▲▲▲

The fire of sunset burned the sky red as storm clouds rolled in from the east. Soon the clouds smothered the last rays of Amaterasu, and dark night enshrouded the keep of the Scorpions.

Dairu had ordered a grand welcoming feast for his parents' return. The Mother of Scorpions herself could not have done better. The food was appealing and plentiful without being ostentatious. The dancers were graceful and the musicians pleasing to the ear. Of all the decorations, only the golden banners outside seemed boastful, and these Dairu had removed as soon as his mother and father entered the keep.

Though the bleak days ahead kept Shoju from enjoying the celebration fully, the Scorpion lord felt proud of the work his son had done. He reminded himself to move the date of the boy's gempuku forward. They would need all the men they had in the time to come.

If Kachiko felt the Scorpion lord's trepidation, she did not show it. The celebration their son had arranged drove the dark clouds from the Scorpion lady's mind. She doted on Dairu during the evening in a way that embarrassed the boy and brought a wry smile to Shoju's lips. Even his lovely wife, with her brilliant mind, could still be an indulgent mother.

The Scorpion had donned a festive mask before the feast, both to compliment his heir and to better hide his uneasy spirit. The sight of his wife and son enjoying themselves warmed the Shoju's heart. As the evening slipped by, he could almost forget what lay ahead.

Almost.

As he allowed sake to dull his senses, the song Shoju had heard outside the castle welled up in his brain once more. The melody sounded more seductive than it ever had before. It twined itself around the Scorpion's soul.

He could almost taste its power—power waiting beneath the red roofs of Kyuden Bayushi. Waiting for him to seize it, to take it up. It lay so very close at hand. Shoju would answer the song's call soon enough. Within the song lay his destiny.

Across the room, Yogo Junzo, who had returned to the castle ahead of the rest, raised his cup in a silent toast to the Scorpion lord.

Shoju nodded and raised his cup in return.

▲ ▲ ▲ ▲ ▲ ▲ ▲ ▲

Deep in the black of night, the revelry exhausted itself. Most of the Scorpion retainers had crept to their chambers by the time Shoju dismissed the entertainers.

Dairu, his head resting on his mother's breast, looked up

sleepily at his father. "Is it dawn already?" he asked. "I ordered them to play until dawn."

"Dawn comes early after a long trip," Shoju said. "Even the Lord of the Scorpions needs sleep—as do you, my son."

Dairu smiled. "Have I done well, my father?"

Shoju nodded.

"Of course you have," Kachiko said, running her fingers through her son's hair. "No man could have done better."

"Am I to be a man, then?" Dairu asked, dreams already clouding his vision.

Shoju laid a hand on his shoulder. "Soon. Very soon," he said, and thought, *sooner than I had hoped.*

The daimyo offered his hand to his son—his *right* hand— and helped the boy to his feet. Dairu took the hand, not suspecting the significance. Nor did any of the other half-awake samurai remaining in the room suspect either.

Only Kachiko knew what the gesture truly meant. Bayushi Shoju rarely offered his hand to anyone, man or woman. When he did, it was always the left hand he offered—the hand attached to his good arm. Because of the weakness of Shoju's right arm, the Scorpion daimyo didn't offer that hand to anyone except those he completely trusted. He'd offered it to her and embraced her with it many times. He'd offered it to Tetsuo upon occasion. If court functions required it, he might also offer that hand to the emperor. However, since left-handedness was a tradition among Scorpions, it was not often that such an occasion arose. Of all Rokugan's people, those were the only three Kachiko had seen Bayushi Shoju offer his right hand. Now there was a fourth—his son.

Kachiko cursed herself for ever having doubted her husband's intentions toward the boy. She had once wondered if Shoju merely kept the child as a weapon against Dairu's blood father. No longer.

The best lie is often the truth, Shoju said frequently. It was a maxim he and Kachiko lived by. But sometimes, as Shinsei had taught, things are merely what they seem to be.

Shoju's love for their son had been genuine all these years, and yet, Kachiko had seen sinister motives behind his actions. She had done him a grave wrong.

Warm love for her husband welled up in her breast. She was proud of him, of the burden he had borne for her all these years—almost since the day of their marriage. She wished, more fervently than she ever had before, that she had been able to bear him another child.

The Fortunes had not been so kind to the couple. Whether the fault lay with him or her, she could not say. Both times she had gotten pregnant after Dairu, she had not been able to carry the baby to term. That fact wounded Shoju as deeply as it wounded her. Being the chief of Scorpions, he hid it well.

There was no hiding his feelings for his son this night—not from her.

"To bed now, Son," the Scorpion said to his offspring. "We have much work ahead of us."

Dairu nodded sleepily. "Hai, Father." He mounted the staircase at the end of the room and went upstairs toward his summer quarters.

Kachiko rose from her cushions and stood next to her husband. "To bed?" she asked, slipping her hand into his.

"Hai," he said, nodding wearily.

Together, they ascended the great staircase. When they reached the top, Shoju turned aside from the corridor leading to their usual chambers. She looked at him questioningly.

He said nothing, but slipped his right hand in her left and led her down the hall. Diverting through several concealed panels, they arrived in the Nightingale Room. It was a small, plain, L-shaped chamber sequestered within the fortress among the topmost floors. A clever arrangement of mirrors usually flooded the room with light from a window in another part of the castle. Tonight, the room was dark, save for the occasional flash of lightning from the storm.

Again, she looked at him, questioning.

"The room's music will make me sleep better," he said, his voice like distant thunder.

Kachiko smiled and nodded. He stepped into the room. The floorboards chirped sweetly, as if nightingales lived in the wood. The music it made was beautiful, but it masked a more practical purpose: no enemy could come into the room without making the floor sing.

The Mistress of Scorpions crossed the room with her lord. She lit a single beeswax candle on a small table near the thick quilt that served as the room's bed. The futon was hidden from the room's fusuma entrance by the bend in the room. This made it impossible to see—or attack—someone in the far end of the room while standing in the entrance.

Despite what Shoju said about music, the *lack* of noise in the room during the night would make her husband sleep better. He lay down on the bed and reclined himself on one elbow. She lay down beside him and whispered in his ear.

"I have never loved you more than I do at this moment," she said, her voice like honey. He reached up and removed the delicate lace mask from her face. Gently, she removed his mask as well. They kissed.

When they separated, she turned and blew out the candle.

▲▲▲▲▲▲▲▲

After the fury of the storm subsided, they lay together in the darkness and listened to the distant thunder. In the back of his mind, Shoju heard faint music as well. It was not the floor of the Nightingale Room that sang, but a different, disturbing music.

He looked at his wife, her pale head resting on his chest, and caressed her dark hair.

"I love you," he said.

She looked up at him, knowing that what he said was not what he intended to say. Still, she drank in the words and savored them.

"As I, you," she replied.

"I need you now more than ever," he told her.

She nodded and ran her hand across his chest. "You know I am with you," she said. "Always."

"The game we must play is more dangerous than any a Scorpion has ever played before."

"And the stakes far higher," she agreed. "What must I do?"

"I have thought things over since I spoke with the Great Dragon," he said. "I can see many paths—though not all. You know the information that our spies brought us while we traveled, but you do not know my mind on these matters."

"Only because you have not shared your thoughts with me," she said, "but I know you only do what you must, and I know the emperor must die."

"Hai," Shoju said softly.

In the distance, thunder echoed off the Spine of the World Mountains.

Kachiko's hand reached up and stroked his face. "Shall I kill him for you? A simple poison would suffice. I could slip it into his food. It would not matter if I was caught."

"You would do that for me?"

She nodded. "Of course."

He stroked her hair. "I will not sacrifice you to my ambition."

They embraced each other for a long moment.

Shoju let out a long breath. "The heir must die as well," he said. "The scroll said the last Hantei would loose Fu Leng on Rokugan. The boy cannot be spared."

"Then I shall kill him as well. For you."

Shoju shook his head. "Again, I say no. If I am to pay in blood, the blood will be my own."

"Someone must lead the empire after the Hantei are gone," she said. "Who better than you?"

"Who better?" he repeated quietly. In Bayushi Shoju's mind, the song of steel grew stronger.

"Who better to lead the world through the dark times ahead? Who is stronger than you? Who more clever? Who more loyal?" Her breathing grew shallow with excitement, and her nostrils flared slightly. Shoju fancied he could see the green flecks sparkling in her black eyes. She leaned up and whispered in his ear, "No one. Together, we are invincible. No one can stand in your way."

"One might," Shoju said.

Kachiko arched her delicate eyebrows. "Who?"

"The Lion, Akodo Toturi," he replied.

"He is merely a cub," she said, biting his left earlobe.

" 'Even a lion cub may someday lead the pride,' Shinsei said."

"But a cub may also be devoured by his own kind," Kachiko replied. "Or brought to ruin by his own follies."

He looked at her, and she smiled. "Have you found such follies in Toturi?" he asked.

"You may not think it," she said playfully, "but my ears are very large. There is little they do not hear."

"Then you have done as I asked? Discovered Toturi's weakness?"

"So great as a general," she said. "So foolish as a man."

"And you can use this to destroy him?"

"You wound me, my lord," Kachiko said with a sly smile. "Of course I can—if you will it."

Shoju nodded, "I do. See to it personally."

"I would trust no other."

"My plans will meet their culmination at the Festival of Fire. It will take us that long to make the preparations." Their eyes reflected the deep darkness of each other. "Your timing must mirror mine," he said.

"Does it ever not, my love?"

"You will leave in the morning?"

"Hai, my lord. But . . ."

"But what?"

She smiled and embraced him. "But first," she said, "I wish to come back to bed."

▲▲▲▲▲▲▲▲

Bayushi Shoju awoke the next morning to find his wife already gone. She had somehow left the chamber silently, without causing the boards to sing. Shoju smiled. Kachiko was the only person he knew who could do this. If she were not, he would never use the room. Someday, he would have to ask her how she did it. For now, he merely felt content that all his wife's considerable skills would soon be brought to bear against Akodo Toturi.

The Scorpion daimyo retired to his usual chambers to bathe and change clothes. His withered arm was amazingly alive this morning; he couldn't remember the last time he'd felt so little pain. He almost decided not to take his potions but recalled the incident with the ogre less than a day's ride from the castle gates.

I must ever be on my guard, he reminded himself, even here.

Shoju lifted the small, blue bottle from the table near his bed and drank. The liquid felt like fire in his mouth, and the tattoo on his right arm burned. He dressed quickly, in somber colors and a grim mask. Anyone seeing him in such a face would know better than to disturb the daimyo's thoughts. Shoju had much to do today.

He went to the gardens for breakfast, but discovered that Kachiko had already eaten. She had left a note for him. It said that shortly before dawn she had departed the castle on her errand. With her went three of her handmaidens and two guards—all of whom Shoju knew to be masters of disguise. In all likelihood, no one would ever guess the Mother of Scorpions was abroad in Rokugan.

If someone did discover her, Kachiko would be well protected. In the small retinue, the guards were the least formidable—mere samurai. The handmaidens, though . . . One was a powerful shugenja. The other two were assassins, ninja-ko. The Scorpion lady had defenses of her own, too.

The Scorpion lord smiled. He knew Kachiko would accomplish the task he had set for her. As he ate, Shoju drew up a list of people he would need to see immediately, among them his shugenja, Shosuro Bantaro and Yogo Junzo, and his half-brother, Bayushi Aramoro.

Bantaro had stayed behind at his own castle when the rest of the host returned to Kyuden Bayushi, but Shoju told him to follow as soon as he was able. On horseback and without a retinue to slow him down, Bantaro would arrive at the Scorpion fortress within the week—possibly in the next day or so if he used magic to quicken his journey.

Junzo was already within the castle walls, of course, though his studies into the artifacts uncovered beneath the castle two years ago kept him sequestered, for the most part, from the day-to-day goings on.

Aramoro could be found in the keep as well. He had been recalled from his usual nefarious missions to watch over Dairu while his parents journeyed to the lands of the Dragon. Shoju had seen Aramoro only briefly at the feast last night, and he wanted to ask where his brother had been when Dairu festooned the castle with banners.

Behind his somber mask, Shoju smiled at the thought. How Aramoro would squirm.

The pleasure of needling his half-brother quickly vanished as grim plans overtook the morning. Tetsuo arrived as Shoju worked on his list; the Scorpion lord had sent for him soon after dressing.

"The essence of conspiracy," Shoju said as Tetsuo bowed and sat next to him, "is to keep as many people in the dark for as long as possible."

"Does this include our own people, lord?" Tetsuo asked.

"To some extent," the Scorpion replied. "Even our people need to know only enough to do their assigned tasks. To tell them more would be an unnecessary burden—it would distract them from their mission."

He dipped his brush into the ink and wrote a few more

names on the scroll. "The Phoenix and the Dragon invite debate, encourage free thought. That is why they are ineffective, impotent," he said. "Our people, on the other hand, know the justice of our cause. They know that ours is a lonely battle, and that we, as Scorpions, must fight it alone—though all the clans of Rokugan are set against us. They know I would never lead them astray. That is why we will be able to save the empire."

"The weakness and excess of the other clans will be our best weapon," said Tetsuo.

Shoju nodded, dipped his brush, and jotted down another name. "Just so," he said, "as it has been for a thousand years. Our key is control: control of the truth, control of our people, control of ourselves."

As Shoju laid the brush down, Bayushi Yojiro arrived in the garden and bowed.

"You sent for me, Master?" he asked.

Shoju rolled up the scroll and handed it to him. "I need to meet with these people. Speak to those within the castle personally. We'll hold council with them tonight. Send messages to those too far away to come. Tell them they will receive instructions from me shortly. These instructions are to be followed to the last detail."

"Of course, great lord," Yojiro said, bowing again. "Where shall the meeting tonight take place?"

"In the eastern tower, the topmost council room, just after sunset."

"It shall be done," Yojiro said. He bowed once more and left.

"He's a good man," Tetsuo said when Yojiro was out of earshot.

Shoju snorted. "Almost too good to be true. I suppose we have his association with my wife to thank for that."

The comment startled Tetsuo a bit. His face flushed slightly, and his slight mask couldn't hide the redness.

Seeing it, Shoju laughed. "Will you blush like a maiden every time I mention the good work Kachiko does for me?"

"N-no, lord," Tetsuo said, feeling his embarrassment rise.

"I promise you, my young cousin—there is nothing my wife does that I do not know about and approve of. You should know that by now."

"I do, my lord."

"And yet, you still hear rumors. . . ." Shoju said it as more a question than a statement.

"I try not to listen, great lord."

Shoju pointed at his lieutenant. "You *should* listen," he said. "Listening is the Scorpions' stock in trade." He leaned back on his low stool. "However, you should not believe even half of everything you hear. I know I don't." This last remark, said in almost a jolly tone, broke the tension.

Tetsuo smiled despite himself. "I'll keep that in mind, great lord."

"See that you do. Funny, Yojiro believed he was to watch Kachiko to protect *me*. In fact, I assigned him the duty so he could learn from *her*."

"Lord?"

Shoju leaned forward and said in a low voice. "Life does not always teach us the lessons we expect, Tetsuo. Nor are the most effective lessons learned in the way we expect them."

Tetsuo nodded.

The Scorpion daimyo suddenly cocked his head. "Do you hear that?" he asked.

Tetsuo listened as well, but heard nothing. "Hear what?"

"Distant music," Shoju said, "as if . . ." He realized what he was hearing. Behind his mask, the Scorpion lord's face grew grim once more. He stood.

"Come," he said, motioning to Tetsuo. "We have work to do."

▲▲▲▲▲▲▲▲

Again, Shoju led his young cousin through the hidden passageways honeycombing Kyuden Bayushi. "Over your nerves, yet?" he asked.

"Yes, great lord."

"Ready to face skeletons and ghosts and spiders once more?"

Tetsuo nodded grimly. "Whole fortresses of them, if need be."

Shoju stopped at an intersection and paused, as if choosing the correct path. "The fortresses will come later. Nor do I expect any opposition in our current task."

"No ghouls?" Tetsuo asked, letting his hand slip from the hilt of his katana. He had noticed that the Scorpion lord had set aside his weapons before their journey, but he had not asked why; it was not his place to do so. "No spiders?"

The Scorpion lord shook his head and started down one of the corridors. "No, the only dangers we face now are the traps our ancestors set against intruders. These traps I know how to defeat."

Tetsuo nodded again and asked, "Then why have I come with you, my lord?"

"Tetsuo, I know more secrets than any man alive. More than any man could tell in one lifetime. It is these secrets that give me my power, not the strength of my sword arm."

"I know this, great lord."

"Some secrets have been passed down to me through the ages from my father, and his father before him. In time, if I am able, I will pass those secrets to my son."

"After his gempuku?"

"Yes," Shoju said. He stopped and manipulated a flagstone before continuing. "I will move the date up," he said. "Dairu will have his initiation into manhood before we go to Otosan Uchi, before the Fire Festival."

"Then you'll pass your knowledge to your son."

"Some of it, yes, but I will not have time to teach him all, I fear."

Again, the Scorpion daimyo managed to startle his cousin. "Your life will be long, great lord. You shall have plenty of time."

Shoju glanced over his shoulder at his cousin. "Perhaps," he said. "If fortune or circumstance prevent me from doing so, teach my son the things I have taught you."

"But, great lord, your brother, Aramoro, is Dairu's guardian."

"Aramoro protects my son's body; I want you to protect his mind. My brother and I are not as . . . close as we might be. We do not always see eye-to-eye. However, you and I do. There are things about this castle that even my brother doesn't know. Things such as the catacombs where we found the scroll, and the hidden room where I will take you presently."

Shoju stopped and cocked his head. "Listen!" he said. "Do you hear it now?"

Tetsuo listened. A strange faint humming drifted to his ears. It sounded as though it came from very far away. The tune was lilting yet powerful, plain yet seductive. "I . . . I can hear it," Tetsuo said.

He looked down the long, stone hallway. They had descended deep below the castle once more. This time, however, with fear pushed out of his mind, Tetsuo had managed to keep his bearings. He thought he could find this hidden corridor again if necessary. He had watched carefully as his master deactivated the traps along the way. Tetsuo felt certain he could pass these secrets along to the young lord, if need be.

"What is that music?" Tetsuo asked. "It tugs at my very soul."

"I've heard it for months," said Shoju, "for years. In quiet moments, as sleep steals over me, it sings softly in my ears. Only two things dull its voice."

"What things, my lord?"

"The love of my wife, and the nearness of my ancestral sword, *Itsuwari*."

"Is that why you are not wearing the sword?" Tetsuo asked.

Shoju nodded. "Hai. For the first time in my life, I've needed to hear the call. Come."

They walked down the corridor only a few dozen steps farther and stopped. Shoju turned to the right-hand wall and counted the stones. When he found the correct one, he placed his hand against it. The stone glowed red around his fingers, but if it burned him, the Scorpion lord did not cry out.

As Tetsuo marveled at this magic, a portion of the wall to Shoju's left slid away. When the wall had completely retracted, the Scorpion daimyo removed his hand. "To place your hand on the wrong stone in this wall would mean your doom," he said to Tetsuo. "Pray you never have to do what I have just done."

Tetsuo nodded, though he was having trouble concentrating. When the wall opened, the music in his mind grew stronger. It compelled him forward, into the room beyond the portal.

"Stop!" commanded Shoju, barring his lieutenant's way by stretching out his left arm. "There is one final trap."

He drew two silver coins out of his kimono. "Payment for passage," he said, flipping the *bu* onto the stone floor of the room, just beyond the threshold. "One for each of us. Without the coins, that floor is no more substantial than a dream, and the pit it covers is bottomless."

Tetsuo swallowed and nodded. The alluring song was still strong in his mind, but good sense had taken over once more. He looked into the room.

Beyond the entrance lay a plain, square room about ten strides across. It was flagged with the same regularly-shaped gray stones as the corridor had been. The chamber was lit, though Tetsuo could not tell how. The light seemed to come from everywhere and nowhere. It was a soft, cool light.

At the far end of the room lay a stone platform, about waist high. The air over the dais shimmered as if with the summer heat. Otherwise, the room stood empty.

"What is it?" Tetsuo asked, his eyes trained on the vague disturbance in the air. It was spectral and fleeting, dancing like colorless fire. The song in Tetsuo's head seemed to come from it.

"It is a Kenchi, a bloodsword. It is *Yashin*," Shoju said reverently.

"A bloodsword?" said Tetsuo. The room had grown cold. The young lieutenant's hands and face went white. "But, my lord, why?"

"I will not stain the sword of my family with the blood of the emperor and his heir. But this," he said gesturing into the room, "this was forged for just such a purpose."

Tetsuo looked at his lord. As always, the Scorpion lord's mask hid his true feelings and intentions.

"Its name means 'ambition,'" Shoju continued, stepping carefully into the room. "It is for the good of the empire that I claim it now."

He walked forward, and Tetsuo followed after.

"For years," Shoju said, "the sword has rested here, calling to our forefathers—calling to me. Our ancestors were wise; they hid this weapon deep within the world for a reason. Its song is seductive . . . and deadly."

"I can't see it," Tetsuo said. "It's less substantial than a shadow."

"Ambition is ever thus. It can never be seen when viewed directly, but always hides itself." Shoju had walked to within a few steps of the dais. He turned and glanced over his right shoulder at his young cousin, and then turned halfway back, toward the sword. Behind the daimyo's mask, Tetsuo could see the Scorpion lord looking at the "sword" out of the corner of his eye.

"But a man who is bold," Shoju said, "may grasp Ambition and wield it to his own ends."

He reached out sideways with his left arm and seized the empty air. Lightning flashed. Bolts of power danced about the room. In their center, clutched in Bayushi Shoju's hand, Tetsuo could see Yashin, the bloodsword.

It was a magnificent, fascinating katana—nearly four feet of highly polished steel with an ebony hilt. It looked as though it had been newly forged. A sinuous wave ran down the length of the blade, and as the sword moved, the wave seemed to change, like swells on the ocean. Arcane symbols decorated the hilt and hand guard, though the lightning and Shoju's hand kept Tetsuo from making out what the characters might be. The blade of the weapon had a vaguely crimson tint—like sunset over the deep sea.

For a moment, the only sound to be heard in the room was the crackling of Ambition's magical energy.

Finally Shoju spoke through gritted teeth. "However," he said, almost grunting the words, "a man who is wise will wield power not for his own gain, but to greater purpose." The bloodsword loomed before him and quivered, as if fighting the Scorpion for control.

Slowly, inexorably, the Scorpion daimyo raised the blade over his head. As he did, he felt the righteousness of his cause. His heart swelled with renewed purpose. He knew that all he hoped for would come to pass. One day soon, Bayushi Shoju would sit on the Emerald Throne. Fu Leng would be defeated.

"I take this sword to save the empire," he said. "I will pay whatever price must be paid. Let no one stand in my way!"

12 WORDS BETWEEN WOMAN AND GIRL

Bayushi Kachiko rubbed her feet and looked at the road ahead. As a lady of high standing, she had grown unaccustomed to walking or riding. This past week she had done a considerable amount of each.

Her small band had moved quickly through Scorpion lands, taking full advantage of their training and magics. The mountains proved little more difficult. The isolation of the area provided a distinct advantage. They traveled openly and saw few people, except as they neared the border at Beiden Pass.

After that, they became stealthier. The roads to Otosan Uchi were well traveled, which slowed them down considerably. The short stretch through Lion lands caused no troubles, aside from the usual border checks. Secure in their strength, the Lions did not feel threatened by their neighbors.

This brought a smile to Kachiko's face. Though traveling unmasked for the first time in ages, she had been forced to disguise her beauty. If the Lions only knew who it was they passed so quickly through their borders . . . if they only knew what she and her lord had in store for them . . . but the Lion slept. The greatest threat to their clan in generations passed unnoticed beneath their noses.

The Crane were more watchful. Bands of samurai patrolled the highways, always on guard against "suspicious types." Most outsiders and *all* Scorpions were included in that broad category. Fortunately, Kachiko's disguise proved more than a match for haughty Crane eyes.

It galled her to have to bow and scrape before people who were so far beneath her. She made a note of the name of each person who treated her badly; later, when she resumed her station, she would make them pay.

On their third day under the "protection" of the Crane, the Scorpion lady's band was accosted by bandits. The thieves came upon them in the dark as they were making camp but did not catch the Scorpions unaware.

Before the leader of the bandits realized what was happening, Yogo Miyuki, Kachiko's shugenja, had turned the man's bones to dust. The samurai and ninja-ko made quick work of the other thirteen—though they left one alive for interrogation.

None of Kachiko's party received any wounds.

After determining that the bandits knew nothing of the party's true identity or mission, Kachiko sent the prisoner to his ancestors. Miyuki used one of her awful secrets to dispose of the bodies.

The party skirted well around the Imperial City of Otosan Uchi. Their destination, Mura Kita Chusen, lay to the capital's north and east. The detour caused a slight delay, but their disguises ran a greater chance of being uncovered in the capital itself. Avoiding the capital altogether, Kachiko led her party circuitously to their destination.

Mura Kita Chusen was a pleasant, beautiful town. One of the villages that encircled Otosan Uchi, it was nearly as well kept as the capital. Long rows of docks lined the town's harbor and provided shelter for fishing boats—the village's main source of income. There were other industries on Mura Kita Chusen as well, most serving the needs of the Hantei capital.

The northern outskirts of the town stretched well beyond the city walls, even to the edge of the Imperial Forest, Fudaraku no Mori, "The Forest of Paradise." Kachiko knew from her spies that the Lion Akodo Toturi cherished those woods. He often hunted in them to escape the cramped existence of life at court.

She knew another reason he liked the town. Mura Kita Chusen held the house where Toturi's geisha worked, and thus it held the keys to the Lion's heart. Kachiko planned to hold those keys in her own delicate hands very soon.

Two of her people scouted ahead of the party and entered the village before her. They secured suitable lodging for their mistress, well away from the usual Scorpion safe houses. The accommodations were not as lavish as her station dictated, but were far better than conditions on the road.

Upon arriving at her rented villa, the Mother of Scorpions sent her ninja-ko to pave the way for their mission. Kachiko bathed and prepared herself for the path ahead.

Months ago when her spies had first learned of Toturi's weakness for the geisha Hatsuko, Kachiko had immediately set on a course of action. She knew such indiscretion could eventually be turned to the Scorpions' advantage, though she had not guessed how soon.

Kachiko's initial step was to gain control of the geisha house from its previous owners. Kitsune Junko, mistress of the house, was fronting for a local merchant. He put up little resistance to the Scorpions' offer, and thus saved his own life. Kachiko had been glad. Though she didn't mind necessary killing, she disliked the publicity caused by assassinations.

Fortunately, a well-placed word and a small amount of

gold was all the silk broker required to relinquish control of Junko's geisha house. The well-placed word had been about a certain youthful indiscretion in the banker's past. The gold had merely been a formality to hurry things along. Victims squawked less if they believed they were paid off, rather than merely blackmailed.

The completion of the takeover had been so easy Kachiko barely considered it a victory. After the buyout, operation of the geisha house had been turned over to Yogo Asami, who had been sent to Mura Kita Chusen specifically for that purpose by the far-sighted Scorpion lady.

Asami shared a unique history with her mistress. When they were both fourteen, Bayushi Kachiko had chanced to see Asami at a geisha house. Noticing the strong resemblance between the two of them, the future Mother of Scorpions immediately purchased the girl's contract.

Kachiko trained Asami in the ways of the Scorpion, and soon the girl was able to impersonate her mistress quite effectively. This allowed Kachiko a measure of freedom she had not possessed previously. No one at her father's court suspected that the young woman walking the gardens at night was not, in fact, Kachiko. Thus, Kachiko had been freed to pursue her own passions.

She treated Asami well. The former geisha never had cause to inform on her mistress. In fact, Asami quite enjoyed the role and the measure of power it brought her. The two young women continued the deception for a number of years, almost until Kachiko's marriage to Shoju—though it had become more difficult as their bodies matured along somewhat different lines.

While the Scorpion lady had since eclipsed the beauty of her former pupil, the two still shared a close working relationship and a more than passing resemblance. Kachiko intended to use that resemblance to her advantage once more, but this time, in reverse.

Asami had done a fine job manipulating the affairs of

Junko's geisha house so far. Things now required a more deli-cate—and persuasive—touch. One of Kachiko's ninja-ko had been sent to fetch Asami.

The other had been sent on a sabotage mission—to keep a love-struck Lion busy.

Asami arrived promptly at Kachiko's dwelling and was ushered into her mistress's inner chambers.

"My lady," Asami said, bowing low. "How may I serve you?"

Kachiko smiled; Asami was ever quick to come to the point.

"Our geisha house—the one run by the Kitsune woman," Kachiko said, "how does it fare?"

"It is a boring enterprise, hardly worthy of the Scorpion," Asami replied, revealing just a bit of her ambitious nature. "I could change that, if you desire, Mistress."

"Until now, I have not seen fit to reveal our interest in the house to you, Asami."

"I suspect it has something to do with the young lion who prowls the grounds like a cat in heat," Asami said.

Kachiko chuckled. "I see you have lost none of your per-ceptive abilities."

"I haven't. You trained me well. But it doesn't take a Scor-pion to see through Akodo Toturi's disguise. Even the woman who runs the house knows that he's more than he seems—though she doesn't realize who he is."

Kachiko frowned. "Hmm. Perhaps she should be removed."

"If you think so, Mistress."

"I'll judge for myself when I see her."

"When *you* see her, Mistress?"

"Yes, I intend to take your place for a while."

Asami smiled. "Have we come full circle, then?" she asked.

"Hardly. I've merely decided to take a personal interest in the house at this point."

"Bearding lions can be dangerous," Asami said.

Kachiko frowned; sometimes her former pupil assumed too much. The Scorpion mistress leaned closer to Asami. "I've played many dangerous games in my life, but this is the most dangerous of all—and the most critical. I know that Shoju and I can count on your unwavering support."

Asami bowed again. "As always, Mistress."

Kachiko leaned back. "Now, then," she said, straightening the folds of her elegant silk robe, "tell me everything you've learned. Start with what false name and background you have been using as the house's owner. Then I want you to send a note to this Junko. Tell her I, that is *you*, want to see her immediately. I'll have one of my samurai deliver the note as you fill me in on the rest."

▲▲▲▲▲▲▲▲

Four hours later, Junko and her assistant Yoko arrived at Bayushi Kachiko's temporary residence. Using a seeing spell, Miyuki told her mistress the two women appeared nervous. This made the Scorpion lady glad.

Asami had told Kachiko she never allowed Junko to visit her lodgings. How could she? The Scorpions valued thrift, and Asami had found it unnecessary to take luxurious accommodations to keep up her deception. The Kitsune geisha mistress could be just as easily deceived by a nice kimono and the occasional visit to her house of business. Kachiko appreciated Asami's frugality and made a mental note to give Asami some small reward at a later time.

It had taken less than an hour for Kachiko to carefully transform herself into the image of her former slave. Clothes and makeup did most of the job. The rest Kachiko accomplished by mimicking the manners of the girl she'd grown up beside. When she had finished, only Bayushi Shoju himself could have told the two apart.

As Kachiko had worked on her appearance, Asami had continued her briefing.

Kachiko's former double had done her job well. She knew

details about the house, its operations, and its clients that Kachiko could not have learned from any conventional source. She also appreciated the role Asami had chosen: Aki, the widow of a well-to-do Crane samurai. Too respectable to work, Aki had spent her inheritance on several small businesses, which provided her enough income to live comfortably. Aki was a respectable woman, impressive in her quiet strength, and as persuasive as a Scorpion. It was a role Kachiko fit into with ease.

As she donned an appropriate wig, Kachiko had thought perhaps she and Asami had not grown up so differently after all.

Kachiko's samurai ushered Junko and Yoko into the inner part of Kachiko's townhouse. As they did, Asami and Miyuki took up positions behind a concealing screen near their mistress. Kachiko, now Aki, seated herself in a small depression in the center of the house's dining room. A low, ornate table sat in the depression before her. There was just enough room on the other side of the table for her guests to sit. Kachiko-Aki nodded at the women as they entered the room, quickly sizing them up.

Time had not been kind to Junko. The trials of the geisha business had aged her beyond her years. Though she'd carefully made up her face, she could not hide the wrinkles. Strands of gray hair peeked out from beneath Junko's black wig.

Yoko was younger, little more than a girl. She wore her own hair tied up in a bun. Her face was pretty, but she smiled too frequently, betraying a lack of intelligence. The girl carefully stayed in her mistress's shadow. Yoko was rumored to be Junko's niece. The resemblance between the two made her more likely an illegitimate daughter. Kachiko made a mental note to have Asami check on it.

Junko and Yoko bowed deeply.

"Mistress, we are honored you allow us to visit you in your home," Junko said, pulling nervously at the hem of her kimono. It was a fine garment, but had not been kept in the best repair.

"I am pleased to have you in my humble abode," Kachiko said graciously. She nodded to her ninja-ko, who played the role of a servant. The ninja woman left the room and returned a moment later with a tray bearing a jar of sake and three cups. She set the drinks on the low table in front of her mistress.

"I hope you don't mind," Kachiko said, indicating the alcohol, "but it helps calm my nerves in this heat." To emphasize, she picked up a nearby fan and waved it at herself.

"Not at all, Mistress," said Junko. She and Yoko practically fell over themselves reaching for the bottle. Junko seized it and poured a cup first for Kachiko, then a smaller portion for Yoko, and then one for herself.

Kachiko picked up the cup and raised it to her lips. The other women did the same, carefully watching to make sure they didn't drink longer than Kachiko did. Inwardly, Kachiko chuckled. She would have no trouble bending these toadies to her will.

"It has come to my attention," Kachiko said, "that our house is doing very respectable business."

"Thank you, Mistress," both women chimed. They bowed.

"However," Kachiko said, putting down her cup, "I believe we could do—we *can* do better."

Junko and Yoko looked at each other, crestfallen. Kachiko reached to refill her cup. Yoko got the bottle first and poured for her.

"Our girls," Kachiko continued. "Are they everything they could be? Beautiful? Talented in conversation and music? Clean?"

"Y-yes, Mistress," Junko said, and both women bowed again.

Kachiko waved her fan. "Then the trouble must lie elsewhere. I know several houses of the same size that are making far more money than we are. Is the quality of our food and drink good?"

Junko and Yoko nodded like birds bobbing their heads. "Yes, Mistress."

"Our prices, they are not too low nor too high?"

"Neither, Mistress," said Junko.

"We charge what the market will bear," Yoko added.

Kachiko nodded knowingly. "I see. I see. Perhaps we are not serving our customers as well as we could."

"Our service is impeccable!" Junko said, shocked at the suggestion.

"No, no, no," Kachiko said sternly, flicking her fan at them. "You misunderstand. I do not mean our service is lacking. What I mean is perhaps there are things our customers want that we are not giving them."

"In what way, Mistress?" Junko asked. She seemed unnerved by the whole conversation, which was exactly what Kachiko wanted.

Kachiko rose and walked about the room, waving her fan like a fluttering bird.

"In the Willow World, the fantasies of men are supposed to come true. Perhaps our clients have special dreams and desires that we could fulfill."

"Oh," said Junko, appearing much relieved. "What kind of things do you mean, Aki-sama?"

Kachiko appeared impatient. "You should know that far better than I, Junko. You and Yoko are there every day. Surely we have regular customers. We must. I have seen them when I check on the house."

"Of course, Mistress," Yoko said.

"Many regular customers," Junko added.

"Well, tell me about them," Kachiko said, finally turning the conversation where she wanted it to go. "Who is our best customer?"

"That would be Inoshiro Toshiro," Yoko said.

Kachiko waved her fan impatiently and stopped walking. "The guardsman? I know all about him," she said. "To serve his desires, we would have to turn the whole house into a brothel." She humphed theatrically.

Yoko and Junko laughed nervously until Kachiko smiled. Then their laughter grew more genuine.

"And we would have to give sake away for free," Yoko added.

Junko appeared about to scold her young charge, but when Kachiko smiled at the quip, Junko stopped short. "We could never do that," Kachiko said. "We couldn't do either of those things. Surely we have more *normal* customers. People we could please without debasing ourselves. People who would pay more for special services, services not provided by brothels."

"Perhaps," Junko said, rubbing her chin.

Yoko chimed in. "There's the wandering soldier," she said.

"Ah!" said Kachiko. "I think I've seen him. He's one of Chuko's customers. The one who always wears the blue armor."

"No, that's not who I mean," said Yoko, slightly embarrassed at having to correct her mistress. "I mean the one who rides the tall horse, and wears simple robes. I'd think him a monk if I didn't know better."

"What makes you think he's a soldier?" Kachiko asked.

"Hatsuko told me so," the young woman said.

"I have seen his dai-sho," Junko added. "The swords are very fine—at least to judge from their scabbards."

"And sometimes he brings a bow," said Yoko, excited that she could add so much to the conversation. "He brings us game, upon occasion. I think he hunts in the Imperial Wood."

"Is the Imperial Wood not forbidden?" Kachiko asked.

"Not to samurai of sufficient rank," Junko said.

Kachiko sat back down and smiled, allowing the robes to fall pleasingly around her form. "Does this high-ranking samurai have a name?"

"He has never told us," Yoko said.

"Though once—a long time ago—he came in with Ikoma Bentai," Junko added. "So I think he must be a Lion."

"Well, it doesn't matter," Kachiko said, waving her fan. "So long as we keep him happy. Good customers bring repeat business and other quality customers as well. Who did you say served him?"

"Hatsuko," said Yoko.

"One of our best girls," Junko added.

"Perhaps I should talk with her," Kachiko said thoughtfully. "First, tell me—is there anything this samurai desires that we have not supplied? Does he have any dreams that the Willow World could fulfill?"

"He likes the gardens," said Junko.

"Sometimes we even let him take Hatsuko for a walk," Yoko said. She covered her mouth with her hands, realizing she may have made a mistake.

Kachiko raised one eyebrow. "That's most unusual, is it not?" she asked.

Junko pulled nervously at the hem of her kimono. "It is," the older woman said, "but he seems a trustworthy sort."

"And he pays well for the girl's time," said Yoko.

Kachiko nodded. "Then perhaps that is just the kind of special service we should give our gentlemen. Perhaps there is even more we could do in that direction. Where does this samurai like to go on his walks?"

"The woods, I think," Junko said. "The edge of the Imperial Forest is not far from the rear of our house, as you know."

"Yes," Kachiko replied. "The beauty of the forest is one of the reasons I bought the house in the first place." It was a lie, but it brought a smile to the faces of the other women. They bowed. "The beauty of nature compliments the beauty of our girls," Kachiko continued. Yoko and Junko bowed again. "So, the samurai likes the woods?"

"Hatsuko told me once that he longs for a cabin in the mountains," Yoko said, pleased to add a tidbit to the conversation once again.

"Does he?" Kachiko said. She was careful not to show any emotion, but the revelation made her heart flutter. This fact could play into her scheme very well. She waved her fan and laughed. "Too bad we couldn't afford anything like that."

The other women laughed as well.

"Perhaps there are other things we could do for him—and our other customers too. The walks in the woods seem harmless enough, if the man is of good standing." Kachiko straightened her robes. "We should do more things like that," she concluded.

Junko and Yoko bowed. "As you wish, Mistress," they said in unison.

Kachiko folded her fan with a swift motion. "I have an assignment for you, then," she said. "You will talk to our other girls and find out what special services we might provide—services unusual for a geisha house, but ones that will not endanger our girls nor damage our reputation."

"Hai, Mistress," the women said in unison.

Kachiko stood, indicating by her manner that the audience was over. Junko and Yoko stood as well.

"I shall interview this Hatsuko myself," she said. "Perhaps there is more she could tell me."

Yoko and Junko nodded.

"My servant shall notify you before I arrive," Kachiko said. "Now I am fatigued."

Both women bowed low to Aki, and a ninja-ko servant ushered them out. When they had gone, Kachiko slid open the panel behind which Miyuki and Asami had been hiding.

"Asami," she said, "I have a new assignment for you."

Asami bowed slightly. "I live to serve," she said.

"I need you to find me a cabin in the woods nearby," Kachiko said. "If you cannot find one within the Imperial Forest itself, one in the adjoining land will do. It must be secluded. It must be nice enough to tempt a daimyo but plain enough to appeal to a monk."

Asami nodded knowingly. "A pretty trap for a young lion," she said.

Kachiko nodded in return. "Just so. Do it quickly."

"As swiftly as the wind," Asami said. She left. Kachiko smiled.

▲▲▲▲▲▲▲

The next day the Scorpion mistress, in her Aki disguise, came to the House of Junko. Her ninja-ko had stopped by earlier to arrange Kachiko's visit. She wanted to make sure she arrived when few customers occupied the house, so she chose the early morning for her visit.

As she approached the gate, Junko and Yoko appeared—as if by magic—in front of the house. They bowed and scraped deferentially and ushered Aki into the house, making excuses for the humbleness of the establishment. Kachiko made all the appropriate responses, though her keen mind was actually elsewhere.

Asami had done her work well. In short order she had turned up a small cabin within the Imperial Forest. It belonged to an imperial gamekeeper, but he had been renting it out to earn extra money.

"The people he has rented it to are either fugitives or poachers or both," Asami told Kachiko. "The cabin is not currently being used." Since Asami possessed persuasive abilities nearly comparable to those of her mistress, it took little effort to convince the gamekeeper to change tenants. The cabin would be rented to Asami—or, rather, her Aki persona—for the purposes of a romantic tryst the "widow" was carrying out.

Kachiko chuckled. Asami had nearly told the truth, though the person involved in the tryst would not be Asami or Aki.

They examined the cabin in the late afternoon, and by evening had determined what renovations would have to be made to render it suitable for their purposes. Asami arranged for a Scorpion repair crew to work through the night. By morning, the gamekeeper would hardly have recognized his own home. Kachiko, who had carefully avoided contact with the work crew, deemed it "perfect."

Then the Scorpion lady, as Aki, had gone to visit Junko's geisha house.

"Our woman Hatsuko," Kachiko said, "where is she?"

"Awaiting your pleasure, Mistress," Junko said.

"Her room is in the back quarter of the house," Yoko added. "Her samurai prefers to be close to nature. Our gardens abut the forest near there."

Kachiko nodded. "Good. I shall see her. Take me to her room. Then you may go."

"Mistress," Junko said flatteringly, "we obtained many good ideas from our other girls."

"I'm sure you have," Kachiko said. "I'll be delighted to hear them after I've talked to this girl."

Junko and Yoko bowed. Yoko led the Scorpion lady to Hatsuko's room and slid back the screen. "My lady," Yoko said, "your geisha Hatsuko."

Hatsuko bowed low, touching her head to the clean tatami mat on the floor. The geisha's room was large but plain, almost monastic. A few simple lacquer tables and brush paintings were the only decorations—in keeping with the character of her lover.

Kachiko nodded to Yoko, and the younger woman left the room. Kachiko crossed to where Hatsuko knelt. The Scorpion mistress opened her fan with a flourish and said, "Let me take a look at you."

Slowly, Hatsuko rose. She did not meet Kachiko's eyes. The Mother of Scorpions looked her up and down. She saw a girl fair of face and form, with shiny black hair and the painted features of a geisha. The girl's kimono was of good quality and accentuated her figure nicely. She had delicate hands and feet and a generous bosom. She could have made a fine woman, but—in Hatsuko's posture, in the stance that revealed one's soul—Kachiko saw an emptiness. The geisha had been beaten down into her station in life, and had no spirit to rise above it.

Kachiko put her hand on Hatsuko's chin, lifted up her face, and looked into the geisha's eyes. They were brown and soulful, but reminded the Scorpion lady of a doe's eyes. Kachiko smiled, but not for the reason Hatsuko apprehended. Good, thought the Mother of Scorpions. There is much I can use here. Hatsuko smiled back timidly.

"Walk with me," Kachiko said.

Hatsuko nodded and followed Kachiko to the outer exit of the room. Kachiko glanced at the shoji and waited. Hatsuko rolled back the screen and the two of them stepped outside. Kachiko led the girl to the woods at the edge of the gardens.

"You know who I am?" Kachiko asked the girl.

"You are my mistress's mistress," Hatsuko said.

"And do you know why I am here?"

"No," Hatsuko said.

Kachiko looked straight at the girl, but Hatsuko turned away from her gaze. "Come now," the disguised Scorpion said, "I'm sure Junko and Yoko spent a good deal of time discussing my visit with you. They probably spent hours asking you questions they thought I might ask and suggesting responses you could give. I suspect they had you up half the night, which is why you look so tired."

Kachiko glimpsed real fear in the geisha's eyes. "No . . . I mean yes," Hatsuko said. "I mean, they spoke to me, but that's not why I was up late."

"Oh?" said Kachiko, arching one lovely eyebrow.

"I was waiting for my . . . for a client."

"And did he arrive?"

"No."

"So you were not paid, then?"

Hatsuko shook her head. "He has never been late before. Always he arrives early."

They had walked very near to the forest now. "I see from your face that you care for this man," she said. "You shouldn't, you know. A man is just a man. A customer is just a customer. They're all alike in the end."

Hatsuko turned her face down, and she blushed behind her white makeup.

"He is . . . different," Hatsuko said softly.

Kachiko frowned slightly. "This young man, is he the soldier that Junko and Yoko told me about?"

Again, Hatsuko blushed. "He is a soldier, yes."

"I too loved a soldier once," Kachiko said, adding just a hint of a wistful sigh to her voice.

"What happened?" Hatsuko asked.

"He died," Kachiko said. "They all either die or move on in the end. That's the way soldiers are. When they go they leave you heartbroken."

"He will not leave me," Hatsuko said.

"Really?" Kachiko asked, arching her eyebrows. "Then he must be something special." She turned to the forest. "Do you know these woods, girl?"

"Not very well," said Hatsuko.

"But you have been in them?"

"Yes. Sometimes."

"With your soldier?"

"Yes."

"Come walk under the boughs and tell me about it," Kachiko said. "It would do my widow's heart good to hear." She stretched out her hand to Hatsuko.

At first, the girl seemed reluctant to take it. Then, timidly, Hatsuko put her hand in the hand of the Mother of Scorpions.

As the girl talked in vague, romantic ways about the man Kachiko knew to be Akodo Toturi, the mistress of Scorpions led Hatsuko ever deeper into the woods. Kachiko agreed politely with the things the geisha said, chatting as if she were an interested older woman who feared she might become a spinster. All the while, Kachiko led the girl toward their true destination.

Suddenly, Hatsuko stopped and gasped.

"What is it?" Kachiko asked, though she already knew.

"This cabin," Hatsuko said.

"What about it?"

"Totur—I mean, my soldier often speaks of a cabin in the woods."

"Is it a cabin he has been to, then?"

"No," said Hatsuko. "It is one he dreams of."

Kachiko laughed. "He dreams of my cabin?"

Hatsuko's brown eyes grew wide. "This is your cabin, my mistress?"

"Yes," Kachiko said simply. "Though I seldom come here." She sighed wistfully as she said it. "My husband built it for me when we were young and in love."

"That's exactly what my love wishes to do for me."

"Does he?" Kachiko asked, arching her eyebrows again. "Maybe he isn't so bad. Why don't you come inside? We'll have some tea."

"Oh, I couldn't," Hatsuko said.

Kachiko frowned. "Who is to say what you can, or cannot do, besides myself?"

"No one, Mistress."

"Then come inside and stop being foolish."

Kachiko slid back the screens and stepped inside the cabin. Inside was a single room, plain white with simple decorations—almost like Hatsuko's room at the geisha house.

The geisha noticed the resemblance. "It's almost like a dream," Hatsuko said.

"Indeed it is," said Kachiko, taking a pot from over the small fire. She'd arranged for the tea to be ready when they got there. Even now, her ninja-ko waited in the woods should she be needed further.

"I put the pot on before I came to see you," Kachiko explained as she poured the tea. "I thought I'd like to have some when I got back, though I had no idea I'd have a visitor."

Hatsuko bowed and took the cup Kachiko offered. "Thank you, Mistress," she said. She put the cup to her lips and drank deeply, trying to quiet her nerves. The geisha never felt the subtle Scorpion herbs that, from that moment on, dulled her will—herbs to which Kachiko had long ago built up an immunity.

"You said this is like a dream," Kachiko said softly. "Whose dream? Yours or your lover's?"

"His . . . I mean both," said Hatsuko, her head suddenly feeling cloudy. "Both of ours."

"The dreams of men and women are seldom the same, you

know," Kachiko said, refilling Hatsuko's cup. "Especially the dreams of samurai and geisha. What is it you want, Hatsuko?"

"I want . . ." Hatsuko began, a faraway look in her eyes, "I want to be with my lover forever, until the Sun Goddess sets behind the mountains for the final time."

Kachiko nodded sympathetically and said, "That will never happen, you know. It never *can* happen."

"It will happen," the geisha said a little too insistently.

"I see in your eyes that you doubt it too," said Kachiko. "My husband died and left me. Your soldier lover will surely leave you, one way or another."

"No! Never! He has promised!"

"But men do not keep their promises."

"Akodo Toturi does," Hatsuko said defiantly.

Kachiko leaned back on her cushion. "So, that is your lover's name?" she said. "Tell me, Hatsuko-san, do you know who your lover truly is?"

"He is a great soldier . . . a general."

"He is the *emperor's* general, a man married far more to his duty than he could ever be to a simple woman . . . to a geisha."

"That's not so!"

"It is so," said Kachiko, leaning in closer to the girl. "It is the way of the world. Men leave, either to death or to the arms of another woman. He has another woman already, this Toturi, you know."

"Yes . . . I mean, no," Hatsuko said softly.

"He's engaged," Kachiko continued, "to an advisor at the Imperial Court."

"He does not love her."

"He cannot help but marry her," Kachiko said. "He will marry whomever the emperor tells him to marry. And the woman he marries shall *not* be a geisha—the emperor would never allow it."

"He will buy my freedom," Hatsuko said, tears welling up in her eyes. "He has told me so."

"And I would gladly sell your contract to him," Kachiko

said. Then she lowered her voice, leaned close, and whispered in Hatsuko's ear. "But he will *never* ask."

"No!" Hatsuko cried, burying her face in her hands.

"He will not ask because he dares not. It would displease the emperor too much. He could have asked me already . . . . But he hasn't."

Hatsuko leaned forward, sobbing, until her head almost touched the floor. "He loves me," she said, pounding her delicate fist on the floorboards.

"But he can never marry you," Kachiko whispered. "*Never.*"

Hatsuko collapsed in a heap, weeping piteously.

"How could a simple geisha hope to hold the heart of the Lion daimyo?" Kachiko asked sarcastically. "He'll use you and cast you aside. That is the way of the world."

Kachiko leaned back and observed the wreckage she had caused. After a suitable pause, she spoke again.

"However," she said, her voice deep and melodious, "it is possible that you and he can be together."

Hatsuko looked up. A glint of hope sparked in her tear-reddened eyes.

"You can be together, *forever*," Kachiko repeated.

"H-how?"

Kachiko leaned back. "I'll tell you presently, but first, I want to tell you what tragedy the future would bring if you were to marry this man. He is the daimyo of his clan, you know that."

Hatsuko nodded, wiping the tears from her eyes.

"But you do not know about his fiancée," Kachiko said. "Her name is Isawa Kaede, and she is a powerful sorceress in the Phoenix clan. She is influential at court—the emperor listens to her. If she found out about your affair with Toturi, it would mean the end for him."

"She would have him killed?" Hatsuko asked.

"The emperor could *order* him killed, for the shame he has brought upon Kaede and his own house. More likely, he would force your beloved to commit seppuku."

Hatsuko gasped, "No!"

"Yes. The shame would be that great. Of course, you would be executed as well. But that might not be the worst that could happen."

"What could be worse than ritual suicide?"

"Seppuku is a way to regain lost honor. That would be the best Toturi could hope for. Far worse would be to be left to the devices of this Kaede."

"What could she do to my Toturi?"

"As a sorceress, there is no end to the horrors she might inflict on him. You've heard that a Phoenix is a bird that dies in flames and yet lives again?"

Hatsuko nodded, fear building up behind her eyes.

"Well," Kachiko said, lowering her voice once more, "I have heard that Phoenix sorcerers can inflict a thousand burning deaths on one man. They call it 'the hell of burning devils.' In this terrible spell, they set a man afire, but their magic makes his skin grow back each time it burns away."

Hatsuko gasped.

"So a man may burn for a day, or a *thousand* days, and yet not die until they let him."

"Surely she would not do this to her fiancé," Hatsuko cried.

Kachiko tilted back her fine nose and looked down at the girl. "What would a woman *not* do to the man who betrayed her?"

"I will take him away," Hatsuko said, looking around frantically. "We will flee from this place!"

"Where could you flee that a sorceress could not find you?" Kachiko asked sympathetically. "And if he were to strike first—if he killed this witch-fiend—the emperor would have him killed just as surely, though probably more swiftly. Either way, it would be a terrible blow to the empire. The Phoenix and the Lion would go to war. It could tear the empire apart. All this because of *love*. Do you want to bring about the end of the empire?"

"No," Hatsuko sobbed.

Kachiko leaned back and took a deep breath before continuing. "Toturi is young. He doesn't see the folly he has brought upon himself—and the empire. To him, you may seem but a simple dalliance, but in fact, you are his death."

"Then I shall kill myself!"

"Too late. The damage has already been done. Or would you kill Junko, Yoko, all your friends, and *me* as well?"

Tears streamed down Hatsuko's face once more. "I would but . . ."

"But?"

"But I *cannot*. I have not the strength." She buried her face in her hands and collapsed once more. "Oh, we are doomed! Doomed!"

"Yes," Kachiko said, stroking the girl's black hair. "As are moths who fly too close to a flame."

"You said there was a way we could be together . . . !" Hatsuko sobbed, her voice almost smothered by robes and tears.

"There is," the Scorpion lady said calmly. "You can be together forever and the empire will be saved."

"Please," Hatsuko said, grabbing the hem of Kachiko's kimono, "please, I beg you . . . tell me how."

From around her neck, Kachiko took a small blue medallion. "With this," she said, holding out the amulet before the frightened girl.

Hatsuko looked up, her eyes spellbound by the glittering blue jewel in its golden setting. Inside the gem, she could see a small amount of white powder. "What does it hold inside?" she asked.

"The Sleep of Eternity," Kachiko said.

"Poison?"

Kachiko nodded. "If you prefer to think of it as such."

"But you said we would always be together."

"How else can one always be together with one's love—except in the afterlife?"

Hatsuko lowered her tear-stained eyes and wept piteously.

Kachiko watched her carefully. "Think of eternity in paradise," she said, her voice calm and soothing. "Surely that is better than pain and death here upon this callow world. Surely it is better than war and the destruction of the empire. Remember, you will be *together*."

Hatsuko sobbed softly on the floor.

"Will you do it?" the Scorpion lady asked. "Do you have the courage to save yourself and your lover? Do you have the courage to save the empire?"

From beneath her robes, Hatsuko said, "I do. . . . I will."

The Mother of Scorpions stood and walked to a nearby wall. She hung the amulet on a small peg there. "When the time is right," she said, "you can bring him here. Put half in his tea, and then take the rest yourself. Sweet oblivion will come swiftly. Do you understand?"

"Yes."

"But you must use the powder soon," Kachiko said. "Its potency will diminish after one month. The gem will be here when you need it. I will be using the cabin for the next week. One of my servants will come and tell you when you may bring your man here. It should be the next time you see him."

"He was supposed to visit me last night," Hatsuko said plaintively.

"So you said. So you said," Kachiko replied, knowing full well that her people would keep Toturi busy for a long while yet—nearly until the time she and Shoju chose to move against the emperor. "The time will come soon enough. When you have your chance, you must take it. You may never have another opportunity."

"Why are you doing this?" Hatsuko asked.

"Because I know what it is like," Kachiko said, "to live without my one true love. I should have killed myself when he died. See that you do not make the same mistake."

Hatsuko nodded, but the tears didn't stop.

It seemed as though Kachiko would leave the room, but she turned back as she slid open the shoji screen.

"And remember," she said, "every moment you tarry is another moment in which Toturi may be discovered— another moment that brings him closer to dishonor and the burning death. Another moment that brings us all closer to the destruction of the Emerald Empire."

Hatsuko shuddered an acknowledgment.

"Come now," Kachiko said. "I need to teach you the path to take back to the geisha house."

Slowly, Hatsuko got to her feet.

▲▲▲▲▲▲▲▲

The next morning Bayushi Kachiko turned the role of Aki back over to Yogo Asami. She left instructions that Hatsuko was to be watched carefully. The Scorpion mistress doubted the girl would need any further encouragement to carry out her task, but if she did, Asami would be there to make sure everything went according to plan.

Akodo Toturi would be dead by the time the Scorpions visited the emperor to celebrate the Fire Festival.

▲▲▲▲▲▲▲▲

In a huff, Toturi cast aside his riding gear and entered Junko's geisha house.

Junko appeared from an alcove and bowed to the wandering soldier. "It is good to see you, my lord," she said.

Toturi growled an unintelligible response.

"When you did not arrive for your last scheduled visit, we feared something might have happened."

"No," Toturi said. "Just got tied up. Affairs you wouldn't understand."

Junko bowed again. "Even in peacetime, the work of a soldier is never done," she said. "You look tired. Shall I prepare a bath?"

Toturi shook his head. "Hatsuko will do it." Then, remembering his manners, he said, "I'd like to see her if I may."

"Most assuredly, my lord. I shall fetch her at once."

Toturi waved her off. "No need to. I know the way."

Junko watched the young general go, wondering for just a moment who he really was. She shook her head and went about her business.

Without announcing himself, the Lion pushed the screen back.

Hatsuko jumped at the sudden noise and movement. "Oh!" she cried, pulling her kimono tighter around her.

"Have no fear, Hatsuko-chan," Toturi said, bowing. "It is only I."

She rushed to her feet and embraced him. "Toturi-sama," she said softly, pressing her face against his broad chest.

"I'm sorry I startled you," he said. "But I was anxious to see you. It has been too long."

"When you did not come," she said, "I feared something had happened to you."

He shook his head. "No. No need to worry. I just got tied up with some business at court."

"What kind of business?" she asked shyly.

Toturi looked at her and sighed. Something was bothering her, though he couldn't figure out what. "Why do you ask?" he said.

"Because I missed you," she answered. "It has been nearly a month since our last . . . appointment and I feared you would not return."

The Lion laughed, full and hearty. "You need never fear that, my love. I would sooner die than desert you."

"Would you?" she asked.

"Of course I would."

"Then what kept you from my side?"

Toturi motioned for her to sit. He sat down beside her.

"Bad luck, I suppose," he said. "Papers—official business— that I had signed were lost. They had to be drawn up and signed again. Then my horse came up lame and needed to be reshod. To make matters worse, several of my people got involved in a teahouse brawl in Otosan Uchi. I couldn't leave until I sorted all those things out."

He put his arm around her. "But, believe me," he continued, "I had no choice. Sometimes I wish I had never become a daimyo."

"I wish . . ." she said, ". . . I wish you could stay with me always."

"As do I," he said. He pulled her to him and kissed her passionately. They separated, and he pressed her head against his chest. "I would give the world if I could."

A shudder ran through her delicate frame.

"Are you cold, my love?" Toturi asked. "A warm bath will change that. Draw one for us both, will you?"

Hatsuko nodded and walked toward the shoji screen to the bathhouse that adjoined her room. Then she turned back.

"Toturi-sama," she said, "if you could have but one wish, what would it be?"

"One wish?" he said, rubbing his chin. "That's easy." He walked to her side and embraced her. "I would wish that you and I could be together forever."

"As you told me before? In a small cabin in the woods?" she asked.

"Yes," he said, smiling down at her. "Together, forever, in our small cabin hidden away in the forest."

She smiled back at him, but she did not meet his eyes.

13 COMING OF AGE

Shoju welcomed his wife and her people home without the elaborate ceremony Dairu would have wanted. It was a warm welcome nonetheless. Shoju had begun setting the wheels of their plan in motion. Only a few points of business remained before the Scorpions' journey to Otosan Uchi. Foremost among these was the gempuku ceremony for Dairu, the daimyo's heir.

They held the ritual on the second day after Kachiko's return. Hundreds of Scorpion nobles, retainers, and honored guests assembled in the great hall at Kyuden Bayushi. Shoju and Kachiko, dressed in their finest masks and kimonos, sat on a dais at the front of the hall. The other Scorpions lined the sides of the chamber. The guests wore their best finery. To do otherwise was to risk execution.

The room itself had been decorated with banners of gold, black, and red. Many of these featured the Scorpion mon. Some of the tapestries were inscribed with blessings and spells to speed the initiate on his road to manhood. The center of the room sat empty, reserved for the ceremony itself. At a signal from Shoju, the hall fell silent.

Bayushi Dairu marched through the great entryway doors and into the hall. He wore a gold kimono and mask, each decorated with red and black filigree. In his left hand he held a katana. In his right, he held a scroll. Two dignitaries escorted the Scorpion heir into the room. On his right strode the priest Mifune. On his left marched the Scorpion swordmaster, Masayuki, a bow and arrows strapped to his back.

Dairu handed the sword to Masayuki and unrolled the scroll. He read:

"Leaves tumble swiftly—rivers flowing ever change—even mountains fall." He followed with two more haiku, both by Scorpion poets. He rolled up the scroll and handed it to Mifune.

Then he recited the verses of Shinsei by heart. Mifune nodded as the boy spoke. Both Shoju and Kachiko felt pride grow within their hearts. Their son had studied well.

After the recitation, Masayuki removed the bow and arrows from his back and handed them to Dairu. Fusuma side screens slid open and servants brought eleven wooden targets into the room, setting them before the great doors. The targets had been painted with the pictures of animals: deer, pheasants, boar, and others.

Dairu nocked an arrow to the bow and pulled the string to his ear. Willing his heart and breathing quiet, he concentrated as he had been taught. When he felt the moment of perfect stillness, he let the arrow fly. The first target fell. The crowd remained silent—as was custom. Only when Dairu felled the last target, a lion, did the Scorpion lord nod his approval.

Dairu bowed to his father. He gave the arrows and bow back to Masayuki. The swordmaster returned Dairu's katana to him.

Dairu tucked the scabbard into his obi and drew the sword. Uttering a martial arts cry, he stalked to the center of the room and held his sword in front of him.

At the sound, the side screens opened again and servants rolled in seven practice dummies made of straw. Dairu waited for the moment of inner silence.

When it came, he moved swiftly about the room, swinging his sword in wide arcs. He cut the arms from the first dummy, the legs from the second. The third he bisected at the waist; the forth he decapitated. The fifth lost both arms and legs, the sixth both middle and head.

On the last, Dairu removed all the limbs and bisected the middle. He cut off the head as the dummy fell. With a satisfied cry, he resumed his starting position. He glanced at his parents.

Shoju nodded once more; Kachiko smiled.

Dairu sheathed his sword and bowed.

Mifune stepped forward. From within his robe he produced four silken handkerchiefs. He tossed them into the air in front of the boy.

Using his iajutsu fast-draw skill, Dairu drew his sword and cut the first silk in two before it hit the ground. He did the same to the others, turning four into the lucky number eight. He then resheathed his katana and bowed, first to the priest, then to his parents. Mifune bowed back; the Scorpion lord and lady nodded.

Two monks stepped forward and handed a piece of rice paper to the priest. Mifune turned and presented it to Dairu. The Scorpion heir took the paper in both hands and held it up over his head for all to see.

He let go of the paper with his right hand and drew his sword once more. Sweat beaded on Dairu's brow. His heart pounded. He willed himself to concentrate, slowing his heart. He stared intently at the paper, dangling from his left hand by one corner.

Slowly, he brought the point of the sword to where his

fingers pinched the rice paper. Deftly he drew the blade of the sword along the paper's thin edge. In a few moments he had turned the one piece of paper into two. Both pieces were of equal size to the original, though thinner.

Dairu let out a long breath. With a flourish, he returned his sword to its sheath once more. He bowed to his parents.

Bayushi Shoju stood and strode toward the center of the hall to his son.

Dairu knelt before his lord.

Shoju looked down on the boy. His ornate mask made it impossible to read the Scorpion daimyo's face.

Dairu bowed his head and waited.

From a secret place within his robes, Shoju drew forth a wakizashi—the samurai's short sword. He held the sword out to Dairu. "Today," the Scorpion lord said, his voice echoing like thunder in the hall, "you are samurai."

Dairu took the sword and tucked it into his belt, completing his dai-sho—the mark of a samurai, the mark of a man. He could not help smiling. He stood and bowed to the only father he had ever known.

As Shoju bowed back, the great hall burst into thunderous applause. The nobles present stood, thrust their fists in the air, and shouted "*Banzai!*" three times.

Dairu blinked back the moisture at the corner of his eyes. He could see his mother wiping the tears from her face. He turned to his father.

Shoju nodded at Dairu. The young man sensed the smile behind his father's mask.

"Come," the Scorpion said, motioning Dairu to join him on the dais. "Let the celebration begin."

Father and son turned to Mifune and Masayuki and bowed. The priest and the swordmaster bowed lower in reply. Both of Dairu's tutors smiled proudly at their student. Shoju turned and led his son to the platform at the front of the hall. They seated themselves beside Kachiko, and the feasting began in earnest.

▲▲▲▲▲▲▲▲

By the end of the evening, the castle staff had exhausted themselves. They went to bed knowing they had done their utmost to serve their master, his wife, and his son.

Most Scorpions slept late the morning after the gempuku ritual. The servants, of course, got to work at their usual times—though no one faulted them if they seemed a bit sleepy.

When they arose, Shoju and Kachiko set about making the final preparations for the trip to the capital. Dairu was given the task of readying the horses, and Tetsuo helped him.

Shortly after sunset, Shoju and Kachiko met with their son in the high tower of Kyuden Bayushi's great keep.

"My son," Shoju began, his face stern behind his mask, "I suspect you've guessed our trip to the capital is not merely to celebrate the Fire Festival."

Dairu nodded. "It was not my place to ask, Father, but I have wondered, yes."

"Now that you are a man," said Kachiko, "you must know the true purpose of our visit."

"You know already," continued Shoju, "that the path of the Scorpion is a difficult one. We are born to do what the other clans cannot . . . *will* not do. Our divine mission is to do the bidding of the emperor, no matter what the cost. Nothing is more important than protecting the empire—not life, not family, not honor. Do you understand?"

"Yes, Father."

Shoju nodded. "Yosh," he said. "Now our credo will be put to the ultimate test. We will risk all, sacrifice all, for the good of the Emerald Empire, indeed, for Rokugan itself."

"We have learned," Kachiko said, her eyes dark and somber, "that a catastrophe is about to befall our world. The return of Fu Leng is imminent."

The young heir to the Scorpion throne gasped. "No!"

"What your mother says is true," Shoju said. He turned and

stalked from where they stood in the center of the room to the edge of the high balcony. "Soon all this," he waved his hand to the lands beyond the castle, "may go up in flames. Our land may be torn, screaming, into the very bowels of Jigoku itself."

Dairu took a step forward, his hand unconsciously straying to the hilt of his sword. "But this must not *be*, Father," he said. "We must prevent this disaster—at any cost."

"We must, we can, and we will," Shoju said grimly, not turning to look at his son.

"We will, though it may cost us everything," said Kachiko. "The cost to the empire will be terrible as well."

"No cost is too great to prevent the resurrection of Fu Leng," Dairu said bravely.

Shoju turned and put his hand on his son's shoulder. "You understand, then," the Scorpion daimyo said. "Good. Now your mother and I must tell you what actions the Scorpion will take to avert this catastrophe."

"A scroll dictated long ago by Uikku, the Serene Prophet, to a Scorpion retainer warns of how the return of Fu Leng will come to pass," Kachiko said. She held her son's dark eyes with her own as she spoke. "The resurrection of the Evil One will be brought about by the last Hantei emperor."

"Hantei . . . !" Dairu gasped.

"Unless," Shoju said, "we stop him."

"But, Father, how can we stop the emperor? We serve him—even unto death."

"We serve him, yes, but we also serve the empire. If the emperor becomes a threat to the empire—" Shoju paused and looked away from his son "—a new emperor is needed."

"An emperor who is not a Hantei," Kachiko added. "An emperor who will not bring about the return of Fu Leng. Perhaps even a Bayushi emperor."

Dairu looked from his father to his mother, disbelief showing in his eyes. His small mask could not disguise his shock and horror. "Kill the emperor?" he asked.

"Would you kill one man to save a hundred? A thousand?

Ten thousand?" the Scorpion daimyo asked. "If taking the life of the emperor would serve the empire best, how can we *not* do it? It is our sworn duty."

"It is what we are bred for," Kachiko said, standing beside her husband and taking his left hand.

"But, Father," Dairu said, "my first battle . . . it should not be against the emperor."

"Fortune seldom sets us on the path we desire, my son," said Kachiko. "Our cause is just. We need you at our side."

Dairu crossed to where his parents stood, and he took Shoju's right hand. A twinge of pain flared up the daimyo's shoulder, but he ignored it.

"Then I am with you," Dairu said. "Tell me how we will accomplish our goals."

Shoju nodded. "Yosh."

The three of them sat down simultaneously.

Kachiko began. "While our retinue travels to the Hantei castle, the real strength of our forces is already in place," she said.

Shoju continued her thought. "For the last month, our people have infiltrated the capital city, posing as tradesmen and artisans. Our safe houses have supplied them with shelter. No one suspects how many Scorpions now dwell within the capital city."

"At the same time, Soshi Bantaro and Yogo Junzo have crept into the hills around the city," said Kachiko. "They have used subtle spells and the arts of the ninja to conceal themselves. The great mass of our weapons is with them."

"But, if our weapons are outside the city . . . ?"

"They are outside now," Kachiko said, "but soon they will be within the walls. Our shugenja will use their magic to make the swords and spears appear to be mere sticks, kindling for the upcoming Fire Festival."

Shoju folded his hands on his lap. "At the same time, Yogo Junzo is using subtle magics to weaken the castle defenses."

"But won't the Hantei shugenja detect this?" Dairu asked.

"No," his father said, "because Junzo is not working to defeat the castle's spells, merely to alter them, so that we may bring our forces in undetected. The spells of the Crane and Phoenix will remain, but they will have been corrupted to our purpose.

"When we arrive," Shoju concluded, "the emperor will hold a feast in our honor. During that feast, we shall strike."

14 ROKUGAN IN PERIL

Early the next morning, the host of the Scorpions assembled inside the eastern gate of Kyuden Bayushi. Shoju stood at the front of the retinue, holding the reins of his magnificent Unicorn-bred steed. Dairu and Tetsuo took up positions next to him. Several ranks back, within sight of the Scorpion heir, rode Bayushi Aramoro—the daimyo's half-brother and the heir's watchdog. He blended in nicely with the crowd of retainers, which was exactly what he wanted.

Kachiko languished in her palanquin, waving an ornate fan to stave off the morning heat. At times like this, she hated the small, lacquered box that custom forced her to ride in. Others in the column may have been discomforted by the torrid weather as well, but no one was ill-mannered enough to show it. Shoju had ordered all of his people to wear their most festive masks, which not only suited a visit to the emperor, but also disguised the true nature of their errand.

Bayushi Yojiro stood beside his daimyo and spoke to the Scorpion lord. "Are you sure you do not want me to come with you, my lord?" Yojiro asked.

Shoju shook his head. "No. You must stay here," he said. "I entrust our castle and sacred homeland to your care. No one else is worthy of the job."

Yojiro bowed low. "Thank you, great lord."

"One other thing," said Shoju. He turned to his horse and from the saddlebag pulled a long, linen-wrapped package. "Here," he said, handing it to the younger man.

"What is it, great lord?" Yojiro asked.

Behind his mask, Shoju's face grew grim. "*Itsuwari*, the sword of my ancestors."

"The royal sword!" Yojiro gasped.

"I will have no need of it on this trip," Shoju said. In the back of his mind, the humming song of *Yashin*, the bloodsword, grew stronger. "Protect it until I return," the daimyo said.

"With my life, great lord," Yojiro replied. He bowed low, reverently holding the package containing the sacred sword.

Shoju swung into the saddle of his horse, ignoring a twinge from his lame arm as he did so. "When next we meet," he said to Yojiro, "the world will be safe once more."

"May the Fortunes ride with you," Yojiro said.

Shoju snapped the reins of his horse, and it strode forward; the rest of the host followed behind.

▲▲▲▲▲▲▲▲

On the afternoon of the twenty-first day, the Scorpion host came within sight of the City of the Shining Prince. It was another oppressive summer day, as most of the days of their journey had been. High, dark clouds rolled toward the city from the west, dimming the light of the setting sun.

To ordinary eyes, the approaching storm seemed nothing unusual. Bayushi Shoju knew the clouds portended the subtle art of his shugenja at work. Soon, it would begin to rain; the rain would build into the early hours of the evening when the city would be engulfed in a cascading thunderstorm.

This storm would hide the movements of his people as they massed both inside and outside the city. The lightning would also add a dramatic flair to the speech Shoju intended to give that night. Such omens were only fitting, given the violence that was to come.

The Scorpion retinue approached the city via the Emperor's Gate—so called because beyond it lay the only paved road into the capital.

In Rokugan, nearly all roads were composed of common dirt. Bad weather made the use of wheeled vehicles nearly impossible—as it would later tonight. The Emperor's Road, however, had been constructed of stone, and once a year, the emperor would ride in his carriage along that road, from the palace to the outskirts of the sprawling city. The carriage was far more impressive than the palanquin that the emperor usually used, and even more impressive than his ornate litter. Unfortunately, the carriage could travel only this one road.

Dairu marveled as his father's retinue rode through the gate. He had been in the city before, but never this way. The Emperor's Gate was immense, composed of timbers wider than the young Scorpion and taller than a three story temple. The doors had been painted white and carved with powerful runes. They were bound with wide bands of iron. The great hinges were iron, too. Golden filigree decorated the dark metal with mythological scenes of samurai and dragons.

A huge *torii* stood just beyond the portal. Usually these decorative arches stood in places of worship, doorways to heaven. The symbolism here was obvious; those who rode through this gate had set themselves on a divine path. At the end of the road sat the great palace of the Hantei.

The castle thrust itself above the rest of the city and into the morning sky. Its white towers seemed to merge with the clouds. Even the approaching storm could not dim its brilliance. It looked to Dairu as if a piece of heaven had fallen to ground. The young Scorpion glanced at his father, wondering if the Scorpion lord felt the same thing he did.

Shoju nodded as he noticed his son's glance. Somehow, the nod reminded Dairu of the grim nature of their errand.

Besides availing themselves of the honor of taking the Emperor's Road, Shoju had chosen the Emperor's Gate for another reason. The parts of the city controlled by the Scorpion Clans abutted the road. The faithful could watch from their houses as their leader entered Otosan Uchi. This would signal the Scorpion people—those who knew of Shoju's plans—that their preparations had entered the final stages.

On their way to the palace, the retinue passed fragments of several ancient walls. In the past the city had expanded often, and as it did, the old outer walls came down to supply stones for the new. Fragments of the former bastions remained where local architecture had attached itself vinelike around them.

The houses of Otosan Uchi followed traditional Rokugani plans. Their frames were timber with rice paper walls. Most had a single wooden door or gate leading from the main road into the house. The houses of wealthy people centered on a garden and perhaps a pool. The rest of the structure was built around this captive bit of nature. All Rokugani houses were well ordered, though some were not well maintained. In Otosan Uchi, even the most modest dwellings sparkled. To keep a household in less that perfect condition—especially along the Emperor's Road—would have been an insult to the Son of the Sun. Such insults led to quick executions.

Soon the Scorpions came within sight of the Forbidden City. The walls of the Imperial Precinct were impressive, tall and white like ivory. They shone brightly, even as thunderclouds eclipsed the afternoon sun. Shoju remembered stories he'd heard of these enchanted walls. One—a true one so near as he could tell—said the emperor who had ordered the wall built had commanded it be made of stones of the same size. Samurai scoured the whole of Rokugan to fulfill the Son of the Sun's wish. This perfect symmetry added strength to the wall's enchantments.

Legends said the wall had never been breached, either by earthquake or enemy. Shoju doubted this was true. In any case, he intended to put the second part of the legend to the test—though not in the way the builders had anticipated.

As the Scorpions drew near, the gates of the Forbidden City opened before them. For a moment, Shoju thought of the dream he'd had so many months ago—his dream of entering the city amid death and carnage.

Beyond the gates he didn't see fire and demons. Instead, a great crowd waited to greet the Scorpion host. At the head of the crowd, on a gold-canopied litter, sat Emperor Hantei the 38th.

The crowd within the Forbidden City cheered as the Scorpions dipped their banners in respect to the emperor. Behind his pleasant mask, Shoju smiled a grim smile.

Shoju recognized most of the people with the emperor. Shosuro Taberu, the Scorpion envoy, stood in his usual place to the emperor's left. He nodded when Shoju caught his eye. Also to Hantei's left stood Kakita Yoshi of the Crane, his hair bleached white in Crane fashion. He was a tall, thin man and good looking, not so offensive as Cranes went, and a fair poet. Though he had never wielded a blade, Yoshi was one of the most powerful men in the empire. He held the ear of the emperor. The Scorpion lord hoped it would not be necessary to kill him. Yoshi had been an ally of the Scorpion in the past.

With the Crane stood Doji Shizue, as fair as a willow even under the shadow of the approaching storm. The girl had been lame since birth but possessed an exceptionally keen mind. Both the infirmity and the intellect were traits she shared with the Scorpion lord. He reminded himself to keep an eye on her.

To the right stood Isawa Kaede, the Phoenix Mistress of the Void, and Seppun Ishikawa, the captain of Hantei's guard. The Phoenix shugenja would bear watching as well. Shoju hoped the trouble with her fiancé, Akodo Toturi, would dull her wits. She would not be easy to deceive, and her powers were formidable. The Scorpion would talk to Kachiko's handmaid, Yogo Miyuki, about neutralizing the woman.

Ishikawa posed less of a problem. Though a fine warrior, he would be no match for Shoju's men, either in prowess or in physical strength. The Scorpion daimyo's brother, Aramoro, could make short work of him if necessary.

There were others in the imperial party, and Shoju catalogued the weakness of each man and woman.

Seppun Bake was a sycophant. He used his knowledge of religion and prophecy to bolster his otherwise tenuous opinions. Otomo Sorai could almost have been a Scorpion. His main purpose was to subtly pit the clans against each other and thereby keep them in the emperor's control. For the emperor's sake, the Scorpions sometimes let him think he had succeeded. In fact, Sorai was an amateur compared to the courtiers of Kyuden Bayushi.

The herald, Miya Yoto, was too old to be of any consequence. Shoju did not see Yoto's young, energetic son Satoshi in the crowd. Seppun Daiori had seen better days. Though he tried to carry himself proudly, in his mannerisms the Scorpion lord detected the weakness of an opium addict. He would pose no threat, either.

Nor would the royal heir stand in the Scorpions' way. To judge from what Shoju saw, Sotorii would be even less a threat than they had thought. Rather than give the visiting lord the attention that courtesy demanded, the young Hantei hung to the back of the greeting crowd and flirted with Miya Matsuo's daughters.

Not only were the girls considerably beneath his station, Sotorii seemed to be unduly familiar with one of them—

Yumika. The boy looked hung over. Better he should die than live to disgrace the empire with his reign, thought Shoju.

Akodo Toturi was conspicuously absent. His spot, next to the emperor's right hand, stood empty. During the final days of the Scorpions' journey to Otosan Uchi, Kachiko's spies had brought news of the Lion's impending demise.

Shoju reined in his horse before the Son of the Sun Goddess and bowed low. The company behind him came to a halt and did the same.

"Your Most August Majesty," the lord of Scorpions said politely.

Hantei nodded to him. "Bayushi Shoju, our most loyal servant and friend, welcome to our city. We rejoice that you have chosen to visit us during the Festival of Fire. We also rejoice at your son's recent coming of age. Where is the boy?"

Shoju motioned to Dairu, and the Scorpion's heir rode forward. "Majesty," he said, bowing deeply.

"We are honored to receive you at court, young Scorpion," Hantei said. "We trust the trials of your gempuku were not too strenuous."

"The heat of the forge determines the strength of the steel," Dairu said somewhat nervously.

The emperor smiled at him.

Dairu's heart grew warm, as if the sun had fallen upon his shoulders. He smiled back and bowed. Deep inside, he prepared for the grave test to come. This day, I am truly a Scorpion, he thought.

"And your lovely wife, Lord Bayushi," the emperor said, "We trust she has made the journey as well?"

In answer to the question, a servant opened the door to Kachiko's palanquin and the great lady stepped out, her movements as graceful as a cat. All eyes followed her. Even Hantei Sotorii stopped flirting long enough to pay attention.

"I am honored to return to the white-walled City of Clouds," she said, bowing.

"Ah, Kachiko," the emperor said jovially, "you chase the fog of age from this old man's eyes. We trust you will join us by our lotus pond after dinner."

Kachiko bowed again, holding the emperor with her eyes. "Of course, Majesty," she said. "Weather permitting."

"Very good, very good," the emperor said, rubbing his hands enthusiastically. "Perhaps we should dispense with formalities and get right to feasting. We understand we have chosen a particularly good menu this evening."

"Your selections have been most excellent, Celestial One," said Seppun Bake, stepping forward momentarily and then melting back into the crowd.

"Good. Good," Hantei said, nodding. Having apparently had his fill of pomp and pageantry, he added, "We should get right to it, eh?"

"As you wish, Your Majesty," Shoju and Kachiko said simultaneously. The lord and lady pretended not to notice the emperor's friendly informality. Shoju and Kachiko bowed, as did Dairu, and—a moment later—the rest of the Scorpion host.

"Well, then, let's go," said the emperor. He waved his fan, and his bearers carried him in the direction of the great tower. He winked playfully at Dairu as he went. Shoju and the others fell into step behind.

Shosuro Taberu dropped back in the procession so that he could speak with the Scorpion lord and lady. He bowed as they reached him. They nodded in reply.

"You will find everything in readiness," Taberu told them. "I've secured some of the finest rooms in the palace for your retinue."

Shoju nodded. "Yosh," he said, realizing his retainer's double meanings.

"I'm sure you've done your usual excellent job, Taberu," Kachiko added. "The lord and I will take time to freshen up before the feast. I expect many of our people have last-minute details to attend to as well."

"I'll see to it," Taberu said, smiling at her. Despite the years they had worked together, he remained enthralled by her beauty and cunning.

▲▲▲▲▲▲▲▲

Taberu's accommodations proved as good as his word. The chambers of the Scorpion lord and lady were sumptuous, with a beautiful view of the palace gardens. They were also easily defended and difficult to spy upon. After their arrival, Yogo Miyuki set up a series of subtle spells to make sure any conversations taking place in the room remained private.

After the shugenja had gone, Shoju and Kachiko bathed in an adjoining room and prepared for the feast.

The Scorpion lord stretched. Noticing a weakness in his lame arm, he traced the intricate design of his tattoo and felt the stiffness slip away. He fetched his blue bottle and drank a draught to reinforce the tattoo's magic.

As Shoju did his kata, Kachiko inventoried her poisons. Because of imperial security, she had not been able to sneak many into the castle. Fortunately, her position as advisor to the emperor had allowed her to secrete a goodly supply throughout the castle during her earlier visits. The poison she chose for tonight would have to be special. She needed something subtle but powerful, something that would dull the mind of the emperor and his guests but not let them suspect they were being drugged.

A diluted form of the black lotus seemed best for this purpose, and Kachiko set about mixing the proper doses. She would make sure the poison found its way into the emperor's food. Fortunately, his food taster had Scorpion ties and was immune to the mixture Kachiko intended to use.

Probably, the poison would not be necessary at all, but neither Kachiko nor Shoju liked to take chances.

Having finished their personal preparations, the Scorpion lord and lady dressed. They chose their most beautiful kimonos and masks for the feast, though their robes were also cut to allow the maximum freedom of movement. In her obi, Kachiko concealed two small folding daggers. She also hid another two in her hairdo as hairpins and a third in her fan.

Shoju secreted a number of *shuriken* within the folds of his garments. Normally, he would have hidden a folding staff as well, but tonight he had a far better weapon.

Just behind his head, suspended in the very air itself, hung *Yashin*—Ambition. The bloodsword's ancient magic made it invisible, hidden even better than it had been beneath the Scorpion Palace. No one could see it now unless the Scorpion daimyo took it in his hand. The enchantments set upon it long ago made it undetectable by any but the most skilled sorcerers.

Realizing this slight weakness, Kachiko added Isawa Kaede to the list of those sure to be poisoned. No one would be allowed to carry weapons at the feast, but *Yashin* would be there anyway, waiting for the perfect moment.

A final item completed the Scorpions' wardrobe. Bayushi's Mask, a delicate silken cloth, had been handed down through the generations to Shoju. The enchantment of the mask rendered the wearer immune to mind-reading and other forms of mental magic, but it served another purpose as well. When worn, the artifact increased the persuasive power of its owner. Anything the wearer said became reasonable under the influence of the mask. Even outlandish things took on some plausibility, and righteous things framed in well-chosen words became tantamount to orders.

In his reign as daimyo, the Scorpion lord had never found it necessary to use the mask—until now. Always the persuasive power of his voice and the logic of his arguments had been enough to sway listeners to his cause. Tonight, if he was to save the empire, Shoju needed every advantage.

He reverently donned the mask of his ancestors and carefully placed a decorative mask over it. The top mask was complex and colorful. When worn one way, it was a cheerful laughing face, but when worn upside down, it became a frightening, almost demonic visage. Shoju turned the mask so that it presented its happy countenance—at least for the start of the evening. Later, he would use the frightful aspect.

Kachiko's silken mask accentuated the beauty of her face, just as her kimono emphasized her perfect body. She wore just enough make-up to be alluring without seeming wanton. She did up her long hair in graceful knots secured with the large hairpin daggers she had chosen earlier.

As the Scorpion lord and lady finished their preparations, the storm outside broke. Great gouts of rain poured down from the heavens, and thunder crashed and echoed through the streets of Otosan Uchi. Summer heat turned the rain into clinging mist almost as soon as it hit the ground. Soon the city lay shrouded in rain and fog.

Shoju and Kachiko smiled; Yogo Junzo and Soshi Bantaro had done their jobs well. Everything was now in its place. Tonight they would save the empire, or sacrifice their lives trying.

▲▲▲▲▲▲▲▲

The feast was a glorious spectacle. The palace's great hall was nearly four times the size of the one at Kyuden Bayushi. A rich man's house could have easily fit inside it. Tall timbers supported a roof so high that four men standing on each other's shoulders could not have touched it. Many-colored lanterns hung from the rafters, dappling the room in rainbow light.

Banners and paintings decorated the chamber. Some depicted the exploits of Hantei's illustrious ancestors. Others had been hung for this occasion and showed the many brave deeds of the Scorpion Clan. Dairu and Tetsuo marveled at these works of art, proud to be part of the Scorpion line.

In accordance with tradition, the tea ceremony was held first, to honor the emperor's guests. The woman who poured the tea performed the movements gracefully, and with great precision, showing her dedication to the art. Shoju and Kachiko sat on the floor and drank alongside the emperor, renewing their friendship and devotion.

Next came the customary presentation of gifts. The emperor gave the Scorpion lord and lady a beautiful scroll painting of the mountains near Beiden Pass. For their part, the Scorpions presented the emperor with a jewel-encrusted ivory horse. "To waft your dreams into heaven," said Kachiko.

Then the celebration began in earnest. The entertainment included a Noh performance, dancers, acrobats, musicians, and a poetry reading. Kakita Yoshi had returned to his homeland earlier in the day, after greeting Shoju's company, so one of his poems was read by Daiori—who also included a verse of his own in the reading. Daiori had the good sense to save the Crane's work for last.

Then came the food: sumptuous, impressive courses, each impeccably timed and perfectly prepared. Each was more wonderful than the last. The feast began with dried fruits and pure white rice, followed by cold turtle soup and hot noodles. Peacock eggs wrapped in seaweed came next.

Sake servers made sure that every celebrant's cup remained brimming with warm rice wine.

Pickled fruit and ginger cleansed the palate between courses. More noodles then, served with abalone sauce followed by octopus, marinated with hot spices. Roast boar stuffed with fruit and herbs finished the feast.

By the time they reached the end, Dairu thought he might burst from pleasure. Surely the kitchens of Hantei had fallen directly from heaven.

Through it all the entertainment continued, though not in so bold a way as to disturb the diners. Undimmed by the fury of the storm outside, the party stretched into the night.

▲ ▲ ▲ ▲ ▲ ▲ ▲ ▲

The feast impressed Isawa Kaede—and she had been in the court long enough not to be impressed easily. It also annoyed her. Surely a visit by the Scorpion daimyo was no more important than a call by the leader of any other clan. Yet, Hantei the 38th always took special steps whenever Bayushi Shoju came to Otosan Uchi. What did the Scorpions do that was so important anyway? They were all liars, thieves, and assassins. Kaede folded her arms across her ample bosom and frowned.

The weather annoyed her as well. Something about it played on her nerves. Perhaps it was the combination of so many Scorpions and the raging storm outside. Scorpions always made her uneasy anyway. Scorpions liked this unsettling influence—it kept their enemies off guard.

Feasting with the Bayushi lord and lady also had a disquieting effect on Kaede's body this night. Or perhaps the incessant thunder caused her head to pound. Kaede hoped the weather would improve in time for the Fire Festival. Bonfires were notoriously hard to light when wet, and as a Phoenix, Kaede always enjoyed a good fire.

She raised her hand to her head and realized she was sweating, sweating far more than the humidity and temperature could explain. Am I ill? she wondered. She tried to summon her powers to vanquish the feeling, but couldn't concentrate.

Seated on the tatami next to her, Ishikawa leaned over and asked, "Is anything wrong?"

"No," said Kaede. "I mean, yes. . . . I mean I'm not feeling well."

"It's the heat," said the captain. "Perhaps you should retire."

"No," she replied. "Not yet. I don't want to be impolite."

"You needn't worry about leaving," Ishikawa whispered. "I saw the royal heir sneak out some time ago."

Kaede frowned. "With that Miya girl?"

"Yes. Matsuo's daughter. Yashika, I think."

"Yumika," Kaede said.

"That's it. She seems perfect for him."

"She's a vain, shallow girl, interested only in her own pleasure."

Ishikawa nodded. "As I said. Have you tried the natto? It's excellent."

Kaede smiled despite herself. "I'm not sure if my stomach is up to it."

"If you need to make a strategic retreat, I'm your man."

She reached out and almost touched his hand. "Perhaps I should. Let me make my good-byes." She got to her feet but brought her hand to her mouth as her stomach lurched.

"Don't worry about it," he said, jumping up to support her. "The emperor is far too busy enjoying himself. No one will even notice you've left."

"That's a fine thing to say."

"You know what I meant."

▲▲▲▲▲▲▲▲

Despite Ishikawa's words, Bayushi Shoju did notice as the Phoenix lady left the hall. Her departure advanced his plans nicely. If she were to cause any trouble later, it would be easy to subdue or eliminate her—and Ishikawa as well.

Shoju thought of the other dignitaries.

Yoshi of the Crane had left before the feast, returning to his home. He could offer no resistance. His young protégée Doji Shizue remained but was lame and powerless. Near her sat Seppun Daiori. Despite his addiction, he was a man of principle and therefore might prove difficult.

Shoju whispered instructions to a retainer to watch Daiori and neutralize him if necessary.

No one else posed a true threat. Miya Satoshi, the herald's son, had the youth to be a problem but not the temperament. His father, Yoto, had neither. Otomo Sorai was the emperor's troublemaker, but he was a politician. Even with a sword in his hand he would be no threat. The rest were minor officials and the sons and daughters of courtiers. They were rabble, all, but rabble in sufficient numbers could be dangerous. Shoju hoped his speech would persuade many of them to his point of view.

Killing might be necessary, but Shoju preferred to do as little as possible. The hum in his mind reminded him that the bloodsword felt differently.

Foremost in Shoju's thoughts, though, was the emperor. He was the key to the return of Fu Leng, and he sat within easy reach on his dais. His drunken heir had meanwhile slipped out with that Miya girl. Shoju had sent word to his ninja to track down Sotorii and kill him. The heir would not survive the night.

As sake washed away the last of the food, Shoju sensed that the time had come. Seizing the moment, he rose from the floor and looked at the emperor.

The hall grew quiet. Even the storm seemed to hold its breath.

The humming in the Scorpion daimyo's head, the siren song of *Yashin*, grew louder.

"Your Imperial Majesty, noble lords and ladies," he began, "I am honored to be among you tonight. The people in this room represent the finest folk in Rokugan."

There was light applause, and a murmur of agreement ran through the room.

Behind his double mask, Bayushi Shoju smiled.

"The road we travel in life is often a difficult one," he said. "It seldom leads where we think it will. My road led me into the bowels of my own castle. Kyuden Bayushi is old, and its secrets are deeply hidden. I suspect many of you would give your lives to discover some of those secrets. Some of you may do so yet—inadvertently, of course."

It seemed to many in the hall as if the grin on the Scorpion's pleasant mask actually grew wider.

Shoju continued. "Those secrets have cost the lives of Scorpions as well. Perhaps most famous of these lost souls is Bayushi Daijin, who plumbed the secrets of Uikku, the Serene Prophet. What he learned drove Daijin mad. He perished in the catacombs beneath the Bayushi palace. No one knew what he had discovered . . . until now."

A whisper swept through the crowd. Bayushi Tetsuo appeared at his daimyo's side and handed Shoju an ornate scroll case. The young lieutenant slipped back into the crowd and surreptitiously left the hall.

The Scorpion lord held the scroll up for all to see. "Behold the testament of Bayushi Daijin!" he said. He began to unroll it. Green sparks flew from the parchment.

The crowd gasped. Even the dozing emperor seemed to become more alert.

Seppun Bake edged forward to get a better look. "Can this be true?" he asked. "Why was I not told? Why was his majesty not told?"

"Would I send a lowly messenger to foretell the end of the world?" Shoju asked, his mask bathed in the scroll's green light. "For that is what this scroll contains, the prophecy of the end of the Emerald Empire."

A cry went up from the assemblage.

Near the front of the hall, Seppun Daiori stood and shouted, "Impossible!"

Shoju turned his gaze on the man, and Daiori almost thought he could see red eyes blazing behind the smiling mask. "Quite true, I assure you," Shoju said. He held the scroll so that the others could glimpse the burning green characters. The scroll fought to roll itself shut. Shoju would not allow it. He was the artifact's master.

"The empire is strong," Daiori replied, folding his arms across his chest, "as is its emperor. We are not impressed by your magic tricks, Scorpion. What could destroy the power of the clans? We are stronger now than we have ever been."

"Strong we may be," said Shoju, "but not invulnerable."

Upon his dais, the emperor stirred. He fixed Shoju with his eyes and sternly asked, "Who could have the power to threaten the empire?"

"Only one . . ." Shoju said, ". . . Fu Leng."

At the name of the Evil One, huge green sparks leapt from the scroll. They shot into the air and disappeared within the vault of the chamber. A gasp went up from the audience, and murmurs of fear filled the room.

"The Evil One is locked away forever in his accursed land," said Bake. "The Crab tends the wall diligently. He will never escape. He will never return to Rokugan."

"Is that what your teachings tell you, Master Bake?" asked Shoju. "If so, they are wrong." Shoju stared hard at the emperor's religious advisor. Bake sat down.

The Scorpion daimyo let the parchment roll itself shut. The green sparks died away. "Listen," he said, lowering the scroll and setting it on the floor before the emperor, "for this is the prophecy of the return of Fu Leng." He waited for silence to settle over the hall.

"The scroll tells us that even now, the Evil One begins his return to Rokugan," Shoju said, turning and looking at all the guests in the room. "Unless we act, we are living in the final days of the Emerald Empire!"

"Are you saying you have the power to prevent this catastrophe?" Seppun Daiori asked skeptically.

Shoju nodded. "Yes. But the price will be terrible."

"Surely there must be another way," Bake said. "If the price is so high, why pay it?"

"The scroll tells us why," Shoju said, pointing to where the artifact lay. "Long hours I have pored over it with the best minds in my service."

Bake huffed. "But not the best minds in the empire."

"Would you debate me on this matter?" Shoju asked, allowing his honeyed voice just a hint of sarcasm. "If so, pick up the scroll; read it. You will forgive me if I continue my story while you do."

Bake scurried forward and picked up the scroll. The move surprised Shoju only a little. The emperor's hunched advisor thirsted for knowledge almost as much as he desired the emperor's praise. Fortunately, even if Bake foiled the ancient magic, even if he deciphered the key portions of the scroll, it would be too late for him to stop what Shoju had planned. The Scorpion ignored the sycophant and continued.

"The language of the scroll is archaic, difficult, but the story it tells is plain. There are signs that the return of Fu Leng is imminent, and you must believe me when I say that all these signs have been fulfilled.

"His return will be terrible indeed. Clan shall set upon clan like famished dogs. The rivers will run red with blood. Cities, and even entire homelands, will burn. That won't be the worst of it, for though Fu Leng's mortal pawns will cause much chaos, not all of the Evil One's minions are human."

Shoju turned slowly, glancing around the chamber, making sure he held everyone's attention. Outside the castle the storm raged in cadence with the Scorpion's words, punctuating his remarks.

"Recently, I fought an ogre not a day's ride from Kyuden Bayushi, the very heart of the Scorpion lands. The beast slew four of my men before my retainer slew it. Its very presence so far from the Carpenter's Wall, from the supposed edge of Fu Leng's territory, proves that the barriers between our world and Jigoku have grown thin indeed.

"I do not blame the Crab. They have fought long and hard against the minions of the Evil One. Rather, I blame all of us, every noble lord and lady in this room, for ignoring the signs that are now so apparent. We became secure in the lives we've led for so long, lives of petty squabbling and clan skirmishes, lives where securing favor at court means more than personal responsibility."

"The Scorpion are not blameless in this!" someone—

Shoju thought it was one of the Moshis—called from the back of the room.

"I will shoulder our share of the blame," Shoju said. "Just as I will shoulder the responsibility for our part in preventing what is to come. What is to come will be like nothing any of us have ever lived through before. Imagine the worst battle, the worst war any of you have ever fought in. Then imagine the Evil One's demons fighting in the battle as well.

"The scroll of Uikku foretells it:

"They will pit clan against clan, fueling the hate that will burn us to bones. They will rape the land, slay our women and children, set fire to our fields, our farms, our homes. The sky will burn orange with the flames of Jigoku. The ground will be stained black with blood.

"Disfigured bodies will litter the landscape. Friends, clan mates, family, mothers, daughters, fathers, and sons—all of them will fall before the Evil One. They will be torn to pieces; they will lose arms, legs, heads. Their eyes will be gouged out, their remains desecrated by Fu Leng's creatures.

"But the dead will be the lucky ones. Those who live will be slaves for the Evil One. Their bodies will be burnt, abused, and corrupted. Boils will cover their flesh; their teeth will rot; their fingernails will be pulled out. Parts the Evil One has no use for will be fed to the dogs.

"By day the survivors will toil in the boiling pits of Jigoku. By night they will sleep in open graves. They will drink blood and eat human flesh.

"The warfare of Fu Leng will be eternal. It will never end so long as there is one living man or woman or child to fight for the Evil One's amusement. They will fight not until death, but until there is no more of them left to fight. They will fight without arms, without legs, without even teeth. The most noble lords and ladies will be reduced to nothing more than *eta*—the unclean.

"When they can fight no more, they will be tossed upon a mountain of similar wretches. Bereft of arms, legs, teeth, they will not even be able to burrow out of the obscene pile. Instead they will wait in unspeakable pain and fear, wait to be taken to the supper table of their captors."

Shoju spun toward the audience. With one swift move, he twisted his pleasant mask upside-down. Now the happy face became an angry, demonic visage.

The guests gasped and shrieked at the sight. Later some swore that Shoju's face itself had become that of a devil. Others said they saw images of blood-covered demons dancing obscenely around the room. A few swore that the very chamber itself became—for an instant—as black as the pits of Jigoku.

Bake dropped the scroll he had been trying to open. In the back of the hall, one of Miya Matsuo's daughters screamed and fainted dead away.

Outside, thunder crashed.

Shoju slowly turned his frightening countenance toward the emperor.

The Son of the Sun Goddess paled and shrank back.

Behind his frightful mask, Shoju smiled. "Picture all this in your minds," the Scorpion said quietly. "Remember it well. This is the fate that awaits all of us when Fu Leng returns. That day is near. All of you in this room will live long enough to regret it if we do nothing." He bowed low, almost touching his mask to the tatami mat. As he rose, he caught the eye of his wife, Kachiko. She smiled.

The emperor drew an ornate fan from somewhere within the folds of his kimono and fanned himself. He looked old, weak, uncertain. "Bayushi Shoju," he said, forcing his voice to remain calm, "you have said that this doom is upon us. Yet you have also said that we are living in our final days *unless we act*. Is there something we can do to avoid this terrible fate?"

Cries of, "Yes! Yes! What must we do?" echoed from around the room.

Shoju nodded gravely. The song of *Yashin* grew strong in his mind.

"Some say prophecy cannot be changed. And yet . . . and

yet . . . Shinsei teaches that we each hold our own destiny within us. Like him, I believe a man—a strong man—can control his fate." Shoju looked slowly around the room once more before finishing. "A single man," he said, "can change the world. The actions of one man alone could save the empire. This I believe with all my soul."

Hantei the 38th looked at him. "Are you this man, Bayushi Shoju? Could you save our kingdom?"

"I could, Majesty," Shoju said, "but to save the empire, I would have to contemplate the darkest deeds, commit the foulest acts. My people would have to sacrifice life and perhaps even honor to support me. No man could sacrifice more, yet I tell you now that, for the sake of the Emerald Throne, I would do it."

"Then you must do so," said Hantei.

Shoju took a step toward the emperor's dais, turning and speaking to the rest of the room.

"I have commission to act in your name?" Shoju asked Hantei the 38th. "To do whatever is necessary by any means possible?"

"You have it."

"I have your support both in this life and the next? I have your word that from this point on what I do I do only as an extension of you yourself? That my hand is your hand, that my sword is the sword of the emperor?"

The Scorpion had approached now to within just a few feet of the frightened emperor.

Hantei fought back the fear and steeled his face. "You are my strong right arm," he said. "What you do, you do by my leave—no, by my *command*. Bayushi Shoju, do what you must to save the empire."

"Then it is done," Shoju said.

In his mind the song of *Yashin* grew to a piercing shriek. All this time the blood sword had hovered at the Scorpion lord's back, invisible and undetectable. It had waited a thousand years, and now its moment had come.

Shoju looked into the aging emperor's eyes and quietly said, "Forgive me, my friend."

The Scorpion reached behind his back with both hands and seized the hilt of the bloodsword.

In that instant, the sword became visible to those in the hall. They gasped as they saw it, shimmering like heat rising over the desert, red like the setting sun. Thunder crashed and shook the very foundations of the castle.

Bayushi Shoju brought the sword down in one long, smooth stroke.

Yashin struck the emperor, cleaving Hantei from collarbone to hip. The Son of the Sun Goddess, leader of the Emerald Empire, fell to the floor, dead.

15 THE SCORPION COUP

Concern written across his face, Seppun
Ishikawa looked at Isawa Kaede. The Phoenix
Mistress of the Void had refused to return to
her own chambers. Instead she had chosen
the night air and the storm. They stood
together on one of the palace's roofed veran-
dahs, buffeted by the power of the tempest.
The rain soaked the hems of their kimonos.

"My lady," Ishikawa said, shouting to
make his voice heard above the thunder, "it's
crazy to be out on a night like this. Retire to
your chambers, I beg you."

Kaede shook her head. "No," she said. "No.
Something is wrong. I need fresh air to clear
my head."

"But the storm will only make your
malady worse," he said.

"I thought that at first," she said, "but now,
with clean air in my lungs, I wonder. . . ."

"Wonder what?"

"I wonder if I am indeed ill, or if something much more terrible is happening."

Lightning flashed again. Kaede glimpsed two figures dashing through the rain to one of the gardens' many gazebos. Even at a distance, she recognized the wardrobe of the royal heir, Hantei Sotorii.

"The weather is playing on your mind, I fear," Ishikawa said. "Come inside, please!"

A bolt of lightning struck the main tower of the keep. Crashing thunder shook the central palace to its foundations. The flash left Kaede and Ishikawa momentarily blind.

A great wailing burst from within the castle.

"What is it?" Ishikawa asked, peering through the storm toward the feasting hall.

Kaede's face had gone as white as rice paper. Though her senses had been dulled by poison, in her soul she knew what had happened.

"The emperor is dead," she said quietly, her voice sounding as though it came from very far away.

▲▲▲▲▲▲▲▲

Bayushi Tetsuo and Yogo Miyuki stood in a small high room in the Scorpion residence within the castle. They'd thrown back the shutters so that they could see the city outside. Rain pelted into the chamber, soaking the floor and the nearby rice paper screens.

"Stop pacing," Miyuki said peevishly. "You're making it difficult to concentrate."

"I just don't like leaving the lord in a time like this," Tetsuo said, stopping only momentarily before resuming his course around the room.

"We all have our parts to play," Miyuki said. "Shoju needs you to lead the forces in the castle; he needs me to coordinate our sorcerers. Rest assured, our lord will fulfill his destiny."

"I know he will, but . . ."

"Wait," said Miyuki, holding up one slender hand. A sly smile of satisfaction crept over her pretty face. "It is done," she said. "Go! I'll signal our forces outside the castle."

Tetsuo nodded, said, "Hai!" and dashed from the room.

Miyuki raised her arm and pointed it out the window. Her fingers traced intricate signs in the air. A ball of energy streaked from her fingertips and into the sky beyond the castle walls. When it reached the outskirts of the Forbidden City, it burst into a bright, white bolt of lightning.

The Scorpion forces outside the castle wall saw the signal and began their carefully planned assault.

"For the empire!" Miyuki said, her voice hardly more than a whisper.

▲▲▲▲▲▲▲▲

For a moment, silence reigned in the great feasting hall. Then a terrible, piteous wail arose from the emperor's guests.

"He's killed the emperor!" someone cried.

In an instant, Shoju's partisans sprang into action. They withdrew their smuggled weapons from their kimonos and laid about them, attacking anyone who posed a threat to their Scorpion lord.

Shoju himself slaughtered two *yojimbo* as the bodyguards raced—far too late—to protect the emperor. *Yashin* sang as it drank their souls.

Kachiko buried her hairpin in the neck of the nearest guard before he even knew what was happening.

In a moment the feasting hall was filled with men and women fighting for their lives. Amid the chaos strode the lord of the Scorpions—calm, controlled, supremely confident.

The revolution spread out from his single sword strike. It filled the great hall and swept beyond the palace.

Even now, Shoju's samurai and ninja were sneaking

through the water tunnels beneath the Imperial Precincts. Soon, they would spring out and take the Forbidden City.

Simultaneously, his samurai outside the enchanted walls were throwing off their false faces. Many had come to Otosan Uchi disguised as peasants. Now they showed their true colors—Scorpion colors. The outer city would soon be theirs.

The Emerald Guardsmen would not be able to stop them. Moments ago, the guards had been relaxing at Scorpion-controlled tea houses. Now they were dying at the hands of Kachiko's ninja-ko geisha.

Most importantly, at this very moment, Junzo, Bantaro, and their men were opening the city's enchanted gates. The shugenjas' subtle spells had subverted the Forbidden City's walls. Unknown to the loyalists that manned them, the city's defenses were now under Scorpion control.

Soon the city would belong to Shoju.

He whirled in the air and split the man nearest him in two. The tattoo on the Scorpion's lame arm burned with lusty fire. *Yashin* sang its glorious song of blood. Behind his mask, a cruel smile drew across the Scorpion lord's face. Victory was close at hand.

▲▲▲▲▲▲▲▲

Seppun Daiori raised himself from the tatami. He'd been thrust to the floor in the initial fight and, until now, had had no room to stand. As he tried to get up, the wound in his side— the one he'd gotten in the battle that killed his brother—flared up again. It had never healed properly. Now it felt as though a knife stuck under his ribs. He grimaced in pain and groped for something to hang onto. He found an offered hand.

Daiori looked up and saw Doji Shizue, pale and shaking with fright. "All is lost! Lost!" she whispered plaintively.

"No," Daiori grunted. She helped him to his feet. "We may yet escape—live to fight another day."

He touched the painted panel behind them. It slid open, revealing a short hallway beyond. "Come," he said, entering the passage and pulling the lame girl after him.

As they ran, Doji Shizue wept.

▲▲▲▲▲▲▲▲

Bayushi Aramoro sat on a lacquered seat near the door to the room. He frowned beneath his mask. It galled him to have to sit while so many were fighting for the future of the empire. It galled the young man Aramoro was protecting as well.

"Why did they bring me if they won't let me fight?" Bayushi Dairu asked.

"Your mother is concerned about your safety," Aramoro said. "And your father—my brother—is wise enough to know that a battle is at its most dangerous in the chaotic opening moments."

"Yes, yes, I know all that. But wouldn't you rather be fighting?" Daimu drew his katana and made a few practice cuts in the air.

Behind his mask, Aramoro smiled. "Of course I would." He fingered the hilt of his sword. "But there'll be enough fighting—enough blood—for everyone by the time this is over. You mark my words."

Aramoro didn't usually like speaking. He was a solitary man, self-possessed and focused on his mission—the perfect ninja. Somehow, his nephew always drew the speech maker out of him.

"But I—" Dairu began

A hand signal from his uncle silenced him.

Shadows fell on the fusuma walls of the room. The figures of samurai danced on the rice paper. Their voices could be heard without.

". . . Killed the emperor!" one cried. "Damned traitors!"

said another. "Don't stand around," said a third. "Kill them all! Let's go!"

With that, the lead man threw back the sliding door to the Scorpion Heir's chambers. Seven samurai charged into the room, their katanas raised high.

The face of the first hit the floor before he had crossed the threshold; his head was no longer attached to his body.

The next three muscled their way inside. Aramoro killed two with swift strokes from shoulder to hip. The third got past the master of ninjutsu.

Dairu ran his sword through the samurai's neck. He fell gurgling to the floor. Dairu felt queasy. He'd never killed a man before.

The fifth attacker proved more worthy than the first four. He was a large, wiry samurai with red hair and a long mustache. Rather than a sword, he wielded a *tetsubo*, a long iron staff. Using the staff to parry, he bore forward, warding off Aramoro's attacks as he came.

The ninja master backed into his nephew. That nearly proved his undoing. The samurai clouted him on the side of the head. Aramoro reeled and fell. The big man whirled his staff and connected with Dairu, hurling him backward.

Before the samurai could finish Dairu, Aramoro pulled a weighted chain from within his robes. He flung the weight at their attacker. The chain wrapped around the man's right wrist. Aramoro pulled.

The samurai staggered and fell forward. Aramoro's sword was waiting. It ran him through the chest. Though dying, the samurai wasn't done. Flailing blindly, he fell full-force on Aramoro. The chain on the samurai's wrist entangled them both. Together they crashed to the floor.

The two remaining samurai stormed into the room, intending to finish off the fallen Scorpions. Dairu and Aramoro struggled up as the samurai raised their katanas.

The swords never descended. The attackers suddenly stood still, confusion written across their faces. Blood leaked from the mouth of one and the nose of the other. They collapsed dead on the floor.

Behind them stood Bayushi Tetsuo, his sword dripping.

Tetsuo smiled at his cousins. "What are you two waiting for?" he asked. "Come join the fight."

▲▲▲▲▲▲▲▲

"The throne room. We must get to the throne room," Seppun Daiori said. He pulled Doji Shizue behind him as he ran through the palace's twisting corridors.

The girl staggered. Her crippled leg made it nearly impossible for her to keep up. Tears streamed down her pretty face. Her long white hair trailed out behind her like a cape, billowing as they ran.

"W-why the throne room?" she asked.

"Because if there are any loyalists left to make a stand," Daiori said, "that is where they shall make it. Perhaps the heir is there as well."

▲▲▲▲▲▲▲▲

The throne room was on Shoju's mind, too. He thrust *Yashin* through the belly of a samurai. The bloodsword sang as it drank the man's soul. The Scorpion lord looked around.

Resistance had died quickly in the great hall, along with many of the revelers. Moshi Seji knelt in the center of the floor, surrounded by Scorpion guards. On his lap, he cradled his dead twin, Taro.

Miya Matsuo, one of the emperor's favorite courtiers, lay dead near his lord. Two of Matsuo's daughters cowered by the door. The third, Shoju reminded himself, had left with the Hantei whelp.

Miya Satoshi, the son of the herald, still struggled against

Shoju's men. His father, Yoto, lay where he sat during the feast. Miya Yoto had collapsed soon after the fighting broke out. From this distance, Shoju couldn't tell whether the old man was dead or alive.

All of the emperor's guards had died fighting. They fought bravely, as true samurai. Shoju felt glad the Emerald Champion had not been there to lead them this evening.

Looking around, Shoju noticed with pride that few of the fatalities in the room were Scorpions.

Most of the loyalists hadn't fought at all. Rather, they had quickly bowed their heads in surrender. Unarmed and outnumbered, they knew they were no match for the Scorpion's host.

Among the prisoners were Sorai, the troublemaker, and Bake, the emperor's toady. The two men stood quietly among the other captives, biding their time. Shoju suspected they were waiting to see how the conflict ended before choosing sides.

When the fighting broke out, Bake had clutched the scroll of Daijin to his breast—apparently willing to shield the artifact with his life. He had been lucky that no one saw fit to kill him for it.

Shoju walked to where Bake stood and held out his hand. Reluctantly, Bake handed him the scroll. Shoju had one of his people hurry it into safekeeping.

At a signal from their master, Shoju's men began to herd captives into one corner of the room, away from the doors and secret exits. As the group passed Shoju, Moshi Seji cried out and lunged for the Scorpion daimyo.

Shoju spun, *Yashin* screaming in his mind. He saw the face of the doomed youth clearly and twisted the sword in his hand. *Yashin*'s pommel crashed down atop Seji's head. The boy slumped to the floor, unconscious.

The song of the sword grew angry. Shoju ignored it. The sword was not his master. There had been enough killing here.

Shoju's men dragged Seji away with the others.

The Scorpion lord turned toward his wife.

Kachiko smiled back at him.

"Any unaccounted for?" he asked.

"Daiori and the girl, Shizue," she replied. "Plus those who left before your speech."

The Scorpion frowned. "Time enough to round them all up," he said. He pointed to one of his samurai and said, "See that the prisoners do not escape. Kill anyone who tries."

The man clicked his heels, bowed, and said, "Hai!"

Shoju turned to his wife. "Find your handmaidens and check on the situation outside. Report to me as soon as possible."

Kachiko nodded and disappeared through a nearby sliding panel.

"Come," Shoju said, gesturing to a number of his followers. "Our destiny lies in the throne room." The group broke off from their fellows and followed the Scorpion as he left the great hall. The moans of the wounded and dying trailed Shoju as he went. Their cries were drowned out by the song of *Yashin*, now safely sheathed at the daimyo's side.

The small band wound their way through the castle's twisting corridors. En route, they encountered Shoju's brother, Aramoro, along with Dairu and Tetsuo. All three sported small cuts and bruises, and their fine clothes had been stained with blood. None appeared to be seriously injured. Shoju nodded at them, and they fell into step with his company.

"The Hantei heir?" he asked.

Tetsuo shook his head. "No one has seen the boy since early in the evening."

"Our plan fails if he lives!" Shoju snarled. "Aramoro, see to it!"

The ninja master bowed. "Hai, great lord." He stepped into a side corridor and quickly vanished from sight.

▲▲▲▲▲▲▲▲

A short distance ahead, Seppun Daiori heard the host of the Scorpion coming. He pushed open the iron door to the throne room. His heart fell.

There was no one inside. No one else had made it this far. There was no one left to resist the coup.

He looked at Shizue's wet, fear-filled eyes.

If anything were to be done, Daiori would have to be the one to do it.

His stomach clenched tight. The wound in his side flared to life. He felt as if he were back on the battlefield where his brother had died.

Daiori never wanted the leadership of his clan, but it had been thrust upon him. Only later did he discover that a Lion partisan had planned his brother's death so that Daiori would become daimyo. Daiori had been in that man's grip ever since. Every day he lived in fear. Had it not been for his young son— whose mother was long dead—he might have given it all up. There were days when life was just too much to bear. Even the opium didn't help.

He was an unworthy man.

Now the fate of the empire rested with him. If he could just keep the Scorpion from the throne, perhaps the day could still be won. He turned to Doji Shizue.

"Go," he said. "Hide yourself. Live. No matter what. Live to tell what transpired here."

She looked at him with tearful, questioning eyes. "But . . ."

"There is no time!" Daiori insisted. He thrust her back through the iron door into the throne room and closed it behind her. With luck she would be able to escape. Seppun Daiori braced himself, ready to meet his destiny.

Destiny arrived in the form of Bayushi Shoju. A small band of samurai, including Dairu and Tetsuo, strode up the corridor with him. All were armed to the teeth.

Daiori assumed a defensive stance. His old wound burned like fire. "You shall not pass," he said. "The throne will not be yours."

Shoju paced forward, his gait graceful and steeped in power, like that of a great cat. "Step aside," the Scorpion daimyo commanded.

Seppun Daiori shook his head. "Never. I challenge you, Bayushi Shoju."

Behind his mask, the Scorpion's eyes narrowed. "You have no weapon," he said coldly. "Step aside."

"Give me a sword to defend my honor."

Shoju turned to one of his retainers and nodded. The man stepped forward and proffered his katana to the late emperor's military advisor. Daiori bowed and took it. He drew the weapon.

The air hummed as Shoju unsheathed *Yashin*. He looked into Daiori's eyes and said, "Surrender, and you will be spared."

Even the power of the Bayushi mask failed to sway his opponent.

Daiori's reply was but a whisper: "Never."

▲▲▲▲▲▲▲▲

Lightning flashed again. An explosion went off near the outer wall of the Forbidden City. Dark figures appeared atop the castle's bastions.

"It's started!" Kaede cried. "Merciful Shinsei! How could I *not* have seen!"

"What's started?" Ishikawa asked. "What's going on?" Bile rose in his gut. He fought to control his fear and confusion.

"Revolution!" she said, looking about in near panic. "The Scorpion is trying to seize the Emerald Throne!"

"We must stop him," Ishikawa said. His hand went to the hilt of his sword.

Kaede placed her dainty fingers on his wrist before he could draw. "No," she said, determination replacing the fear in her voice. "We must protect the heir."

"But where to find him?" Ishikawa cursed. "The young fool! He could be anywhere!"

"No," Kaede said calmly. "I saw him just moments ago in the garden. Come! We must act quickly."

▲▲▲▲▲▲▲▲▲

With wide, graceful strides, Shoju approached his opponent. His garments moved deceptively, making anticipation difficult for the Scorpion's enemy. The Master of Secrets held the bloodsword wide and low in his left hand. His right hand was held open before him, as if in a welcoming gesture.

Behind him, the Scorpion lord could hear the anxious breathing of his companions—Dairu and Tetsuo foremost among them. The song of the bloodsword grew louder.

Daiori shifted position, always careful to keep his back to the closed throne room door. He wanted to give Shizue as much time as possible to escape.

The Scorpion closed in, advancing in a deadly dance. He brought the sword up and held it in both hands, his arms cocked so that the blade ran parallel to his face. From behind the demon mask he said one word: "Come."

With a cry of defiance, Daiori charged forward. He aimed his blow at the Scorpion's breast. Shoju easily parried it. The Master of Secrets danced aside and sliced at his opponent's back. The blade of *Yashin* cut through Daiori's kimono and drew blood, but it did not strike home.

Daiori cried in pain and staggered forward. He turned just in time to see Shoju glide sideways, opening his stance into the welcoming gesture once more.

"Surrender!" the Scorpion said.

Daiori's reply was an inarticulate roar. He charged, cutting at the Scorpion's waist.

Shoju spun away and thrust his sword backward, under his arm, as if he were striking with the butt of a staff. The point of *Yashin* found its mark.

The blade pierced Daiori's back between the ribs. It struck

deep. The Seppun daimyo gasped and slumped to his knees. Shoju yanked his sword free and turned in time to see his opponent fall face first to the floor.

The borrowed blade slipped from Daiori's hands. It skidded across the wooden surface, coming to rest against the great doors of the throne room. A low moan escaped Daiori's mouth.

Shoju sheathed his blade and stepped forward. He knelt and gently turned the dying man over. "You fought well," the Scorpion said.

"You are the master of lies," Daiori said, blood trickling from his lips. "At least I won't live to see you take the throne."

Behind his mask, Shoju frowned. "You heard my tale. Can you not see the justice of my cause?"

"Ambition has blinded you, Scorpion lord. A man as steeped in bloodshed as you would never see another way. You have doomed all of us as surely as you have doomed yourself."

Shoju stood. "The blood I have shed," he said, "has always been to serve the empire."

"And whom do you serve now, Master of Secrets?"

Before Shoju could answer, a fit of coughing seized Daiori. Blood bubbled from his mouth. The dying man fixed his eyes on the Scorpion and said, "Promise you will not slaughter my son."

The Scorpion nodded. "You were a noble opponent. I will vouchsafe him from the city. He will be taken to a place of safety."

"Do you swear?" Daiori said, pain washing over his face.

"I swear."

"T-tell him his father fought bravely," the Seppun daimyo said, and then he died.

Shoju looked at the corpse resting at his feet. "I will," he said. He turned to the throne room doors.

▲▲▲▲▲▲▲▲

Inside the throne room, Doji Shizue heard all that had taken place. She knew her time was running out. Try as she might, she could not find the secret panel she knew was hidden in the throne room. Her carefully ordered thoughts had become frantic.

"Where is it?"

▲▲▲▲▲▲▲▲

Hantei Sotorii stepped outside the gazebo to see what was happening. Lightning flashed all around, and he could hear explosions in the distance.

"What's going on?" Yumika asked, pulling her kimono around her body and following him out into the rain.

Sotorii shook his head. "I don't know," he said. His young eyes scanned the garden before him. The river ran nearby, but its serene music was completely smothered by the fury of the storm.

In a sudden flash of lightning, Sotorii saw something that made his blood run cold. A dark shape rose out of the river just a few yards away. He knew only one word for the shape, a word he'd heard in whispered legends since he was a boy.

"Ninja!" he gasped.

The girl shrieked.

The black-garbed figure noticed the young lovers. He drew his sword and charged.

Sotorii backed away, pushing the girl before him as he went. The ninja aimed his sword at the Hantei heir's neck. Sotorii ducked.

Instead of a victim, the blade of the *ninjato* struck one of the gazebo's pillars and stuck.

Sotorii and Yumika turned and ran for the castle.

For a moment, the ninja tried to yank his blade from the wood. Then he reached into a fold of his billowing black costume and pulled forth a shuriken.

The ninja flicked his wrist. The small, star-shaped dagger flew through the air. One point lodged in the calf of Sotorii.

The royal heir screamed and fell to the ground. Yumika stopped and looked at the boy, unsure what to do.

The ninja retrieved his sword and charged once more.

Yumika took Sotorii's hand and tried to pull him to his feet. As he struggled to rise, Sotorii looked back over his shoulder and saw his death closing in.

The ninja raised his sword high. The blade never fell.

Another figure stepped out of the darkness. His blade met the ninja's and parried. With a twist, the larger sword flipped the ninjato from the hands of its master. The ninja's sword flew through the air and landed beside a goldfish pond.

In a flash of lightning, Sotorii recognized his savior: Seppun Ishikawa.

The captain of the guard cut at the ninja's midsection, but the lithe figure hopped back, out of harm's way. Ishikawa advanced. The ninja seemed made of darkness itself. When next the samurai lunged, the ninja had already darted away.

Reappearing from the shadows, the black-garbed assassin reached into the folds of his robes once more.

"Shuriken! He has shuriken!" Sotorii gasped, holding the wound in his leg.

Ishikawa's face grew grim, and he assumed a defensive posture.

The ninja drew out a throwing dart with each hand. Before he could throw them, though, the ninja's whole body suddenly jerked, like a puppet on a string. He slumped to the ground and moved no more.

Ishikawa glanced sideways to see Kaede standing nearby, concentrating. She let out a long, slow breath and brought her outstretched arms to her bosom, drawing the deadly Void magic back inside herself.

"Remind me never to get you angry," Ishikawa said to her.

Kaede ignored him and went to the heir. "Are you all right?" she asked the boy.

"No, I'm not all right!" Sotorii snapped. "What's going on here? We demand to know!"

"Your father is dead," Ishikawa said testily. "The Emerald Throne is yours, if you can convince the Scorpion to give it back to you."

Sotorii staggered as if he had been struck. He sat down abruptly. "Y-you're sure?"

"I felt it," Kaede said. "I *know* it. The city is under siege by Scorpion forces."

"B-but why . . . ?" the boy asked. He appeared to be on the verge of tears.

"Ask the Scorpion your riddles if you like," said Ishikawa. He knelt beside the ninja and pulled off the assassin's black mask. Behind the hood he found a boy, hardly older than the heir. The boy ninja was dead. "You did your job well, Lady Isawa," Ishikawa said.

"Our job now is to save the heir," Kaede replied. "If we do not escape the castle, he will surely be killed."

"Desert the castle?" Sotorii asked, the shock still sinking in.

"You must," Kaede said. "The Scorpion will not rest until you are dead."

"B-but where will I go?"

"Your father has many supporters," Ishikawa said. "Even Bayushi Shoju cannot kill them all. First, we must get out of here. Every moment we linger is another moment your life— the life of the empire—is in peril."

"But they will know I'm not dead!" the boy emperor said. "You said they wouldn't stop coming after me. Where can I hide from the Master of Secrets?"

"Oh, Sotorii," Miya Yumika cried, throwing her girlish arms around the boy's neck. "We are doomed!"

Ishikawa nodded and looked grim. "The boy has a point," he said. "So long as he lives, the Scorpion will track him down. I, for one, doubt our ability to protect him."

"Where are the ones who should have protected my father? Why did our best samurai fail to save him?" Sotorii asked angrily, wiping tears away from his face. He removed Yumika's arms from his shoulders.

"I assume they are dead, Your Majesty," Ishikawa said. "And we may soon join them."

"Not necessarily," said Kaede. The excitement had cleared Kachiko's poisons from her mind. "If we could convince the Scorpion that our young Hantei is dead, we could buy ourselves time."

Ishikawa looked at the corpse of the ninja. "That boy," he said, "that ninja, is nearly the same size as Sotorii. If we were to mutilate the body . . ."

"No," Kaede said. "There is a better way." She stepped toward the body and cleared her mind. She let the power of the Void fill her once more as she stooped beside the corpse.

Kaede laid her hands on the face of the dead boy. Gradually, the features flowed and changed until the ninja resembled the heir to the throne. She lingered a few moments more, hiding the effects of the spell and making sure they would not fade.

Hantei the 39th, Ishikawa, and Yumika stood slack-jawed.

"Will it fool them, do you think?" Ishikawa asked.

The Mistress of the Void nodded. "It has a chance, especially amid this chaos. I've made the spell hard to detect, though probably Yogo Junzo could discover it."

"We'll have to dress the corpse in the heir's clothes," said Ishikawa.

"M-my clothes?" said Sotorii.

"Be quick about it!" Ishikawa barked. "The Scorpion won't give us all night." He took off his kimono and handed it to the new emperor.

Hantei quickly began to undress. Yumika walked tentatively to Kaede.

"What about me?" she asked. "People saw the heir leave the feasting hall with me."

"You could run back to the hall," Kaede said. "Say you fled when the ninja attacked."

"But . . . but that would disgrace my family. Couldn't I go with you?"

"If you did, people would wonder what had happened to you," Ishikawa said. "It would make our ruse more difficult. We cannot take any chances while traveling with the heir."

"I could lay a spell on your mind," said Kaede, "erase your memory of what happened after the attack."

Sotorii had finished removing his robes and dressing in Ishikawa's outer kimono. He handed his old clothes to the captain of the guard. "If the Scorpion sorcerers question her, they will discover your spell."

"Most likely," Kaede conceded.

"Then I see no other option," Sotorii said, turning suddenly cold. "Yumika must sacrifice her life for me."

Ishikawa stopped dressing the ninja's body and glared at the heir. Kaede and Yumika were doing the same.

"Your Majesty," Kaede said, "surely there is a better way—"

"You and Ishikawa are prepared to sacrifice your lives for mine," the young Hantei said. "Everyone loyal to me should be willing to do the same. Finding her body next to the body you've made to look like mine will reinforce our story."

"That's true, but . . ." Ishikawa began.

The new emperor turned to Yumika and looked her in the eyes. She began to cry again. "Will you do it, Yumika?" he asked. "Do you love your emperor?"

"I . . . I do, but . . ." she said, tears streaming down her face.

"Emperor Hantei, don't . . ." Kaede said, stepping forward.

Yumika waved her away. "*Iie!* No," she said, wiping back tears. "My young lord is right. I will give myself up for him." She turned to Sotorii and said, "But promise me, Emperor Hantei . . . promise me you will look after my father and sisters."

"I will," he said.

"Then, one last thing I ask."

"Name it."

"A kiss," Yumika said. "One last time."

"Granted," said the boy emperor. He took her in his arms, embraced her, and kissed her long upon the lips.

When they parted, Ishikawa stepped forward. "I will have to use the ninja's sword to do it," he said. Already he had recovered the weapon from where it lay.

Kaede said, "Ishikawa—"

"The emperor is right," said the captain of the guard. "Her life may buy us the time we need."

Isawa Kaede stepped forward and kissed the girl on the cheek. "I'm sorry," the Mistress of the Void said softly.

"I . . . I shall be brave," Yumika said, sniffing back tears. "Come morning, I will be with my mother in paradise."

Kaede stepped back.

Ishikawa addressed the girl. "I've run this sword through the body of the ninja, to appear he—that is, *the heir*—was killed with it," he said. "Thank you for your sacrifice, Yumika-san. I'm sorry it is necessary."

"Please," the girl said. "Do it swiftly." She held her arms rigidly at her sides, her fists clenched so tightly that her fingers went white.

"I promise you," said Ishikawa, "there will be no pain." As he said it, he ran the sword cleanly through her heart. He withdrew the weapon.

Yumika's body slumped softly to the ground. The rain washed over her face, carrying away the trickle of blood that leaked from her mouth.

"Come!" the young emperor said. "We can waste no more time."

"We must take the ninja's sword and clothes with us," Ishikawa said, gathering the things, "and hope the rain will erase the traces of our passage."

"I know a secret way out of the gardens," said Kaede. "Follow me."

The others trailed after the Mistress of the Void. As she

went, Kaede couldn't help stealing one last look back at the girl who had died to save the heir to the Emerald Throne.

⋏⋏⋏⋏⋏⋏⋏⋏

Doji Shizue found the secret panel and slipped through, just as Bayushi Shoju entered the throne room. Shizue sealed the panel tightly behind her, realizing only then that the small chamber had no other exit. She was trapped.

Her heart pounded so loudly, Shizue feared it would betray her to the Scorpion.

Beyond a thin panel of wood, the emperor's killer stalked proudly about the throne room.

⋏⋏⋏⋏⋏⋏⋏⋏

Shoju passed the threshold of the great iron doors and drank in the sight of the throne room. The chamber was beautiful, almost enough to take the Scorpion's breath away.

Golden sunbursts spangled the high-vaulted ceiling. Each sun was painted in a small coffer on an azure, star-flecked background. Great wooden beams supported the curved ceiling.

The walls of the hall were made of wood panel and plaster. Painted scenes of natural splendor decorated the walls: stately mountains, winding rivers, crashing waterfalls, twisted trees. These panels covered the solid stone of the castle's foundations. Beauty hadn't compromised security.

Two wings of the room had been set aside for the emperor's audience. Here the advisors would sit, awaiting their master's pleasure. Currently the smooth wooden floors sat empty.

On the far side of the room was a low platform, and on the platform sat the Emerald Throne—the only piece of furniture in the room. The throne had a low seat and a high back. It was made entirely of carved jade. Dragons and other mythical beasts twined themselves lovingly over every surface of the imperial chair.

Shoju walked to the throne and seated himself on it. The great carved seat felt uncomfortable.

"It is with no great pleasure that I do this," he said to his son and Tetsuo. His lame arm throbbed, and Shoju felt as though the months of planning, the battle, the bloodshed, had drained his very life away.

"What next, Father?" Dairu asked.

"What next?" Shoju replied. "What next, indeed?" He seemed more weary than either Dairu or Tetsuo had ever seen him before.

"Surely next we consolidate our position," Tetsuo said. "Secure the city. Send representatives to the other clans to explain our position."

"Of course," the Scorpion lord said, glad—not for the first time—that his people could not see his face behind the mask. They would have seen a face plagued by uncertainty and the terrible cost of his actions. Even the song of *Yashin* had grown softer in his mind. Shoju said a silent prayer and gathered himself.

"Tetsuo," he said, "see that the palace is secure. Once it is, bring the noble hostages before me. Include at least one representative of each of the six other major clans. Any minute now, Kachiko should have a report on the fighting outside the castle."

"I am here, my lord," Bayushi Kachiko said, gliding into the throne room as if she owned it. She walked the short distance to the throne and stood at her husband's left elbow.

"We have secured the outer walls. The inner enchanted wall will soon be completely under control as well," she said. "There is still fighting, especially among our people and the Emerald Guard, but I have no doubt it will be quelled soon. Most of the embassies have already fallen to our forces." Here Kachiko paused and smiled at her husband. "By morning the city will be ours," she said proudly.

A "hurrah!" went up from the small band of Scorpions.

Shoju quieted them by raising one finger. "We do this out of necessity," he reminded them. "Not for personal gain or aggrandizement. Our plan is necessary for the safety of all Rokugan."

He looked at Tetsuo, who had lingered in the room to hear Kachiko's report. "Well?" he said.

Tetsuo bowed and hurried off.

The Scorpion lord turned to his son. "Find your uncle," he said. "If we don't kill the heir, our plan is undone."

"Hai!" Dairu said, bowing and turning to go. Before he could leave the chamber, Bayushi Aramoro entered.

"Great Lord, I have found the heir," Aramoro said. "He is dead."

Shoju leaned forward on the throne. "You're sure?" he asked.

"I saw the corpse myself. He was in the garden with a girl. One of our ninja must have taken them by surprise. Their bodies both show the same, telltale cuts."

"Where is the person who killed them?" Shoju asked.

"I do not know," Aramoro said. "Likely he or she didn't know who they were. In the dark, the Hantei heir could have been any courtier out for an intimate rendezvous."

Shoju slumped into the Emerald Throne.

"Then it is over," he said wearily. "We have won."

He closed his eyes. The throne felt cold and hard against his back. The seat's ornate carvings dug into his lame shoulder. The fires of exhaustion ran up and down his spine. Images of blood and battle plagued him. That part of Shoju's nightmare, at least, had come true.

16 POISON

Hatsuko looked at the pale face of her lover and wept until she could barely see.

Toturi was handsome. So handsome, even now—even as he lay still upon their bed in the small cabin Aki had provided for the rendezvous.

How happy he had been when Hatsuko told him of the place. How thrilled that, perhaps, his dreams were finally coming true.

They had gone to the cabin immediately when he came to see her. He had marveled at the tiny house's beauty and simplicity, declaring it "perfect." They made love on the plain wooden floor.

They lingered there in the forest, not far from the spot Toturi had named Hatsuko Falls. It seemed they might stay in that place for all eternity.

Such a serene and beautiful place, even now, even with Toturi lying so still.

Toturi had never wanted to leave. Nor did Hatsuko. This was the place where they were meant to be together. This was the time they had together. She knew things would never be so perfect for them again. This was *their* moment, as Aki had told the young geisha.

Soon, very soon, the moment would pass.

Hatsuko had not worked up the nerve to use the blue gem on the first day. Then she had been swept up in the moment, in Toturi's happiness, in the glory of their love.

Nor had she been able to brew the poison on the second day. That day they walked in the forest, they talked, they laughed. They bathed naked in the pool below Hatsuko Falls. At long last, Toturi had seen her without her white geisha makeup.

He told her the paint didn't matter, but without it, Hatsuko felt as if part of her identity—her soul—had slipped away. She found she didn't know who she was anymore. Her relationship to him encompassed her entire world.

Toturi seemed to like that; but it made Hatsuko more afraid than ever.

That realization had given her the strength to do what she needed to do on the third day. Also, Toturi planned to leave her on the next morning, returning to Otosan Uchi and his fiancée—a woman Hatsuko would never meet, could never know.

The geisha wondered what the woman, Isawa Kaede, was really like. Was she as beautiful and terrible as Aki had described? Could she really burn a man for all eternity?

Hatsuko determined that the Phoenix would not burn Akodo Toturi.

On the evening of the third day, Hatsuko slipped the poison out of the blue gem and into Toturi's tea. The remainder she reserved for herself.

Toturi drank the tea, laughing and joking, as happy as she'd ever seen him in his life.

What a perfect moment for life to end, Hatsuko thought.

She stood to brew the poison for herself. The time was right. The perfect moment had come.

As she got to her feet, a strange look came over Toturi's face. He stared into space as if he didn't see her, as though he were in a completely different world—just as he had looked that first day at the falls.

Then his mouth and eyes opened wide. "Hatsuko," he said—the name both plea and accusation.

She reached for him. His body tumbled to the floor.

"Toturi!" she cried, tears welling up in her eyes and pouring down her face like rain. She held him, kissed his face, his mouth. Already, he had grown terribly cold.

As cold as he was now, much later, as he lay upon their bed where Hatsuko had brought him, the bed where they had made love earlier that day and all the night before.

So cold. So still.

In the end she had not been able to do it. The blue amulet hung around her neck, ready for her to act, but she had not been able to. The gem still held a large measure of its poison, more than enough for one—but not enough for two.

Hatsuko wondered, through her tear-stained thoughts, if she had done the right thing.

If half the poison was enough to kill a man, or woman, surely one quarter was too little to do so.

Surely there was no poison that powerful. Surely cutting the dose in half would cause only sleep—prolonged, peaceful sleep. Sleep for a week, or a month, or perhaps more.

Time in which Hatsuko might find the courage to finish the job—prolonging the perfect moment forever. Time in which the Fortunes might deliver the lovers from the terrible fate that descended on them. If the Fortunes had such plans, they had—so far—not seen fit to share them with Hatsuko.

So she wept. Piteously. Night and day. Unsure of herself, unsure of her love, unsure what to do.

She had cut the lethal dose in half before giving it to her

lover, but she had never considered what might happen after that—what she would do now.

Perhaps she would stay in the cabin and tend Toturi forever as he slept. No. Sooner or later, she would be forced to finish the job.

If she had not finished him already.

He lay there beside her, so still, so cold. Her tears splashed his face like a tiny waterfall.

If half the poison would kill a man, what would one quarter do?

How much was too much?

17 THE WAY OF THE UNICORN

Shinjo Yokatsu reigned in his magnificent horse and tossed his black hair in the morning sun. The horse snorted and pawed the ground with its powerful hooves.

The champion of the Unicorn clan surveyed his troops and smiled. Even this early in the day, they had mustered out quickly, formed up precisely. They were fine men and women, every one of them.

Despite months of unannounced drilling, they had not grown lax in their performance. Though they had never been given a reason for the maneuvers, they had not questioned their lord and master. This was what it meant to be samurai.

Now, two weeks into the current set of drills, Shinjo Yokatsu looked at his troops and felt proud. Over the last fortnight, the hooves of Unicorn horses had churned the soil of the land near Toshi Sani Kanemochi Kaeru into a rich loam. His army was as ready as it ever would be.

The question remained, did the army *need* to be ready?

The other clans had speculated about the meaning of these drills ever since Yokatsu had first ordered them. People didn't believe the maneuvers were just practice. If they were, why were they so elaborate? Why the supply trains? Why the siege equipment?

Most people believed the Unicorn were getting ready to fight, but no one knew whom. Popular opinion said the clan was making ready to take sides in the Crane-Lion dispute, but who knew on which side the Unicorn would ally?

Others thought the Unicorn would march to the lands of the Crab, either to bolster the defenses against the Shadow-lands or to quell an uprising by Hida Kisada, the Crab leader. Rumors abounded that the Crab was displeased with the emperor—though few believed he would strike against the Emerald Throne.

A third opinion said the Unicorn prepared to make war on their own behalf, to expand their territory. Holding their drills just outside their recognized boundaries did little to dissuade this rumor.

Of all those in the field that day, only Yokatsu himself knew the truth. He had heard the prophecies of the Unicorn shugenja. He had listened to the whispers coming from the dark parts of the Unicorn cities. He alone had noticed the movements of peasants throughout the empire—peasants whom Yokatsu knew to be pawns of the Scorpion.

Though he knew the Scorpion was secretly mobilizing, Yokatsu could not guess the intent of the Master of Secrets.

So he sat on his tall steed that afternoon, watching the southern sky. A massive thunderstorm rolled out of the Spine of the World Mountains and blew toward Otosan Uchi. Yokatsu wondered what, if anything, that storm might mean.

By morning, he knew.

In the hours just before dawn, news of the Scorpion's coup

spread like wildfire. Shinjo Mariko, a young shugenja, woke the lord with the news.

"The emperor is dead," she said, out of breath from running. "The Scorpion are taking control of Otosan Uchi. Our people got the word out, but then communications went silent."

Yokatsu cursed under his breath. "Sound the alarm! Form up the troops! We leave immediately! Tell my generals there is no time to waste!"

Fifteen minutes later, Yokatsu was dressed and seated on his horse. He wheeled the animal around and addressed the troops, ready to march.

"What man may know his own destiny?" he shouted. "This is the moment we feared, the moment we prayed would never come. The emperor is dead and the usurper, Bayushi Shoju, sits on the Emerald Throne. Will we stand for it?"

As one, the assembled Unicorn host raised its weapons and cried, "IIE! NEVER!"

"Will you follow me, though fire and death and all the assembled armies of the other clans may stand in our way?" Yokatsu asked.

"HAI!" came the unanimous reply.

The Unicorn Champion raised his katana high. "Then ride like the wind!" he said. "To Otosan Uchi! Let no one bar our way!"

The Unicorn army roared with approval. Yokatsu wheeled his horse and galloped off toward the capital. His army fell in behind him and did the same.

⋀⋀⋀⋀⋀⋀⋀⋀

Late the second night after the coup, Dairu found Tetsuo atop one of the outer walls of Otosan Uchi. Beyond the battlements, great bonfires and torches painted the waning darkness red and orange. The Scorpion heir crept toward his cousin along the wall.

"Get down!" Tetsuo hissed.

Dairu crouched just in time. An arrow flew over his head, barely missing him.

"You shouldn't be here," Tetsuo said. He grabbed the boy's shoulder and pressed both their backs against the battlement. Looking into the Scorpion heir's eyes, Tetsuo saw no fear, only determination. Dairu had grown up.

"I thought I'd find my uncle here," he said.

Tetsuo shook his head. "I haven't seen Aramoro since we finished off the Emerald Guard yesterday."

"Do you know where he is?" Dairu asked. "Father wants to see him."

"Outside the walls, I think, scouting," Tetsuo said.

A clattering sound came above, and the top of a ladder protruded over the battlement.

Quickly, Tetsuo and Dairu rose and pushed the ladder off the wall. The climbers fell to the ground. In the firelight, Dairu glimpsed hundreds of soldiers milling below. Several took shots at the cousins. The Scorpions ducked away before they could be hit.

"Who are they?" Dairu asked. "I don't recognize their banners."

"Irregular troops from the other clans," Tetsuo said. "Phoenix and Crane mostly. They must have had patrols nearby when we took the city. Some Unicorns, too—more every hour. I've seen others as well, even Dragons. The only ones missing are the Crabs."

"Why are they fighting us? Surely the other clans can see that Father did the right thing."

"They are like blind, headless snakes," Tetsuo answered. "They react without thinking. Angry and afraid, they lash out, heedless of the damage they cause. The justice of our cause doesn't matter."

Dairu nodded.

A black-garbed figure suddenly crested the wall nearby and dropped into a crouch. A torrent of arrows followed him.

Dairu and Tetsuo reached for their swords, and then recognized the familiar form of Bayushi Aramoro.

Aramoro's black garb had been torn and stained with the blood of his enemies. His Scorpion mask hung in tatters, barely covering his handsome face.

Dairu looked at his uncle. Is that what my father looks like? he wondered. In all his years, the Scorpion heir had never seen his father's true face.

Aramoro sprinted to where his relatives hid.

"Does your mother know you're out here?" he asked Dairu.

"Father does," the Scorpion heir replied. "He sent me to find you."

"What did you find out?" Tetsuo asked.

"We've been lucky so far," Aramoro said. "Our enemies seem as interested in fighting among themselves as in attacking us. The Phoenix and Crane don't trust each other, and neither of them trust the Unicorn. They're riding great circles around the walls, killing, looting. They've lost their minds. They think they have us contained."

A call drifted up from the other side of the wall. "Scorpions!" a man shouted. "We've captured another one of your spies!"

"Is it true?" Dairu asked.

"I doubt it," Aramoro said. "These fools see Scorpion spies everywhere."

The three Scorpions peered over the edge of the battlement.

Below, a ragtag group of samurai held a lone woman. She was tied in heavy ropes and looked to have been badly beaten. She sobbed and struggled feebly.

A scraggly bearded samurai called up to the unseen Bayushi. "This is what happens to all Scorpion traitors!" he said. He drew his sword and ran it through the woman's neck.

Aramoro stood, a shuriken in his hand. The loyalists below spotted the ninja master and began to draw their bows. Aramoro threw the dart. It struck the scraggly bearded samurai in the forehead, and he toppled backward, dead.

Aramoro and the others ducked behind the battlement in time to avoid a hail of arrows.

"Who was she?" Dairu asked, his eyes wide.

Aramoro shook his head. "Never saw her before. Just some peasant. I told you, these people are insane."

"We should report to the lord," Tetsuo said. "There are enough men here to hold the wall."

Aramoro and Dairu nodded. All three crept back toward the palace.

"Matsu Tsuko has joined the others," Aramoro told his relatives, "as if her Lions could do any good."

"Is she ineffective?" Dairu asked.

"A fair warrior," Tetsuo replied, "but not trusted by her clan."

"They trust her even less now," said Aramoro. " 'Where is Akodo Toturi?' her people ask. 'Hiding like a monk in his temple,' she replies, though no one believes her. Her forces have been searching high and low for him, but they'll never find him."

The ninja master looked at the other two and smiled behind his tattered mask. "I started a rumor that Tsuko had him assassinated so she could assume clan leadership."

"Will her people believe it?" Dairu asked. They reached a watchtower and descended its staircase to the city streets.

"She's always hated Toturi," Tetsuo said, "so they may."

"Even if they don't," said Aramoro, "she'll have to spend precious time dispelling the rumor."

"What about the Crab? Any sign of them?" asked Dairu.

"Just rumors," Aramoro replied. "They say Hida Kisada and a great army have begun marching toward the capital."

"He comes to join us," Dairu said.

Aramoro and Tetsuo looked at each other.

"Or our enemies," Tetsuo replied.

"Assuming they haven't killed each other for traitors before Kisada gets here," added Aramoro.

Sunrise peeked over the vast ocean, casting pale yellow light on the besieged capital. Pyres of "traitors" filled the morning sky with greasy black smoke, blotting out the sun. Hungry crows circled the outskirts of the city.

The Scorpions hurried to the palace.

▲▲▲▲▲▲▲▲

Hantei the 39th's scream was smothered by a hand that clamped over his mouth.

"Your Highness!" hissed a harsh voice.

The heir to the throne looked around, panic in his dark eyes. For a moment, he didn't know where he was. Then the song and the smell of the rain, the sound of voices and horses in the background, reminded him.

"You must be quiet!" the voice said.

"You've had a dream—a nightmare," said a more friendly voice. His pulse was still racing, but Hantei recognized Isawa Kaede. "Screaming could get us all killed," she said.

The young emperor mutely nodded his head. The hand withdrew from his face, and Sotorii realized it belonged to Ishikawa, captain of the palace guard.

"A thousand apologies, Majesty," Ishikawa said. "But your scream could have given away our position."

"I-I dreamed of demons," Hantei said breathlessly. "They were calling my name. They sounded so close."

"The voices of the Scorpion, most likely," said Ishikawa. It had taken days, but they had finally escaped the city walls. Even now, the three refugees kept to themselves. They sat huddled in a copse of trees near the city. The underbrush in the small stand had provided the shelter they needed for the night, both from the rain and from the eyes of Scorpion spies.

"Are those Scorpions I hear on horseback?" Hantei asked.

Ishikawa shook his head. "No. Crane by the look of them. They seem to be hunting Scorpions."

"Or anyone who looks suspicions," Kaede added.

"We should make our presence known," the new emperor

said. He started to stand, but Kaede put her hand on his arm and restrained him.

"No!" she whispered harshly. "We do not know these people. They seem to be killing stragglers on sight. For all we know, they could be in league with the Scorpion."

"But I'm tired," the heir said. "My leg aches from this accursed shuriken wound. These are our people. Surely they will help us."

"Kaede is right," Ishikawa said, leaning close to the boy. "We don't know who to trust right now. Caution may yet save your life. Impatience will surely get us all killed."

"We can find my people," Kaede whispered. "They will get us to safety."

Hantei crossed thin arms over his chest. "Very well," he said. "But we will not crawl through the mud for much longer."

▲▲▲▲▲▲▲▲

On the third day, Doji Satsume, Emerald Champion, returned from the field. He cursed the business that had called him so far from the city when his emperor had needed him most. Nor did he understand why his son, Doji Hoturi, had absented himself as well.

"You should have been there!" the older man barked. He rode up to his son outside the city wall, and the two of them glowered at one another.

"Someone needs to run our clan," replied Hoturi, the Crane heir. Years of bickering with his father made the Crane daimyo's anger boil quickly. "Surely you're not suggesting I leave that task to my bride! Besides, Toturi was supposed to be there. He *should* have been there. Where is he?"

"Out whoring, from what I've heard," said Satsume, his green armor gleaming in the afternoon sun. "They say he loves some geisha more than the emperor."

Hoturi nodded grimly. "Hai. I've heard it said, also."

"Nevertheless," Satsume said, pointing at his son, "protecting the emperor is *your* job as well. You have failed."

"Perhaps, then, you would prefer to follow Yokatsu of the Unicorn?"

"Ha!" said Satsume. "Me, pledge loyalty to that barbarian-tainted . . . ! He should follow *me*. As should the Lion Tsuko. As should *you*."

"We must stop this in-fighting," Hoturi said. "With the Phoenix gone, we need every samurai."

"The Phoenix, gone?" Satsume asked, startled.

"They marched away a few hours ago," Hoturi said. "No one knows why."

Satsume spat. "Perhaps they've taken up with the Scorpion."

"Perhaps they tired of this constant bickering," Hoturi said, holding his voice tight.

"As do I," Satsume snarled.

He turned his back on his son and rode away into the body of his army. Hoturi stared after him, his eyes narrow with anger.

▲▲▲▲▲▲▲▲

At sunset, the Master of Secrets stood alone in the high tower of the palace, watching fires ravage the outskirts of the city.

"The peasants have their Fire Festival after all," he said to no one in particular.

Despite the animosity between the competing armies, the meeting of their generals had stirred something within the city walls. Small pockets of rebellion broke out in Otosan Uchi. As the Unicorn and their tenuous allies encircled the outer walls, resistance within the city grew stronger.

Since Aramoro's return, no Scorpions had left the city and lived. Even the envoys Shoju sent to explain his actions to the other great lords were slaughtered. Shoju sent more ambassadors to take their place.

As the Scorpion daimyo stood, trying to read his future in the smoke, the fusuma entrance to the room slid open. Tetsuo entered.

"Master," he said breathlessly, "I have word of your latest envoys."

The Scorpion turned toward his cousin. Behind his mask, Bayushi Shoju's brow furrowed. "And?" he asked.

Tetsuo bowed low. "Dead, my lord. All of them."

"Did any reach their intended destinations?" Shoju asked.

"One, I think, was killed by Matsu Tsuko herself," Tetsuo replied.

Shoju's eyes blazed, and his hand stole to the hilt of his sword, *Yashin*.

"They should have a care," he said, his voice strong and deep, like the purr of a tiger, "lest I ride from this tower and show them the true strength of the Scorpion."

Tetsuo bowed.

Shoju let out a deep breath.

"Try one more time," he said wearily. He turned back to the window again and watched the city burn.

L

18   HATSUKO FALLS

The dragon in Akodo Toturi's mind
writhed and coiled in agitation.

"Fool! Imbecile!" it hissed. Great blasts of
steam escaped its wide mouth.

Toturi looked around, wondering where
he was. Blackness enshrouded him. Not even
stars shone. Only the brilliance of the dragon
illumined the darkness.

Toturi began, "Great One—"

"You have failed! You are undone!" the
creature said, its voice like thunder in the
mountains. "The empire is in flames and
you—" the dragon paused, and lightning
flashed from its eyes "—you lie asleep, insen-
sate, satisfied, having quenched the fire of
your loins. You are a fool, Akodo Toturi."

"I . . . I did not mean—"

"No one ever means to bring about his
own destruction—or the destruction of
those he loves. Yet, you have done it. You

ignored my warnings, and now your destiny is upon you." The dragon scowled. "Never has a mortal more deserved his fate."

Alone and naked in the darkness, Toturi felt even smaller.

"I can make amends," he said.

"Never!" cried the dragon. "If you were to live a thousand years, you could never undo what your selfishness has done!"

"I *will!*" Toturi said. "Just show me the way!"

"I *have* shown you the way; you did not follow it! You must keep your own counsel now. Let us hope it serves you better than it has thus far. An empty throne and bitter defeat await you, Akodo Toturi. Go!"

With that, the dragon twisted and coiled and vanished into the darkness.

As it went, Toturi found himself falling. Wind whistled past his face. The world around him grew brighter. Gray gave way to swirling colors. Sound assaulted his ears.

Crying. Someone was crying.

Toturi sat up suddenly.

Hatsuko jumped back and gasped.

The Lion tried to rise to his feet, but his body rebelled against him. Hatsuko rushed to his aid. Hope and love played across her tearstained face. Toturi's limbs felt wooden, heavy. Movement brought a tingling fire to his entire body.

"M-my lord," Hatsuko gasped. "My love . . ."

"What have you done to me?" Toturi asked, his voice filled with accusation.

Hatsuko shied back, as if he had struck her physically. Still, she supported him under his arms.

"I . . . I . . ." she began. "She said you would leave me. She said we could be together only in death."

"Who?" he asked, turning his blazing eyes on her. "Who said?"

"Aki," she replied, tears streaming down her face once more. As she looked at him, she felt something in her soul shatter. "She said your fiancée would kill you if you married me."

"Kaede?" Toturi asked, confused.

Hatsuko nodded, her hair flailing around her face like tiny black whips. "I had to protect you from the burning death," she said.

"You poisoned me," he said.

Again, she nodded. "But I could not . . . could not . . . ."

"How long?" he asked.

She looked at him, uncomprehending.

He seized her by the shoulders and shook her. "How long have I lain here?"

"A-a week," she said, sobbing. "Perhaps more. I . . . I don't know."

He pushed her aside and rose, fighting the tingling fire in his limbs. Stumbling to the wall, he took his swords from where he had laid them and thrust them into his obi.

As he turned back to her, he saw her fumbling with a blue gem on a long chain. The gem opened; inside, it held a white powder. She put the gem to her lips.

"Oh, no!" he roared, slapping the amulet from her hands. The gem smashed against the wall. Its contents burst into a small, white cloud. "Poison is too good for you!"

She brought her hands up to protect herself, but he grabbed both her wrists with one large fist. Pushing backward, Toturi thrust her to the floor. She lay there, head on the tatami mat, weeping. The Lion daimyo drew his katana.

She looked up at him, tears running down her plain, unpainted cheeks. Toturi marveled that he had ever found her face lovely.

"Kill me, Toturi-sama," she said. "I beg you." She lowered her face to the floor, exposing her neck to him.

Toturi raised his blade high.

He looked down at the quivering mass before him.

She had destroyed him, just as the dragon had said. She had poisoned him, kept him here—in this accursed cabin—for who knew how long. Probably his reputation had been damaged beyond repair. But that was not all. The dragon had hinted that far more dire consequences lay before him.

Toturi's lips curled back from his teeth. He tightened his grip on the sword.

Hatsuko, his geisha, had ruined him. And yet . . . and yet . . . he could not bring himself to destroy her.

The remnants of passion clung to his heart, and though he no longer loved her, he did feel pity. He could not kill her.

As he stared at her pitiful, huddled form, a vision of fire and blood and death filled his mind. A black dragon danced in the sky over the capital city, and demons leered in the background. Great armies massed outside Otosan Uchi.

Toturi swung his blade and cut a large hole in the shoji wall of the cabin. He stepped through the opening and walked outside, sheathing his sword as he did so. Behind him, he could still hear Hatsuko weeping.

Turning down the hill, he strode into the forest in the direction of Junko's geisha house.

Hatsuko rose from the floor and staggered to the hole. "No!" she cried. "Come back! End my life, I beg you! Please!"

Toturi didn't stop; he didn't look back.

For a long time, her plaintive cries echoed after him.

Half an hour later, Akodo Toturi sat astride a haggard, borrowed horse and rode toward the column of smoke on the horizon. He knew it came from Otosan Uchi.

▲ ▲ ▲ ▲ ▲ ▲ ▲ ▲

Hatsuko collapsed on the cabin's threshold as soon as Toturi was out of sight. She cried and called after him for an endless time. He did not return. The shadows in the Imperial Forest grew long and dark.

Eventually, she could cry no more. Hatsuko raised her unpainted face off the cabin floor.

The world outside looked lovely in the light of the late afternoon. To Hatsuko, the beauty brought only pain.

She had lost him. Just as surely as if she had killed him,

she had lost her one true love. No—*more* surely. If she had been brave, had done as Aki had told her and not lowered the dose, Toturi and Hatsuko would have been together for eternity. She had not been brave enough, for his sake or hers.

Now Toturi would face the flaming death of his fiancée's wrath. Perhaps the empire itself would fall.

Hatsuko rose to her feet, leaning against one of the cabin's posts for support. Her limbs felt stiff. At the same time, her bones seemed made of jelly.

Slowly she steadied herself.

Feeling chilled, she pulled her kimono tight around her frail body.

She had lost everything.

The realization hit her and she nearly fell to the ground again. Only her grip on the post kept her upright.

If only she had been more brave.

Now there was nothing left.

Her future was empty—like her soul.

She staggered off the porch of the cabin and into the woods beyond.

The tears came again. Hatsuko found herself running through the forest blindly. She ran; she wept. Thorns and bracken tore at her kimono, at her skin. They flailed at her face and body but failed to scourge the pain from her soul.

She ran for an endless time, neither feeling the pain nor caring about the wounds.

A sound made her stop, a soft, melodic sound. She caught her breath. Opening her eyes, she brushed away tears and long strings of her tangled black hair.

The waterfall. The waterfall was singing to her from nearby.

"Hatsuko Falls," Toturi had called them in happier times.

She took a tentative step forward, and then another. She pushed the thorny underbrush aside as she walked. Stones and sticks cut her bare feet. She didn't mind.

Before her lay the falls. She stood at their top, their head. The small river rushed by her and cascaded over the cliff, singing as it met the rocks below. The song called to her.

Surely the Fortunes had guided her steps.

Hatsuko walked carefully to the edge of the cliff and hung her bruised and bloody toes over the precipice. She looked down.

Sweet oblivion waited below. She heard it calling her name.

Hatsuko smiled and embraced it.

For a moment she felt as though she were flying.

The air rushing past tickled her skin and thrilled her insides. She opened her mouth to scream with joy.

Then, darkness claimed her.

19   THE COUP IN PERIL

Otosan Uchi continued to burn. The great River of the Sun ran red with blood. Bloated bodies floated over the Fudotaki Waterfall near the palace.

Dairu and Rumiko ran from the High Gate by the river. Arrows chased them, but none struck home.

A Phoenix archer stepped from a building just ahead. He fired at Rumiko.

The arrow stuck in Rumiko's shoulder guard. In midstride, she swung her katana. The archer brought his bow up to parry. Rumiko's sword cut it in half. Her followthrough sliced the archer from shoulder to hip, and he fell, dead.

A samurai leapt out from behind the archer. He was older than Rumiko and far larger. He brandished a two-handed *no-dachi* sword.

"Don't wait for me," Rumiko called to Dairu.

Dairu didn't listen. Instead, he jumped forward to fend off the samurai's attack. The no-dachi hit Dairu's katana with such force that the Scorpion heir staggered backward. The samurai looked surprised to be facing two opponents rather than one.

Before he could recover, Rumiko sliced open his belly. The samurai tried to lift his huge sword, but doing so spilled his guts. He crumpled to the ground.

Dairu and Rumiko turned and ran again.

"If anything had happened to you," Rumiko said, "your father would have killed me just as surely as that samurai."

"Forgive me," Dairu said, trying to gaze beyond the samurai-ko's mask. "I did not mean to impugn your honor."

Rumiko laughed.

They turned a corner and nearly knocked over Aramoro, who was running in the opposite direction. The three of them paused.

"What's happening?" Aramoro said. "Dairu, why are you away from the castle?"

"I came to inspect the troops," the young man replied.

Rumiko bowed. "Aramoro-sama," she said. "The loyalist forces have pushed inside the High Gate. Our forces are holding them, but . . ."

Aramoro cursed. "I feared as much. Go back to the front. I'll take the heir to safety."

Rumiko bowed again. "I live to serve." She turned and ran back toward the conflict.

"There are Lion, Unicorn, Crane," Dairu said breathlessly. "Even a few units of Dragon and some Phoenix stragglers."

"They've united?" Aramoro asked.

"No," said Dairu. "They still squabble like cats and dogs—but there are many of them."

Aramoro nodded. "Too many for you to battle single handed," he said. "Come. Your father will need us both."

▲▲▲▲▲▲▲▲

In the high tower of the palace, Bayushi Shoju feared all his plans would come to naught.

The foray Aramoro and Dairu reported at the High Gate soon became an alliance foothold in the city. Loyalists within Otosan Uchi rallied. Soon, all those devoted to the late emperor's cause had gathered near the High Gate.

Despite the disarray of the allied troops, the Scorpion found it nearly impossible to dislodge their enemies.

Shoju's talks with the captives went little better. Despite the clear hand of fate, those whom he kept prisoner still refused to believe the Scorpion had acted for the greater good of the empire. Even Seppun Bake held steady to his position, even after Shoju allowed him a room of his own and free access to the Scroll of Bayushi Daijin. The Scorpion lord suspected Bake was waiting to see who finally won the day.

Once a toad, always a toad, Shoju thought.

The battles to hold the city became fiercer every day, as did the Scorpion lord's battles against the siren song of *Yashin*.

Wield me! the sword whispered. *I will deliver the day unto you!*

Those closest to the Scorpion lord—Kachiko, Dairu, Tetsuo—noticed a change in his demeanor. He rarely spoke, and when he did, his temper was short. The transformation worried the daimyo's friends. Not even his wife spoke to him of it. Often, Shoju walked the ramparts of the palace alone. It was on one of these battlements that Tetsuo found him, just as the sun slipped behind the Spine of the World Mountains.

"Great Lord," Tetsuo said, kneeling.

Shoju continued to stare at the billowing black smoke rising from the city's western fringes.

"Am I emperor?" the Scorpion asked in his quiet, melodious voice.

Tetsuo seemed surprised by the question. "Who else, great lord?" he asked.

Shoju shook his head. "I do not feel like the emperor," he said. "I have the palace. I have the throne. I have the mirror, the jade, the sword, and yet . . . somehow, it is not enough."

Tetsuo rose and stood by his lord. He, too, looked out over the burning city.

"They will understand," the younger man said. "You will make them understand."

"Will I?" Shoju asked. His voice was impassive, and his grim mask disguised whatever true feelings he might have. He pointed to where the fire spread. "They're doing better since Satsume arrived. I think we might lose the outer city."

"I pray not, Majesty."

Shoju turned and looked at his young cousin. "Why have you come?" he asked.

"We have confirmed the reports," Tetsuo said. "The Crab is on the march."

"How far?"

"Within three days."

Shoju nodded and turned back to the burning city.

"For which side does he march?" Shoju asked.

"No one knows, great lord."

"If Kisada joins our enemies," the Scorpion emperor said, "we may fall." He took a deep breath. "We need to send an envoy to the Crab—secure his aid."

"But, how, my lord? Our enemies' shugenja daunt our communications outside the city. We were lucky to receive this intelligence at all. Most of our spies are discovered and killed as soon as they approach the outer walls."

"Then I will have to send better people," Shoju said. "I will have to make sure they reach their goal." He put his long-fingered right hand on his younger cousin's shoulder. "You will go to the Crab for me," he said. "Explain to Kisada our position."

"I, Your Majesty?"

Shoju nodded. "Don't worry, I will give you a message, tell you what to say. I will see that the loyalist clans are kept busy while you slip away. Come, we need to talk to Kachiko, Junzo, and the others. I have a plan."

In the back of the Scorpion lord's mind, the song of *Yashin* grew strong once again.

▲▲▲▲▲▲▲▲

The Emerald Champion, Doji Satsume, rode beside Matsu Tsuko of the Lion. They patrolled the outer precincts of Otosan Uchi near the High Gate. Night was rapidly descending, and fires within the city lit the darkening sky.

"Where's that son of mine?" Doji Satsume called, cursing under his breath.

"His forces are conducting a foray toward the Temple of the Sun," Tsuko replied.

"*What* is he doing?" Satsume asked. "That's too close to the Scorpion quarters. We could never hold an outpost there. We should reinforce our position here, and then move north—retaking the quarters of our own clans."

"I agree," said Tsuko, her long white mane blowing in the wind. "But Yokatsu agrees with your son. They want to bring the fight to the Scorpion directly. They think perhaps they can break his back."

"Anyone on the back of the Scorpion is sure to be stung," said Satsume. He spat dust from his mouth and turned to one of his lieutenants. "Inoshiro, find my boy and tell him to retreat to this position."

The man bowed, "Hai, my lord." He rode off.

Tsuko smiled at Satsume. "I guess you don't get to be Emerald Champion without having some sense," she said.

Satsume snorted. "Apparently, you need less to be clan champion."

Tsuko nodded. "I would agree with that. I always said Toturi was a mistake."

"Hai. At least Hoturi's here, even if he won't listen to good sense."

A cry went up among the loyalist forces. "The Scorpion!" they shouted. "The Scorpion has left the castle!"

Satsume wheeled around, trying to see from which direction the cry came.

"Surely he would not be so foolish," Tsuko said.

Something exploded to the east. A crowd of panicked loyalists retreated into the square, sweeping the armies of the Lion and the Emerald Champion apart.

Behind the retreating wave came a Scorpion host on thundering steeds. Their red and black mon flapped in the wind. At their head rode the usurper, Bayushi Shoju. He wore a frightful, demonic mask. His red and black kimono billowed around him like an ebony ghost. In his hand he wielded *Yashin*.

Beside him rode Kachiko's handmaiden, the sorceress Yogo Miyuki, and on the other side, his brother Aramoro, the Master of Assassins. With them also came Dairu, the heir.

The Scorpion counterattack had been well-planned. Yogo Junzo's powerful magics had hidden the army from detection until they passed beyond the walls of the Forbidden City. Now the Scorpion force caught the loyalists almost completely by surprise.

The Scorpion host fanned out as they came, driving the disorganized allies before them.

Satsume reared his mount, trying to rally his fleeing troops. He could see Matsu Tsuko and her forces being swept away before the Scorpion tide. The Emerald Champion knew he had to do something or the day would be lost.

Boldly he called to his men and charged his horse into the mass of onrushing Scorpions. Many of his green-armored compatriots rallied to his side. They hit the usurper's forces in the left flank.

Satsume killed the first two samurai he ran into, lopping off their heads. He pulled a third from the saddle. Satsume's horse finished the job, trampling the man. Around him, the Emerald Champion could see that his men were having similar success.

He drove for the heart of the Scorpion force. Bayushi Shoju rode there, directing the vanguard of the Scorpion cavalry to meet them.

Satsume ordered his men back. They would regroup and charge the Scorpion lord head on. Satsume smiled in grim determination.

The Scorpion sorceress Miyuki did something terrible. She stretched out her hands, and black dust blasted forth like a swarm of insects.

Satsume heard a hideous cracking beneath him. His steed collapsed, its bones shattered. The horses of those who rode beside him sprawled in similar piles.

Satsume scrambled to his feet. His men did the same, forming a protective circle around the Emerald Champion. The Scorpion host pressed forward.

Doji Satsume ripped off his helmet. He tossed his graying head back and bellowed, "Bayushi Shoju! Face me!"

Miyuki raised a finger and pointed at the Emerald Champion. At a glance from her lord, the sorceress let her hand fall back to her side.

Shoju dismounted his black steed and strode gracefully to where Satsume stood. Their forces parted before them, allowing each passage. The two men eyed each other, the Scorpion's face hidden behind his frightful mask.

"Usurper bastard!" Satsume said. "Would that you had never been born."

The Scorpion emperor said nothing, but merely assumed a defensive posture, his sword raised crosswise over his head.

With an enraged scream, Doji Satsume charged.

Shoju parried the Crane's cut easily and danced aside, dark fire playing in his masked eyes.

Satsume growled and swung around, slashing. His sword found only the Scorpion's billowing costume, and it slid through the robe without causing any harm. The Scorpion's kimono seemed to be woven of shadow itself.

Shoju's blade flashed and jabbed Satsume's left shoulder. A thin line traced down the Emerald Champion's deltoid and began to leak blood.

Behind his mask, Shoju smiled. How like his dream this was.

Satsume thrust and cut again.

The Scorpion merely danced away.

"Damn you!" Satsume cried. "Fight like a man!"

Behind his mask, the Scorpion's eyes narrowed. "What I have done," he said, "I have done for the empire—to save the empire from Fu Leng."

"To save it for yourself, you mean!" Satsume said, and charged again. He aimed a cut at the Bayushi's midsection, but Shoju easily parried it. Before the Crane could recover, the Scorpion's boot found his gut; Satsume fell back, sprawling.

"You know I'm right," Shoju hissed, his teeth clenched behind his mask.

Before the Crane could answer, a cry went up from the crowd. "Hoturi! Hoturi!"

The champion's son had returned. His forces rode hard into the fray. That broke the spell that had held the combatants' men. Fighting resumed on all sides.

In the center of the maelstrom stood Satsume and Shoju.

"Surrender," said the Scorpion. "I will be lenient. You don't have to die this day." He took his sword in his left hand and drew it back across his body, like a bowman readying an arrow. His right hand he held outstretched, as if Satsume might take it in friendship.

The Crane spat. "Insect!" he cried, charging forward. He aimed his attack at the Scorpion's neck.

At the last instant, Shoju spun aside, dodging the blow. The Scorpion's blade twisted in his hand and rammed backward into the Emerald Champion's gut, slipping deftly between the armor at Satsume's side.

For a moment, the two of them stood frozen, almost side by side. Satsume's eyes widened in disbelief. Shoju stood next to the Crane's shoulder, holding his pose like a dancer who had reached his finale. The Scorpion withdrew *Yashin* with one swift move, and the Emerald Champion slumped to the ground, his blood staining the dirt.

"Father!" cried Hoturi.

Shoju turned to find the Crane daimyo mere yards away. The fighting had slackened momentarily as the Emerald Champion fell, but now it resumed, more furious than before.

The Scorpion emperor flicked the blood from his sword in the ancient shiburi motion.

"Archers, fire at will!" Hoturi screamed. Arrows blackened the air as the Crane daimyo ran forward, a wild look in his eyes. He charged directly toward Shoju, swinging his sword in a wide arc.

The Scorpion emperor danced aside, and the Crane's blade found only empty air. Shoju thrust *Yashin* at Hoturi's neck, but the younger man recovered from his charge and parried just in time.

The tides of battle swept all around them, a mass of churning, fighting bodies, swords clashing, arrows flying. . . .

Hoturi's sword chose targets in quick succession: neck, thigh, gut. Shoju parried them all. The Bayushi Lord danced aside gracefully, a demon-faced shadow in the flickering firelight. Hoturi pressed forward, rage filling him. Behind his mask, the Scorpion emperor smiled.

Suddenly, a cry went up. "Father!"

Shoju turned at the sound of his son's voice. Dairu held the body of his uncle, Aramoro—Shoju's half-brother. A Crane arrow had lodged itself deep in the shoulder of the Master of Assassins.

Hoturi took advantage of the distraction. He thrust his sword at the Scorpion lord's midsection.

The billowing costume saved Shoju. The Crane's blade traced only a small scratch along his ribs. Shoju spun, fire and hatred blazing in his eyes. Hoturi thrust again, but the Scorpion effortlessly batted the blade aside.

Shoju twisted and cut. His sword found the armor straps at Hoturi's shoulders. Hoturi's chest plate fell forward, exposing his breast.

Before the Crane could react, Shoju lunged. *Yashin* found flesh. Hoturi cried out and reeled back, blood splashing from his chest.

The fighting crowds surged forward, separating the two. Shoju was swept backward, toward his son and brother. The battle carried Hoturi toward the body of his father. The Crane Lord was not mortally wounded, though he would carry a scar on his breast for the rest of his life.

So close, Shoju thought, the song of *Yashin* screaming in his mind.

He looked to his son, still supporting Aramoro. The arrow had struck the ninja master close to the bone, but it was the Scorpion heir who looked as pale as death.

Seeing the gaze of his half-brother, Aramoro said, "I'm all right."

Shoju nodded. "Dairu?" he asked.

"I'm fine, Father," the boy managed, though he looked sick.

Shoju glanced toward the fighting crowd once more. Scorpion, Crane, and Emerald Guards whirled around each other in the tides of battle.

In their midst, Shoju could see the Crane daimyo kneeling beside the body of his father. A fire welled up in the Scorpion's belly. He had been within moments of his long-anticipated revenge on Hoturi . . . !

The Scorpion emperor pushed the emotion aside.

"Fall back!" he called to his embattled troops. "To the Forbidden City!"

"Brother, we could destroy them," Aramoro said, his teeth clenched behind his Scorpion mask.

Shoju surveyed the situation once more. "Perhaps," he said, "but their reinforcements are greater than ours. See how the thrice-cursed Lion rallies her troops even now?" The Scorpion emperor shook his head. "No," he said. "Our objective has been accomplished with this foray. We have given Tetsuo the distraction he needed to escape the city without detection. Now we retreat, hold our position, and await word from the Crab."

20   THE WAY OF THE CRAB

The death of the Emerald Champion proved a setback to the allies, but not a serious one. Though the loyalists missed his fighting prowess, Satsume's death helped unite the allied forces. What remained of the champion's troops quickly rallied to the banner of his son, Hoturi—though the two men had not been close in life.

As the Scorpion host fell back, the allies consolidated their position near the High Gate. The next day, loyalists mounted a furious counterattack into the southern section of the outer city.

Rumiko retreated once again, though without the Scorpion heir to keep her company.

Twice she thought she would die. The first time, she turned into a blind alley and found herself trapped. Three burly Lion samurai chased her into the dead end.

She turned to face them and cut the first man across the neck as he charged her. The second she ran through with her katana. The sword stuck in the Lion's ribs, and before she could pull it out, the third man nearly cut Rumiko's head off. She ducked and lashed out with her foot. The man staggered. He stumbled over the body of his dead comrade. Rumiko drew her wakizashi from her obi and thrust the short sword through his eye. She picked up her katana and ran out of the alley the way she had come.

Rumiko's second brush came when she neared the Temple of the Sun. She fought in the rearguard as the Scorpion forces fell back. Houses burned all around, and falling timbers crashed everywhere. One nearly crushed Rumiko's skull. She spun away from the flames, the smoke stinging her eyes.

Through tears, she barely glimpsed a Crane samurai-ko charging her. Out of the shimmering black haze the woman came, her katana raised high.

Rumiko drew quickly and turned her foe's blade aside.

The Crane countered with a thrust to Rumiko's face. The sword traced a red line down her cheek. As she staggered back, the Crane advanced, swinging her katana in a wide arc.

The blade connected with Rumiko's side, finding the weak point between the armor plates. Rumiko dropped her sword and fell to the ground. White pain flashed before her eyes.

The Crane came in for the kill.

Rumiko groped with her right hand, trying to find her sword. Instead, she found a handful of hot ashes. She seized them and flung the cinders into her opponent's eyes.

The Crane shrieked, lashing out blindly.

Rumiko rolled aside, and the blade struck ground where her head had been. She grabbed her wakizashi and thrust it into the Crane's exposed armpit.

The Crane staggered back but didn't die. The short sword fell out of the wound to the ground.

Rumiko tried to stand. Her side screamed in pain. Light

flashed before her eyes. She couldn't find either of her weapons in the smoldering chaos.

The Crane raised her sword once more. She jerked backward suddenly, clutched at her neck, and rose into the air. It seemed she had been plucked from the ground by an invisible hand. The Crane kicked her feet uselessly in the air. In the fire and smoke, the thin chain around her neck was nearly invisible.

Rumiko looked up and saw Aramoro standing on the roof of the Temple of the Sun, holding the other end of the chain. He wrapped the chain around one of the temple's cross posts and leapt to the ground, landing lightly at Rumiko's side.

"Fall back to the next street," he advised her. "Our people are strong there, and these rabble aren't organized enough to push us any farther."

Rumiko nodded and said, "Hai!"

Aramoro disappeared into the smoke.

Rumiko watched the Crane strangle for a few moments. She found her weapons and resheathed them. Clutching her injured side, the Scorpion samurai-ko limped off after the Master of Assassins.

▲ ▲ ▲ ▲ ▲ ▲ ▲ ▲

Shoju watched the battles alone from his vantage point in the high tower of the palace. In his soul, he longed to ride forth once more, to slay Hoturi and the other daimyo who stood in his way. *Yashin* urged him on in this ambition, singing sweetly in his ear night and day.

At most times, the Scorpion emperor was strong-willed enough to resist the call of the sword. He knew he would not catch the loyalist forces unaware twice. If he rode out once more, chances were good they would be waiting for him. He doubted Hoturi would be so foolish as to face him again in personal combat.

No, Shoju's chance to kill his enemy man-to-man had passed, at least for the moment.

As battles raged in outer Otosan Uchi, the Scorpion emperor's forces had no difficulty securing the Forbidden City. With the magic of the walls on his side, the enemies' siege machines could do nothing.

In each of the five days since the emperor's death, the Scorpion had spoken to the hostage representatives of the other clans. Despite his persuasive abilities, they remained unconvinced of the righteousness of his cause. This irked Shoju, and he could feel *Yashin* in the back of his mind, urging him to kill everyone who would not cooperate.

Still, the Scorpion held out hope the other clans could be brought to his side or at least brought to rein.

The Crab would arrive soon, and their arrival would change everything.

On the sixth morning after the coup, Hida Kisada and his army closed in on the city. Fighting between the Scorpion and the allied clans trailed off. Each faction gathered its forces, waiting to see on which side the Crab would enter the war.

As the Crab crested the hills outside Otosan Uchi, Kachiko found her husband and went to stand beside him. She looked out past the burning city to the approaching army.

Like well-ordered ants, Crab forces swarmed the hills surrounding the city. They were a vast mass of black-shelled warriors. Even from this distance, Kachiko could see their order and discipline. Every samurai knew his place, every man followed Kisada's commands to the letter.

Look at them, Kachiko thought. Kisada must have emptied every Crab garrison and brought them here. It's a wonder he still has samurai left to man the Carpenter's Wall.

Kachiko shuddered and pulled her kimono tight around her. She moved closer to Shoju.

"Perhaps you should speak to Kisada in person," she said, twining the fingers of his right hand with hers.

Shoju felt a sudden stiffness in his limb and touched the

burning tattoo to restore its subtlety. "How would I do this?" he asked. "Parade myself to the gate like some commoner? Ride forth and hope I can slay all those who stand in my way?" He shook his head. "No. Tetsuo has carried my words to Kisada. I trust him as I trust you, or our son, or Aramoro."

"But if he should fail—"

"If he should fail, we are doomed," Shoju said. "At least we have saved the world from the Evil One."

She gazed at his mask. He had chosen a passive, contemplative face for the day. The mask hid his worries—worries enough for all of Rokugan. The two of them stood silently, watching the advance of the Crab armies.

The Crab forces marched directly toward the western gate of the city, the High Gate. As they came, the allied forces fell back, waiting to see what the Crab would do.

Shoju and Kachiko both held their breath.

The flag of the Crab went up. The Crab planted his banner with their enemies.

Kachiko turned away from the window, blinking back her anger. "Would that you had sent me instead," she said ruefully.

Bayushi Shoju let out a long sigh.

"We must try to hold out as long as we can," he said. "Make them see we are right—the Hantei had to die."

She turned back to him; tears stained her silken mask. "We should kill them all!" she cried. "All the ambassadors, all the hostages! They're fools! They don't deserve your generosity or your sufferance. You should stain the land dark with their blood and make the rivers run red."

He put his hands on her shoulders and embraced her.

"Then who would we rule over?" he asked. "A destroyed world? A nation of the undead? Do you think I am the Evil One himself?"

She hung her head and said nothing.

A great hurrah went up outside the city. The Bayushi lord and lady knew the forces of their enemies had been joined.

"At least," she said quietly, "Toturi will not lead them."

Shoju nodded. "Without the Lion to unify the clans, we may still stand a chance." He looked into her eyes. "Get word to our commanders. They are to hold their positions as long as possible. Tell them to burn the city if they must to keep the clans from advancing. If need be, they are to fall back to the Forbidden City. The enchanted walls are still under our command. We can hold the palace a long time if necessary."

Kachiko bowed. "Hai, my lord." As she raised her face, he lifted his mask and kissed her on the forehead. She turned to leave.

At the door, she was nearly bowled over by a pale, haggard figure. The man stumbled into the room, looking more like a beggar than a samurai. When he crossed the threshold, he fell to the floor, pressing his head to the tatami mat.

"My lord," he said plaintively.

In the dirty, unkempt form prostrate before him, Shoju recognized his cousin. "Tetsuo!" the Scorpion emperor said. "Get up!"

"I cannot, my lord," Tetsuo said. "I have failed you. I have failed us all."

Kachiko paused as if to stay, but a glance from Shoju sent her away on her errand. She slid the door closed as she left.

"I spoke your words, but Lord Kisada did not hear them," Tetsuo continued. "I fought my way back into the city, but too late. The Crab has sided with our enemies, my lord. I have failed."

He looked up from where he knelt. "I beg you, do not let me live with this dishonor. Slay me. I have brought nothing but shame to our clan."

The Scorpion's eyes looked out from behind his mask and took in the face of his cousin. Behind the dirt and grime he saw a noble man, crushed by shortcomings that were not his own.

"What did the Crab say?" the Scorpion emperor asked.

Tetsuo rose somewhat, though he remained on his knees.

"Lord Kisada said he would never side with the weak. He had thought, perhaps, when you killed Hantei, it was a sign of strength—a sign that the time had come for a new imperial line.

"But when I came to him, he changed his mind. Had I not asked, he would have given you his support gladly—because it would have proved you did not *need* his support. By asking for his aid, I doomed our cause."

Tetsuo collapsed on the tatami once more.

"Please, Great Lord," he said, "if you do not kill me yourself, allow me to commit seppuku. Nothing else will erase the stain of my failure."

Shoju looked down on his young cousin. In his mind, the Scorpion emperor could hear *Yashin* crying out for blood—always more blood. His hand went to the hilt of the sword, but he did not grip the hilt.

Instead, he knelt beside Tetsuo and put his hand on the broken man's shoulder.

"No," the Scorpion emperor said quietly. "It is not your fate to die now."

"My lord . . . ?" Tetsuo said, looking up with tearstained eyes.

The Scorpion extended his right hand to help his cousin rise. "The fault is mine," Shoju said. "The words you carried belonged to me. It was I who miscalculated. I should have realized the only way to obtain the Crab's support was *not* to ask for it. I was a fool."

Tetsuo took Shoju's hand, and the two of them stood. The Scorpion lord's shoulder twinged as he helped his cousin up.

"Never, my lord," Tetsuo said. "It was I who failed to convey your words properly."

Shoju shook his head. "The failure is mine."

"But the stain . . ."

"It will fade with the passage of years," said Shoju. "The stain is largely on me. The time has not come for you to die. Not yet. I sense you have another part to play in this drama before it is over."

Tetsuo dropped his head and looked at the floor. Shoju put his hand on the younger man's shoulder.

"Come," the Scorpion emperor said, "there is much we must do."

21 THE LION ARRIVES

Inside a pavilion near the High Gate, Hida Kisada studied his fellow daimyos. His gaze finally settled on Doji Hoturi. The Crab lord scowled.

"Saving the outer city from fire is futile while the Scorpion holds the Forbidden City," Kisada said. He crossed arms over his great chest. His armor made a sound like scuttling crabs.

Hoturi stood firm. "We've forced the Scorpion back within the inner walls," he said. "Only a few stragglers remain, and we'll soon sweep them up. If there is to be anything left of the city, we need to put out these fires. The peasants can't do it on their own. They need our help." The Crane daimyo turned and paced the pavilion. "That bastard Shoju can wait. He has no place left to run."

"Just what I'd expect from a Crane," said Matsu Tsuko, acting head of the Lion. "You have no stomach for fighting. Some problems—this problem—can't be solved with politics, though. Only force will pry the Scorpion from the palace."

"I'm not disagreeing with that," Hoturi said impatiently. "But the city is still burning. We're only now getting it under control. We need to concentrate on saving Otosan Uchi. It's what Hantei would have wanted. Would you have the new emperor rule over a city of ash?"

"Better a city of ash than a city of Scorpions," Kisada said. "What say you, Yokatsu?

The Unicorn daimyo scratched his chin. "The inner wall still holds. Its enchantments are strong. You haven't dented it with flames or rams or magic. Ladders set against it catch fire. Men trying to climb it die screaming. Even the River Gate, where the water flows through the wall, appears impregnable. My samurai can't ride over walls. More force is obviously necessary."

"Hear that, Hoturi?" Tsuko said triumphantly.

Yokatsu held up his hand to quiet her. "But now may not be the time for force," he concluded.

Matsu Tsuko looked at him and snarled, "It's taken us six days to get this far. I won't give up now. Fight fires with Hoturi if you want. I'll be fighting the Scorpion."

Kisada nodded in agreement.

"What do you plan to do, Yokatsu?" Hoturi asked.

"The Phoenix concern me," he said. "We still don't know why they left. Some of my scouts say the Phoenix may rejoin the war on the side of the Scorpion. We should be wary. Someone needs to set patrols, keep the city free from invaders within and without. My people are best suited to the job. You can fight the fires, Hoturi, and the Crab and Lion can bang their heads against that wall. My people will keep the city secure and keep watch."

Hoturi kicked the dirt floor. He went to the front of the pavilion and pulled back the silk. Gazing out over smoke-stained Otosan Uchi, he wondered if the city would ever be the same.

▲▲▲▲▲▲▲▲

Bayushi Aramoro fell to his knees and bowed low before the Scorpion emperor.

"My lord," he said, "I beg you . . . let me return to the battlefield."

Shoju looked hard at his half-brother. Sweat dripped down the brow of the Master of Assassins, though the room was not hot. Aramoro trembled. His breathing was ragged. He was not well, despite receiving the best medicines and treatments available.

"Brother," Shoju said. "Your wound burns with infection. You are not suited for battle. I won't sacrifice your life foolishly, and I forbid you to do so as well."

"Brother . . . please," Aramoro said.

Shoju shook his head. "No. I make you yojimbo to Dairu once again. He needs a bodyguard now more than ever. Besides—" the Scorpion looked to Kachiko on the other side of the chamber "—my wife desires it. Dairu has taken too many reckless chances lately."

Aramoro took a deep, shuddering breath. "Hai, Otennoo-sama," he said. He rose and left the room.

Kachiko crossed the smooth wooden floor and stood by her husband.

"Thank you, my lord," she said, taking his hand.

Shoju nodded. "What news?"

She took a deep breath. "Our lines of control are fraying," she said. "Enemy shugenja block many of our magical communications. Sneaking out of the city has become impossible, even for the best ninja. The assassination attempts I've coordinated against the allied leaders have failed. If only Aramoro were well!"

"Hai," Shoju said grimly. He looked at his wife's face and read the worry behind her silken mask.

"At least," she said, "our enemies do not sleep well, either."

Shoju merely nodded and gazed out over the city. The fires had died down, but the sounds of the dying still echoed over the walls.

▲▲▲▲▲▲▲▲

Tetsuo crept to the edge of a burned-out Scorpion safe house, just beyond the wall of the Forbidden City. No one had discovered the secret passage below the house. Tetsuo had used the tunnel to take several small bands of samurai through to harass the enemy.

Tonight, they had done their jobs well. His first band killed some Lion sentries. His second stole supplies from the Lion's camp. The dimming fires made the Scorpions' stealthy jobs easier. Hidden by the darkness, their training made them nearly invisible.

Shoju would be pleased with the raid's results.

It still wasn't enough.

Standing in the ruins of the safe house, Tetsuo spotted a Unicorn patrol. Their route would take them right by the Scorpion position. There were only four of them.

Tetsuo looked at his samurai. They were battered and bruised, still catching their breath from the evening's skirmishes.

"Five of you," he whispered. "Come with me. The rest, back in the tunnels." Five samurai, Rumiko among them, hurried forward. "If we don't return," Tetsuo said to the others, "tell the lord of our failure."

The remainder of the group nodded. Silently they disappeared into the trapdoor. Tetsuo's allies crouched low beside him.

The young Bayushi looked at Rumiko. Pain was written on her face. The wound in her side troubled her. Yet, she had volunteered for this mission. They all had.

Tetsuo felt proud of his people. He steeled his mind for the attack.

The Unicorn patrol rode closer. At a signal from Tetsuo, the Scorpions sprang.

Tetsuo took the lead rider. He slashed across the man's chest, sundering his lacquered armor and dashing the horseman to the ground.

A red haze drew over Tetsuo's eyes. In his mind, he could hear the song of *Yashin*, Shoju's bloodsword. He chopped the rider's head from his shoulders, but he didn't stop there.

Again he stabbed the Unicorn's body. Again and again. *Yashin*'s song screamed in his mind. He could hear the sound of battle raging around him—the clash of swords, the screams of horses and men—but it came as if from a great distance.

A hand fell on Tetsuo's shoulder. He spun, ready to kill.

It was one of his own men. "They're dead, Tetsuo-san," the man said. "I hear more coming. We must go."

Tetsuo nodded and took a deep breath. Rage seeped out of him. His ears still pounded with blood, but now he could hear more horses coming.

He looked around. All of the Unicorns lay dead. One of his people had lost an arm; the man clutched the bloody stump as his brethren tried to tourniquet it.

Nearby, Rumiko lay in a pool of her own blood. She was dead, her skull crushed by a horse's hoof. Her black hair was splayed about her head like a sunburst.

The sight made Tetsuo's gut clench tight. He couldn't stand the thought of leaving her there in the mud. Not caring that he touched an unclean thing, Tetsuo took hold of her armor and began to drag her away.

"There's no time!" his man said. "Quickly, Tetsuo-san! We must go!"

Tetsuo nodded and dropped Rumiko's body. Her cold, dead eyes stared up at him, reflecting the light from a distant fire.

Tetsuo retreated inside the trapdoor and pulled it shut behind him. Though rites could cleanse his hands of the taint of the dead, nothing would ever wash the sight of Rumiko from his memory.

▲▲▲▲▲▲▲▲

In the hours before the dawn of the seventh day, a lone figure rode silently past the outskirts of the allied position. His coming was hidden by heavy rain. He rode directly to the tent of Matsu Tsuko and dismounted. Recognizing him immediately, the guards allowed him to pass within. One man ran to spread the news of his arrival.

Matsu Tsuko glared at the map of the city. She pounded her fist on the low table. She had been unable to sleep and, at the same time, unable to plot some strategy to defeat the Scorpion. With bitter vindictiveness, she hoped the other generals were having no more luck than she.

The man's entry into her tent startled her. She jumped to her feet. Her hand went to the hilt of her sword.

The man removed his broad-brimmed hat and cast it to the floor near the pavilion's entryway.

Tsuko gasped. "Toturi!"

The Lion general bowed.

Tsuko snarled at him. "Idiot! Where have you been?"

"Poisoned," he said simply. "Held by our enemies."

"I suppose you expect me to turn leadership of my troops over to you," she said angrily.

"Of course," he replied. "I'll need to talk to the other generals as well. Please summon them."

Tsuko's hand strayed once more to the hilt of her sword. She slid it out a few inches. "I should kill you where you stand, traitor."

Toturi's eyes narrowed, but he made no move for his katana. "You can try if you like," he said, "after this is over."

The Lioness pushed the sword back into its scabbard. "With pleasure," she said. She left the tent.

Twenty minutes later, the heads of the clans had gathered in the Lion's pavilion. Of them all—Hoturi, Kisada, Yokatsu, Tsuko, a Mirumoto captain from the Dragon, and a Shiba sergeant from the Phoenix—only the Lions seemed fully awake.

The others looked tired and somewhat stunned by Toturi's sudden appearance—even Kisada.

All wanted to know more of what had happened to Toturi—why he had not been present when the emperor needed him. The Lion General brushed these questions aside, saying there was time for answers once the Scorpion had been defeated.

"After I escaped my captivity," Toturi said, "I rode directly here. During the trip I collected intelligence from those I met on the road. Citizens have fled the capital in great numbers, and many had vital information to tell.

"As I crested the final hill and came within sight of the city," he said, "a vision came to me. I saw the rain and the fire and the smoke engulfing the City of the Sun, and—suddenly—I knew a way to pry the Scorpion from his perch."

Kisada scoffed. "You ride into camp having spent the day listening to peasants, and you expect us to follow you?"

Toturi fixed the Crab with his eyes. "Only if you want to win," he said. "The Scorpion took the city by a combination of force and subterfuge. They planned this for months. We do not have that luxury."

Toturi stood and, like a huge cat, paced the room. "Our forces are greater than Bayushi Shoju's—though his have been better prepared. He expects us to make frontal assaults. That is what we are best at, and that is what we have done so far. You can see the good it has done.

"Shoju sits on the Emerald Throne, his troops secure within the walls of the Forbidden City. He has our people held captive. Why he has not killed them, I do not pretend to understand. It is his mistake. This error means that we have allies within his walls.

"It may be," Toturi continued, "that others of our people still lie hidden within the Forbidden City, or even in the palace itself, waiting for the right moment to strike."

"When will that moment come?" Hoturi of the Crane asked. "If they did not strike when my father fell, when will they?"

"They will strike when we are there to support them," Toturi said.

"Within the palace walls?" Tsuko scoffed. "How?"

"Using the means of the Scorpion himself," Toturi said.

Kisada folded his arms across his broad chest and leaned back. "We're listening," he said.

"Rain and smoke and fire are not just destruction," said Toturi. "They can also be an ally. They can mask an army's true intentions. Is it true that when Shoju left the Forbidden City, he did it by the River Gate?"

Yokatsu nodded. "As impossible as that seems, he did. The wall's defenses are impenetrable at that point, but . . ."

"Obviously they are *not* impenetrable," Toturi said. "The walls are under the Bayushi's command, and they do his will. Probably, he subverted them to that purpose even before he slew the emperor."

The generals around the pavilion nodded.

Toturi slapped his hand on the map table. "We can do the same!" he said.

"The walls are too well guarded," Tsuko complained. "We can't possibly take control of them."

"We don't need to take control of all of them," Toturi said. "We need only one small section—the section the Scorpion will least suspect, the least vulnerable section."

"The River Gate," said Hoturi.

Toturi nodded. "Hai. So far, your most successful forays have been to the south. Now we will pull back. We will go north and east to the Fudotaki Gate, by the waterfall. We will mass the bulk of our forces there, as if to make a large assault.

"As they go, our people will set fires throughout the city."

Some gasped at this. Hoturi said, "We've only just brought the fires under control!"

Toturi looked at the Crane daimyo and replied, "It is sometimes necessary to remove a limb to save a man's life. The fire and smoke and rain, if it holds, will help to mask our true purpose.

"While the Scorpion concentrates his forces to defend the Fudotaki Gate, all our best shugenja will work a subtle spell. They will regain control of the wall near the River Gate, without alerting Bayushi's people.

"The Scorpion shugenja will be distracted by the very real assault we will mount on their eastern sector. We will fight all through the night, giving no quarter.

"Then, just before sunrise tomorrow, I will lead my people through the River Gate. Smoke, fire, and even the Imperial gardens will provide cover for our forces. Most of us will go directly to the palace to carry the assault home, but enough will stay behind to hold the section of wall we have won.

"When I give the signal, the rest of you must come as quickly as you can. You will flood through the wall behind us and take the Forbidden City. You will crush the Scorpion beneath your heels." Toturi folded his arms over his chest and waited for comments from the others.

The Crab spoke first. Kisada rubbed his graying chin and said, "Acting like the Scorpion would bring dishonor upon my clan."

Toturi leaned toward him.

"Then you can storm the Fudotaki Gate until we open it for you."

Kisada leaned back and nodded. "Yosh."

"Are you all with me then?" Toturi asked, placing his hand on the low table in the center of the room.

One by one, the others nodded their assent.

Toturi nodded. "Good."

▲ ▲ ▲ ▲ ▲ ▲ ▲ ▲

"They have gone mad," said Shoju, looking out over the vast fires spreading through the outer city of Otosan Uchi. All day, the combined forces of the allies had swept north, around the enchanted wall, toward the Fudotaki Gate. It seemed they set fire to everything as they went.

Soon, most of the city had been set ablaze. Wind wafted smoke toward the imperial palace, making noon seem twilight and twilight seem midnight.

The Scorpion emperor shifted his forces to fend off the concentrated effort being made by the Crab and the others— but he could make no sense of the attack.

Yashin sang for blood. The sword urged him to ride out, to destroy his enemies. The Scorpion resisted.

The walls by the Fudotaki Gate held, even though the allies threw powerful spells and endless numbers of men against it. The Scorpion marveled at the workmanship of the wall—built by the clans in a joint effort so long ago. Now not even the combined power of the other houses could bring the walls of the Forbidden City down.

Something about the attack troubled the Scorpion emperor, though he could not determine exactly what.

Late in the evening—an evening as black as the pits of Jigoku—Kachiko brought disturbing news to her husband.

"My lord," she said humbly, "the forces outside the wall . . . they say the Lion leads them."

"Tsuko?" Shoju asked, incredulous. "She doesn't have the mane."

Kachiko bowed and said, "No, my lord. Not Tsuko, *Toturi*."

The Scorpion's eyes grew wide behind his mask. "How is that possible?" he asked.

"I do not know," Kachiko said, "though I have sent Asami to find out. It took many of our shugenja to get the message to her."

Shoju nodded. "When Toturi went to see his geisha and did not appear at court, we assumed him dead. It appears we were wrong."

"It seems so, my lord. If the rumors are true," Kachiko said, bowing.

"Find out," said the Scorpion emperor, seating himself before the window.

"Hai, my lord." Kachiko bowed again and left the room.

When she returned three hours later, she found her husband sitting in the same place.

"The rumors are true, my love," she said quietly. "Toturi is with the other clans, leading the assault on the Fudotaki Gate."

Ride out! sang the bloodsword. *Crush him!*

"Asami reports that she did not find his body in the gamekeeper's cabin," Kachiko continued, "though she did find the remnants of the poison."

"The geisha?" Shoju asked coldly.

"Gone as well, though the bloodstained tatters of her kimono were found at the bottom of a waterfall nearby. Whether she jumped or was thrown, Asami could not say."

Shoju stood suddenly and roared as if he were an animal trapped in a cage. He drew *Yashin* and stalked around the room, slashing at the empty air, dancing a kata of destruction.

Kachiko fell to her knees and put her head to the floor. "I am sorry, my lord," she said. "I beg your forgiveness."

Shoju stopped and looked at her where she lay quivering. His face drew tight behind his mask.

Strike out! Kill her! urged the sword. *Betrayer! Whore!*

The Scorpion emperor sheathed the ancient weapon. He walked to his wife's side, making no more noise than a cat.

"You have never failed me," he said quietly, "not since our son's birth."

The reminder of her previous infidelity stuck in Kachiko's gut like a knife. "I am sorry, Great Lord," she said, surprised to find herself crying.

He reached down and lifted her so that she stood and looked into his eyes. Suddenly, he embraced her, so tightly that he took her breath away. Then, just as suddenly, he let her go and stepped back.

"Send our best people to the Fudotaki Gate," he said. "Tetsuo, Aramoro, your woman Miyuki, even Junzo if you must."

Kachiko wiped the tears from her face and nodded. "Junzo is already there," she said. "But your brother is wounded, my lord."

"Send him anyway," Shoju replied. "Tell them to find and kill Toturi, no matter what the cost."

She bowed, "Hai, my lord."

▲▲▲▲▲▲▲▲

Toturi's plan worked just as he had hoped. Throughout the day and into the night, he fought with the others at the Fudotaki Gate. Then, under cover of darkness and smoke, he returned to the western wall, near the River Gate. A carefully chosen double wore his armor and maintained the deception that he fought with the rest of the army. Clothed in simple robes, Toturi blended in with many other unarmored samurai.

The allies' shugenja had done their job well. Distracted by the eastern assault, Shoju's people failed to notice the subtle manipulations of the wall near the River Gate. They didn't detect the spells that slipped in to deceive their senses. Nor did they realize it when their lines of communication came under the control of Toturi's people.

Quickly and carefully, the loyalist shugenja gained dominion of the great gate itself. Their willpower replaced the willpower of the Scorpions sealing the gate shut. With their best wizards at the Fudotaki Gate, the Scorpions never even suspected their mastery of the River Gate had been subverted. The allies' counterspells hid their actions completely.

In the hour before dawn, Toturi's samurai struck. The River Gate opened to the will of the Lion's shugenja. Toturi's forces rushed through. Before any could raise the alarm, the allies killed the Scorpion guards and shugenja controlling the gate. Toturi's shugenja quelled suspicion by keeping the telepathic bonds intact, though allied sorcerers now filled the gaps in the mental circuit. This, too, Toturi knew would be to his advantage.

Using the cover of the gardens, Toturi's forces came upon the palace gates undetected. A powerful spell shattered the outer doors and shook the very palace. The deafening *boom* signaled those outside the walls that the real assault had begun.

At once, Hoturi and the others rushed to the River Gate, leaving Kisada and his men to hold the assault on the eastern wall. The Crane forces charged the palace only slightly behind the Lion. The Unicorn rode swiftly to open the Fudotaki Gate and let the Crab in.

The liberation of the Forbidden City had begun.

▲▲▲▲▲▲▲▲

By the time Doji Hoturi reached the palace doors, the Scorpion guards already lay dead—killed by advancing Lions.

"Follow me," Hoturi commanded. "Find the hostages. Kill any who oppose you."

The Crane forces rushed after their young daimyo. Hoturi knew the palace as well as any man alive. The twisting corridors baffled him not at all.

He headed straight for the inner chambers. The Scorpion would want to keep his prisoners close at hand. Dungeon rooms would be too insulting if the Scorpion hoped to persuade the captives to his cause. Instead, the Bayushi usurper would choose to keep his enemies nearby, where they could be watched.

In ones and twos, Scorpion retainers jumped from concealed corridors, attacking the Crane. They were no match for Hoturi and his troops, though they did slow the progress inward. It took precious time to slay them. Hoturi took the time.

Finally, deep within the palace, near where the hostages must have been, Hoturi and his band rounded a corner to confront a small band of Scorpions. Hoturi smiled. A mere boy commanded these guards of last resort.

"I am Bayushi Dairu," the boy said bravely from the midst of the crowd. "You shall not pass."

The Crane's lips drew back in a sneer. "The son of the Scorpion," he said through gritted teeth. He gestured to his men on either side. They leapt forward and engaged the Scorpion samurai.

"Leave the boy to me," Hoturi cried over the clashing of swords.

He advanced quickly, a smile drawing across his handsome face. The faces of the Scorpions remained hidden behind their masks—the better to hide their lies.

Hoturi beat back the sword of the man opposing him and cut him down with a slash from collarbone to heart. Another man stepped between the Crane and his intended victim.

Bayushi Dairu waded into his foes without fear. He wouldn't wait for the Crane daimyo to come to him. For years Dairu's father had told him of Hoturi's undisciplined, selfish ways. In this battle, Dairu could see what the Scorpion lord meant. Hoturi's carefully polished armor and weapon fairly screamed self-importance. Even in the midst of the fight, not a hair was out of place on the Crane's head. He looked as though he'd never suffered a battle scar in his life.

Dairu brought his sword up and parried the attack of a Crane samurai. He slashed down, opening the man's chest. The Scorpion heir kicked the dying samurai away and moved to the next man.

Hoturi's smile widened. His men were winning the battle. Clearly they'd caught the Scorpions by surprise. The usurpers didn't even have any armor. Only a few men stood between him and the Scorpion heir—and most of those men were his own.

He plunged his katana into the gut of a Scorpion samurai-ko and twisted. The woman gasped out her life and fell. Hoturi strode atop her.

The Crane daimyo and the Scorpion heir drew nearer.

Dairu found himself glancing from the man he was fighting to the Crane leader. If I can kill him, Dairu thought, the day will be ours. Father, lend me strength!

He spun as he had seen Shoju do, leveled his blade, and took off a Crane samurai's head. Dairu flicked his blade in the shiburi motion, cleaning the blood from it. He saw the Crane close by. Dairu looked Hoturi in the eyes.

I'm coming for you! the young Scorpion thought.

In the face of the Crane daimyo, Dairu saw something unexpected. Hoturi did not look as Dairu imagined he would. The face returning his gaze was familiar, handsome. Dairu had seen a face like it many times, staring back from his own mirror.

"Back away!" Hoturi cried to his people. "Leave the pup to me!"

The Crane samurai did as their daimyo commanded.

A few moments later, Dairu stood alone in a circle of dead samurai. His sword and kimono were stained with blood—though none of it was his own.

"I will not surrender," Dairu said, assuming a defensive stance.

"I won't ask you to," the Crane replied, smiling. Hoturi leapt forward, swinging his sword as he came.

Dairu parried, turning aside the blade with enough force that Hoturi winced from the wound Shoju had given him.

Dairu spun, dancing like his Scorpion father. He aimed his blade at the Crane's back.

Hoturi turned and parried; their blades slid apart. He thrust at the boy's midsection.

Dairu batted the sword away and lashed out with his foot. The Scorpion's toe connected with the Crane's knee, and Hoturi staggered back. A lock of hair fell from Hoturi's topknot and caressed his brows. The Scorpion heir smiled. Not so perfect anymore, he thought. He lunged, aiming at the Crane's chest.

Hoturi parried and counterattacked, thrusting his katana at Dairu's neck.

Dairu parried high. Before he realized his mistake, Hoturi made a slashing cut downward. The blow opened the young Scorpion's belly, and he collapsed on the floor.

"For Satsume," Hoturi said, stepping over the body. He wiped the blood from his blade onto Dairu's kimono and motioned his men to follow.

As they left, the Crane turned back to the dying boy. "Tell your father 'hello' when you see him in hell," he said.

▲▲▲▲▲▲▲▲

"The Lion is in the palace! The Lion is in the palace!"

The cry shattered the Scorpion emperor's sleep. He hadn't realized he had dozed off. Behind him, the Emerald Throne felt cold and hard.

Instantly Shoju was on his feet, drawing his sword. His lame arm ached in complaint, and the fire from his tattoo burned his shoulder.

Not now, he thought. Not now!

Kachiko ran into the room. "My lord," she cried, "our defenses are breached!"

"How?" he asked.

"I don't know, my lord," she said. "But the Lion is in the palace. The River Gate has fallen."

"Curse me for a fool!" Shoju said. "The assault to the east was only a feint! Summon my people!" he said. "Tetsuo, Aramoro, Miyuki, Junzo."

Kachiko shook her head. "They have not returned from the battle," she said. For the first time, her husband saw worry and possibly even *fear* in her face.

"Where is the Lion?" he asked.

"On his way to the throne room," she said breathlessly. "I don't know if our forces can stop him."

Shoju's face grew grim behind his mask. He sheathed his sword and embraced her, crushing her body against his chest. She returned the hug and lifted up her face to kiss him. He pushed back his mask.

Frantically their lips met, and then parted.

"We are undone," Shoju said. "Find our son. Take him to safety. Spread the word among our people. They are to scatter, hide, assume new identities. They should do whatever is necessary to survive, and pray that history will prove out our cause."

Kachiko nodded, blinking back tears. "And you, my lord?"

"I will face the Lion alone," he said. "If the head of the enemy is removed, the body also will fall."

Kachiko embraced him, and they kissed again. When they parted, he pulled down his mask once more.

The Scorpion emperor had worn his favorite face today. The mask was neither happy nor sad. Instead it showed a grim resolve. The face said, "I shall not be defeated."

He opened the door to the throne room, and Kachiko passed into the corridor beyond. She slid open a secret panel and slipped inside, taking one last, lingering look before she closed it. She mouthed the words, "I love you."

He nodded. Then she was gone.

Moments after she had left, footsteps clattered up the corridor. Lion retainers met and slew Scorpion samurai.

Gracefully, Bayushi Shoju crossed to the Emerald Throne and seated himself on it, the sword *Yashin* hanging at his side. Blood pounded in Shoju's temples, but the song of *Ambition* almost smothered the sound. Almost.

Quietly the Scorpion emperor sat as Toturi's forces charged up to the throne room door and skidded to a halt.

The Lion spotted his enemy and took a step forward.

One of Shoju's long fingers stabbed a hidden stud on the arm of the throne.

Weights and counterweights fell into place. The iron doors

to the throne room suddenly slammed shut, trapping the Lion inside.

Toturi's men pounded on the door, to no avail.

Behind his grim mask, the Scorpion emperor smiled.

22 WORDS BETWEEN MEN

As well as Hoturi knew the palace corridors, Bayushi Kachiko knew them better. Long ago, while the other clans built the great walls, Scorpions had built the palace and its defenses. Among these were the twisting maze of corridors that Hoturi had taken to secure the hostages. Intertwined with the corridors were a second set of passageways—secret ones known only to members of the emperor's family and, of course, to the descendants of the Scorpions who built them.

It took little time for the Scorpion mistress to find her way from the throne room to the chamber where the hostages were being held. Unfortunately, Hoturi had gotten there first.

By the time Kachiko found her son, there was little life left in him. She let out a soft cry and raced to his side, lifting Dairu from the gore-spattered floor.

"Who?" she asked, cradling his bloody head in her arms. "Who did this to you?"

"Hoturi," was all the boy had time to say. He reached for her tearstained face. Then he was gone.

A small cry escaped Bayushi Kachiko's lips.

She bowed her head and wept long and piteously. Only when she heard the noises of the returning Crane did Kachiko gather her resolve.

She carried her son into a secret passage, so the Crane would not find him. Then she closed the panel and left him there. She still had a mission to complete.

Dairu's fair face haunted her dreams ever after.

▲▲▲▲▲▲▲▲

Bayushi Shoju stood as his foe entered the room.

"These doors will not save you, assassin," Toturi said.

Shoju shook his head. "I am not the one who needs saving," he said.

Toturi drew his katana. "Defend yourself, Scorpion."

Shoju bowed. "If you insist." He drew *Yashin*, and the room suddenly grew dark.

"Power is a sword with two edges," the Scorpion lord said. "Even wielding it carefully, you may still get cut. You have not been careful, Akodo Toturi."

Like a dancer, Shoju moved gracefully around the room. Ignoring the stiffness in his right arm, he swung *Ambition* in long arcs.

"Your lust for power shall be your death, Scorpion," Toturi said. He assumed a defensive stance and watched the Scorpion lord for weakness—as he had done with Ishikawa not long ago.

Unfortunately, the Master of Secrets was not so easy to read as the captain of the guard.

Toturi realized with sudden shock how little he knew

about the man he faced. Bayushi Shoju was reputed to be one of the best swordsmen in all Rokugan—but almost no reports of his technique or style had ever reached the Lion's ears.

Toturi had seen Scorpion swordsmen in battle—even left-handed samurai. He'd faced a number of them himself. Left-handed warriors were always more dangerous because Rokugani swordsmanship was based on fighting right-handed opponents. Still, Toturi had overcome the handicap before.

As this graceful black cat of a man stalked around the throne room, Toturi realized he'd never seen anything like Bayushi Shoju in his life. It wasn't just the Scorpion's left-handedness that made a shiver run down the Lion's spine. It was the way the Usurper moved: fast, agile, twirling on the balls of his feet.

Shoju had slain the Emerald Champion only a few days before. He'd also given Hoturi a nasty scar across his chest.

Hoturi could've taught me how to get killed by Shoju, Toturi thought, but I need to know how to win.

Hidden behind his grim mask, the Scorpion's face betrayed none of his intentions.

"I don't lust for power," Shoju said, his voice quiet and sonorous. "I live only to serve." He continued to circle the room; Toturi followed the Scorpion's movements.

"You serve only your evil self," Toturi said, almost spitting the words.

"Not true," Shoju said calmly. "I serve Rokugan. What I have done, I have done for the greater good."

"What good can come from killing the emperor?"

"The good of saving the empire. By slaying the Hantei, I have preserved Rokugan. I have prevented the return of Fu Leng. Uikku prophesied that the last Hantei would bring the Evil One back to Rokugan. Even the emperor himself charged me to do whatever I must to save the empire."

"More Scorpion lies," Toturi said.

Shoju shook his head. "The truth. Hantei would have considered his life, and the life of his son, a small price to save all of Rokugan."

"Madman!" Toturi cried. He charged, aiming a cut at the Scorpion's throat.

Shoju parried easily and danced aside, putting some space between himself and the Lion.

"The only madness," he said, "is pursuing a path that will lead to destruction. You should know that, Toturi."

The way he said the words made Toturi think of Hatsuko and her betrayal. The fire in his belly grew. He charged the Scorpion again; again, Shoju whirled aside. This time he left a slashing cut on the Lion's right shoulder.

Shoju now stood in front of the Emerald Throne. The long blade of *Yashin* gleamed red in the light of the room's lanterns. "Fortune has been kind to you once, Lion," Shoju said. "Perhaps you have an even greater destiny than I. But I have met my fate, fulfilled my destiny. *Never* have I shirked my responsibilities, not even when they called for the death of the emperor."

"You may deceive yourself with lies," Toturi said, "but you will not deceive me."

He rushed forward again and thrust his sword high. Shoju parried and stepped aside. The Lion had expected it. Toturi counterthrust low, piercing the Scorpion's black kimono. The Lion's sword found only billowing silk.

Shoju twisted and brought the pommel of *Ambition* crashing into the side of Toturi's head.

Toturi reeled back; he stumbled against the throne.

Shoju backed away from his fallen foe in long, graceful steps. He twirled his sword in an intricate kata. "You may rest on the throne, Toturi," he said in his musical voice, "but it will never support you."

"Are you a man or a demon?" Toturi asked. He thrust himself off the throne and toward his foe.

The move caught Shoju by surprise; he took a step back.

Toturi swung his right leg forward in a sweeping motion, making contact with the Scorpion's shins. Shoju tottered back. Toturi thrust upward with his sword.

The Lion's blade caught between Shoju's face and his mask. The Master of Secrets flinched away. The sword cut the straps that held the grim mask to the Scorpion emperor's face. The mask fell to the floor and shattered. Shoju leapt back, *Yashin* parrying a second thrust by Toturi.

Both men paused to catch their breath. The dim lantern light revealed Shoju's true aspect. His face was thin and skull-like, with waxen skin and pale, crooked lips. His large eyes bulged slightly, making the red pupils even more menacing. His brow slanted down toward a long, hawklike nose. The whole formed an arrow to the daimyo's pointed chin.

"A demon after all, then," said Toturi. He let out a soft breath and adjusted his grip on his sword.

"Has your beautiful visage won you so much, Lion?" the Scorpion asked. "Sometimes truth is ugly and deception beautiful. I fight for the empire. For whom do you fight? Some geisha? For adoration of the masses? For the emperor's approval? Of the two of us, whose motives are more pure? Which one of us truly wears a mask?"

Toturi shook his head to clear it. The Scorpion's words had begun to wear on him as much as the fight. Could there be any truth in what the Bayushi said?

Shoju beckoned with long fingers. "Come, then," he said softly, "let us see if truth is indeed beauty." He stretched out his sword behind him and held out his right hand.

Toturi charged forward, an incoherent scream on his lips. He cut high, then thrust low. Shoju spun, just as he had with the Emerald Champion. Toturi was ready for the move and parried the thrust.

Shoju whirled away and traced a thin gash across the Lion's exposed back.

Toturi turned in time to parry the cut aimed at his neck. He thrust forward.

Shoju danced back, easily beating the Lion's blade aside. The Scorpion whipped his sword in a circle, catching Toturi's katana just below the hand guard. The impact ripped the blade from the Lion's hand and sent it skidding across the throne room floor.

Toturi ducked to avoid the follow-up blow, but it never came. Instead, Shoju withdrew, gesturing for Toturi to retrieve the weapon.

"Is truth beauty?" the Scorpion asked as Toturi fetched his sword. A hideous smile creased Shoju's face. "To think, I once feared you," he said with a laugh. "Sheep in lion's clothing. Pretender. *Whore master*."

Toturi snarled and charged again. Shoju parried his blow, and the next, and the next. Toturi turned aside the Scorpion's thrusts and forced the emperor back toward the Emerald Throne. All the while, Shoju smiled at him, as if privy to some secret joke.

"Perhaps fate saved you from the poison so I could kill you myself," the Scorpion said. Wickedness permeated his sweet voice.

Toturi realized he was sweating. His breath came in labored gasps. Perspiration dripped into his eyes. A knot of fear twisted inside his gut. Still he pressed forward.

As they reached the imperial dais, Shoju's heel caught the edge. He toppled into the seat of the throne. He reacted quickly, spinning out of the way. Toturi's sword crashed down, splitting the back of the Emerald Throne in two before the blade caught in the seat.

Toturi gasped. Both men stood silent for a moment.

Slowly, Toturi withdrew his sword.

Shoju let out his breath first. "I understand now," he said quietly. "My dream . . . it has come true. I have rent our people as surely as you have rent the throne. I can be the emperor, but I will sit on a throne of skulls and rule over a land of the dead. I have saved the empire but destroyed the throne! Such a price, honor! Such a price, ambition!"

With that he charged, dancing, twirling his sword over his head as he came.

Toturi leapt back, fear building in him. He saw his death in the Scorpion's red eyes. He parried wildly, but Shoju's sword never touched his.

Instead, the Scorpion emperor mounted the dais in two quick steps. He brought the sword down swiftly, as though stabbing his own heart, thrusting *Yashin* into the cleft in the seat of the throne. The sword sparked and screamed with rage. Shoju twisted with all his might.

Yashin broke. The wailing of a thousand lost souls filled the room. Blood gushed from the shards of the bloodsword, splattering the white plaster walls with indelible crimson. Shoju's lame arm screamed in pain, and his tattoo spread burning fire through the limb.

Shoju felt as though lightning coursed through him, but still he twisted—still he persevered. For long minutes, blood gushed from the sword, as though a red river had been dammed within it. At last, the spouts of blood stopped, and the broken sword fell from the Scorpion's hands.

Covered in the gore of his own ambition, Shoju threw his arms wide and turned his hideous face to the sky. "Forgive me!" he cried.

Awestruck and gasping for breath, Toturi faced the throne. Fear of the Scorpion twisted like a dagger in him.

Shoju stood with his back to the Lion, wrapped in his own reverie.

Desperate, Toturi ran forward and thrust his katana through the Scorpion's body. The point came out Bayushi Shoju's chest. For a moment, the Master of Secrets stared at it.

Toturi withdrew the blade.

Shoju turned and gazed into his killer's eyes. In the Bayushi's blood-red orbs, the Lion thought he saw relief.

Then the Scorpion emperor spun, dancerlike one last time, and fell gracefully to the floor, dead.

23 THE THRONE OF SKULLS

For a long moment, Toturi stood over the body of his slain foe. The Lion heard the shouts of his men outside and their fists pounding the iron doors.

Shoju's dead eyes stared at the ceiling. His twisted lips wore a final smile. Even in death, he seemed to claim victory.

Toturi crossed to the remains of the Emerald Throne and pressed the stud that Shoju had activated earlier. Weights and counterweights moved again, and the great doors slid open.

The Lion's men rushed into the throne room, greatly relieved to find him alive. Among them came Ikoma Bentai, Toturi's general and old friend. Bentai and the others glanced around the gore-spattered chamber and, when they saw the Scorpion's body, shouted with joy. They laughed and clapped each other on the shoulders and congratulated their leader for his victory.

Toturi barely heard their words. Instead, he stared at the man he had killed. Toturi now saw the nobility in Shoju's monstrous form. The Scorpion daimyo had given everything for the empire. He may not have been right in his actions, but he had believed them, and he had given his life—and the lives of his clan—for them.

Truly Bayushi Shoju had been samurai.

Guilt over what he had just done welled up in the Lion's breast. Shoju had beaten him, just as surely as if he had run *Yashin* through Toturi's heart.

The sound of footsteps and voices came at the door. Doji Hoturi arrived in the throne room along with a small contingent of Crane samurai.

"What has happened here?" he asked, surveying the bloody scene.

"Toturi killed the Scorpion," Bentai said proudly.

Lion samurai nodded enthusiastically at their daimyo and grunted their approval.

Hoturi sheathed his sword, threw his arms wide, and laughed. "Ha ha! Tell me how it happened!" he said to Toturi.

Slowly, the Lion brought his gaze from Shoju's body to the eyes of his old friend and rival. The joy in Hoturi's eyes made the guilt in Toturi's breast even greater. The Lion looked away.

"He closed the great iron doors, trapping me in the chamber with him," Toturi said. "My men were locked outside. Long we fought." The Lion glanced at the cleft throne, rent by Yashin. He could not bear the thought of what he had done. "Bayushi's sword caught in the throne. It shattered. I slew him."

Ikoma Bentai laughed. "Our leader has grown suddenly modest! Is this the teller of stories known throughout all Rokugan?"

Hoturi crossed the room and smiled at the Lion daimyo. "Why so grim?" the Crane asked. "It seems to be a good day to slay Scorpions! I slew the Bayushi pup myself. We should rejoice in our victories!" He noticed the wounds on Toturi's back and shoulder. "I guess you didn't escape unscathed. To tell the truth, I'm amazed your wounds aren't worse. I guess the Bayushi's skills were overrated."

Toturi shook his head. "No. He was a noble foe."

"You mean he fought nobly—for a traitor," Hoturi said. "But never mind. Rest here while I spread the news. The day is ours!" The Crane daimyo turned. He and his retinue left the room.

"My lord, wait!" someone cried softly.

The delicate voice startled the Lion troops. Toturi's samurai scoured the throne room with their eyes, searching for the source of the sound.

"There, my lord!" Bentai said. He pointed to a slender hand protruding from a crack in a nearby wall.

The Lion's men rushed forward and seized the hand. "A secret panel," one cried. They pried it open and roughly pulled the owner of the hand into the room.

Doji Shizue spilled onto the floor of the throne room. She looked pale and weak, like a frail butterfly, barely able to raise herself up.

Bentai poked his head into the secret room. "No other exits, my lord. Just a few empty water jars," he said. "She must have been here for a while."

Shizue looked into Toturi's eyes. "Yes," she said quietly. "Long enough . . . I have remained hidden a long time."

Toturi gazed at the Crane courtesan's sallow face and saw that she knew the truth. She had seen the battle with Shoju, seen the Lion stab his foe in the back. She knew of Toturi's treachery, his fear, and his self-serving lies.

"She could be a Scorpion spy," one of Toturi's men said. "We should kill her." He looked at the Lion, anticipating the command.

Toturi knew he could silence Shizue forever with one simple word. Whatever secrets she knew would go to the grave with her, but the Crane's almond eyes held him. The guilt in Toturi's breast deepened.

"Do you know her, my lord?" Bentai asked.

"I am Doji Shizue," she said, not waiting for Toturi to reply. "Hoturi is my daimyo. Please, take me to him."

"She could be lying," said one man.

"Should we do as she says, my lord?" Bentai asked. He was watching Toturi's face carefully.

Does he suspect my shame? Toturi wondered.

Before the Lion daimyo could answer, Doji Hoturi and his men returned to the throne room. "We are securing the castle, General Toturi," he began. "Only a few stragglers remain." Seeing the girl, he froze, and his jaw dropped. "Shizue!" he said.

She bowed weakly. "My lord."

"How did she come here?" Hoturi asked.

"We found her in a secret chamber near the throne," Bentai replied.

"Then this day is doubly blessed," said Hoturi. He turned to the girl and smiled. "Beyond all hope you return to us. We had given you up for lost." Two of Hoturi's men rushed forward to help her stand.

"I nearly was lost," she said, looking from Hoturi to Toturi and then back again.

Toturi felt as though a fist had tightened around his heart.

Unaware of his friend's inner turmoil, Hoturi clapped the Lion on the shoulder.

"You have done a great service to us all this day," he said. "You have rid the world of the Scorpion, and you have delivered a favorite daughter back to my house."

"But the throne sits empty," Toturi said.

Hoturi brought his hand to his face and rubbed his clean-shaven chin. "Hmm, you're right," he said. "This could be a problem. Hantei is dead, but what of his heir? Could the boy still be alive?"

"The heir is dead as well," said Shizue. "I heard them speak of it on the night of the coup. Scorpions killed him while he walked in the gardens." Bitterness and anger filled her young voice.

For a moment, visions of fire and destruction danced

before Toturi's eyes. He saw clan set against clan once more—worse than during the siege. Leaderless, the great houses would turn against each other and vie for supremacy.

In death, the Scorpion would destroy the empire just as surely as he had in life. Toturi had only one choice.

"Then, as commanding general of the allied forces," he said. "I claim the throne."

Hoturi and the Crane looked shocked, but Toturi stood firm. He drew himself up to his full height, shaking off his doubts so that no one would suspect the conflicts that lay in his heart.

"By my wisdom and the might of the combined clans, we have defeated the Scorpion Coup," he said. "The unity of our peoples has served us well, and I pledge that it shall continue. I promise to treat all fairly and equally—even our vanquished foes.

"For the good of the empire, I claim the Emerald Throne until such a time as the leaders of the great houses can establish a new line of succession. I pray that all of you will support me in this."

As Toturi finished his speech, all those in the room bowed. The Lions did so first, and then the Cranes, even Hoturi. "Until such a time . . ." the Crane daimyo said.

The last to bow was Shizue. When she did so, she did not bow as deeply as the others.

When everyone stood, Toturi spoke again.

"Go now," he said. "Spread the news that the dark reign of the Scorpion is over. The Lion's justice is now the rule of the land."

The others turned and left. Doji Shizue held the new emperor with her almond eyes for a long time before she went. Ikoma Bentai, the Lion general, lingered behind.

"Go as well," Toturi said to him. "See that Otosan Uchi is secure. Set details to quench the fires that we spread in our haste to reclaim the throne."

"Is that the royal 'we' or we as Lions?" Bentai asked, arching one eyebrow.

Toturi smiled at him. "We as the free people of Rokugan," he said wearily.

Bentai bowed and left.

As the iron doors swung shut behind the general, Toturi collapsed into the rent and bloody throne. A throne of skulls, Bayushi Shoju had called it.

In the end at least, the Scorpion had been right.

The weight of the empire bore down on the Lion general.

He couldn't help but think of the terrible cost this throne had exacted. His mind turned first from Hatsuko, who had betrayed him, to Shizue, who might yet betray his secret shame.

In the wreckage of the Emerald Throne, Akodo Toturi found little rest.

24 RETURN OF THE PRINCE

He's done what?" Matsu Tsuko asked, almost screaming.

"Claimed the throne," Ikoma Bentai repeated. "Until such time as a new succession can be decided on."

"Oh, that's *good*," Tsuko said, her lips curling back in anger. "As if the rest of the clans could ever agree on anything."

"They fought well enough under Toturi," Bentai pointed out.

"I'm sure my illustrious 'cousin' is counting on that," she said. "He may be able to sit on that throne, 'keeping it warm' forever."

"I don't think he relishes the job," Bentai said.

"He didn't relish becoming daimyo either," Tsuko said. "Yet, somehow, he came to lead our clan—even though there were . . . *are* others more qualified to do so."

"Others such as yourself?"

Tsuko wheeled like a caged tiger. "Why should I deny it? If Toturi's brother hadn't died before we could marry, it would be *my* line leading our clan."

"And would you have been able to defeat the Scorpion, then?" Bentai asked.

"Have a care, old man," Tsuko said, fingering the pommel of her katana. "If I had been in charge, the emperor might never have been slain. At least *I* would not have been off whoring when the Hantei were assassinated."

Bentai bowed. "Despite your feelings, the other lords have agreed to follow Toturi's plan," he said. "Even Kisada."

"Crabs!" Tsuko said, making it sound like a curse. "They've dwelt so long in the shadow of darkness, they can no longer recognize the light."

"Be that as it may . . ."

"Very well," Tsuko said. "Tell the Lion I will call on him, though I will *not* make obeisance."

"Our daimyo is a simple man," Bentai said. "I'm sure he does not expect you to stand on ceremony . . . any more than usual."

Tsuko frowned. "He better not—or we may have a second coup."

▲▲▲▲▲▲▲▲

Whispers about the new emperor surrounded the Emerald Court like a wall of fog. Where had Toturi been during the coup?

The people seemed to forget that the Emerald Champion, his son Hoturi, and a number of the other lords had not been present either. The suspicions of the populace focused on the Lion sitting on the throne.

More forgiving souls said that even had Toturi and the others been present, the emperor would still have been slain. Probably, they insisted, the Scorpion would have killed all those who opposed him that night, and then there never could have been a counterrevolution.

Akodo Toturi tried to believe that point of view with all his heart. Yet, deep within his soul he felt a black emptiness. He knew he had betrayed his duty to the emperor for Hatsuko. He also knew he had defeated Shoju, the new emperor, only through dishonorable means. His fear had driven him to it, and now fear gnawed at him.

Doji Shizue held her tongue, though Toturi saw accusation in her eyes.

The allied forces continued to root out straggling Scorpions and put them to the sword. Strangely, none of Bayushi's high command turned up in the sweeps. Soon, the Scorpion section of Otosan Uchi was all but deserted.

Though the Forbidden City had survived largely intact, the damage to Otosan Uchi was considerable. Rebuilding the rest of the city began immediately after the Lion took the throne. It would be many years before the City of the Shining Prince recovered from the Scorpion Coup. If nothing else, Toturi's rule had restored order to the once-peaceful capital.

On the third day after assuming the throne, Toturi stood in the high tower of the palace and looked out over the Scorpion districts, where the fires of retaliation still smoldered.

Ikoma Bentai entered the room and bowed; Toturi bowed in return.

"Majesty, I have news of the Phoenix," the Lion General said. "They have gathered a great army and are even now marching on the city."

"What?" asked Toturi, genuinely shocked at the news. "How far?"

"Two days at most."

"Why did our scouts not spot them previously?"

"We suspect powerful magic, great lord."

Toturi nodded grimly. He had hoped not to have to defend the throne so soon.

"There is more, my lord," Bentai said. Toturi gestured for him to continue. "People are saying the Hantei heir is among the Phoenix retinue," Bentai added.

Toturi's mouth dropped open. "How is that possible?"

"I do not know, great lord—but that is what our scouts say."

"He is dead! Shizue confirmed it. I never would have . . ." Toturi's sentence trailed off. Already the possibilities played over in his mind. Perhaps Shizue lied, knowing the embarrassment it would cause him—embarrassment he richly deserved, if not for taking the throne, then for stabbing Shoju in the back.

Or perhaps it was some kind of mistake or ruse. The Phoenix had withheld the main part of their army from the assault to retake the city. Perhaps they had their own designs on Otosan Uchi. Perhaps they were in league with the Scorpion. Certainly they had been little help in overthrowing the coup.

Bentai cleared his throat. "There is more, my lord," he said. "Your fiancée is with them."

"Kaede?" Toturi asked. "I thought she had been killed in the coup."

"So it was generally believed, though her body was never found."

Toturi didn't know whether to laugh or cry. He felt relieved Kaede was not dead, but terrified at what her return might hold for him. True, Hatsuko was no longer a factor in his thinking, but Toturi had treated the Phoenix Mistress of the Void badly. Would she hold it against him? Would anyone?

Fighting down the fear gnawing at his stomach, Toturi said, "Make all necessary preparations. Their intent may be peaceful—though it may not. If the Shining Prince is with them, we must be ready to give him all due respect."

Ikoma Bentai bowed and said, "Hai!"

⋏⋏⋏⋏⋏⋏⋏⋏

Two days later, Toturi stood before the Emperor's Gate, dressed in his most formal kimono, ready to greet the Hantei heir.

The Scorpion districts had been swept clean—the houses nearest to the road razed—as soon as they confirmed that the Hantei was among the Phoenix. The heir would want to enter the city by his father's sacred road.

With Toturi came the other great lords who were present in the city: Hoturi, Kisada, and Yokatsu, along with Tsuko and representatives of all the other clans, both major and minor. The retinue that turned out to greet the heir looked impressive indeed, though a late afternoon shower threatened to dampen the ceremony.

The great gate swung open, and Toturi gazed out over the Phoenix host. At their head came the young Hantei, carried on a large, open litter by a dozen bearers. He was dressed in the robes of an emperor and wore a circlet of jade on his head. There could be no mistake—he truly was the heir, not some impostor.

Seppun Ishikawa, the captain of the guard, rode at the boy's left, keeping a watchful eye on the crowd.

To Hantei's right, Isawa Kaede rode on the back of a Unicorn-bred steed. She looked proud, powerful, and even tall in the saddle. She was beautiful enough to break Toturi's heart. The Lion emperor felt his chest grow tight at the sight of her.

Suddenly, the world dissolved around him, and time stood still. A white, cloudlike dragon danced in the sky, behind the advancing retinue.

"So, Toturi," it hissed in a thunderous voice, "you have placed yourself on the throne."

"Not by choice," Toturi replied quietly, unsure if anyone else would hear him.

"We all have choices, Akodo Toturi, and yours have brought you to this."

"I did not seek the throne," Toturi said.

"Yet," said the dragon, "every choice you made has led you down this path. Your quest for love, for glory, for respect, all are now culminated in this most logical outcome. You are emperor."

"No," Toturi said. "The boy before me is emperor."

"Have a care," the dragon said, its words buffeting Toturi like the wind. "You have not yet paid the full price for your hubris and, sadly, neither has Rokugan."

With that, the dragon disappeared and Toturi turned to face the new emperor.

25 THE JUDGMENT OF HANTEI

"Akodo Toturi," the young Hantei said, looking down his round nose at the Lion General. "We understand that in our absence you have declared yourself emperor." He fixed Toturi with his dark eyes and scowled.

Toturi bowed. "It was beyond our hope that you lived, my prince. . . ."

The boy cut him off. "*Your Majesty*," he said testily. "We have been crowned in Phoenix lands, following the death of our father."

". . . Your Majesty," Toturi said, correcting himself. "I took the throne only to maintain stability until proper succession could be determined. I renounce it now, gladly." He bowed low, nearly touching his head to the ground.

"We take the throne from you, Toturi," the boy said, sitting in the golden chair upon his litter. "Though we maintain that you, indeed, never held it any more than did the vile usurper."

The comparison to Shoju stabbed Toturi like a knife, but he remained bowed and showed no emotion on his face.

"Indeed," the young emperor continued, "we would ask you by what *right* you claimed the throne when, previously, you had failed so grievously to protect the man who sat upon it?"

"I apologize for my shortcomings, Majesty," Toturi said. "I only did what I thought best for the empire."

"Best for the empire?" said the boy, his voice growing more shrill by the moment. "*Best for the empire!* How is it best for the empire that you cavort with geishas, with *whores*, while my father is being assassinated?"

The knife in Toturi's gut grew cold. He glanced up and found both Kaede and Shizue looking at him. "Your Majesty, I . . ." he began.

Emperor Hantei flicked his fan open and waved it dismissively. "We will hear none of your excuses, Lion," he said. "Our *loyal* servants have told us what you were about while our father died. We do not care what you have to say. There can be no words to defend what you have done.

"We have even heard," the boy said, leaning forward in his chair, "that perhaps you and the Scorpion betrayer were secretly allied—and that is why you were not in court the night my father died!"

Toturi scrambled to his feet, his heart fluttering, the dagger in his gut twisting tighter. "Majesty, that is not true!"

"*Silence!*" bellowed the boy emperor. "You will bow and hear our judgment, or we shall have you slain where you stand." He glanced to one of his guards, and the man stepped forward.

Toturi dropped to the street and bowed once more.

"If he gets up again, kill him," the boy said to his guards.

"We think," the emperor continued, "that perhaps you were in league with the usurper. Why else were you not here? But perhaps you and the demon Scorpion had a falling out. You returned to the city and betrayed him, only to claim the throne yourself."

Hantei stood now and glowered down at Toturi from his litter. "But you did not know that we still lived," he said, his lips drawing into a cruel smile. "You did not know our *faithful* servants had smuggled us to safety." Here he turned and looked at both Kaede on his right and Ishikawa on his left. They nodded, though it seemed to Toturi that both of them looked increasingly uncomfortable.

"I should have you executed right now," the emperor hissed.

"Majesty, no," Kaede said in a soft voice.

From the other side, Ishikawa supported her suggestion. He leaned on his long spear, looking uncomfortable as he spoke to the new emperor. "It is true he has much to answer for," the captain said, "but you can not wring the truth from a dead man."

"And," Kaede added, "he gave up the throne willingly."

"Very well," the emperor said, flicking his fan shut and sitting back down on his golden perch. "Lion, we strip you of your rank and title as our general. Any further punishments will be decided later."

The boy paused and rubbed his head as if to chase away pain. "You should know, however," he said, "that your Scorpion friends no longer exist. We have ordered the clan disbanded. Even now, our forces march to strip them of their homelands."

Toturi looked up, unable to believe what he had heard. He noticed that many of the others present looked shocked as well.

"Otennoo-sama," Toturi said, choosing his words carefully, "surely you cannot punish the children for the actions of their fathers. I'm sure many Scorpions remain loyal to the Hantei."

"It is already done," the emperor said, continuing to rub his forehead. "Even now, our loyal supporters are rounding up the traitors. They shall be brought here to face our judgment. Leaderless and in disarray, they are no match for our might."

"But destroying a Great House," Toturi said, still feeling his betrayals, "surely it will upset the balance of power." In his mind, Toturi saw the man he had slain, a man willing to give up his life and clan for the good of the empire, a man Toturi had stabbed in the back. "Bayushi Shoju . . ." Toturi began, but the new emperor cut him off.

"We shall never hear his name again!" Emperor Hantei snapped. "Anyone who speaks it shall be killed! We order that Bayushi Shoju's name be excised from all records. His line shall be utterly destroyed; no trace of them shall exist, now or ever more! As for you, Lion . . ."

Before Hantei could finish his judgment, a breathless man ran through the gate and knelt before the emperor's litter.

"We have her, Majesty," the man said, bowing low. "She is on her way here even now."

"Who?" the boy emperor asked impatiently.

"The Mother of Scorpions," the man replied. "Bayushi Kachiko. Our patrols caught her on the way to Beiden Pass. She fought fiercely, but she is subdued and unharmed."

The crowd gasped at the news. The boy on the golden perch merely smiled a cruel smile.

"The Lion can wait. Bring Kachiko to our throne room," he said. "We shall see her bow before us, and then we shall see her executed."

26 WORDS BETWEEN WOMAN AND BOY

Emperor Hantei the 39th gazed down from his sundered throne as the guards dragged Bayushi Kachiko into his presence. A hush fell over the blood-stained hall, and the great lords glanced at each other from where they sat on the smooth wooden floor.

Kachiko looked anything but the former empress of the Emerald Empire. Her kimono was dirty and torn, her hair unkempt, and her delicate mask missing entirely. Still, as she struggled against the ropes that bound her, she exuded an aura palpable to everyone in the room. In this most humiliating condition, the Scorpion mistress was still a woman of grace and power.

Miya Satoshi, the young herald, looked at her and thought of his father, still lying in bed, recovering from the coup. His lips grew tight across his teeth, and he announced, "Kachiko, formerly of the Scorpion."

"Majesty," Kachiko said with her nightingale's voice, "I regret that I cannot make proper obeisance before you, but these ropes restrict my movements." As she said it, she turned her face up and looked into the emperor's eyes.

The boy gazed deep into Kachiko's black orbs and saw the dancing sparks of green within. For years he'd watched her at his father's court, admiring her beauty. There was no other woman in the palace to compare with her, no other woman in Rokugan. Despite the grime, she was still the most beautiful woman in the world.

The moment lingered, but then the boy's face grew stern. How it pleased him to have her prostrate before his throne. "Bayushi Kachiko," he said, "you are a traitor. It will give us great pleasure to see your head hung on the palace gate."

"If that is your wish, Majesty," Kachiko said softly. "But first, I request my right as leader of the Scorpion Clan."

"Your husband was daimyo," the boy replied. "And he is dead. Your clan has been disbanded."

"According to ancient tradition," Kachiko said, keeping her demeanor humble, "a clan cannot be disbanded until its daimyo is either executed or tried and stripped of power. When Shoju died, I became daimyo. I inherited his rights. You cannot execute me without trial. Under the law, I insist that you hear my case and render judgment."

"You *insist?*" the boy said, his voice growing shrill again.

"It is my right," Kachiko said, "as laid down by your fathers of old."

Isawa Kaede leaned forward and whispered, "She is right, Majesty."

Seated on the other side, Ishikawa said, "To kill her without trial would be to flout the law of our ancestors." He tried to keep his face neutral, but Kaede saw him frown at Kachiko's suggestion.

Inwardly, Kachiko smiled.

"Very well," the emperor said, leaning back in the sundered throne. "We begin your trial, now."

Kachiko bowed lower and said, "Tradition insists that the trial of a daimyo be private. I trust you to try me." She looked up and cast her gaze around the room, her eyes lighting on Kaede, Yokatsu, Toturi, Tsuko, and Hoturi. She felt fire grow in her breast but fought it down. "No one else here is worthy. You, and you alone, my emperor, must be my judge."

Hantei the 39th looked at Kaede, and she nodded to confirm it. The boy did not notice how uncomfortable the Phoenix lady looked.

"Very well," the emperor said. He gazed around the room once before his eyes settled on Kachiko. "We order the room cleared of all save Ishikawa, our chief yojimbo."

The others in the room rose, bowed, and quietly made their way to the exit.

Toturi glanced back as he left, his heart heavy. Ishikawa occupied a spot formerly reserved for him. It is no more than I deserve, he thought. The great iron doors slammed shut behind him.

Emperor Hantei took a deep breath and looked at the prisoner. "Vile Scorpion!" he began, but Kachiko looked up at him so plaintively that he stopped in midthought.

"What is it?" he asked testily.

"The ropes have cut off my circulation," Kachiko said plainly. "I do not know how much longer I will be able to sit without falling over."

"Loosen her ropes!" the boy commanded Ishikawa.

"Is that a good idea, Majesty?" the captain asked.

"Rebind my hands in front of me, if you like, and leave my feet tied," Kachiko suggested. "That way I could pose no threat."

Hantei nodded, and Ishikawa rose from his low seat. He moved forward and, with his wakizashi, cut the majority of ropes binding the Scorpion lady. He left the knots at her feet, and retied her hands in front. Despite these precautions, Ishikawa felt sure the Scorpion lady had not yet lost her sting.

As the captain finished the job, Kachiko set about straightening her hair and adjusting her robes. "Thank you, Majesty," she said. She glanced up at the boy and could see that he appreciated the changes. He squirmed slightly in his seat.

Ishikawa returned to his seat beside the throne. The boy emperor leaned forward to interrogate his prisoner.

Kachiko bowed her head slightly and slowly closed her eyes. When she opened them again, she was looking directly at the boy. A subtle smile tugged at one corner of her mouth.

"Y-you tried to flee our justice," the boy said. Suddenly, he felt warm. "You have committed grave crimes against our empire."

"I have never betrayed the empire," she said softly, "though I have obeyed the wishes of my husband . . . my *late* husband."

"But you took part in the slaying of my father," Hantei said.

"I was there, yes," she said softly, "but I did not take part. A woman is but a leaf who flies before the typhoon of her husband's will. I had nothing to do with your father's death."

"You deny all involvement, then?"

"I do, though I protected myself in the melee that followed," she said, leaning forward, still holding him with her sparkling black eyes. "Look at me. I am a simple woman, wife to a dead husband, mother to a slain son."

As she said "mother" she moved her neck as if stretching, but the shift also loosened her kimono across her chest.

"I have suffered terribly," Kachiko continued, "though no more than you have, Your Majesty. We have both lost loved ones to terrible tragedy—yours to assassination, mine to madness and retribution. We are alone in the world. I beg your forgiveness for actions that were not my own."

She bowed and touched her head to the floor before rising again. Tears stained her eyes.

". . . If I had *other* hands to guide me . . . !" she said.

Hantei licked his lips nervously; his mouth had suddenly gone dry. "I . . . We . . ." he began, but her purring voice quieted him.

"Destroy the clan of my husband if you must, I would not

blame you for it, though I beg you not to do it." She stretched languidly against the ropes that bound her. The sight had a profound effect on the boy.

The young emperor felt hot. A tingling sensation worked its way up from his loins to the base of his neck. He reached up with one hand and tugged the collar of his kimono.

"You are young and strong and wise," she continued, blinking again slowly before returning to meet his gaze, "and if you see no other way. . . ."

"Other way . . . ." Hantei said sleepily. Though she moved hardly at all, in his mind her body danced before him. He imagined the secrets held beneath her kimono. He felt the soft touch of her flesh against his.

"The wisdom of our ancestors is yours," she said firmly. "Can you not find another way?"

"Another way?" he said. "Our ancestors knew another way?"

She nodded. "You are wise, Emperor Hantei," she said.

The sound of his name from her lips sent a shiver up the young emperor's spine.

"I am nothing before you," she said, bowing again. "Your conquest of me is complete. Past emperors who took their slain foes' vassals, lands, and wives could have no more of a victory than you have over me. My life, my strength, the strength of my people are yours."

She rose up again, taking a deep breath as she did so. "I beg you, judge me. Do with me what you will," she said.

A cunning thought grew in the young emperor's mind. "I should not disband the Scorpions," he said. "I should make their strength my own. I should fold their house into mine, as my ancestors did to their enemies."

"Majesty, no," Ishikawa said. He had listened carefully and watched Kachiko as she moved. For long moments, she had held him spellbound as well. Now, though, the spell broke, and he could restrain himself no longer.

The boy emperor focused his blazing eyes on the captain of the guard and said, "Silence!"

Ishikawa retreated to his spot and stood silently, hand clutched tightly around his spear.

The emperor turned back to Kachiko and said, "I shall take this woman, her lands, and her people. My house will grow stronger from the Scorpions' disbanding."

Kachiko looked up, tears running down her face, washing away the grime. "I beg you, do not," she said. "Judge us, exile us, even execute us. Do not destroy us utterly!"

"Silence, woman!" the boy snapped. Kachiko looked so pitiful and helpless before him; he knew he had won. He turned to Ishikawa as if for advice. "Can I do this?" the boy asked.

Before the captain could answer, Kachiko said, sobbing, "How can you not? He cannot stop you. The great lords cannot stop you. I cannot stop you. You are Emperor Hantei the 39th. There is precedent in our ancient laws. Our lines shall become one. I am powerless before you. I am but a leaf before the typhoon of your will."

Ishikawa started to open his mouth, and then closed it.

The boy looked at her, feeling the fire in his body grow. He wiped the sweat from his brow. Kachiko dried her eyes on her kimono and licked her parched lips.

"Yes," the emperor said. "Yes, I will do it." He turned to his yojimbo. "Ishikawa, tell the others to return. We shall render our judgment of this woman."

Ishikawa rose, walked to the great iron doors, and opened them, calling to those outside to return. Then he strode back into the room and took his place on the boy emperor's right.

When the others had come in and seated themselves on the floor, Hantei the 39th stood.

"The Scorpions shall be destroyed, utterly and forever," Emperor Hantei said. "But we shall do it in such a way that incorporates their strengths into our own." He turned to Ishikawa. "Cut her bonds," the boy emperor said, glancing at Kachiko.

The crowd gasped as Kachiko stood, holding her tied hands out before her. Ishikawa stood. He raised his spear and looked into her eyes. For a moment, he thought about running her through—but his will failed him.

He brought the spear down, cutting first the ropes at Kachiko's wrists and then those at her ankles. The Scorpion lady stepped free of her bonds.

"In accordance with ancient tradition," Hantei said, "I take this woman to be my bride." Another gasp rose from the crowd. In the back of the hall, Seppun Bake fell off his stool.

The boy gave no notice of the display. "Her people shall be absorbed into my own. Their loyalty will therefore be assured. The line of the Scorpion is ended; the House of Hantei grows stronger."

Recovering his wits and his seat, Bake raised his fist in the air and shouted, "Long live the house of Hantei!" The others in the room echoed the sentiment.

As the last of the echoes died away, Kachiko mounted the dais and seated herself beside the throne, on the emperor's left. Ishikawa watched her like a hawk.

Kachiko's eyes swept the room once, lingering only a moment on Doji Hoturi. In a brief flash, she saw her son Dairu's face interposed on the countenance of the man who both conceived and killed him. She blinked, and the image vanished. Deep within her mind, the Mother of Scorpions began to plot her revenge against the man who had murdered her son.

The boy emperor smiled, looking from his new fiancée to the cheering crowd, and then back again. Though some of those present looked nervous, the emperor didn't notice it.

Then his gaze fell on Akodo Toturi, seated near the throne room doors. The Lion didn't applaud. He didn't smile. Hantei felt his anger rise.

He fixed his dark eyes on the Lion daimyo. His heart grew cold, and he said, "As for you, Lion . . ."

27 THE LION'S FALL

The boy sat down in the sundered throne and leaned back before continuing. Kachiko reached up from where she sat and placed her hand in his. Fire stirred within the young Hantei once more. He fixed Toturi with a cold gaze.

"We have considered your case and have come to the truth," Hantei said. "Though none dare speak against you, your own words have betrayed you, Lion. You alone among all our advisors spoke against the destruction of the Scorpion house. By that action you prove yourself their ally—as we suspected."

Toturi stood. "Your Majesty," he said, his voice almost pleading, "I would never betray you!" He took a step forward.

"You already have, by betraying our father," the boy snapped. "You are judged; prepare to receive our sentence."

Toturi knelt and bowed his head.

"Akodo Toturi, we strip you of all rank and title," Hantei said. "No longer are you Lion Champion, or even daimyo. We dissolve your betrothal to Isawa Kaede, who has proved herself a worthy servant—unlike you. We cast you out, Toturi, you and all those who follow you. You are now ronin."

The assembled crowd gasped, but Hantei the 39th continued. "In your place, we appoint Matsu Tsuko head of the Lion Clan. We pray that she will serve us better than you served our father."

Tsuko rose and stepped forward. Toturi glanced at her. Though the two had never liked each other, he found himself surprised by the look on her face. Though proud, she was clearly not happy with the turn of events.

"As head of the Lion Clan," she said, "I most humbly request that our brother Toturi and his people be allowed to commit seppuku to restore their honor."

Toturi felt the dagger in his gut vanish, and the Lion's pride return. Perhaps he had judged this woman too harshly. Here, at last, was an honorable way out.

The Lion pressed his head to the tatami mat covering the floor. "Your Majesty," he said. "I beg you to let me redeem myself. Let my death restore my people in your sight. Allow me this final honor."

What the boy emperor said next froze Toturi's soul.

Hantei leaned back in the remains of the Emerald Throne and said simply, "No." A murmur rose from the crowd; the boy seemed not to notice. "Out of gratitude to your former fiancée," he said, "we allow you to live."

Toturi looked at Kaede and saw the tears welling up in her eyes. She would not have wished it this way. The emperor's punishment was far worse than death. Kaede hung her head.

Toturi turned, taking in the entire room, seeing the shame on the faces of all those present. Finally, his gaze returned to the boy emperor. He looked into Hantei's eyes.

Suddenly, the room grew dark. The floor shook and buckled as if with the power of an earthquake. The boards bulged, and beneath them, Toturi saw fire.

Everyone in the room stood still as the floorboards erupted, sending splintered fragments to the vaulted ceiling. A huge, fiery shape loomed up behind the throne.

The dragon that appeared was the most terrible Toturi had ever seen. Its eyes were blazing coals, its fangs white-hot daggers. Tongues of flame flickered down its back, threatening to singe the great timbers of the throne room. It roared, and the castle's very foundations shook.

Then, before his eyes, the creature of light transformed into one of darkness. Quickly the shape of the dragon melted, like steel in an overheated forge. It grew smaller, but no less powerful; its wise face metamorphosed into a hideous mockery. In moments, the dragon became one of Fu Leng's thrice-damned minions.

The demon belched fire and laughed loud enough to shake Rokugan to the core. The creature reached beneath the throne and brought forth two captives, clutching a man in each burning hand. One victim the Lion recognized as Bayushi Shoju; the other, Toturi knew, was himself.

While Toturi watched in mute horror, the demon seated itself upon the Emerald Throne. As it did so, the creature assumed a more familiar shape—that of the boy emperor. The monster gazed into Toturi's eyes; within the orbs, the Lion saw only death and darkness.

With a start, Toturi realized his vision had ended. He found himself gazing into the eyes of Emperor Hantei the 39th once more. The blackness behind those eyes frightened him.

The nightmare had just begun. Bayushi Shoju had killed the wrong Hantei.

Toturi's own actions—and inactions—had brought the empire to this terrible point. Had he done his duty, had he been by the true emperor's side, all this might never have come to pass. He fell on his hands and knees and wept. No one in the throne room could have guessed the true reason.

The boy turned away from him. "Now," he said with thinly disguised contempt, "what of his geisha? We can't punish the whore master without punishing his trollop."

"Dead, Majesty," Kachiko said from near the boy's left ear. "Our spies discovered her fate while searching for the Lion Champion. She had been thrown off a waterfall near her geisha house—though whether by Toturi's hand or her own, we do not know."

Toturi heard the words, but they did not take hold in his mind. Instead, they echoed inside his skull until Hatsuko's beautiful face appeared before him. He wept to see it.

"Well?" the emperor asked Toturi. "Did you kill her?"

Toturi shook his head. "Not I," he said quietly.

"Oh, well," the boy said, flinging up his hands. "At least she's saved us the trouble of an execution." He gestured to his guards and then to Toturi.

"Strip him," the emperor commanded. "Remove all signs of his former life."

Toturi stood, and two men stepped forward to do as they were told. First, they removed his swords, casting them at the feet of Matsu Tsuko. Then they ripped Toturi's fine robes from his body, making a great show of their actions. Had Toturi paid attention, he would have noticed that most of the court looked away as the guards stripped him.

Not the emperor or his fiancée, though. The Hantei lord and his new lady seemed to enjoy every minute of Toturi's humiliation. Soon the former Lion Champion stood before the Emerald Throne wearing nothing but sandals and a loincloth.

The boy emperor stood and pointed to the door. "Go!" he commanded. "Let no one speak to him. Let no one give him comfort. Let no one bar his way."

Toturi turned and looked around, but no one met his glance. Even Ikoma Bentai had turned away.

Solemnly, the formerly proud Lion walked out of the throne room and left the Castle of the Shining Prince forever. Not once did he look back.

EPILOGUE: MEETINGS ON THE ROAD OF LIFE

The beggar strode down the forested road on his way to the Spine of the World Mountains. He was not looking for anything in particular except peace of mind. So far, it had eluded him.

People who encountered the beggar got out of his way. It seemed clear he was mad, both from the frantic way he moved and the strange things he muttered to himself as he went.

Two Crane guards met him on the road but left him alone when they realized who he was. Other people knew as well—though few dared linger in the beggar's presence.

One of those who did linger was Bayushi Tetsuo. He had followed the man through the forest for two days, trying to decide what course of action to take.

Had he been Bayushi Aramoro, or Yogo Junzo, he probably would have killed the man immediately. But Tetsuo had grown weary of war and death. And so, he followed the beggar at a discreet distance, trying to decide what the honor of his clan demanded, and trying to reconcile those demands with his own soul.

As he watched, a furtive movement in the brush close by caught his eye. He recognized a swift form that few others would even have seen. Picking up a stone, he tossed it in the figure's direction and quietly called, "Aramoro!"

The Master of Assassins turned, a deadly shuriken in his hand. Immediately, he recognized his cousin and stole through the woods to Tetsuo's side. Aramoro made no more sound than a bird as he came.

"Tetsuo!" he said. "I'm glad to see you alive."

"As I am glad to see you," Tetsuo replied. "I thought you dead in the final assault on the palace."

"No," Aramoro said, shaking his head. "I was trapped outside the castle walls, like you. That's the only reason I escaped."

"Dairu?" Tetsuo asked.

"Gone," the older man said, hanging his head. "As are many others. If I could save but one, though . . . ."

"I know," Tetsuo said. "I would have given up my life for the boy as well."

"I should have been at his side, rather than facing the Crab."

Tetsuo nodded. "We both should have been there. What of the others? Do you know what's happening back home?"

"Many of our shugenja escaped, I believe," Aramoro said, "including Junzo and Bantaro. They'll be safe in our own lands, Bayushi Yojiro will see to that."

"Not for long, I fear. I've heard that the Crab, the Lion, and the Crane are sending armies to destroy the Scorpion homelands."

Aramoro shook his head. "There are always more rocks for Scorpions to hide under. I've heard that Taberu and a number of others escaped as well."

"And the Lady Kachiko?"

Aramoro laughed. "They've made her empress! The fools!"

Tetsuo nodded, and a sly smile broke across his face. "Yosh. So long as the Mother of Scorpions lives, our clan may yet be reborn."

"We're not destroyed, lad," Aramoro said. "We're merely laying low for a while."

"Laying low. Is that why you're following this beggar?" Tetsuo asked.

"I'm just making myself useful until it's safe to rejoin Kachiko," Aramoro replied. He nodded toward the beggar. "Do you know who he is?"

"Of course," said Tetsuo. "A lion can't hide beneath sheep's clothing."

"Then you'll help me kill him?"

Tetsuo leaned back and let out a long breath. "Our lord once told me I had another part to play in this drama before I died. I sense that the same is true for Akodo Toturi. Why else would Shoju have let the Lion live? Toturi could never have beaten our lord, unless Shoju let him."

"But honor demands . . ."

"Shoju sacrificed his honor and his life for the good of the empire. Neither one of us is as wise as he. 'Even the Fortunes cannot see all ends.' "

"Quoting Shinsei won't get you anywhere with me," Aramoro said. "What I believe in is *revenge*."

Tetsuo leaned close to his cousin. "Then take comfort in this: What Toturi is going through is the best revenge a Scorpion could wish for. He is ronin, a samurai without a master. All those who followed him have been cast out. The Akodo are destroyed. He has no army, no status, no castle, no home.

"All he has are dreams of what once was, and what might have been. Even an honorable death is denied him. *That* is a fate far worse than you or I could imagine for him."

Aramoro folded his arms across his chest and nodded. "For a youngster, you're pretty wise," he said.

"That wisdom has come at a terrible price," Tetsuo replied.

"I guess Shoju was right about you. Shall we travel together?"

"I'm going west, to help Yojiro protect our homeland," Tetsuo said.

"East for me," Aramoro countered. "I'll hide near the capital and await orders from our mistress. She needs me now more than ever."

They clasped hands. "Our separate ways, then," Tetsuo said.

"Until we meet again."

They nodded to each other. Then each man vanished into the woods.

Unmolested, the beggar continued down the road of life.